Walk on Earth a Stranger

WALK

on

EARTH

a

STRANGER

RAE CARSON

Greenwillow Books
An Imprint of HarperCollins*Publishers*

Walk on Earth a Stranger
Copyright © 2015 by Rae Carson
Map copyright © 2015 by John Hendrix

The text of this book is set in 11-point Hoefler.
Book design by Paul Zakris

Library of Congress Cataloging-in-Publication data is available.

ISBN 978-0-06-224291-4 (hardcover)
"Greenwillow Books."

16 17 18 19 20 PC/RRDH 10 9 8 7 6 5 4 3 2
First Edition

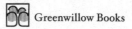 Greenwillow Books

For Martha Mihalick, editrix extraordinaire

Dramatis Personae

IN DAHLONEGA, GEORGIA

The Westfalls

Reuben "Lucky" Westfall, a gold prospector

Elizabeth Westfall, his wife

Leah "Lee" Westfall, their fifteen-year-old daughter

Hiram Westfall, Reuben's brother

The McCauleys

Mr. McCauley, a gold prospector from Ireland

Jefferson McCauley, his sixteen-year-old son

The Smiths

Judge Smith, Lumpkin County judge and landowner

Mrs. Smith, his wife

Annabelle Smith, their sixteen-year-old daughter

Jeannie Smith, their slave

James "Free Jim" Boisclair, a storeowner

Abel Topper, unemployed mine foreman

TO INDEPENDENCE, MISSOURI

The Brothers

Zeke Tackett

Emmett Tackett

Ronnie Tackett

The Flatboat Crew

Captain Rodney Chisholm

Fiddle Joe

Red Jack

The Joyners

Andrew Joyner, a gentleman

Rebekah "Becky" Joyner, his wife

Olive Joyner, their six-year-old daughter

Andrew Joyner Jr., their four-year-old son

Matilda "Aunt Tildy" Dudley, their cook

THE WAGON TRAIN

From Missouri

Frank Dilley, leader of twenty wagons of Missouri men

Jonas Waters, Frank Dilley's foreman

From Arkansas

Major Wally Craven, the wagon train guide

Josiah Bledsoe, a sheep farmer with ten wagons

Hampton, Mr. Bledsoe's slave

The Illinois College Men

Jasper Clapp, studied medicine

Thomas Bigler, studied law

Henry Meek, studied literature

From Ottawa Valley

Charles Robichaud, a ranch hand

Lucie Robichaud, his wife

Jeremy and Samuel, their five-year-old twin sons

From Kentucky

Reverend Ernest Lowrey, a Presbyterian pastor

Mary Lowrey, his wife

From Ohio

Herman Hoffman, a farmer from Germany

Helma Hoffman, his wife

Therese, their fifteen-year-old daughter

Martin, their thirteen-year-old son

Luther, their twelve-year-old son

Otto, their nine-year-old son

Carl, their eight-year-old son

Doreen, their five-year-old daughter

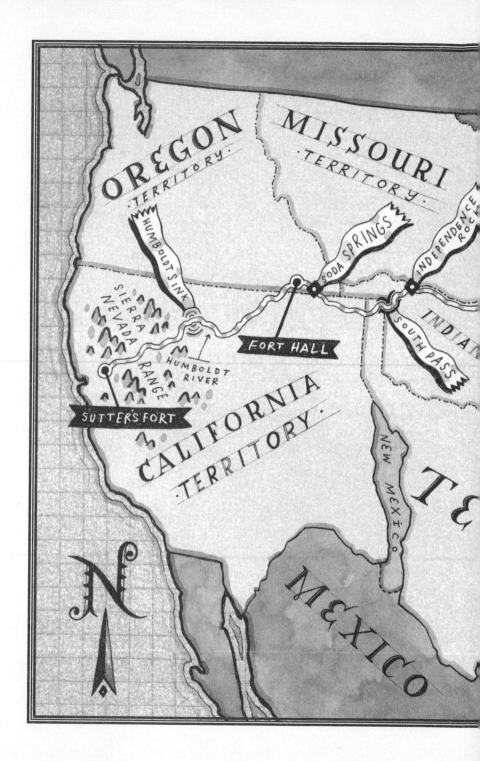

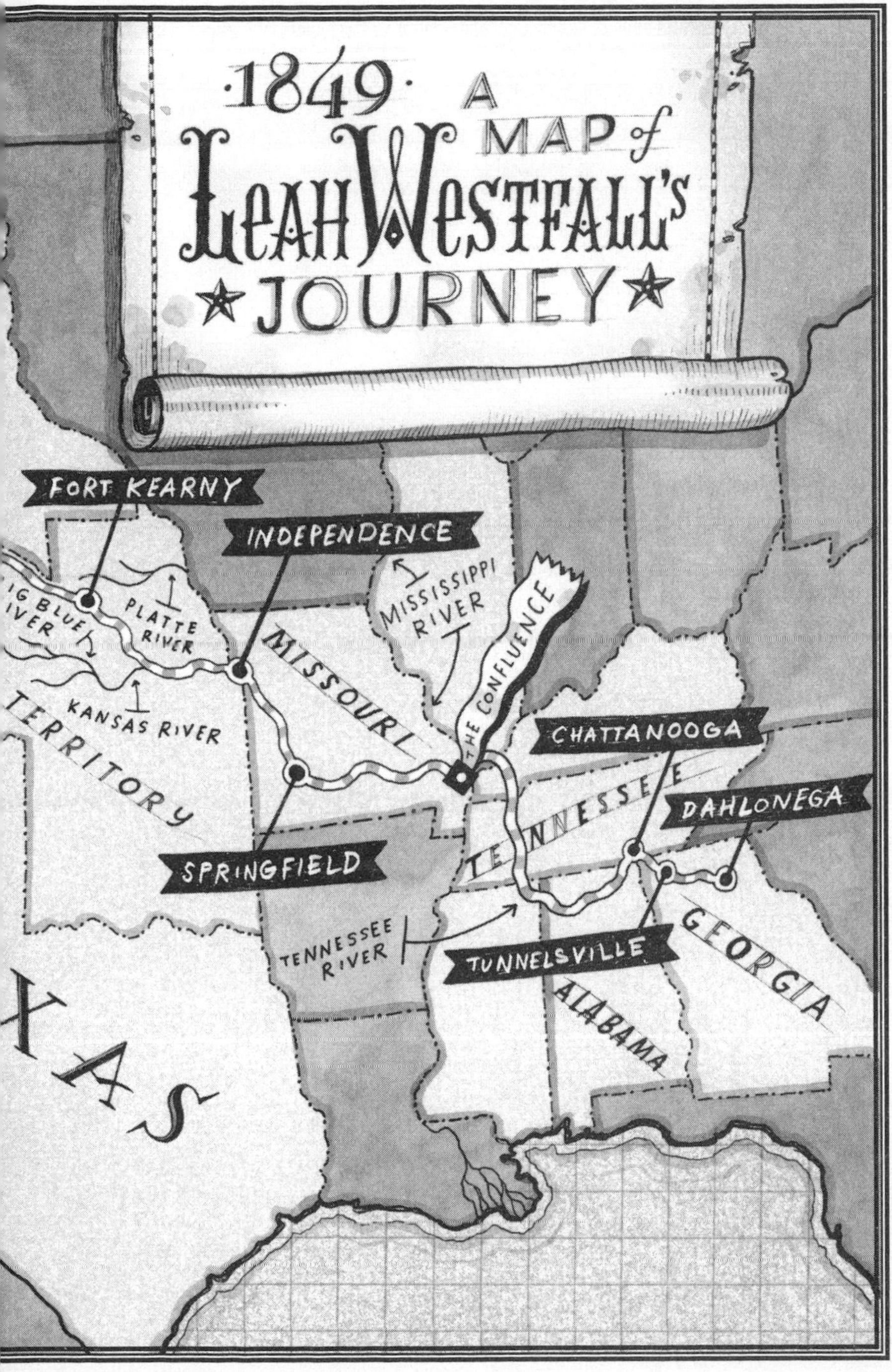
1849 A MAP of
LEAH WESTFALL'S
JOURNEY
FORT KEARNY
INDEPENDENCE
MISSISSIPPI RIVER
THE CONFLUENCE
PLATTE RIVER
MISSOURI
KANSAS RIVER
TERRITORY
CHATTANOOGA
TENNESSEE
DAHLONEGA
SPRINGFIELD
TENNESSEE RIVER
TUNNELSVILLE
GEORGIA
ALABAMA

JANUARY 1849

Chapter One

$\mathcal{I}$ hear the deer before I see him, though he makes less noise than a squirrel—the gentle crunch of snow, a snapping twig, the soft *whuff* as he roots around for dead grass. I can hardly believe my luck.

As quietly as falling snow, I raise the butt of my daddy's Hawken rifle to my shoulder and peer down the muzzle. A crisscross of branches narrows my view. The deer must be allowed to wander into my sights, but that's all right. I am patient. I am a ghost.

I've tucked myself into a deadfall, the result of an ancient, dying oak looming above me. Snow fills the cracks between branches, creating a barrier to the wind. I can barely see out, but I'm almost warm. The snow around me clinks and tinkles like bells, melting in the early morning warm snap. The hem of my skirt and the petticoats underneath are ragged and soaked. If the girls at school saw me now, I'd hear no end of it, but it doesn't matter. We have to eat.

Which means I have to make this shot. If only I could conjure up fresh game whenever we needed. Now *that* would be a useful magic.

Finally, a deep, tawny chest and a white throat slide into view. He bends a black nose to the ground, and I glimpse tall, curving antlers—at least three points on each side. His neck is long and elegant, feathered with winter fur. He's so close I can almost see the pulse at his neck. A beautiful animal.

I pull on the rear trigger—soft, steady pressure, just like Daddy taught me. The click as it sets is barely audible, but the buck's head shoots up. I refuse to breathe.

I am patient. I am a ghost.

He takes a single dancing step, nose twitching. But I'm downwind, and after a moment he returns to grazing. I shift my finger to the hair trigger. The deadfall blocks my view of his skull, so I aim for the lungs.

It will only take the slightest pressure now, the effort of an exhale.

Church bells clang. The buck startles a split second before my gun cracks the air. He crumples, flails in the snow, scrambles to his feet, and darts away, tail sprung high.

"Blast!"

I rip off the ramrod from the barrel as I plunge through the windfall. In good conditions, I can load and shoot again in less than half a minute. Though my fingers are chilled, I might still bag him if I'm quick.

Of course, I wouldn't need to reload if someone was hunting

with me, ready with a second shot. Everything's harder when you do it alone.

I'm reaching into my satchel for my powder horn when crimson catches my eye. Bright red, sinking wet and warm into the snow. He left a puddle where he fell, and a trail of lighter drops to show me the way. I flanked him good.

I follow at a brisk walk, loading as I go—first gunpowder, then a ball nestled in paper wadding, all shoved down the barrel with my ramrod. I won't waste another shot on the deer, but there's a big catamount been prowling these hills. In a winter this mild, the scent of fresh blood might even draw a bear. It's not quite the hungering time—when a critter that's naught but fur and fangs and ribs will attack a near-grown girl—but I'll take no chances.

The trail veers sharply to the right. I pass a bloody depression in the snow where the deer's legs must have buckled again. I stop to load the cap and rotate the hammer carefully into place, then I lift my skirt and petticoats with my free hand and run—smooth as I can so as not to jostle my gun. I have to reach that deer before anything else does. *Never bring home meat that's already been et on,* Daddy always says.

The blood trail plunges down a steep bank thick with young birches. Crimson smears darken their white trunks. My wounded deer is heading toward the McCauley claim, where Jefferson lives with his good-for-nothing da. No sense paying a visit after my hunt, because they're certainly not home. Jeff's da attends church every single Sunday, no matter what, on the misguided notion that regular bench sitting makes him decent.

The slope ends at a shallow but swift creek. The water's edge glitters with ice, but the creek's center runs clear and clean. My boots are well oiled. If I'm quick, I can cross before the water seeps into my stockings. I hitch my skirt and petticoats higher and plunge in.

Midway across, I freeze.

The gold sense sparks in the back of my throat, sharp and hard. It creeps down my throat and into my chest, where it diffuses into a steady buzz, like dancing locusts. My stomach heaves once, but I swallow against the nausea. We don't have enough food in the cellar for me to go wasting a meal.

I force my belly to relax, to embrace the sensation. Best to let it wash over me, through me. Allow it to settle in like an old friend come to stay.

It's only bad like this the first time I'm near something big. A nugget, usually, but sometimes a large vein. From habit, I close my eyes and focus hard, turning in place to find where the sensation is strongest. If I hit it just right, it will be like a string tugging my chest, like something sucking . . . There. I open my eyes. Just across the creek, behind a young, winter-stripped maple. The blood trail leads in the same direction.

All at once I'm shivering, my feet icy with cold. I splash through the creek and scramble up the opposite bank, which is slick with snowmelt. How long was I standing in the water? It seemed like only moments. I wriggle my toes inside my soaked stockings, hoping I haven't ruined my boots. We can't afford another pair right now. Good thing I wore my old hunting skirt. The hem is already a disaster and won't suffer much from being dragged through the stream.

At the top of the bank, I check my rifle, and it seems dry. At least I had sense enough to not let it dangle in the water. As I step around the maple's trunk, the gold sense grows stronger, but I ignore it because the deer lies in a small depression banked with bloody snow.

He pushes up with his forelegs, antlered head straining in the opposite direction. I whip up my rifle just in case, but he collapses back into the snow, his sides heaving.

I prop my gun against the tree and pull the knife from the belt at my waist. "I'm so sorry," I whisper, approaching cautiously. Neck or kidney? He'll fight death until the very last moment. They always do. I know I would.

His antlers still pose too great a threat for me to slice his jugular. He squirms uselessly as I near, head tossing. It needs to be a quick thrust, aimed just right. I raise the knife.

My hand wavers. The gold sense is so strong now, its buzzing so merciless that I feel it down to my toes. It's almost *good*, like being filled with sunshine. It means gold is somewhere within reach.

Deer first, gold later.

I plunge the knife into his left kidney. He squeals once, then goes still. Hot blood pumps from the wound for mere seconds before slowing to a trickle. It steams in the air, filling my nose and mouth with bright tanginess. I'll have to work fast; if that catamount is anywhere near, she'll be here soon.

He's too large for me to carry over my shoulders. I'll have to skin and butcher him and take only the best parts. The great cat is welcome to the rest, with my blessing.

I place the point of my knife low on his soft white underbelly. The gold sense explodes inside me, so much hotter and brighter than the scent of fresh blood. I can't help it; I drop the knife and dig furiously at the snow—dig and dig until I've reached a layer of autumn rot. Muddy detritus jams under my fingernails, but still I dig until something glints at me. Sunshine in the dirt. Warmth in winter.

The nugget unsticks from its muddy resting place without much effort; this time last year I would have had to dig it out of frozen ground. I scrape away mud with the edge of my sleeve. It's the size of a large, unshelled walnut and rounder than most nuggets, save for a single odd bulge on one side. Must have washed down the creek during last spring's flood. I gauge its heft in my palm, even as I let my gold sense do its work. Close to ninety percent pure, if I don't miss my guess.

Worth at least a hundred dollars. More than enough to buy meat to last the winter.

I sit back on my heels, nugget clutched tight, staring at the animal I just killed. I don't even need it now. _Waste not, want not,_ Mama always says. And Lord knows Daddy could use a fresh venison stew.

Today is my luckiest day in a long time. I shove the nugget into the pocket of my skirt, pick up my skinning knife, and get to work.

➤ ➤ ➤

The sun is high over the mountains when I finally haul my venison up the stairs of the back porch. Everything I could carry is wrapped in the deer's own skin, tied with twine. My shoulders ache—I carried it a mile or more—and though I bundled it up tight as I could, my blouse and skirt are badly stained.

"Mama!" I call out. "Could use a hand."

She bangs out the doorway, a dishrag in her hands. A few strands of hair have already escaped her shiny brown bun, and the lines around her eyes have gone from laughing to worried.

"Daddy's not doing so good, is he?" I ask.

Her gaze drops to the bundle in my arms and to the rifle balanced carefully across it. "Oh, bless your heart, Leah," she says. She shoves the dishrag into the pocket of her apron and reaches out her arms. "Give it here. I'll get a stew on while you tend your gun and feed the chickens."

As I hand it over, I can't help blurting, "There's more, Mama. I had a *find*."

She freezes, and I leap forward to catch the package of meat before it slides out of her arms. Finally, she says, "Been awhile. I thought maybe you'd outgrown it."

"I reckon not," I say, disappointed in her disappointment.

"I reckon not," she agrees. "Well, take care of your business, and we'll discuss it with your daddy when you're done."

"Yes, Mama."

She disappears into the kitchen. I hitch the Hawken over my shoulder and head toward the henhouse. Just beyond it is a break in the trees. We keep the land clear here, so nothing can sneak up on the chickens easily. It's a good hundred-yard stretch—all the way to the scar tree, a giant pine I use for discharging my rifle. I whip the gun down and cradle the butt to my shoulder. The wind is picking up from the north a bit, so I aim a hair to the right. _Best aim I ever saw from such a wee gal,_ Jefferson's da once told me, the only compliment I've ever heard him give.

Rear trigger, soft breath, hair trigger, _boom._ Splinters fly into the air as my shot hits its target. The chickens squawk a bit but settle quickly. They're used to me.

I lean the gun against the side of the henhouse. I'll clean her while I'm at the table talking with Mama and Daddy. It will give me an excuse to avoid their worried gazes. "You hungry?" I say, and I hear my chickens—who are not nearly as stupid as most people think—barreling toward the door for their breakfast.

I lift the bar and swing open the door, and they come pouring out, squawking and pecking at the toes of my boots, as if this will summon their breakfast even sooner. They forget all about me the moment their feed is scattered on the ground. Except for my favorite hen, Isabella, who flaps into my arms when I crouch. I stroke her glossy black tail feathers while she pecks at the seed in my hand. It hurts a little, but that's all right.

I have a strange life; I know it well. We have a big homestead and not enough working hands, so I'm the girl who hunts and farms and pans for gold because her daddy never had sons. I'm forever weary, my hands roughed and cracked, my skirts worn too thin too soon. The town girls poke fun at me, calling me "Plain Lee" on account of my strong hands and my strong jaw. I don't mind so much because it's better than them knowing the real trickiness in my days—that I find gold the way a water witch divines wells.

But there's plenty I love about my life that makes it all just fine: the sunrise on the snowy mountain slopes, a mama and daddy who know my worth, that sweet tingle when a gold nugget sits in the palm of my hand. And my chickens. I love my loud, silly chickens.

Only four eggs today. I gather them quickly, brushing straw from their still-warm shells and settling them gently into my pockets. Then I grab my rifle and head inside to face the aftermath of witching up another nugget.

Chapter Two

*D*addy always says I was born with a gold nugget in my left hand and a pickax in my right. That's why Mama had such a hard time birthing me; she had to squeeze a lot more out of her belly than just a bundle of baby girl. The first time I heard it told, I gave my rag doll to Orpha the dog and announced I would never have children of my own.

It didn't take me long to figure it for a fancy lie, like the one about St. Nicholas bringing presents on Christmas, or how walking backward around the garden three times would keep the aphids out of our squash. But that's Daddy for you, always telling tall tales.

I don't mind. I love his stories, and his best ones are the secret ones, the mostly true ones, spoken in whispers by the warmth of the box stove, with no one to hear but me and Mama. They're always about gold. And they're always about me.

After shucking my boots and banging them against the

porch rail to get off the mud, I walk inside and find Daddy settled in his rocking chair, his big, stockinged feet stretched as near to the box stove as he dares. He starts to greet me but coughs instead, kerchief over his mouth. It rattles his whole body, and I can practically hear his bones shake. He pulls away the kerchief and crumples it in his fist to hide it. He thinks I don't know what he's coughing up.

The bed quilt drapes across his shoulders, and a mug of coffee steams on the tree-stump table beside him. The house smells of burning pine and freshly sliced turnips.

"Mama said you found some gold today," Daddy says calmly as I set my boots next to the stove to dry.

"Yes, sir." I head back to the table, where I reach into my pocket for the eggs I gathered and set them beside Mama's stew pot.

He sips his coffee. Swallows. Sighs. "Did I ever tell you about the Spanish Moss Nugget?" he asks. Then he doubles over coughing, and I dare to hope it's not so violent as it was yesterday.

"Tell me," I say, though I've heard it a hundred times.

Mama's gaze meets mine over the stew pot, and we share a secret smile. "Tell us," she agrees. I pull up a chair, then lay my rifle on the table and start taking it apart.

"Well, since you insist. It happened in the spring of '35," he begins. "The easy pickings were long gone by then, and I'd had a hard day with nothing to show. I was walking home creekside, trying to beat the coming storm, when I chanced on a moss-fall under a broad oak. A wind came up and blew away the moss, and there she was, bright and beautiful and smiling; bigger than my fist, just sitting there, nice as you please."

Never in my life have I seen a nugget so big. I've heard tales, but I'm not sure I believe them. Still, I nod as if I do.

He says, "But the storm was something awful, and night was falling. I couldn't get to town to get her assayed, so I brought her home. I showed her off to your mama, then I hid her under the floorboards for safekeeping until the storm passed."

He pauses to take another sip of coffee. The fire inside the stove pops. As soon as I'm done cleaning my gun, I'll take off my stockings and lay them out to dry too.

"And then what happened?" I ask, because I'm supposed to.

He sets down his cup and rocks forward, eyes wide with the fever. "When I got up in the morning, what did I see but my own little Lee with that nugget in her chubby hand, banging it on the floor and laughing and kicking out her legs, like she'd found the greatest toy."

Mama sighs with either remembrance or regret over the first time I divined gold. I was two years old.

He says, "So I re-hid it. This time in the larder."

"But I found it again, didn't I, Daddy?" I cover the ramrod in a patch of clean cloth and shove it down the muzzle. It comes out slightly damp, which means I might have faced a nasty backfire the next time I shot.

"Again and again and again. You found it under the

mattress, lodged in the toe of my boot, even buried in the garden. That's when I knew my girl was special. No, *magical*."

Mama can't hold back a moment more. "These are rough times," she warns as she drops pieces of turnip into the pot. She has a small, soft voice, but it's sneaky the way it can still a storm. Mostly, the storm she stills is my daddy. "Folks'd be powerful keen to hear tell of a girl who could divine gold."

"They would, at that," Daddy says thoughtfully. "Since there's hardly a lick of surface gold left in these mountains."

This is why we are not rich, and we never will be. Sure, the Spanish Moss Nugget bought our windows, our wagon, and the back porch addition. But the Georgia gold rush played itself out long ago, and it turns out that not even a magical girl can conjure gold from nothing or lift it from stubborn rock with just her thoughts. We've labored hard for what little I've been able to divine, and I've found less and less each year. Last summer, we diverted the stream and dug up the dry bed until not a speck remained. This year, we attacked the cliff side with our pickaxes until Daddy got too sick.

There's more gold to be found deep in the ground—my honey-sweet sense tells me so—but there's only so much two people can accomplish. Daddy refuses to buy slaves; he was raised Methodist, back in the day when the church was against slavery.

Today's nugget is my first big find in more than a year.

Lord knows we need the money. Which is a mighty odd thing to need, considering that we have a bag of sweet, raw gold dust hidden beneath the floorboards. Daddy says we're saving it for a rainy day.

But Mama says we hid it because taking so much gold to the mint would attract attention. She's right. Whenever we bring in more than a pinch or two of dust, word gets out, and strangers start crawling all over our land like ants on a picnic, looking for the mother lode. In fact, I've earned my daddy a nickname: Reuben "Lucky" Westfall, everyone calls him. Only the three of us know the truth, and we've sworn to keep it that way.

In the meantime, the barn roof is starting to leak; the cellar shelves are still half empty, with the worst cold yet to come; and we owe Free Jim's store for this year's winter wheat seed. A big nugget like the one I found could take care of it all. It's a lucky find, sure, but not so lucky as an entire flour sack of gold dust worked from a played-out claim.

"So, Leah," Daddy says, and I look up from wiping the stock. He never calls me that. It's always "Lee" or "sweet pea."

"Yes, Daddy?"

"Where *exactly* did you find that rock?"

"By a new deer trail, west of the orchard."

"I heard the rifle shot. Sounded like it came from a long ways off."

"Sure did. Longer still before I got him. I nicked him in the flank, and he ran off. I tracked him down the mountain and across the creek to . . . Oh."

I had crossed over onto McCauley land.

Daddy's rocking chair stills. "It doesn't belong to us," he says softly.

"But we need—" I stop myself. Jefferson and his da need it as bad or worse than we do.

"We're not thieves," Daddy says.

"I found it fair and square!"

He shakes his head. "Doesn't matter. If Mr. McCauley came by and 'found' our peaches in the orchard, would it be all right to help himself to a bushel?"

I frown.

"She should put it right back where she found it," Mama says.

"No!" I protest, and Daddy gives me the mind-your-mother-or-else look. I swallow hard and try to lower my voice, but I've never mastered the gentle firmness of Mama's way. I'm a too-loud-or-nothing kind of girl. "I mean, if we can't keep it, then the McCauleys should have it. Their cabin is in bad shape, and their milk cow died last winter, and . . . I'll take it back. I'll give it over to Jefferson's da."

Mama carries her pot to the box stove and sets it on top. "What will you tell him?" she asks, giving the stew a quick stir.

"The truth. That I was hunting, that I tracked my wounded buck onto his claim and chanced upon a nugget."

Mama frowns. "Knowing Mr. McCauley, the story will be all over town within a day."

"So? No one needs to know I witched it up."

She slams the pot lid into place and turns to brandish her

wooden spoon at me. "Leah Elizabeth Westfall, I will not have that word in my house."

"It's not a bad word."

"If anyone hears it, even in passing, they'll get the wrong idea. I know we live in modern times, but no one suffers a . . . that word. There's no forgiveness for it. No explaining that will help. I know it full well."

Mama does this sometimes. She alludes to something that happened to her when she was a girl, something awful. But I know better than to press for details, because it won't get me anything but more chores or an early trip to bed.

"And I'll not remind the entire town that we send our fifteen-year-old daughter out hunting on the Lord's Day," she continues, still waving that spoon. "Our choices are our choices, and our business is our business, but no good will come from throwing it in people's faces."

"I'll take it back," Daddy says. "I'll tell him I was the one out hunting."

"Reuben, you can hardly walk," Mama says. "No one will believe it."

"I'll wait a few days. Let this cough settle. Then I'll go. Maybe I'll do it right before heading to Charlotte."

This is what Daddy tells us every day. That when his cough "settles," he'll take to the road with our bag of gold. He'll have it assayed at the mint in Charlotte, North Carolina, where no one knows us and no one will ask questions.

"Sure, Daddy." I don't dare catch Mama's eye and give space for the worry growing in both our hearts.

I rise from the table and walk with heavy steps to Daddy's rocking chair. I pull the nugget from my pocket and place it in his outstretched palm. The gold sense lessens as soon as it leaves my hand, and for the briefest moment I am bereft, like I've lost a friend.

"Well, I'll be," he says breathlessly, turning it over to catch the morning light streaming through our windows. "Isn't it a beauty?"

"Sure is," I agree. It's so much more than beautiful, though. It's food and shelter and warmth and *life*.

His bushy eyebrows knit together as he looks at me, straight on. "This nugget is nothing, Lee. Even your magic is nothing. You're a good girl and the best daughter. And that? That's something."

I can't even look at him. "Yes, Daddy."

I return to the table to finish cleaning my rifle. It's a good time for quiet thinking, so I think hard and long. If Mama won't let us sell our gold dust, and Daddy refuses to let me keep that nugget, then I need to figure out another way to make ends meet.

I pause, my rag hovering over the wooden stock. "I could do it," I say.

"What's that, sweet pea?" Daddy says.

"I could take our gold to get assayed in North Carolina. I'll drive Chestnut and Hemlock. The colts'd be glad for—"

"Absolutely not," Mama says.

"It's nice of you to offer," Daddy says in a kinder tone. "But the road is no place for a girl all alone."

"You'd be robbed for sure," Mama adds. "Or worse."

I sigh. It was worth a try.

Mama's gaze on my face softens. "You are such a help, my Leah, and I love you for it. But you would do too much if I let you."

"Tell you what," Daddy says. "When this cough settles, maybe your mama will let you come with me."

"Maybe I would," Mama says unconvincingly.

"I'd like that," I say.

When this cough settles, when this cough settles, when this cough settles. I've heard it so many times it's like a song in my head.

Maybe I'll set traps this winter. Maybe we'll have another big flood, which will give us an excuse to say we found more gold. Maybe our winter wheat will do better than expected. Maybe I'll escape to Charlotte with that bag of gold and beg forgiveness afterward.

Maybe I'll become a real witch, who can cast a spell that will keep our barn dry and fill our cellar.

Chapter Three

*B*y morning, the air has warmed enough that fog slithers thick and blue through the creases of my mountains. Because of yesterday's hunting success, Daddy lets me hitch Peony to the wagon and drive to school.

As soon as I pull up, I can tell something is amiss. Instead of pelting one another with snowballs or playing tag or hoops, the little ones stand clutched together for warmth, holding tight to their dinner pails, speaking in hushed tones. It's like someone important has died, like the governor. Or even the president. But no, the courthouse flag is not at half-mast.

I hobble Peony and scan the schoolyard for Jefferson. He has a knack for seeing everything around him, and if anyone can speak truth to me, it's him.

Annabelle Smith, the judge's daughter, finds me first. "Well, if it isn't Plain Lee!" she calls out. "Driving to school like the good boy she is." The girls my age are clustered around her, and they giggle as I approach.

"You seen Jefferson?" I ask.

"Shouldn't you be out hunting?" Her smile shows off two adorable dimples. God must have a wicked sense of humor to make such a devil of a girl look like such an angel. "Or mucking around in the creek?"

"Please, Annabelle," I say wearily. "Not today. I just want to talk to my friend."

Her smile falters, and she indicates a direction with a lift of her chin. "I think he has something you'll want to see."

I'm not sure what that means, but I nod acknowledgment and head off toward the outhouse.

Behind it is Jefferson, surrounded by a gaggle of braids and skirts, which is odd because the town girls—even the younger ones—usually avoid him. He stands at least a head above them all; tall enough so the hem of his pants sits high, revealing feet that are bare, even in winter— He must have outgrown his boots again. His face is framed by thick, black hair and a long, straight Cherokee nose he got from his mama. An old bruise yellows the sharp line of his cheekbone.

He sees me, and waves a bit of paper. He extricates himself from the girls and meets me halfway, at the entrance to the small white clapboard that serves as our schoolhouse. The girls eye me warily, but they don't follow.

"It's *gold*, Lee," he blurts before I can open my mouth to ask. "Discovered in California."

My stomach turns over hard. "You're sure?"

He hands me a newspaper cutout. It's already smudged

from too many fingers, and it's dated December 5, 1848—more than a month ago.

"President Polk announced it to Congress. So it has to be true."

Thoughts and feelings tumble around too hard and fast for me to put a name to them. I sink down on to the slushy steps, not caring that my second-best skirt will get soaked, and I rub hard at my chin. Gold is everywhere. At least a little bit of it. How much gold would it take for the president to make a special announcement?

"Lee?" he says. "What are you thinking?" His usually serious eyes blaze with fever, a look I know all too well. A look that might be mirrored in my own eyes.

"I'm thinking you're going to head west, along with this whole town." That's why everyone's so somber. Dahlonega was built on a gold rush of its own, and every child for miles will understand that change is coming, whether they want it to or not.

He plunks down beside me, resting his forearms on skinny knees that practically reach his ears. "They're saying the land over there is so lush with gold you can pluck it from the ground. Someone like me could . . ."

Silence stretches between us. He hates giving voice to the thing that hurts his heart most; he hardly even talks about it to me. Jefferson is the son of a mean Irish prospector and a sweet Cherokee mama who fled with her brothers ten years ago, when the Indians were sent to Oklahoma Territory. Not a soul in Dahlonega blamed her one bit, even though she left her boy with his good-for-nothing da.

So when Jefferson says "someone like me," he means "a stupid, motherless Injun," which is one of the dumber things people call Jefferson, if you ask me, because he's the smartest boy I know.

"Daddy will want to go," I whisper at last. And I want to go too, to be honest. Gold is in my blood, in my breath, even in the flecks of my eyes, and I love it the same way Jefferson's da loves his moonshine.

But, Lord, I'm weary. Weary of trying to be as good to Daddy as three sons, weary of working as hard as any man, weary of the other girls scorning me. And I'm weary of bearing this troubled soul, of knowing things could go very badly if someone learned about my gold-witching ways. If we moved west, to a place where there was still gold to be had, it would start all over again, harder and more troublesome than before.

Then again, maybe California is a place where a witchy girl like me wouldn't need an explanation for finding so much gold. Maybe it's a place where we can finally be rich.

"Da will want to go," Jefferson says. "But we don't have enough money to put an outfit together. Look at this."

He unfolds the newspaper, and the bottom of the article is a list of all the items a family needs to go west: four yoke of oxen, a wagon, a mule, rifles, pistols, five barrels of flour, four hundred pounds of bacon . . .

"That'd cost more than six hundred dollars," I say.

"For a family of three, like yours. But even one person

needs at least two hundred." He shakes his head. "There's got to be a different way."

I know from his tone, as surely as I know Mama's locket doesn't contain a lick of brass, that Jefferson wants to go west more than anything. "You're going to run away," I say.

"Maybe. I don't know." He scuffs his bare foot against the step, sending a wave of sludge over the edge. "I could take the sorrel mare. Hunt my way there. Or work for somebody else, taking care of their stock. It's just that . . . It's just . . ."

"Jeff?" I peer close to try to figure him. He has a wide mouth that jumps into a smile faster than lightning. But there's nothing of smiling on his face right now.

"Remember the year the creek dried up, and we caught fifty tadpoles in the stagnant pool?" he says softly.

"Sure," I say, though I have no idea why he'd bring it up. "I remember you dropping a handful down my blouse."

"And I remember you screaming like a baby."

I punch him in the shoulder.

He jerks backward, staring at me in mock disapproval. "Your punches didn't used to hurt so much."

"I like to get better at things."

His gaze drifts far away. Rubbing absently at his shoulder, he says, "You're my best friend, Lee."

"I know."

"We're too old for school. I only come to see you."

"I know."

All at once he turns toward me and grasps my mittened hands in his bare ones. "Come west with me," he blurts.

I open my mouth, but nothing comes out.

"Marry me. Or . . . I mean . . . We could tell people we're married. Brother and sister, maybe! Whatever you want. But you're like me. With your daddy sick, I know it's really you working that claim, same way I work Da's. I know it's your own two hands as built that place up." His grip on my hands is so tight it's almost unbearable. "This is our chance to make our own way. It's only right that— Why are you shaking your head?"

His words brought a stab of hope so pure and quick it was like a spur in the side. But now I've a sorrow behind my eyes that wants to burst out, hot and wet. Jefferson is partly right: I'm the one who makes our claim work. He just doesn't know how much.

"Leah?"

I sigh. "Here's where you and I are different. I _love_ my mama and daddy. I can't leave them. And yes, it's my claim as much as anyone's. I'm proud of it. I can't leave it neither."

He releases my hands. Together, we look out over the snow-dusted yard to find the others staring at us. They saw us holding hands, for sure and certain. But we ignore them. We're used to ignoring them.

"You might not have a choice," he says. "If your daddy wants to go to California—"

That stab of hope again. "Mama will convince him not to. He's too sick."

"But _if_ you go—"

The school bell peals, calling us inside.

"We'll talk later," I say, more than a little glad to let the subject go. I've lots of thinking to do. In fact, I do so much thinking during the next hours that I'm useless for helping the little ones with their sums, and when Mr. Anders calls on me to recite the presidents, I mix up Madison and Monroe.

I drive home as soon as school lets out, not bothering to say bye to Jefferson, though I wave from a distance. I need to get away, and fast, find some open air for laying out all my thoughts about California and gold and going west, not to mention the stunning and undeniable fact that Jefferson just asked me to marry him.

As offers go, it's not the kind a girl dreams about while fingering the linens from her hope chest. I'm not even sure he meant it, the way he stumbled over it so badly.

I've thought about marriage—of course I have—but no one seems to have taken a shine to me. It's no secret I spend my days squatting in the creek bed or hefting a pickax or mucking the barn, that I have an eagle eye and a steady shot that brings in more game than Daddy ever did, even during his good spells. I might be forgiven my wild ways if I was handsome, but I'm not. My eyes are nice enough, as much gold as brown, just like Mama's. But I have a way of looking at people that makes them prickly, or so Jefferson says, and he always says it with a grin, like it's a compliment.

One time only did I mourn to Daddy about my lack of prospects. He just shrugged and said, "Strong chin, strong heart." Then he kissed me quick on the forehead. I never complained again. My daddy knows my worth.

I suppose Jefferson does too, and my heart hurts to think of him leaving and me staying. But the truth is I've never thought of him in a marrying kind of way. And with an awful proposal like that, I don't know that Jefferson's too keen on the idea either.

A gunshot cracks through the hills, tiny and miles distant. A minute later, it's followed by a second shot. Someone must be out hunting. I wish them luck.

By the time my wagon comes in view of the icy creek and the faint track that winds through the bare oaks toward home, I decide there's no help for it but to talk everything out with Mama and Daddy. The three of us have some shared secrets among ourselves, sure, but we have none from one another.

Peony tosses her head, as if sensing my thoughts. No, it's the surrounding woods that have put a twitch in her. They are too silent, too still.

"Everything's fine, girl," I say, and my voice echoes back hollowly.

As the leafless trees open up to reveal our sprawling homestead, right when I yell "Haw!" to round Peony toward the barn, something catches my eye.

A man's boot. Worn and wrinkled and all alone, toppled into a snowbank against the porch.

"Daddy?" I whisper, frozen for the space of two heartbeats.

I leap from the bench, and my skirt catches on the wheel spoke, but I rip right through and sprint toward the house. I don't get far before I fall to my knees, bent over and gasping.

Because Daddy lies on his back across the porch steps, legs

spread-eagled, bootless. Crimson pools beneath his head and drips down the steps—tiny rapids of blood. His eyes are wide to the sky, and just above them, like a third eye in a brow paler than snow, is a dark bullet hole.

"Mama!" I yell, and then I yell it again. I can't take my eyes off Daddy's face. He seems so surprised. So alive, except for that unblinking stare.

What should I do? Drag him away before he ruins the porch, maybe. Or put his boots back on. Why did Daddy go outside without his boots?

My hands shake with the need to do something. To fix something. My eyes search the steps, the porch, the wide-open doorway, but I can only find the one boot, shoved into the snowbank. "Mama? Where are Daddy's boots?" My voice is shrill in the winter air, almost a scream.

I use the porch railing to pull myself to my feet. If I can just find that blasted boot, everything will be fine. Why isn't Mama answering?

The world shifts, and I stumble hard against the railing.

Two gunshots. I heard two. "Mama," I whisper.

I start running. Through the drawing room, the bedroom, the kitchen still messy from supper. Upstairs to the dormer room where I sleep, then back down again. Sunshine has broken through the clouds, streaming light through our windows. Mama's touches of love are everywhere—the blue calico curtains of my bedroom, the pine boughs winding our otherwise plain banister, and poking from the vase on our mantel, flowers made from wrapping paper and stained yellow with wild mustard. Yesterday's venison stew, still warm on the box stove.

But Mama is nowhere to be found, and the place feels so bare it's like an ache in my soul.

Still calling for her, I race outside and bang on the outhouse. I search the barn. I splash through our tiny stream and sprint into the peach orchard.

Under the trees, I stop short. The world is so empty and quiet. Too quiet, as if even the trees need to be hushed and sad for a spell. Which is just as well; I must stop panicking and start thinking. *You're a smart girl, Lee,* Daddy always says, especially when I struggle with algebra. *You can figure this.*

Winter chill works its way through my boots, which aren't quite dry from yesterday's hunt, and I wrap my arms around myself against the cold and the dread. In the distance, Peony snorts at something. I left the poor girl hitched to the wagon. She'll have to keep.

I close my eyes and concentrate, turning in place like a compass.

Gold sings to me from north of the orchard, from the vein that Daddy and I started working before the snow hit. Fainter, as if very small or from very far away, comes the one I'm looking for: a hymn of purity, a lump of sweetness in my throat. A nugget, maybe, but I'm hoping it's Mama's locket.

It's in the direction of the barn. I've already been to the barn. What did I miss?

That lump of sweetness pulls me back through the bare peach trees, through the icy brook. The sensation strengthens as I approach. It's not coming from inside the barn, but behind it. Beyond the henhouse and near the woodpile.

The ground outside the henhouse is littered with down; something panicked the poor birds bad enough to send their feathers through the breathing holes. The sweetness in my throat turns sour. I force myself to walk the remaining steps.

I find her there, sitting with her back against the woodpile, legs outstretched, her skirt ridden up enough that a sliver of gray stocking shows above her boots. The locket that led me to her rests above her heart, sparkling in the sunshine. Below, her waist is soaked in blood. She's been gut-shot.

Her eyes flutter as I approach, and she lifts one hand in my direction. "Leah," she whispers. "My beautiful girl."

I rush forward and grab her hand. "I'll get Doc," I say. "Just hold tight." I try to pull away, but her grip is strong, though her gaze is so weak it can't seem to alight on anything for more than the space of a butterfly's touch.

"My strong girl. Strong, perfect . . ."

"Who did this to you?" Tears burn my eyes.

Her head lolls toward me, as if moving her neck can force her gaze in the direction her eyes cannot. "Trust someone. Not good to be as alone as we've been. Your daddy and I were wrong. . . ." Her words are coming slower and quieter.

"Mama?"

"Run, Lee. Go . . ."

Her chin hits her chest, and she says no more.

Chapter Four

$\mathcal{I}$ need help. I should get the sheriff. Or Judge Smith. I *know* I should.

But all I can do is sit back on my heels and stare. It doesn't matter what I do next. Not a single thing in the whole world will make my mama and daddy any less dead. And once I get up and walk away, everything will be different. I want this moment, this in-between time, when I'm not quite an orphan and I'm not quite alone.

She's wearing her winter dress, the black wool. Her chin rests in the ruffles of the high collar. I avoid looking at her belly, instead letting my eyes drift down to the mud-splattered skirt. She tried to run.

I gently lower her skirt to cover her stockings and tuck it under her ankles so the breeze won't blow it back up. The shiny brown bun of her hair skews to the side. I reach up to rearrange a hairpin or two, but my shaking fingers just make a mess of everything.

I swallow hard. Mama had the most beautiful hair. Shimmering light brown, with hints of bronze and gold. It fell past her waist when it wasn't pinned.

The locket winks at me, bright against the black wool. She'd want me to have it. But removing it will be so final.

A twig snaps, and I shoot to my feet. The sound came from the woods behind the barn. It could have been a raccoon, or even a deer. Still, I imagine murderous eyes on me as I reach behind Mama's neck for the clasp. My hands struggle to make sense of it. I'm too afire with listening, ready to dart away at the slightest noise.

My fingertips tingle from gold as I work the clasp. It comes free, and I barely catch the charm before it slips off the chain. I shove both chain and locket into the pocket of my skirt.

"I'm so sorry, Mama," I whisper. "I have to go."

But go where? Everything is foggy and strange. All I know for sure is that Mama told me to run.

I can't just leave her here. It wouldn't be right. I need help. I need—

Jefferson! He'll know what to do. I could be at the McCauley claim and back in twenty minutes.

I shouldn't go unarmed.

I dash to the house and bang open the back door. Daddy has a special rack above the mantel for hanging our guns. We own three—an old long rifle with a bayonet, the newer Hawken rifle I always hunt with, and a cap-and-ball revolver. The long rifle and the Hawken give me distance and accuracy, but they can be awkward to load while bareback, especially with my fingers trembling like they are. That leaves the revolver.

I grab it from the rack and palm the ivory grip. Something niggles at me while I stare down at it, like mosquitos in the back of my head. I think about Daddy, lying in a pool of his own blood. Bile rises in my throat, but I force it down.

That hole in his forehead. So tiny and perfect. The back of his skull is probably in tatters, but except for that hole, the front is as white and pristine as Mrs. Smith's alabaster vase.

No rifle would make such a tidy hole. My daddy was shot with a revolver, like the one I hold in my hand. No, maybe even a smaller gun, like one of those fancy new Colts. Do I know anyone who owns a new Colt revolver?

I sift through memories of everyone I know, but my mind fogs up again, and I can't do it for all the gold in the world.

Jefferson. I need Jeff.

I run out the front door, leaving it swinging in the wind, and I leap over the steps and over Daddy's body. I unhitch Peony, hike up my skirts, and use the wagon wheel to vault onto her back.

The McCauley homestead is tucked into a dark holler between two birch-thick hills. Jefferson half cleared one of the hillsides and planted corn, now brown and shriveled with winter. But the rest of the land is so wild and dense that most of the ground never sees the sun. It's a dank, dark place made for hiding things like moonshine and heartbreak.

Peony and I splash across the frost-edged creek, passing a

rotting, abandoned sluice. I pull her up at the house—a small log cabin with a sod roof. Smoke curls from the chimney, and wind whistles against the cracked glass of the single window.

"Jefferson!" I swing a leg over and slide off. I sprint through dead weeds to the stoop, where I leap to avoid the sagging steps, and pound on the door. "Jefferson!"

Their dog, Nugget, barks from inside the house. Booted footsteps hurry toward me. The door swings wide, revealing Jefferson's da, a small man with wild gray hair, rumpled clothes, and a bright red nose.

He shrugs on his right suspender strap, blinking against the gloomy day, which is downright perky compared to the murk of the cabin. "Miss Lee," he slurs.

The air wafting out the door is warm and sour, like rising bread gone bad. "I need to see Jefferson," I say.

"Dunno where that boy run off to." Nugget pokes her yellow head out beside his legs, floppy ears perked forward.

"Where do you think he might've—"

"I said I dunno."

"Did he come home after school?"

"Mebbe."

Something snaps inside me. "Think for one *lousy* minute, will you? I'm in a heap of hurt, and I need to talk to your boy."

Mr. McCauley recoils. "Watch your swearing tongue, girl."

My fists clench with the need to bust his bright red nose. It's a testament to my fine character that I turn tail and jog away. I'll find Jefferson myself.

The door slams behind me, so I'm surprised to feel Nugget's damp nose in my palm as I head toward the outhouse.

I pause at the door. It's powerful improper for me to bang on it with Jefferson inside. No help for it. I raise my fist to knock when the crack of an ax rents the air.

Relieved, I lift my petticoats and run toward the ramshackle building that was intended to be a barn but never got finished and became a woodshed instead.

Jefferson is behind it, sleeves rolled up past his elbows and ax in hand, splitting firewood on one of the larger stumps. The moment he sees me, he frowns and drops his ax. "Lee?"

And suddenly I'm clutch-hugging myself, and my words are jumbling all over one another, and I hardly know what I'm saying except that the word "dead" hangs in the air, sharper and more final than the crack of an ax on a chopping block.

His arms come up around my shoulders, and he pulls me close. He smells familiar and safe, like fresh woodchips and loamy soil, and finally I cry—great gulping cries that dampen his shirt.

"All right, Lee," he says at last. "Slow down. Start over and tell me everything. Every single thing."

So I do. His face is grave as I talk. Even though my dinner is turning round and round in my belly, and my words come spilling out all over themselves, Jefferson just stands calm and ponders like a man twice his years.

"Maybe it was bandits," he says, though I can tell he doesn't put much stock in the idea.

"They didn't take anything. Only thing missing was one of Daddy's boots."

"How long ago were they shot, do you think?"

"I heard the shots when I was on the way home. Mama was still alive when I found her. And Daddy's . . . The blood hadn't froze. Jeff, he rushed out the door with his boots still in hand. Why would he do that?"

Jeff's hand finds the small of my back and guides me toward the cabin. I stumble keeping up with his long legs. "Where—"

"I'm getting my gun," he says. "Maybe your daddy heard a shot and ran outside."

Nugget trots along beside us. "Wouldn't he have grabbed his own gun first? He just ran outside. Like . . . like . . ."

Jefferson stops cold, and I almost bang into his shoulder. "Like he knew the person. Someone he was powerful glad to see."

I nod up at him. "Who would Daddy . . ." A sick worry wriggles around in my chest. "Mama said . . . before she . . . She told me to run."

"She thought the murderer was still nearby."

We stare at each other.

"This is bad, isn't it?" I say.

"We'll figure it, I promise. Did you bring a gun?"

"The cap and ball. Loaded it on the way here. All five shots."

"Good. Nugget, stay here with Lee. I'll be right back." He flings the door open and disappears into the murky cabin.

Jefferson never lets me in. He doesn't want me to know how bad it is between him and his da, and he doesn't realize I've already guessed about the moonshine still that's hidden inside. There are things even best friends don't tell each other.

Nugget leans against my leg, and I bend down to scritch her neck. We've always gotten along, Nugget and me.

A thump echoes inside the cabin, then Mr. McCauley yells something loud and angry. Jefferson strides out a moment later, rifle in hand. He won't meet my eye, just heads over to the goat pen, Nugget and me at his heels.

He grabs the sorrel mare; they've never named the poor girl, just call her "the sorrel mare," and they keep her penned for lack of a proper barn. Jefferson mounts up, and I use the fence to climb up on Peony, and off we go. Jefferson leads us southward, toward my house.

"We're going back?" I thought we'd go for help.

His voice is gentle as he says, "No use getting Doc now. And no murderer with a lick of sense would stick around after doing the deed."

I stare blankly.

"Surely you know, Lee?" Jefferson says. "'Lucky's gold' is practically a legend. Once word is out that your mama and daddy have gone to Jesus, the whole town will come poking around. Everyone thinks your daddy stashed—"

"Oh." Tears threaten to spill again. I can imagine it now. Annabelle Smith and her mother coming by with their peach pie and their slick words of sympathy and their darting eyes.

Sheriff Weber searching the whole homestead for "clues," opening cupboards and shifting hay bales and maybe even prying up floorboards.

"I need to hide . . . until everything's settled." The words make me feel heartless and cold. *Necessity is a harsh master,* Mama used to say. Bet she didn't anticipate that necessity would make me look to our gold even before giving her a proper burial.

"It's true, isn't it," Jefferson says, his voice suddenly wistful.

"It's true," I whisper.

"All right, then." He nods, as though to himself. "We'll have to be careful and quick. Just in case your mama was right and whoever did this decided to stick around."

"I'm glad Nugget is with us."

"She'll let us know if someone happens by."

We pass the ridge where Daddy and I started working the new vein, then I cross the tiny cemetery that only has two headstones—one for Orpha the dog, and one for my baby brother who lived three days. Daddy carved them himself. There'll soon be two more, and I don't know who will carve them.

Our pace slows even more as we ride through the orchard. Jefferson sits tall on his mare, alert for the slightest strangeness. As we pass the henhouse, something in me screams not to look, but I can't help glancing that way. The woodpile blocks my view of everything except Mama's legs. Her skirt is still tucked beneath her ankles.

A shadow passes overhead, and I duck before realizing it's

a great buzzard circling. The first of the scavengers, coming to get what's mine.

"Let's go in the back door," I say. I'll have to face Daddy's body again soon enough. But not just yet.

Jefferson guides our horses past the garden and to the back porch. He hands me the reins to the sorrel mare, puts a finger to his lips, and whispers, "I'll check the house. Wait here." He hefts his rifle and slips inside.

He's in there a long time while the cold sun beats down on my head and the buzzards circle and the silent woods watch my back. The world feels empty and quiet. Too empty.

My breath catches. Our gold.

I do sense something—the tiniest spark of sweetness. Probably just the nugget I found yesterday, hiding wherever Daddy stashed it. But the usual, ever-present thrumming in my head whenever I'm near our bag of dust is completely gone.

Strange how you don't notice things until they're taken away.

Chapter Five

*F*inally, Jefferson peeks his head out the doorway and says, "I think it's clear."

I slide off Peony and loop the reins of both horses through the porch rail. "Let's get this done," I say, and my voice is heavy with the knowledge of what I won't find.

Jefferson makes Nugget stay outside. She whines as the door shuts behind us, but I feel better knowing she's out there keeping an eye on things.

"This way," I say to Jefferson, and I lead him into the kitchen. The pine table I used last night to clean the Hawken rifle is askew, the braid rug beneath it wrinkled. One of the four chairs lies toppled on its side.

Jefferson helps me lift the table. I get down on my knees and peel back the rug to reveal two floorboards that almost-but-not-quite match the others.

"This isn't a very good hiding place, Lee," Jefferson says over my shoulder.

Tears are already streaming down my face. I push down on the boards just so, and the opposite ends pop up so I can grab them. "Guess we never figured on actually getting robbed." I reach into the hole.

"Anything?"

"It's gone," I say in a dead voice. I pull out an empty flour sack, the one we were going to start filling next. It's still folded into a neat square.

"What's missing?"

"A three-pound flour bag."

"Of gold?"

"Yes."

"Like that one there? Except full?"

"I said yes."

"Oh, heavens, Lee," Jefferson says. "Three pounds of flour . . . That would be the same as . . ."

"Almost six pounds of gold." I sit back on my heels, holding my hands in my lap to keep them from shaking. "That bag was worth well over a thousand dollars."

Enough to take a whole family to California, easy.

"Where did you find it all?" Jefferson's voice is filled with breathless wonder, and maybe a little anger.

"Here and there," I say, avoiding his gaze. The lie sets ugly in my heart. "We got lucky."

"And now it's gone."

I wipe my eyes quickly and get to my feet. "I have something for you."

"What?"

I close my eyes and turn in place. "Just have to remember..."
There. On the shelf above the box stove, where Mama's
wrapping-paper flowers sit in their plain wooden vase. I walk
over, upend the vase, and the nugget drops into my hand. I
hand it to him. "This one is yours. I . . . chanced upon it after
I chased a white tail onto your claim."

He grips the nugget tight, saying nothing. He's still staring
at the empty flour sack on the floor by the hole. It's stamped
CULBERT & SONS, LTD. FLOUR MILLERS.

"We had to import sacks special from England," I say. "To
get the small size. Daddy hoped people might think they
were really filled with flour at first glance."

Jefferson tears his gaze from the sack to stare at my face
instead.

"Please say something, Jeff. Daddy was going to take it all
to the Charlotte mint, where no one knows who we are, but
he got so sick. It's just been sitting here for more than a year
and . . . Well, Mama said people would hate us for being too
rich too quick. I couldn't stand it if you were one of them."

Jeff shakes his head. "It's not that." Finally, he shoves the
nugget I gave him into a pocket. I thought he'd forgotten it.

"Then what is it?"

He squats down beside the empty sack, brushes the top
with a finger. The fever burns in his eyes. He's picturing it
full of sweet, raw gold. All of a sudden, he snatches his hand
back like he's bee-stung.

"Let's go get Sheriff Weber," he says. We head out the back
door, where Nugget greets us with a little yip.

"Don't tell!" I say, and he freezes on the porch step. "About the gold, I mean. People might think there's more. They might . . ."

His shoulders rise and fall with a breath. "If you say so." Before mounting up on the sorrel mare, he turns to me and adds, "But, Lee? You could have trusted *me*."

I nod, even though shame makes the back of my throat hot. There's so much he still doesn't know. So much I can't say.

"We should grab a few of your things," Jefferson says. "I'm sure someone in town would take you in while—"

"No."

"Lee—"

"I'm getting help, and I'm coming right back. This is my *home*, Jeff."

He frowns. "Promise me you'll keep your guns handy. I'll stick around as much as possible."

"Thank you."

As we ride toward town, I can't shake the feeling that someone is watching us. Maybe it's the continued dead silence of the woods, or the way Nugget keeps her ears perked and sticks so close to Peony that she nearly gets stomped.

Not that it matters. Anyone who's watching is wasting his time. I've already lost everything.

News of the murder sends the town of Dahlonega into a frenzy, and the next few days are a blur. I have visitors every waking minute, which makes me feel a lot safer but puts a terrible ache in my head. Everyone's condolences have an edge of excitement to them. When Mr. Cooper, superintendent at the U.S. Mint, lends all his assayers and other staff to Sheriff Weber for a search of the woods around town for the murderer, it becomes almost like a holiday.

Mama said to run, but I've no place to go. This is my home. I've worked just as hard to build it up as Mama or Daddy ever did, and I won't let anyone scare me away. So I sit in my house for days, pretending to be grateful for company, waiting and waiting for news that doesn't come. I keep the five-shooter close by and ready, breaking a rule about loaded guns in the house. I hope to hear that bandits have been raiding the mountains, that mine isn't the only house they hit, because that would mean I'm probably safe now. It would mean Mama wasn't trying to warn me about anyone in particular.

The search of the woods reveals nothing. Sheriff Weber asks around at Mrs. Choice's hotel and Free Jim's store, where they say a steady stream of strangers have been passing through all week on their way to the gold fields of California. He eventually concludes that the awful deed was perpetrated by bandits looking for Lucky's secret stash—which I assure him never existed—and that they're probably well west of here by now, along with all the other good-for-nothings.

I'm not convinced he's right, and it makes me a little sick for my parents' murders to be put to rest so easily. But God help me if I'm not a little relieved too. I don't know what I'm going to do next or how I'll run a homestead all by myself. Maybe after the funeral I'll finally have time and space to think it all through, away from prying eyes and wringing hands.

Everyone inquires politely about my parents' relations, as if somehow their asking will conjure up the kin everyone knows I don't have. Mama's family cut her off when she married my daddy, and she hasn't talked to them since moving away from Boston. Daddy has no blood left but his brother, Hiram, a fancy lawyer way down in the state capital of Milledgeville. In a place where family connections spread out like wild grapevines covering the trees, I'm all alone.

Or not quite all alone. There's still one person I can turn to for help.

Jefferson and a couple other boys from school spend an afternoon digging graves for Mama and Daddy. I found out it would cost me twenty dollars to have headstones made, and maybe I could witch up enough gold dust given a little time, but not without raising questions. So I ask Jefferson to make a pair of wooden crosses for now.

The day of the funeral dawns icy clear. Meltwater from the warm snap froze overnight, leaving the trees, the eaves of the barn, and even the henhouse dripping with tiny icicles. The whole world sparkles so bright in the winter sun it's almost hard to look at.

After finishing my morning chores, I wash up and don my best dress—a brown wool with lace cuffs, and a pointed waist with pretty yellow piping. Mama and I finished it just last week.

I can't get the corset very tight without help, but the dress buttons up with surprising ease. It has the fullest skirt I've ever owned. I remember twirling in place during my final fitting, admiring how high the hem lifted in spite of the fabric's weight. Mama scolded me for showing off my petticoats.

I stand before our tiny mirror to put on her locket, and I see her face staring back at me. Everyone says I have her eyes—widely spaced and mostly brown, a little too deep-set. But I look like her more than ever today. I seem older, with thinner cheeks and sunken eyes. I haven't eaten much these past few days.

I reach around the back of my neck and clasp the locket in place. I flip out the lace collar to cover the chain. The pendant rests just above my heart. It's a relief to feel the gold sense come back, even a little. I may never take off the locket.

Someone knocks at the door. I glance at the table to make sure my revolver is still there. I've been keeping it handy these past few days, because whoever killed my parents is armed with at least a Colt. If my visitors have found it strange that I never open the door unarmed, they haven't said.

I grab the revolver and head toward the door, feeling a stab of embarrassment; the steps leading up the front porch still have bloodstains on them, though I've scrubbed and scrubbed. They're brown-black now, not like blood at all. Still, if I don't replace them soon, I'll see Daddy's body in my mind's eye every time I step outside. Maybe Jefferson will do it for me.

And it's like I've summoned him with a thought, because I swing the door open and there he is, his gaze downcast and his wrinkled hat in hand. Nugget sits at his heels, her tail thumping.

He blurts, "I'm going west, Lee."

It's like a kick in the gut. "What? When!"

He looks up finally, and I gasp, for his right eye is the color of spring violets and swollen shut. "Now," he says.

"Oh, Jeff, what happened? Was it your da? I'll kill him if he—"

"Come west with me."

The sorrel mare is tethered at the bottom of the steps. Two saddlebags hang over her sides, and Jefferson's long rifle rides high in its saddle holster near her withers. "That nugget you gave me. I should've given it back, but . . . I just came from Free Jim's store. He bought it off me. Gave me enough to buy a stake in a wagon train."

"It never belonged to me. It was yours to do with as you wanted."

"Then come to California with me. You could sell this place to Mr. Gilmore today."

A vision passes before my eyes: clear mountain brooks sparkling with gold flecks, nuggets winking up from pine needle–choked earth, game so plentiful you'd hardly have to leave your back porch to shoot. For a girl like me, California is the Promised Land.

"Leah, we'd have enough money to buy our way there if you sold—"

"I . . . I don't know." Is that what his marriage proposal was about? Finding someone to help him buy his way there?

"Mr. Gilmore has had his eye on this place for years," he insists.

I shake my head. "Doesn't matter. I'm just a girl, and I can't sell what I don't own until I get my hands on Daddy's will, proving the place is mine." I'm not sure how I'll do that. Uncle Hiram was the one who drew it up, years ago. "This is my home, Jeff. I've worked so hard to build it into something nice. I don't know what's going to happen to me, or how I'll run this place, but . . ."

He steps forward until his body fills the doorway. When did Jefferson become so large? "Then let's just go."

Oh, dear Lord, but a hole is opening up in my heart again, just like the one that started gaping wide when I saw Daddy's boot in the snow. "I have to go to the funeral, and then I have to sort through Mama's and Daddy's things, and then there's my chickens, and . . ."

He plunks his hat back on his head. "I know you, and I know you want this. When you change your mind, find me in Independence, Missouri. I'll wait a spell for you. Can't head west until the prairie grass starts to grow, anyway. Otherwise, the sorrel mare will starve. But I can't wait too long either, else I meet winter in the mountains." His lips press into a firm line. "I'll wait for you in Independence as long as I can."

I watch him walk away, the hole growing wider and deeper. Sunshine falls onto his shoulders, lighting him up like a torch, and for a moment I can hardly breathe.

He pauses. Turns. Sadness tugs at his eyes as he says, "Seems like I've been waiting for you to come around my whole life, Lee. But a man can't wait forever and stay a man."

And with that, my best friend in the whole world is gone.

Chapter Six

I've hardly closed the door on Jefferson's retreating back before another knock sounds. I smooth down my hair and check my hairpins before opening it again. It's Mrs. Smith, wife to the judge and mother of Annabelle.

"Oh, Leah dear, I was worried something had happened to you." She frees one spindly, gloved hand from its fur muff to pat my cheek, but her gaze moves beyond me, roves the interior of the house. Looking for untidiness to gossip about, I'll wager. Or hoping giant sacks of gold will magically appear on the kitchen table.

"Everyone is waiting for you graveside," she explains at last.

She's wearing a funeral-appropriate black gown with velvet panels, but it's her locket that catches my eye and makes my throat buzz a little. It's gold, like Mama's, and etched with interlinking hearts. It contains photographs of her husband and Annabelle, taken when the Smiths visited Charleston on holiday. I know this because Annabelle told everyone at school about it when they got back.

Mama would never have allowed such an expense. The locket I now wear contains a tiny tuft of my baby brother's hair.

"Aren't you coming, dear?"

Does Mrs. Smith realize how lucky she is to have a whole family? "Yes," I say to the locket. "I . . . I just needed a moment to myself."

"Of course." Her tone holds a whiff of disapproval. "I'll walk with you."

"Thank you."

She grabs my hand and yanks me out the door. Judge Smith waits in the walkway, and he tips his hat as we descend the stairs. "Glad to see you, Miss Leah," he says.

I mumble something polite as the Smiths take up posts at each shoulder. They are both long and lanky, and they walk with unerring purpose and perfect posture, certain of their significance in this world. I am towered over. Hemmed in. Imprisoned.

Jefferson's words return to me like a clanging church bell. *I'll wait for you in Independence.*

When we arrive, others are already gathered around the snow-dusted mounds that mark my parents' graves. The air smells of freshly turned earth. Almost everyone wears black. They huddle in groups, bundled against the cold, their breaths frosting the air. It's more people than I'd like to see right now, but less than my parents deserve.

Annabelle Smith is the height of fashion, even in mourning black, with a rabbit-fur cape and a poke bonnet with blue silk flowers and long, trailing ribbons. Her young slave, Jeannie, stands a pace behind her, shivering in a thin muslin dress. Reverend Wilson has already taken up his post behind the twin wooden crosses, his huge Bible in one arm and his huge wife under the other.

I'm surprised to see Jefferson's da. He wears his buckskin coat over stained trousers, and he stares dolefully as I approach, his red nose brighter than ever. Does Mr. McCauley realize Jefferson has run away?

Beside him is Free Jim Boisclair, the richest Negro in Lumpkin County and a great friend to my daddy. He speaks in hushed tones to a few others I recognize from our infrequent visits to the Methodist church. He points to something in his hand. A leaflet, with writing I can't make out. Several others are clutching leaflets too. There's a buzz in the air, like when everyone is worked up to hear a new preacher. I can't shake the feeling that the leaflet is the main attraction and the funeral a mere afterthought.

Upon seeing me, the reverend clears his throat. Conversations die around me. My face warms under the scrutiny of silence, and I'm almost relieved when he launches into his eulogy.

To my dismay, it turns out to be a sermon. He speaks of the toils of this life and how sometimes our troubles make us want to escape to far-off places instead of standing strong in the Lord's grace. He says the love of gold is the root of all evil and we should be storing up treasures in heaven instead.

Tears prick at my eyes. No one would blame me for shedding a few, but I hold them back anyway, because I don't want to let rage tears flow when my parents deserve grief. It's not right, the reverend using their deaths as an excuse to give us all a talking-to.

I'm in a bit of a haze and grateful for it when Annabelle Smith—who wrongly thinks she has the voice of an angel and always sings loudest in church—barrels through all six stanzas of "Amazing Grace." Everyone comes to shake my hand and tell me how sorry they are and that God is looking out for me as one of his sparrows and do I need anything?

Mr. McCauley hangs back. Gone is his angry scowl. He wrings his hat in his hands and glances around as if searching for something. Finally, he approaches.

"You seen Jefferson?" he asks.

I echo his own words back at him. "Dunno where that boy run off to."

My mockery is lost on him. "Sorrel mare is gone. And my rifle. I found this by his bed." He shoves one of the leaflets in my face. "Dog's gone too."

I snatch it from his hand and look it over. It's an advertisement for the Pacific Mail Steamship Company, promising to take passengers to California, beginning in the spring, for the sum of two hundred dollars. This is what everyone's so excited about. This is what the reverend is speaking out against.

Mr. McCauley says, "You think he went to catch a boat?"

I pin him with a gaze, and he shifts uncomfortably.

My heart starts to soften toward him, but then I remember Jefferson's busted eye. "He's probably halfway to Savannah," I say. "If you leave now, you can catch up." Keeping the leaflet, I turn my back on him.

Annabelle Smith finds me next. She clasps my hands and says, "I'm so sorry, Lee. I wish . . . I mean . . . I'm just sorry." She can't meet my gaze, but her words have a ring of sincerity.

"I'm glad you came," I say automatically. But suddenly it's true. I watch her back as she walks away, wondering what it would be like to have a girl for a friend.

Free Jim is next in line. His dark hand closes around my cold, pale one—too tight and too warm—and I blurt, "I'll make good on Daddy's credit, Mr. Boisclair, I promise. I just need a little time to—"

"No need, Miss Leah," he says gently. "The account was brought up-to-date just this morning."

"What? How?"

He frowns. "Your uncle Hiram paid it. Apparently he's done well for himself down in Milledgeville."

My stomach drops into my toes. How did my uncle get here so fast? How did he know?

"That man's a born politician," Free Jim says, and it doesn't sound like a compliment. "Anyway, I'm praying to the good Lord every day on your behalf. Your daddy was a fine man; one of the finest I knew. The world is a poorer place today, but heaven is all the richer."

"Yes, sir," I say, swallowing hard. "Thank you, sir."

Free Jim and my daddy have a history, going back to the first discovery of gold in these parts. Daddy always considered him a friend, and we've gotten through many a tough winter thanks to Free Jim and his generous negotiating. We'd have owed him even more for that winter wheat seed if he'd demanded fair market price.

"I thought your uncle would be here," Free Jim says, glancing around. "He said he had a few errands, but afterward he'd— Oh, there he is. Mr. Westfall!"

My heart races as he calls out my uncle's name. Slowly I turn.

The conversation around us dies as Uncle Hiram bears down on our little group, tromping through the winter-gray trees like he owns them. He's followed by Abel Topper, a shovel-faced man with keen eyes, who used to be a foreman before his mine dried up and closed down.

Hiram exchanges greetings with Free Jim, who afterward tips his hat to me and nods in solemn farewell. He and Abel walk off together. Uncle Hiram turns in my direction.

Dread curls in my belly, and I'm not sure why. Maybe it's because he looks so much like my daddy, though he's more dashing, truth be told. Thick lashes rim sharp brown eyes, and neat sideburns frame a solid jaw. His long nose would be the bane of any lady, but on him, it fits proud and strong. He wears a shiny top hat and a fine wool suit with silver buttons, and the sparkling silver chain of a hidden pocket watch loops across his left breast. His sweeping, knee-length overcoat is unbuttoned, revealing a black leather holster with white stitching slung across his hips. The revolver is partly hidden by the holster, but I can plainly see that it's tiny, ivory-gripped, and sparkling new.

A Colt.

I'm sure of it.

It doesn't mean anything. Lots of folks have bought Colts recently. Still, my hand creeps to my imaginary holster before I remember that I'm dressed in funeral finery, that my five-shooter lies lonely on the table.

I glance around. Everyone is clearing out, except Mrs. Smith, who lingers. I edge closer to her.

"Hello, sweet pea," Hiram says in a slow, sleepy Milledgeville drawl.

Daddy's endearment, coming from him, feels as false as hearing a cat bark. "Why are you here?"

His smile is just the right amount of sad. "Judge Smith wrote to me with the terrible news. I came right away to put Reuben's affairs in order."

Uncle Hiram doesn't seem all that shaken by "the terrible news." When my baby brother died, I thought the pain in my chest would never go away, even though I only knew him for a few days.

He says, "I'm here to help you put—"

"I don't need your help." He hasn't bothered to visit since I was eight years old.

"I don't think you understand. I'm your guardian now."

I blink. "Oh."

I'm still staring up at him when he reaches out with his

fine gentleman's hand and caresses my cheek.

The gold sense wells inside me, so startling and quick that tears spring to my eyes. I lurch away from him, swallowing hard to keep down my breakfast.

"There, there, sweet pea," he says, as though talking to a recalcitrant horse. "We'll get accustomed to each other in time. Everything's all right now, I promise."

My skin is crawling. Everything is not and never will be all right. Because my uncle is carrying a new Colt revolver, and he's covered in gold dust.

Sure, he probably brushed it off. Wiped his hands. And I can't *see* the gold caught in his knuckles, or trapped beneath his fingernails, maybe even lingering on his overcoat. But I can sense it. I can always sense it.

"Leah?"

Grief washes over me in waves until I'm dizzy with it. Jeff was right: Daddy rushed out of the house to greet someone. Someone he was glad to see.

And my uncle killed him. His very own brother.

"It's okay to cry, baby girl," he says.

I blink against tears and clench my fists, imagining what it would be like to feel his nose bust under my knuckles. But my rage dribbles away, and my legs twitch as if to flee. Is he going to kill me too? Who would help me? Not Mrs. Smith, who even now gazes up at my uncle like he's the second coming of George Washington. She would never believe me. No one would.

"You have room in the barn for my horse?" he asks, and

for the first time, I notice the tall black gelding hobbled behind him in the woods. It's snowing again, and the horse's back is powdered with white. "Poor boy could use a bit of pampering."

There's not a hint of regret or shame in his face. No fear of discovery in his voice. And maybe that's what will keep me safe, for now. I can't let on that I know what he did.

I force my voice into perfect blandness. "I have two empty stalls. Put him in the one by the door, or Peony will give him a nip."

"We'll talk more in a bit," he says. "I'll come back later to pay my respects." He tips his hat to Mrs. Smith, who stands enthralled beside me, and he heads back toward his gelding.

"I'm not moving to Milledgeville!" I call out after him.

He looks over his shoulder. He's still wearing that slight smile. A whole world I don't understand is in that smile. "Of course not," he says.

Why did you do it? I want to scream at his back.

"A very fine man, your uncle," Mrs. Smith says.

"I hardly know him," I murmur, still staring after him.

"Well, you're lucky to have him."

I say nothing. Mrs. Smith has known me my whole life. But she's delighted to see me given over to a perfect stranger, for no other reason than I'm a young girl and he's a fine gentleman relative.

There's no proof Hiram murdered my parents—not unless I lay my secret bare, the one I swore to Mama and Daddy I'd never reveal. There's nothing I can do.

Well, maybe there is one thing.

I'll wait for you in Independence.

I return to the house and discover that several people dropped off food before heading back to their own homes. I count three jars of jam, two baskets full of biscuits, a meat pie, some baked ham and smashed potatoes. More than I can possibly eat. Warmth swells in my chest, surprising me. The people of Dahlonega are a gossipy, small-minded lot, but we've always taken care of our own.

Boots tromp up the stairs outside. The braid rug covering our hidey-hole has puckered at the edge. Quick as a snake, I put my toe out and stomp the wrinkle down. I almost laugh aloud at myself. Hiram already stole my gold. Keeping secrets is such a habit.

He doesn't even knock, just swings the front door wide and strides inside like the house has been waiting for him. He whips off his gloves and whacks them against his thigh, sending powdery snow falling to the floor.

I don't bother to hide my glare. "Hang your hat and coat there by the door," I say, indicating the iron hooks in the wall.

"What culinary delights are conspiring to make my mouth water?"

If he's trying to sound like a fine Southern gentleman, he's failing. "I don't know. Whatever folks left for us?"

"I smell baked ham," he says, shrugging off his overcoat. "Fix a plate for me?"

I consider storming off, but I can't shake my upbringing. When you have a guest in your house, you fix them something to eat. I grab a clean plate from the hutch and cut him a slice of ham, then surround it with potatoes and biscuits. I hope he chokes on the first bite.

Hiram makes himself at home. He has a heavier step and quicker movements than my daddy, and the tobacco scent of him swells, pushing everything out of its way, making the air of my home seem unfamiliar and strange. He settles into Daddy's chair by the cold box stove, and I put the plate on the side table next to him.

"Help me with my boots," he says.

My gut churns as I approach, careful like a cat. I kneel at his feet, and my fingers squelch in lingering mud as I grab and yank. The boots come loose easily enough that he could have done it himself. He sits back, sighing like a man well and truly satisfied. "Thank you, sweet pea."

I ignore him, setting the boots by the door. I wipe my hands on a rag. Then, standing straight as I can, my chin in the air but my face as void as a snow-blanked hill, I ask the question that's been squeezing my soul: "How long are you going to stay?"

He pulls a pipe from the breast pocket of his vest. It's carved with vines, and the sick-sweet scent of tobacco gets even stronger, though the pipe remains unlit. He contemplates it a moment, smiles a small, secret smile, then shoves it back into his pocket. "Forever, Leah," he says finally. "This is my home now."

"It belongs to me. Daddy left it to me in his will." My fists clench at my sides again. "You know it. You're the one who drew it up."

"He left this homestead—everything—to me," he says.

I open my mouth, close it. Try again. I imagine I look like a brook trout, tossed onto the bank and gasping.

His voice gentles. "You need proof; I can see that." He puts his stockinged feet up on Daddy's stool and leans back. "My boy will be here soon with all my belongings. When he arrives, I'll unpack my office first and show you my brother's will, signed by Reuben himself."

It takes a moment for me to realize "boy" refers to his slave. If Daddy knew that his brother owned slaves . . .

My eyes prick with tears all over again. I won't cry in front of him. I *won't.*

"Be reasonable, sweet pea. Such a will would have been invalid, anyway. The law, in its wisdom, protects the weaker sex from the hardships and vicissitudes that attend the ownership of property."

"I'm not weak."

"Of course not. You're a Westfall." His smile is all teeth. "But you *are* a young lady, one who has just suffered a terrible tragedy, no less. It's a good thing I came when I did."

"Why? So you can . . ." I almost say "kill me too." "So you can take what doesn't belong to you?" I finish lamely.

"It's mine, lawfully and morally. And so are you, sweet pea. My very own charge." His gaze on me softens. It's the same look of affection Daddy gave me when he said I had a strong heart, and it chills my bones.

"This is a hard time for you; I understand that," he continues. "But you and I, we are much alike, I think. We're going to get on swimmingly." Keeping his eyes on me, he picks up his plate, stabs the ham with a fork, and crams the first large bite into his mouth.

I ignore him, pulling on my own boots—Daddy's castoffs from years ago—and head toward the door. I have plans to make.

"Where are you going?"

I whirl to find Uncle Hiram still peering at me. He seems nervous all of a sudden, and I'm pleased to have shaken that smug composure, though I'm not sure how I did it.

"I'm going to muck stalls."

"That's man's work."

"There's no man here willing to work, far as I can see."

He frowns. "That barn is the cleanest I ever saw."

"Because I don't shirk my daily chores."

We stare at each other, our chins set equally hard, and the thought niggles like a worm in my belly: Maybe we are alike. Maybe just a little.

Finally, he says, "You're too valuable to waste on farmwork, Leah. I know what you can do. And I intend you to keep on doing it."

I do a stink-poor job of keeping the shock off my face. Daddy told him. Hiram knows about me. My knees turn as wobbly as pudding. I need to get away to the barn fast, before I fall apart completely.

"But when my boy gets here, I'll start making a lady out of you. I know Reuben and Elizabeth let you run wild as a colt, but no longer."

"Whatever you say."

"I care about you, Leah Westfall. More than you know. I'll make sure you have the best of everything. The best gowns, the best grooming, the best—"

I walk out and slam the door behind me.

Uncle Hiram tricked my daddy, for sure and certain. He drew up the will, and Daddy signed without question. Hiram was the one person Daddy had trusted and loved enough that he let his guard down.

Trust someone, Mama said. Her dying words, burned into my heart. But she was wrong. When there's gold to be had, you can't trust anyone. Not a single soul.

Snow has started to pile up against the barn, and I scoop some of it out of the way so I can swing open one of the barn doors. It's not until I'm wiping snow from my hand on to my skirt that I realize I'm still wearing my brand-new dress.

Peony greets me with a snort and a head toss. I shove the locket under my collar so she doesn't accidentally break it, then I slip into her stall and put my arms around her neck. Finally, I let the tears flow.

"You want to go west with me, girl?" I whisper into her mane.

My shoulders relax and my jaw unclenches as she snuffles at my hair and neck. We lived in the barn for two years before Daddy built our house. *The animals come first*, Daddy always said. *They're our lives and livelihood.* I don't really remember that time—I was too little—but I've always felt at home here with Peony. Always felt safe.

Our wagon sits braked in the center of the barn. On each side are four stalls containing Peony and the rest of the team, two milk cows, and now Uncle Hiram's black gelding. Tack hangs on wooden pegs at the opening to each stall. Hay is stacked against the back wall and in the loft—not enough for winter, not with Hiram's horse here.

I cast around for our missing gold, but I don't sense it anywhere. I'd bet all the hay in our barn that Hiram took it to get assayed already. He probably used some of it to pay our debt to Free Jim and then put the rest in the bank. There's no way I'm getting it back now.

"How do you feel about wearing a saddle again?" I say to Peony. It's been years since she's worn anything but a soft halter for riding; I've always been able to direct her with my knees. But a trip across the continent will demand a lot more of us, and I'll need finer control and a firmer seat.

It's tempting to take the wagon; I could carry more, and Peony is used to that bridle and harness. But if Hiram knows what I can do, he'll come after me, for sure and certain. I'll travel so much faster on horseback.

I stumble against Peony with a sudden realization, my knees threatening to betray me. *I'm* the reason he killed my parents. He wants me. Or rather, my gold sense.

I should leave. Right now. No, tonight when Hiram is sleeping. Maybe I can still catch up with Jefferson. My heart squeezes at the thought. In the space of a week, I've lost my parents, my home, and my best friend. But if I catch up to Jeff, I'll get one thing back.

Daddy has saddlebags around here somewhere. And horse blankets for winter. My neighbors left enough food to give me a fine start. I'll bring one change of clothes, an extra canteen, Mama's old tinderbox . . .

Thinking of Mama sends her voice into my head. *Nothing slows a girl down faster than haste,* she always said when she saw me hurrying my stitches.

I step away from Peony and take a long, slow breath. I need to be smart about this, not fast, and there's no way in heaven or hell I'm making it to California with nothing but a gun, a horse, and some leftover funeral food. Jefferson, at least, could hire on as protection or even a hunter. Anyone would be glad to have him along. But I'm just a girl. Which means I need money. Enough for almost a year's worth of supplies. I ought to hire a chaperone too, or no wagon train will have me along. I need to look neat and respectable. I need . . .

I need to be a boy.

My pulse hammers in my throat. Could I do it? I'm strong. I can shoot better than any man in Dahlonega. Maybe if I cut my hair. Wrap my chest tight. It will take a day or two to alter some of Daddy's clothes to fit me. I have handsome eyes, sure, but some boys do. I'll just keep Daddy's hat brim pulled low. When I find Jefferson, I'll ask him to say I'm his little brother, even though we don't look a thing alike.

Annabelle Smith would be scandalized to hear what I'm

thinking now. But it's my best shot; I know it is. Once I run off, Hiram will be searching for a girl. And if I look like a boy, no one will think twice about me riding astride or bringing down a deer. I won't have to be neat and proper all the time. I could travel alone, and no one would pay me any mind.

Even as a boy, I could sure use some money. My hand goes to the locket at my chest. No, not that. But Mama has a nice bracelet. Hiram won't notice if a few of the chickens go missing.

My chickens. Who will take care of them?

It hits me like I've been mule-kicked: I'm leaving home. Once I'm gone, never again will I wake to sun shining through my dormer window. I'll never again bake a cobbler with peaches picked fresh from my very own orchard. My parents will never get proper headstones.

I'll just have to make sure it's all worth it. Find a new way for myself. Maybe California is a place where a woman can have her own land, her own life.

I'll wait for you in Independence.

I'm coming, Jeff.

Chapter Seven

I've spent the last two days being agreeable to my uncle. Not friendly, mind you. Just blankly pleasant enough not to arouse suspicion. I made him breakfast both mornings, helped him take off his boots each night, and let him sleep in my parents' bed without batting an eye. I've also been altering some of Daddy's clothes to fit me, and I'm exhausted from staying awake so late, peering at blurry stiches by the light of a single candle.

It's the third morning after the funeral. I'm leaving today. I still don't have any money, but I've scrounged up a few things to sell. I'm trying to decide whether to sell them to Free Jim's store or head out of town first.

Uncle Hiram sits across from me, eating the breakfast I made. He's mopping up egg yolk with a biscuit when he raises his head and says, "I'm sending you to finishing school in the spring."

I sit quietly, hands in my lap, gaze cast down so my eyes

don't give me away. It shouldn't matter what he says, now that I'm running off, but his declaration makes me feel like a cat with fur being rubbed the wrong way. "The school in town is just fine. Everyone likes Mr. Anders."

"It was a place to start," he says around a mouthful of biscuit. "But it's no place to finish. I suppose letters and sums will be useful to us, but you need to learn style and comportment."

I'm not sure what he means by "useful to *us*," but I nod and say, "If you think it's best."

"Which isn't to say you won't be busy here when you're home. I'm sure there's plenty of gold still to be found."

He wipes his hands on a dishcloth, then puts them into the pockets of his vest. When he pulls them out, they're both fisted. He reaches them toward me and says, "I have a gold half eagle in one hand. Which is it?" There's a twinkle in his eye that reminds me so much of Daddy that my chest hurts.

The coin sings to me clear as spring runoff from his left fist. I point to the right.

He smiles. "You can't keep secrets from me, Leah."

I sigh and point to the left.

"That's my girl." He opens his fist, and there it is, shining yellow-bright. "Here. You can have it."

I snatch the coin from his palm.

In the next instant, I almost give it back. Hiram just made me divine gold. He asked me to do it, and I did. Without question. But I can't say no to five whole dollars right now, even if they come from the devil himself.

A horrid thought occurs to me. "You thinking of taking us west?" I ask. That's the last thing I need—to go where he intended all along.

"Yes," he says. "Though not for at least a year. Everyone else can help themselves to the surface and placer gold. I have bigger plans in mind for us, but we'll need to put some polish on you first."

I can't imagine what that means. Maybe I'd rather never know. Unable to make nice a moment more, I rise from the table. "I have chores need doing."

"And I have some errands to attend to today." He pulls his silver watch from his breast pocket, flicks it open for a look, then closes it and shoves it back in. "My boy will be here with my things by the end of the week, and I'll need room in the barn. I want you to sell two of the horses."

I gape at him, marveling at my luck.

He misunderstands. "I know you're fond of them," he says gently. "But I don't want to pay to feed more horses than we need, and my own are much better stock."

"Not Peony," I say.

"I might sell that one later. Abel Topper was asking about her. Thought he might get a deal, since Reuben passed."

My fingernails dig into my palms.

Maybe I imagine the sympathy that flits across his face. "Take two of the others for now. With so many people heading west, Free Jim can turn them around for a quick profit. I've already talked to him. He's expecting you."

Uncle Hiram has just unwittingly paid my way to

California. "Yes, sir." My mutinous lips want to smile more than anything, but I won't let them.

"Bring me whatever you get. It will help pay your tuition."

"Yes, sir."

I busy myself with cleaning as he rises from the table, and I refuse to look up as he buckles his holster and dons his overcoat and hat. *Go, go, go,* I say in my own mind, like a prayer, but Lord Almighty, does he take his sweet time about it. Finally, the door closes, and I allow that grin to go slipping all over my face.

I whip off my apron and hang it by the washtub. I run upstairs to my dormer, where I grab Daddy's castoff boots from under the bed—the ones I wear for hunting and mucking stalls. I've already stuffed extra stockings into the toes, but I won't put them on for good until after I've sold the horses. After lacing my own boots tight, I pull the leaflet from where I hid it under my straw mattress. It's wrinkled and damp, and the upper right edge has a tear because I've handled it so many times. Mama used to say the water of the Atlantic goes on and on—to the edge of the world. I want to see that someday; I surely do. But Jefferson is heading toward Independence, so that's the way I'll go too.

I lay the leaflet on the floor. With the toe of my boot, I edge it slightly under the bed. I want it to look natural. Like I left it there on accident. Hopefully, Hiram will find it and think I'm heading to California by sea.

For the last two days I've been silently saying good-bye to everything in the house—the box stove, the worn table where we ate so many meals together, the porch where Mama and I used to sit on summer evenings, and especially my bedroom with its beautiful window. The patchwork quilt, though, I'm taking with me. It's already wound tight in a saddlebag, hidden in the hayloft.

My new-to-me shirt and trousers are in the barn too, along with some supplies and Mama's sewing shears. It all has to wait a few hours more.

The town square is packed with people when I arrive with the colts, Chestnut and Hemlock, pulling my wagon. There's no way I'm getting through this noisy crowd, especially without Peony to keep the colts in line, so I steer around behind the courthouse and the general store. It's muddy back here, but quieter. I throw the brake lever, grab my skirts, and jump from the wagon.

I give Hemlock a pat on the nose, tie the colts' reins to the store's back porch rail, and walk through the gloomy alley between courthouse and store, toward the square. Hundreds are gathered on the green—all miners by the wiry, sunless look of them, a few of them slaves. They're listening to someone lecture from the steps of the courthouse, and as I approach, the speaker's words ring out: "Why go to California? In that ridge lies more gold than man ever dreamt of. There's millions in it!"

I almost laugh aloud. It's Dr. Stephenson's voice; I know it well. He's from the mint, and he's assayed our gold plenty of times.

Everyone in the crowd mutters. Some are nodding. But others, like me, are tickled by the fact Dr. Stephenson considers this a compelling argument. Sure, there's plenty of gold in Findley Ridge; you don't need to divine it like me to know that. But it all belongs to the mine, and Dr. Stephenson is wasting his breath. These men are going west, for sure and certain. There, they'll work just as hard as they do now, and at the end of the day, they'll have sore backs and blistered hands and coughs that won't quit—but they'll get to keep their gold.

Good thing I'm leaving today. Most of these folks will be a few months saving money and selling their belongings, but soon enough, there won't be anything left of this town. I edge away from the crowd and mount the steps to Free Jim's store.

"Leah Westfall," he says as I enter. He stands behind a counter painted bright white. Beside him is a glass jar full of hard candy, a large scale for weighing dry goods, a smaller scale for weighing gold, and—new to my eye—a half-dozen large pickaxes. The shelves behind him are filled with pairs of boots; some new, some not. "What can I help you with?" he asks.

Gold pricks at my throat. He's got dust lying around somewhere, in addition to coins from the mint. "Hello, Free Jim. Uncle Hiram wants me to sell two of our horses. A matched pair. Know anyone in the market?"

"The colts, right? The ones Reuben broke?"

"Yes, sir."

"And now your uncle wants them gone."

"Yes, sir."

He studies me close, rubbing at his jaw. Softly, he says, "That Hiram Westfall owns you right proper now, doesn't he?"

His words give my belly a squirm. Too loudly, I say, "Seems like everyone around here is making plans to head west."

"Indeed. The sooner you get to a gold field, the better you'll do. Folks in this town remember that."

Free Jim glances around the store, but we're alone. Everyone is outside listening to the speech. He says, "McCauley was asking around town after his boy. Seems to think his son ran off to Savannah, hoping to catch a boat and sail halfway round the world. Don't suppose you know anything about that."

I pretend to misunderstand. "Mr. McCauley spoke to me at the funeral, said the same thing."

"Might have been a mistake for Jefferson to go."

I step toward the counter, getting right in his face. "You *know* he has reasons to strike out for himself."

He holds up his hands. "That's not what I'm saying."

"Then what?"

He considers me, as if deciding something.

Free Jim reaches beneath the counter and pulls out an old farmer's almanac, the kind Daddy always kept lying around for easy reference. He opens the cover, revealing a square of thick folded paper tucked inside. He unfolds the square and spreads it out. "This is Mitchell's Reference and Distance Map, the 1846 edition, with an inset for Texas, California, and Oregon."

I peer at it. "Oh?"

"We're right here." A large blunt finger drops onto the section labeled "Georgia." The states are marked in bold outline, each one filled with brightly colored counties. His voice drops to a whisper. "Now, when someone leaves Georgia, and they don't want anyone finding them . . ."

His voice trails off. I swallow a lump in my throat. "Like Jefferson, you mean."

"Sure, like Jefferson." His fingertip traces across Georgia to the ocean. "Say the rumors are true and Jefferson is going to Savannah. That's trying to get to California all in one jump. A temptation, to be sure. But he'll have to wait there to find passage, and waiting somewhere is asking to get caught. Even if he does find passage, the ships will have records. Passenger manifests that anyone could look at."

"How should he do it?" My next words are timid. "Head for Independence?"

"Sure." The map keeps trying to fold back up. Free Jim grabs a boot from the shelf behind him and plunks it on the counter to hold down the edge. "If Jefferson is smart, and I reckon he is, then he should consider his journey in stages. The first thing is to get to Chattanooga. There's only one road across the mountains. Now, let's say somebody's looking for him."

"Like . . . his da."

"Like his da. Any store or tavern or farm he stops in, people might recognize him. So he's got to camp out. But the local pattyrollers know all the places to hide. So the faster he gets away from here, the better." He pauses, leans forward. "The most dangerous part of the journey is close to home."

Daddy always said the slave patrols were little better than bandits. For the right price, they're happy to go after just about anybody, and Uncle Hiram wouldn't think twice about sending them after me. I bend over the map, memorizing the towns on the way to Chattanooga—Prince Edward, Ellijay, Dalton.

Jim slides his finger westward over the mountains. "Let's say Jefferson makes it to Chattanooga. From there he's got two choices: He can go overland, through Kentucky and to the Ohio River. Or he can get on a flatboat or steamer and ride down the Tennessee River."

"Which is better?"

"He should go by land. He can keep moving, not get tied down where someone might catch him. It's hard to run when you're on a boat, unless you can walk on water like our Lord."

I choke on a laugh.

Free Jim's return smile quickly fades as he indicates a twisting blue line that cuts the map in half.

"The Mississippi River?" I ask. It looks huge. Even on paper.

"Yep. Everyone going west must cross the Mississippi eventually. By ferry or steamer."

"Is that . . . expensive?"

He nods. "The steamer surely is. And bound to get more expensive every month. By this time next year, fares will be double, at least. But once the river is crossed, Independence is just a state away."

I study the roads that lead from Chattanooga, but there are too many places to remember. As long as I go north and west, I'll get there.

Jim spreads his hands on the map, one thumb on Dahlonega and the other on Independence. "If Jefferson's all alone for this part of the journey, he'll need to be full of care. You understand me?"

"I understand."

"But if he reaches Independence and joins a wagon train, the guides will take him the rest of way."

"So, the wagon journey is the easy part," I say.

He shrugs. "I wouldn't say that."

I fall back on my heels, shoulders slumping. The country is bigger than I thought it was, and I'm going to need more money than I realized.

Chapter Eight

*T*he bell on the door chimes. Free Jim quickly folds the map, stuffs it inside the almanac, and slides it under his counter. A fellow I don't recognize crosses the threshold and goes straight for the gold mining tools.

"I'll throw in the wagon too," I say, as though we've been haggling this whole time. "Hiram wants them all gone to make room for his own team."

"So you're saying I can get a bargain."

"I'm saying you can get a fair price."

"I'd be happy to take them off your hands," he says. "But I'll have to stable them at the hotel until I find a buyer, so the best I can offer is seventy-five each. Ninety if you throw in the wagon."

"They're a matched driving team and saddle-broke to boot!" The man perusing mining equipment glances our way. I force calm into my voice. "Worth at least two hundred and forty for the pair."

Free Jim leans forward, resting his arms on the counter. His voice is so low I must strain to hear: "I don't keep much money on hand. Man like me has no place to put it."

It's a split second before I realize he's talking about the bank. They won't open an account for a Negro.

"So I mostly trade in goods and store credit, understand? If you want to hear the jangle of gold eagles, and I suspect you do, you'll have to let it all go for one hundred and eighty dollars, and I'll be doing that as a favor to your late father."

"Oh."

His gaze softens. "Tell you what. I'll throw in a few men's shirts."

"Men's shirts?"

"I'm sure your uncle could use some new ones." Whispering, he adds: "Light. Easy to carry. They'll be worth ten dollars or more to the right person at the right time."

"I see."

The stranger picks up a pan, turns it over in the light, as if pondering how such a thing could possibly help in the search for gold.

Free Jim asks, "Ever heard a mockingbird?"

I'm not sure what he's getting at. "We had one last summer, sounded just like an oriole. Mama would get so excited, then she'd look and look and never see it."

"You understand what I'm saying, then. If someone's looking for an oriole, that mockingbird is going to slip right by them." He pauses. "Anyway, I'll throw in some men's shirts. I'm sure your uncle will find a good use for them."

I swallow hard. "I appreciate that, sir."

"So. People might come around asking after . . . Jefferson. Which way should I say he went? By land or sea?"

"By sea. He went by sea. I'm sure of it."

"All right, then." I'm not sure why Free Jim is so keen to help me out. Maybe it's because he was such good friends with my daddy. Maybe he has his own suspicions about Uncle Hiram. Regardless, I need to get out of town fast, before Free Jim isn't the only one who figures what I'm about.

He writes down the total on a piece of a paper. "I'll need your signature on this bill of sale," he says. "For when Hiram Westfall comes asking after his horses."

The bill of sale does not mention the shirts. I sign my name.

Jim counts out a huge handful of eagles and half eagles. One hundred and seventy dollars total, which he bundles up inside four long-sleeved, linsey-woolsey shirts in such a way that they don't jangle even a little bit. The final ten dollars he breaks into smaller coins and hands to me.

I'm pocketing the coins when he says, "Best of luck, Leah Westfall. Lord willing, I'll be seeing you very soon."

My gaze snaps to his. He winks at me.

Free Jim is planning to go west too. I smile, and it feels like my first genuine smile at a fellow human being in days. "I surely hope so, Mr. Boisclair." I have at least one friend besides Jefferson, and that's no small thing.

◆　◆　◆

Chestnut and Hemlock were never my favorite horses. Still, I can't bear to say good-bye. On a promise from Free Jim that he'll have them tended right away, I leave them behind the store and circle around the crowd on foot. As soon as I'm out of sight of the town proper, I hitch my bundle of boughten shirts and hidden coins under one arm, pick up my skirts with my free hand, and run as fast as I can. It's three miles till home, and I run the whole way.

Once inside the barn, I pull the doors shut and lean against them to catch my breath. My uncle said he had errands, but I don't know exactly what that means or how long he'll be gone.

I race up the ladder to the hayloft and shove a bale aside to reveal my stash of clothing and supplies. My fingers are clumsy on the buttons of my dress, and I force myself to slow down. Good thing I'm wearing my old day dress, which buttons down the front.

I shrug the dress to the ground and unlace my corset. I fold them up and stuff them inside one of the saddlebags. Shivering, I wrap Mama's old cotton shawl around my chest as tight as I can and tuck in the edges. It doesn't feel very secure, but it does flatten what little there is. Hopefully, I'll get better with practice. Hopefully, my chest won't grow any larger.

I pull on the trousers and shirt I altered, then shrug the suspenders over my shoulders. Daddy's boots feel way too large on my feet. I've tended the garden and mucked stalls in them, even hunted a little, but walking and riding all day long will be a different matter. I'll just have to make do.

Only thing left is my hair. I grab Mama's shears.

I've always liked my hair. It's long and thick, gold-brown like my eyes. I was so proud the day Mama let me put it up, knowing it would shimmer in the sunshine. I didn't bother putting it up today. Before I can think about it a second longer, I grab my braid and start hacking away.

Hair is stern stuff. It takes some effort before the braid comes away in my hand. My head immediately feels lighter. Remembering how Mama always trimmed Daddy's hair, I snip along the top and sides too, so it's short all over. I'm probably making a mess of it without a mirror to guide me, but my hat will cover the worst of it.

I shrug the saddlebags over my shoulder. Braid in hand, I start to descend the ladder, but wisps of gold-brown hair catch my eye. They almost blend into the hay, but not quite. I can't leave my hair for Hiram to find.

I gather it all up, quick as I can. I'll hide it in one of the stalls. No—too risky. I should dump it somewhere in the woods, along with my women's clothes.

My saddlebags are already fit to burst, but I shove the shiny mess down inside one anyway, then I spread loose hay around to blur the sight of any stragglers. I drop the saddlebags to the ground and follow them down the ladder.

I toss the bags beside Peony, and I grab her bridle from its peg outside her stall.

The unmistakable *clop-clop* of hooves nears the barn entrance.

I dart inside Peony's stall and swing the door shut. I crouch in the front corner as the barn doors creak open and light fills the space, along with a rush of fresh, icy air.

The creak of a saddle as someone dismounts. The jangle of a bridle. "There, there," Hiram says. "That's a good boy."

Will my uncle wonder why the wagon is gone, even though he didn't ask me to sell it? Will he see that Peony's bridle is missing from its peg?

I hardly dare to breathe as I strain my ears. He's unsaddling Blackwind, far as I can tell. Now he's removing the bridle. Blackwind stomps, and Hiram chuckles. "You'd like that, wouldn't you, boy?" he says. "Fine. A rubdown it is."

No, no, no.

Peony snorts and tosses her head. My uncle's footsteps approach. "Hullo, girl," he says.

Don't look down, don't look down.

Above me, a thick arm in a black woolen sleeve snakes out. Peony allows her muzzle to be rubbed, though her nostrils remain flared. "You'll get used to us, girl," Hiram says. "So will your mistress. I promise."

The arm disappears. Footsteps retreat. I wait, quiet as a mouse, my heart in my throat, as he rubs down his gelding. Is it twenty minutes? An hour?

Finally, *finally*, he sets the curry brush back on the shelf and closes Blackwind's stall. The barn doors shut behind him, leaving me in safe, blessed gloom, and I loose a single sob of relief.

I stay frozen, waiting for him to get out of earshot. When

I can stand it no more, I spring to my feet and toss Peony's blanket over her back, followed by the saddlebags and saddle. As I buckle on the rifle holster, I whisper, "We have to move fast and quiet, girl. Won't be more than an hour before he starts to wonder why I'm not home yet." And sooner or later, he'll figure out what the missing wagon means.

She bears the saddle without complaint, and I heap praise on her and kiss her nose. After one last tug on her girth strap, I take her reins and pull her from the stall. Gradually, quietly, I crack open the barn door and peer outside. A light snow is beginning to fall. Hiram's footprints, crisp in the fresh snow, lead toward the house.

The barn door isn't visible from anywhere in the house except the back porch, so I probably have a few minutes to get out, close the door, and get into the cover of the woods. I'm about to yank her forward when I get an idea.

Blackwind's saddle hangs over the side of one of the empty stalls. I grab my knife from the belt at my waist and saw through the girth strap. It takes longer than I care for, but unless Hiram's a dab at bareback riding, it'll be worth it.

I grab Peony's nose strap and lead her from the barn. The door squeals when I close it behind us. I swing up onto her back. She dances a little, but I dare to hope it's with anticipation rather than nervousness over the unfamiliar saddle. I check that Daddy's Hawken rifle is steady in its holster, and give her flanks a light kick. She lurches forward, eager to go, but I keep her at a quiet, patient walk.

The world is smothered in soft white. Fresh flakes continue

to drift down, and I twist in the saddle to make sure they're filling Peony's tracks. No birds call, no rodents rustle in the barren underbrush, no wind whistles through the bare branches. The winter-still world holds its breath, waiting for me to give myself away with a sound.

I nose Peony behind the barn and into the woods. I bend over her neck to avoid low branches as we twist through the maze of chestnut and red oak and digger pine. The trees break wide too soon, revealing the white ribbon of open road. I pull Peony up short.

If I take the road, I risk being seen by someone who knows me. If I keep to the thick woods, I can't go fast enough to outrun Hiram.

With a kick and a "Hi-yah!" I urge my horse into a gallop. I refuse to look back.

Chapter Nine

Peony and I fly down the road. The wind sweeps my hat from my head so that it flaps like a sail at my back, the chin strap strangling my neck. The icy air on my face makes the corners of my eyes tear. Or maybe it's the fact that I'm leaving home forever, as fast as I possibly can.

We reach the fork, and Peony slows, sides heaving. She noses toward the familiar route into Dahlonega. I steer her left, on to Ellijay Road, but she tosses her head and veers right again. "Please don't fight me, girl. Not today." When she feels the reins against her neck a second time, she gives in.

I resist the urge to spur her back into a gallop. Though she pulls our wagon almost every day, I haven't been running her regularly. I need to take care of her if she's to stay sound all the way to California.

But this is precious, precious time; the only part of my journey when I can put distance between myself and Hiram before he realizes I've run away. Which means I'll have to run Peony again once she cools off. I'll have to.

The most dangerous part of the journey is close to home.

"We might make Prince Edward by dark if we hurry," I explain, my voice sounding hollow and lonely in the empty winter woods. "Daddy's been there."

My plan is simple: stay on the big road until I get to an even bigger road, and head off into the woods if I see someone familiar. If I'm lucky—very lucky—the gathering at the courthouse will last awhile, leaving the road empty.

An hour passes. I urge Peony into a gallop again. This time, she pulls up even sooner, and I dismount to walk beside her for a spell, giving her a chance to rest.

I feel smaller when I'm not on Peony's back. Smaller, lonelier, colder. The woods loom to cither side, dotted with adjoining paths that all look the same—gloomy tunnels through leafless forest, barely wider than deer trails. What if I've missed an important turn? I hope I'm going in the right direction.

Any direction is better than back, I tell myself firmly. Soon enough, with the sun low and me still not home, Hiram will realize I'm gone. He might be searching already. I did my best to misdirect him toward the sea route, but what if it wasn't enough? There could be men on the road right now, pattyrollers or borrowed miners, coming to ride me down. Maybe they'll ambush me, bursting out of one of these silent, gloomy trails.

I can't help myself; I swing back into Peony's saddle and

urge her forward. She tosses her head in protest. "It's just a few days of hard travel. Once we're out of Georgia, we can slow down a little." I reach down and pat her neck. Even in the fading light, she's a beautiful animal, with a shimmery golden coat and a flaxen mane and tail.

"Peony," I say, pulling her up and sliding off again. "We've got a problem."

Everyone for miles knows "Lucky's palomino." She's even more recognizable than I am, with a coat bright enough to shine in the twilit gloom. I whip off my gloves and stash them in my pocket. With my bare hands, I shove aside some slushy snow and scoop up the mud beneath it. When I lift it toward Peony's neck, she twists her head away.

"Sorry, girl, but everyone knows that pretty coat of yours."

Working fast, I smear mud down the side of her neck. She nips the space near my ear in warning. That's the thing about Peony—she's sweet most of the time, but if you do something she doesn't like, she'll let you know. Daddy used to say she and I got along so well because we had a few things in common.

"Hold still!" I rub a little mud on her flanks, wary of an impending kick. When I smooth it down her rear legs, she whips her tail around to swat my face.

I give her reins some slack and step back to see how she looks.

"Blast."

It's only my first day on the road, and I've already made a huge mistake. She's exactly the same horse as before, with her proud bearing and corn silk mane and a glorious tail that almost brushes the ground. Now, she's muddied up in a way that will draw even more attention, and the precious time I spent disguising her is a total waste.

I start to climb back on, but I pause, foot in the stirrup. There's another bit of business I should take care of while we're stopped. The delay might add up to another huge mistake, but ignoring the task could be worse.

Every decision I make right now feels like the wrong one. I'll just have to be quick.

I hobble Peony and grab my woman's clothes and shorn braid from the saddlebag. It's an armful, even rolled up tight as it is, with the corset, the full skirt, and the petticoats. The whole mess is probably worth a decent sum, and for the hundredth time I consider selling it somewhere. For the hundredth time I come to the same conclusion: It would seem mighty odd for a young boy to walk into a store with a bundle of female fixings to sell. They'd take him for a thief for sure—which might make them look close enough to realize he wasn't a boy at all.

Using a small branch and the heels of my boots, I dig at the ground, squelching up mud and rotting leaves. I don't have time to make a proper hole, so I settle for a small depression. I drop in my parcel of hair and clothing.

I stare down at it too long, feeling strange. The edge of the skirt's ruffle has started to escape the bundle, and the shiny braid winks up at me. It's like I'm burying half a girl here.

Peony's snort moves me to action. I cover it all up best I can with more mud, add a few deadfall sticks and rocks, which ought to hold if a big rain comes this way. My saddlebags are a lot lighter now. I mount up and kick Peony forward, but my back twitches, like that buried bundle is staring after me and my ill-fitting trousers.

The mud dries on Peony's coat, making her skin twitch like it's covered in flies. She shows her annoyance in a hundred tiny ways, from fighting her bridle to flicking her tail.

"That was a bad idea, and I'm sorry. I promise I'll clean you up as soon as I can."

She tosses her head as if to yank the reins from my hands. "Stop it!" I snap. "I'm doing the best I can, you ungrateful, mule-headed . . ." My tirade fades as quickly as it came. Yelling at my only companion won't do me any good.

Night falls. I don't dare gallop her in the dark, but neither do I dare stop. At least Peony's shiny coat is becoming a colorless gray in the gloom. No one would recognize her now.

My tiny spark of relief is doused by the *clop-clop* of hooves. Someone approaches.

Everything inside me yearns to dash for the woods and hide, but I have to face people eventually. I nudge my hat brim low, sit straight in the saddle, and trust the moonlight to hide what it must.

A silhouette appears around the bend and rides toward me at a leisurely pace. Not anyone I know, thank the stars. He's gray and heavily whiskered, and he stoops low over a swaybacked mare. A huge tear in his hat has been hastily stitched with dark thread.

"Howdy," he says, with a tip of his hat.

"Howdy," I reply, tipping my own hat. One little word, but it sets my heart pounding fit to tumble out of my chest.

We pass each other. I stare straight ahead as if I haven't a care in the world, as if I've every right to this road. I imagine him calling out at my back. *What's a young lady like you doing out here all alone? Why is your horse so muddy?*

He doesn't. The sound of his mount's hooves fades, but it's a while before I breathe easy. "We did it," I whisper after a spell. "I don't think he suspected a thing."

We press on. The air chills. Peony's steady steps echo around us. Except for that man with the mended hat, I haven't seen a single soul, which is odd, even for winter. I'm fretting all over again that I've gone the wrong way, when I catch the sharp scent of burning pine. Sure enough, we round the next hill and find Prince Edward.

Houses cluster along a western slope, smoke rising from their chimneys and lanterns glowing in their windows. Below them are a white clapboard church, a small store, and a two-story tavern. Lanterns swing from the tavern's front post, illuminating the double doors and wooden stoop. Everything I need is there—oats for Peony and supper for me. But I don't dare go inside.

A group of men stagger from the tavern door, where they pause to don their hats and pull out their pipes. Coals glow in their pipe bowls, and sickly sweet tobacco smoke fills the air.

Quickly, I aim Peony away. We'll circle the town, keeping

to the shadows. Then we'll find a place to camp for the night.

Too late. "Hey, boy," one calls out.

I pretend not to hear, but my neck prickles, and my grip on the reins tightens. Peony sidesteps in response.

"Boy, I'm talking to you. What's your name?"

I recognize his voice now— It's Abel Topper, from the funeral. The one I saw talking to Uncle Hiram.

I hold Peony to a smooth, casual pace, but my mind races. Topper was a foreman at one of the mines before it dried up. His men—all desperate for work—could be here with him. My uncle might have hired them to look for me. *Why* did I waste time with that awful mud?

"Leave the boy alone," someone says.

Topper's voice drifts toward me. "That looks like Lucky Westfall's mare, is all I'm saying. Hiram said he'd sell her to me."

"Topper, you're too drunk to know a mare from a mosquito."

"Not that drunk. What's she doing out here? I'm telling you . . ."

Abel Topper's voice fades with distance, but I feel his eyes boring holes into my back, and I don't know what to do about it except to keep us walking. We pass the stable, the church, the store, and a few more small houses. Once we're out of sight, I kick Peony into a run, urging her to go faster and then faster still.

After a minute or two, Peony pulls up in protest, and I let her. I dismount and wrap my trembling arms around her sweaty neck. "That man won't take you," I choke out. "You're not going back to Uncle Hiram. No matter what."

The most dangerous part of the journey is close to home.

The woods hemming the road are dense and black, and I lead Peony into the cold thick of it. She needs time to walk off her sprint, so I don't stop until we find a stream with a trickle of water; nighttime makes it look like an inky scar slashing through the ground. I work mostly by feel, feeding Peony what little oats I've got in my pack, rubbing her down, checking her over. Galloping her was a stupid and dangerous thing to do in the dark; we're lucky she didn't injure herself.

I take my time, making sure to brush away every speck of that stupid mud. When she bumps her head against me, I know she's finally forgiven me for this terrible day and is ready to rest. I shiver with cold as I hobble her beneath the trees.

Good thing Daddy made me learn how to start a fire in the dark. I scrape a small hole in the ground, rooting around for dry wood as I go, then I pull out my tinderbox and coax up a fire. I hunker over the flames until I stop shivering.

There's nothing to eat except the trail food in my saddle-bag, but I don't want to touch it. What if it has to last? There could be Abel Toppers in all the taverns, general stores, and boardinghouses from here to Independence.

What's she doing out here? Abel Topper said. He wasn't expecting to see Peony. Which means my uncle didn't send him. In fact, Topper probably arrived hours ago. Maybe even yesterday. Long before I left.

The thought frees me to grab some hardtack and force myself to eat. As I chew, my thoughts drift to Jefferson, who set off with even less than I did. I hope his supplies are lasting and the sorrel mare is doing well by him. I hope he's safe, with a cheery fire of his own. And to be honest, I hope Jefferson's soul is giving him a sting that he ran off on me, leaving me all alone.

No, he couldn't help it. He was in a bad way as much as me, with a daddy who is worse than no daddy at all. It wasn't Jefferson's fault. It wasn't.

The hardtack turns to grit in my teeth, and my stomach rolls over in protest. Turns out, I don't have room for much inside me except worry and anger and tears that haven't been given leave to see daylight.

Speak of the devil and you summon it, because just thinking about tears invites them to spring to my eyes. I blink rapidly, trying to tamp them down because they feel like angry tears, not sad ones.

There, I've said it. I'm mad.

I'm mad at my parents for not being here, I'm mad at Jefferson for leaving without me, and I'm mad at myself for not going when he asked. I'm mad at everyone back home for brushing off my parents' murders, and I'm mad they turned the funeral into a church social. Most of all, I'm mad at Uncle Hiram for being a slimy, villainous beast and taking every single thing I ever loved. I'm scared and I'm mad, and both keep me awake in the dark for a long time.

The cold wakes me before dawn. The fire has burned down

to nothing. I'm shivering, teeth chattering, and my blanket is soaked with dew.

My stomach is truly empty, and my tears have dried; I won't be shedding more. I chew on another bit of hardtack as I saddle Peony.

The only way to go is forward. "C'mon," I say. "We have to keep moving."

Chapter Ten

The sun is still low enough to brush the hilltops when I see a woman off to the side, collecting eggs from a coop. I keep to the far edge of the road and try not to attract attention.

"Do you want to buy some eggs?" she calls out.

My heart races, but my stomach rumbles. Reluctantly, and maybe eagerly, I turn Peony toward her.

She cradles the eggs in her apron. Her straw-colored hair peeks out of her bonnet, which hasn't done a thing to keep the freckles from her cheeks. "How many do you want?" she asks.

"I'll give you a dime for a dozen." As soon as the words are out, I know I've offered too much.

Her eyes narrow. I resist the urge to check the wrapping around my chest or lower my hat brim even more. "Don't have that many today," she says, "but I'll give you a half dozen for three pennies." Which is a fair price.

After eating so little last night, I need a good meal, and

badly. "Do you have a burning pit nearby where I could fry them up?"

"Come on in, and I'll fry them myself. Split an armful of wood and bring it inside with you." She nods toward a stack out by a shed. A maul leans against the wall.

I'm not keen to delay. Or go inside a cozy cabin where someone might get too close a look at me. Then again, I can't afford to turn down a good meal.

I hop down and hitch Peony to the post beside the watering trough. I work hard and fast, one eye on the road. The effort loosens my cramped legs and makes my shoulders sing. When I'm done, I split and stack a little extra, just by way of saying thanks.

I carry my armful of firewood to the house and find the door propped open. A chubby baby, not even a year old, plays in a rail crib. Bacon pops in the frying pan on the box stove. A plate of fried eggs and a steaming bowl of grits wait for me at the table.

The woman reminds me of my mama, with hair that won't stay neat and a skirt hem that won't stay clean. Her husband is probably off at work somewhere, maybe panning in a nearby stream or working one of the smaller mines.

"Drop that wood in the basket," she says when she sees me hovering. "Then have a seat. I made extra since you seemed so determined to work up an appetite."

"Thank you, ma'am." I tip my hat to her, which reminds me that I ought to take it off while inside.

Her gazes catches on my ragged hair, and I suddenly feel

like a rabbit about to bolt, but the moment passes and she scoops some bacon onto my plate. "Eat up."

My mouth waters as I sit down and grab a fork.

"It's early to be on the road," she says. "Getting cold out there too, though your pretty mare looks to be putting on a nice coat."

Stopping here was another mistake. She'll remember Peony for sure, if someone comes asking. "She's always been a good winter horse," I say around a mouthful of food. After swallowing, I add, "Heading to Dalton to see family. Guess I'm in a hurry to get there."

"Oh. Thought for sure you were heading west after gold. Anyway, pace yourself. You won't make Dalton today, no matter how early you start or how hard you go."

"No, ma'am."

I eat so fast it gives me a bellyache. We say a few more general words to each other, mostly about the weather and the roads, all very polite, neither of us volunteering anything personal. I compliment her on her tidy house and her fat baby, which is always safe, and she observes that Peony looks sturdy and strong. After eating every single bite, I rise to clean my plate, just like I would at home, which seems to take her aback.

"Way my mama taught me," I say.

She laughs. "Well, you tell your mama she raised you right, next time you see her."

I hesitate a space too long. "Will do, ma'am," I answer softly.

She opens her mouth to say something else, but changes her mind. She wraps up some extra food in a handkerchief and hands it to me, along with a couple of wrinkled winter apples.

"For your pretty mare," she says.

"How much do I owe you for all this?" I ask, reaching for my change.

"Three pennies for the eggs."

"But—"

"You earned it. That's enough firewood to get me through the rest of the week."

"Well, all right."

I can't get back on the road fast enough. At least my belly is full and my horse is rested.

As the morning passes, I encounter more travelers, and it's a little easier each time. Most want to stop for a friendly chat, but I try to keep our interactions to a quick howdy. Twice, when the way is clear, I urge Peony into a run.

By midafternoon, I catch up to a woodcutter, whose slow mule cart is loaded with firewood. A farmer rides beside him, his saddlebags filled with bright red crab apples. As with everyone on the road, I search their faces for a spark of familiarity and am relieved when I don't recognize either one.

"Afternoon, son," the farmer says.

"Hey, you're coming from Lumpkin County, right?" the woodcutter says to me. "You hear tell of Lucky Westfall's murder?"

My words freeze in my mouth. "I . . . No, sir. Haven't heard a thing."

The woodcutter turns to the farmer. "Him and his wife was both murdered. Might be the same gang that killed those Indians out by Dalton."

"Westfall was an Indian?" the farmer asks.

"No, but they was after gold both times."

I wait for him to add, "The Westfalls had a daughter. She's missing now." Instead, the conversation shifts to unsolved murders from a decade ago, and then to a debate about whether it's really murder to kill an Indian, and then to the price of winter wheat. I keep pace with them, as they'd expect this close to town, but I'm silent the whole while, and my hands grip Peony's reins so hard I feel them through my gloves.

It's early evening when we get to Ellijay, which has several crooked house–lined streets to go along with its white clapboard church and two-story tavern, all tossed around a messy intersection. I count five roads coming together at the center of town, but not a single sign indicating which is which. I work up my nerve and ask the woodcutter to point out the Dalton road.

"There's not another town until Spring Place," he says. "And that's a day's ride. Come on up to the tavern with us and stay the night."

"No! I mean, I've got a place to stay."

With a shrug, he points the way, and I hurry off.

Peony and I put a few more miles beneath our feet. The

country is so thick with winter-stripped branches and dead-fall that it's nearly dark before I find a good place to steer her off the road and into cover. After a cold, damp night and a breakfast of deer jerky, I hustle Peony through the town of Spring Place. The road beyond is even busier, and saying howdy to so many people is terrible on my nerves. I remind myself that lots of traffic makes it easier to blend in.

I'm not far from Dalton when I'm walloped by the presence of gold. My throat constricts as I blink through fuzzy vision. I pull Peony up short, waiting for the sense to turn sweet on me. It takes longer than usual. Maybe it's because the gold is on the move. Or maybe, in the days since Hiram stole every speck of my family's fortune, I've gotten out of practice.

Peony dances beneath me, snapping me out of my daze. I hope I didn't lose time again. I look around to see if I've embarrassed myself, but no one seems to care that we've stopped dead in the middle of the road. Perhaps it was only a few seconds.

I urge her forward, even as I cast out for the source. A scraggly man approaches, leading a wagon with fresh-cut lumber for the sawmill. Both knees of his overalls are patched, but I'm sure he's the one who triggered my twitch.

He reaches into his pocket and pulls out a shiny golden watch, flips it open, and checks the time. More gold is some-where close—maybe a handful of eagles. If he's wealthy enough to afford that watch and carry a stash of coins, he could afford decent overalls. I guess folks aren't always what they look like on the outside, which is something I think I ought to know by now.

He grins at me with tobacco-stained teeth. "Almost time!" he says.

"For what?"

"You'll see."

Not a minute later, a whistle shrieks and a column of dark smoke rises above the trees. It moves closer, picking up speed until the column stretches long, like reins trailing a runaway horse.

"Is that the train?" I ask.

"Well, it sure ain't a steamboat," he says with a wink. "It'll be there when you get into town. You should take a gander."

"I'll do that, sir."

"It's going to change everything!" he says. "Once that tunnel's done."

"That's what my daddy always says." Said. That's what my daddy *said*.

Sure enough, an hour later I steer Peony into Dalton and discover that the town's main feature is the train.

I stare agape. It's a metal behemoth, bigger than any machine I've seen or imagined. It makes me glad I'm not an iron scryer, if such a thing exists, because if it set off my witchy powers, it would leave me dead senseless for a day.

When the train chugs away from the station, Peony and I set out on the Chattanooga road, which follows parallel to the now-empty tracks. I imagine how fast we could get to California if a train headed that way. It might only take weeks instead of months. Truth be told, I'm not sure it's safe to ride in something so huge and fast.

I'm a mile north of town when horses clop up behind me. I've been swift, passing lots of folks on the road. But no one has been passing me. I glance back, just quick enough to mark three riders—men in thick beards, weathered coats, and slouched hats.

They gain on me slowly. The first comes up on my right and gives me a friendly nod. The second fellow pulls even on my left. The third rider closes in at my rear.

Peony's ears go back.

They have a rangy look about them, with sun-blasted skin and unkempt hair. But their guns are shiny and new.

The one beside me grins, and I feel like a deer in his sights. "Howdy," he says.

"Howdy," I say with forced cheer.

"Saw you at the station in Dalton. That train is something else, ain't it?"

"Never seen anything like it," I say, because it seems like a safe thing.

"Ever seen those steamboats on the Mississippi?"

"Never been to the Mississippi."

He whistles. "They're a sight too, blowing out a cloud of smoke and running down the water like a thousand horses. We're headed that way. Go down to the Mississippi every winter. Where you headed?"

"North to see some cousins."

"Whereabouts? If it's around here, me and my brothers probably know 'em."

"Oh, I don't think you would. They're up close to Chattanooga."

His eyes narrow. "Know pretty much everybody around those parts. Ain't that so, Ronnie?"

"You know it is, Emmett," says a voice behind me, and the back of my neck prickles.

"Don't think we've ever seen you around here before," the first one—Emmett—says.

"I reckon not," I say. "My family's back in Ellijay."

The fellow grins like a cat with a mouse, and I don't know what I said wrong, but I immediately regret it. My thoughts spin fast, trying to figure out my options.

"Shoot, Ellijay's not that far, is it, boys?"

"Never been there myself," Ronnie says behind me.

"Neither have I," says the one beside me. "But I hear it's nice."

"So, you fellows know the area pretty well?" I have a peculiar urgency to keep them talking.

"Nobody knows it better than us, from Dalton to the Mississippi," Emmett says.

"Then maybe you can tell me something. Man at the train station said the next town is Tunnelsville, less than a day's ride. Thought I'd reach it by now."

"That's fourteen, fifteen miles away," Emmett says.

"At least," Ronnie adds.

"Oh," I say. "So I won't get there tonight?"

"Not a chance."

Without warning, I jerk Peony around. Ronnie's horse whinnies as it sidesteps to avoid us, and I breeze right past. The men pull up their horses and turn to stare at me.

"You fellows saved me a lot of trouble," I say. "But it puts a burr under my saddle for the fellow who misled me back at the station. Figure if I hurry, I can get back to Dalton in time for supper."

Emmett frowns. "Sounds about right."

"Well, you did me a kindness, and I'm grateful," I say.

I kick Peony into a fast walk. I don't hear their horses following behind, and I resist the urge to look over my shoulder to make sure. I'm halfway back to Dalton when I finally risk a glance, and when I don't see them on the road behind me, my hands start shaking something fierce.

I slide from Peony's back and lead her uphill into the woods. The ridge is thick with birch, a place where I can observe the road unnoticed. I sit down, knees to chest, and watch the winding track below me while Peony lips hungrily at bare branches.

Nobody shows before dark. I hope the brothers kept on going to wherever they were headed. If they stop for the night, I might encounter them again tomorrow. Maybe I can find other folks to ride with before I do.

I lead Peony deeper into the trees and find a sheltered spot beside a stream. Snow blankets the ground up here, and my breath frosts as the temperature drops. I crunch through a caul of ice with the heel of Daddy's boot so Peony can drink.

I hitch her to a tree instead of hobbling her so we can take off quickly if we need to.

The wood is damp, and it smokes something awful, so I keep the fire small and hope it doesn't show much against the sky, which is a bit too moonlit for comfort. I load Daddy's Hawken rifle and lay it out at my side. I hate letting it rest on wet ground, but I'm not sure what else to do. The fire, small already, burns low even before I drift off.

Peony's nicker wakes me.

Branches crunch under heavy boots.

I reach for my rifle, but it's gone.

Before I can jump up, the cold end of a gun barrel presses against my scalp. I don't have to look at it to know it's the Hawken, and it's loaded.

"You should have gone back to Dalton for the night," Emmett says.

"Heck," says Ronnie. He's a looming shadow on my left, hemming me in so I can't escape. "You should've stayed in Ellijay."

Chapter Eleven

I'm in big trouble if these brothers were hired by my uncle to bring me home. But I'm in bigger trouble if they weren't.

Mama warned me about men like these. She knew a few when the Georgia gold rush was young, when times were rough and she was one of the only women in Dahlonega. So I know they'll rob me blind, at least. If they're not working for my uncle, they'll do worse.

"Zeke," Emmett says. "The fire's gone out. Fetch us some wood, will you?"

"Make him do it," Zeke says, indicating me.

Him. They're not working for Hiram.

"Shut your trap and do what I tell you," Emmett says. As his brother sulks off, he says, "You, sit up."

I do as he asks, slowly, keeping an eye on the Hawken.

"And give me that blanket," Ronnie says, yanking it from my shoulders. He wraps it around his own and steps back again, keeping me trapped between him and Emmett.

"How'd you find me?" I ask to stall more than anything.

"Smelled your campfire," Emmett says. "Ronnie here spotted the place where you left the road. He's a dab at tracking, my brother."

I left tracks, and I made camp upwind of the road.

Zeke returns. "Why're we wasting time here?" he says, dumping a few branches beside the fire.

"Ain't no rush," Emmett tells him. "Might as well pass the night."

Emmett squats beside my fire pit, the Hawken across his knees. He keeps the barrel aimed my way, one hand resting on the stock within easy reach of the triggers. With his free hand, he stirs the coals and stokes the flames. "You got that bottle on you, Ronnie?"

Ronnie retrieves a jug from his horse. Corn liquor, if I don't miss my guess. He pulls the cork and takes a swig, then passes it to Emmett, who does the same before handing it off to Zeke.

My saddlebag lies on the ground beside me, where I was using it as a pillow. Ronnie grabs it and reaches inside.

"Stop that," I holler before I think better of it.

Ronnie grins. Holding my gaze, he slowly and deliberately rummages around inside. He pulls out Free Jim's bundle of shirts. "Hey, there's a shirt in here for each one of— Holy ..."

The gold eagles spill out, clanking as they fall, then roll silently into the dead leaves. Ronnie drops the shirts and scrambles for the coins. Zeke runs over to help. Emmett remains where he is, watching me like I'm a snake.

I'm worse than a snake. I am patient. I am a ghost.

"There must be sixty or seventy dollars here," Zeke says.

"More!" Ronnie says.

"How much?" Emmett asks me.

"Didn't stop to count."

"You think this is Lucky Westfall's gold?" Ronnie asks.

Emmett raises an eyebrow at me.

"What if it is?" I say, clenching my hands into fists to keep them from trembling. If everyone knows about Daddy's murder, it's only a matter of time before they hear tell of his missing daughter.

Zeke is down on his hands and knees, scattering leaves and branches. Ronnie upends my saddlebag and shakes out my few belongings. Peony's grain spills everywhere. Thank the stars I got rid of my women's clothes.

"Reminds you of the old days, don't it?" Emmett says, still studying me.

"This kid don't look anything like a Cherokee," Ronnie says.

"But us, out in the woods at night, looking for someone stupid." His chuckle is ugly and mean. "Remember that first fellow?"

"Didn't have anything on him but a bearskin," Zeke says.

"And that rifle, remember? You carried that rifle for three years."

"Heck, I hated that gun. Never shot straight for me."

"Because you hit too many Indians in the head with it," Ronnie says.

"Maybe we should head west like everyone else," Zeke says. "We won't find a richer treasure trove of stupid than on the road to California."

They're pretending to ignore me, but I know better. I saw it a dozen times with Jefferson's da, the way he'd coyly provoke Jeff into being heedless or clumsy, then use the excuse to yell at him. If no one was around, he'd do more than yell. So I'm watching them close and waiting for my chance to escape, but I'm not going to give them any excuse.

The fire is going strong now. The brothers gather close and pass the bottle around again. Ronnie has found most of the coins, and he lays them out before the fire, counting them over and over again. Anger makes it hard to see straight. I fled one thief only to find another, and soon I'll have just as much nothing as I did before.

"We got lucky tonight," Emmett says.

"We did," Zeke agrees.

"But think of those flatboats, drifting down the Ohio," Ronnie says. "It's like money at a fair, waiting to be picked up off the ground, and it's a lot closer than California."

"Eh," Zeke grunts, and takes another drink.

"How about it?" Ronnie asks, looking at me. Whatever comes next, it's how he plans to set me up. "You've a talent for robbing, at the very least. Murder, if you're the one who killed Westfall. You want to go to Memphis with us, head down the Mississippi?"

Zeke sits up straight. "Hey, now, I don't want to split shares four ways."

Ronnie scowls and pokes at the fire, sending up a spiral of sparks. Its warmth is seeping back into me. My limbs twitch with readiness.

"I thought you didn't want to come with us this year, Zeke," Emmett says.

"Aw, I was just letting off steam," Zeke says.

Emmett turns back to me. "So how about it? All these farmers from Ohio, Indiana, Pennsylvania—they complain about slavery, how bad the South is, how we ought to change our ways. But come early winter, they slaughter their hogs, fill their barrels full of pork, and float down the Mississippi. They stop at every plantation along the way, selling off their goods until they get to New Orleans. Then they walk back home, their pockets full of southern money. They're a bunch of hypocrites."

"God hates hypocrites," Ronnie says.

"Amen," Zeke says.

Emmett smiles. "So you see, we're instruments of God's justice. How would you like to be an instrument of God's justice?"

I say nothing.

"A lot of these northern hypocrites like to gamble their way back home," Emmett continues, "where their families can't see them being hypocritical. And my brothers and I like a fair game of cards as well as the next man."

"Not a fair game," Ronnie amends.

Emmett says, "If they lose a little money to us, that's fine. Keeps it here in the South where it belongs."

"Some of 'em like to drink," Ronnie says. He takes the jug from Zeke and tilts his head back for a swallow.

"That they do," Emmett agrees. "And we happen to be drinking men too, and good company besides. But these northern fellows are weak, and if they can't hold their liquor, and they fall down and hit their heads—"

"Or fall into the river," Ronnie says.

"Why, then, it's our civic duty to empty their pockets and take their wages, to return them to their families."

"If we ever see their families," Ronnie adds.

I make myself breathe slow and easy, or else I'd scream and run. These men aren't just robbers, they're killers. Freebooters, just like Colonel Plug's boat-wreckers down the Ohio River or Mason's gang at Cave-In-Rock.

Emmett grabs the jug from Ronnie and tilts it to his lips. Peony is tugging at her hitch, which shakes the branches of the small birch she's tied to. She doesn't like the smell of this either.

"I have to admit that northern folks are unjustly suspicious of me and my brothers, on account of their deep and hypocritical prejudices," Emmett says. "But you? You look as innocent as a sacrificial lamb with those big, wide girlie eyes. We might be able to use that."

They're starting to relax. I can see it in their shoulders. In the easy way they tip back their heads for a swig. *Just a few more drinks, boys.*

"On the other hand, if you don't want to join us as our long-lost cousin Tackett from Ellijay, no hard feelings. We'll just take what we need and leave you here in the woods."

Leave me dead in the woods, he means. Zeke's hand is too near the big knife on his belt. Ronnie seems to be gazing off the other way, but Emmett still aims the Hawken at me. My belly squirms to think that after everything, I might get killed by Daddy's own gun.

Emmett holds out the jug, offering me a drink. "So what's it going to be?"

I'm supposed to beg them to take me along. If I do, they'll have a laugh at my expense, then murder me anyway. If I don't, they'll use it as an excuse to be extra mean.

The jug hangs in the air, along with Emmett's question. I figure I'm dead no matter what I answer. So I pull a trick I learned watching Jefferson deal with his father: I change the subject.

"My horse. Sounds like she got snarled up."

At my voice, Peony whinnies and struggles harder. I say a silent blessing to her.

I add, "She spooks easy. If she doesn't get unsnarled, she could hurt herself. And then she's no good—can't ride her, can't sell her."

Ronnie frowns. Emmett shuffles closer to the fire, trying to get a better look at me. His hand inches toward the triggers. Staring me down eye-to-eye, he says, "Zeke, go untangle the horse."

"Why me?"

"Because I told you to."

Zeke stomps over to Peony, spewing a string of curse

words. He draws his knife and cuts her hitch.

"There, you satisfied?" he says.

Peony thanks him by biting his cheek.

Zeke screams. Peony rears, and Emmett and Ronnie leap after her because she's worth even more than the coins. The rifle is no longer pointed at my head.

I launch to my feet and kick the fire. Glowing coals fly up and hit Emmett and Ronnie in the back. Emmett drops the jug. Liquid spills and whooshes into flame.

I turn and flee. The Hawken rifle cracks the air; the shot splinters a tree beside me. I can't see where I'm going, and I don't care. I trip, falling to my knees, but I scramble up and keep going.

My instinct is to run for the shadows where the moon can't touch, so I skid downhill. I'm probably leaving muddy marks in the hillside, but I can't worry about that now. I trip again—a big, fat log this time—which sends me flying. I hit the ground hard, and pain shoots from my shoulder and up into my neck. I roll down the hill, faster and faster, and come to a soft and sudden *thunk* in a collection of damp leaves.

I lie gasping, detritus filling my mouth. How long since the shot was fired? Thirty seconds? Forty? Any man worth his salt would have that rifle reloaded by now.

Their voices echo through the trees, but I dare to hope they're moving farther away. I glimpse the fire's orange glow on the slope above, flickering between swaying branches, but I kicked it good, and its light fades.

It's too dark to sneak away; I'm as likely to run right into the brothers. Best to stay in one place. Being hunted is like being a hunter, really. Either way, you have to be as silent and still as death.

Mold pricks my nose as I scrape leaves to cover myself, until their weight feels like a blanket over my body. Now I've nothing to do but wait silently, my mind spinning. I should hide here at least until morning. Poor Peony. I hope she got away. If not, they might hurt her just for spite.

"He came down this way."

I startle at Ronnie's whisper, causing the leaves around me to rustle.

"I heard crashing and mucking about. See that spot there, where he slipped?"

Be patient. Be a ghost.

"I hope he hit his head on a rock and killed hisself," Zeke says. "He should pay for what that horse did."

"It's your own fault, you fool," Emmett says. There's pain in his voice too; I hope the fire burned him good. "Why'd you go and cut it loose for?"

"You said untangle, and I untangled."

"Shut up, both of you," Ronnie says. "I heard something."

Footsteps shuffle through underbrush on the hillside just above. Someone steps on a log, which creaks hollowly and sends dirt and leaves pattering down on top of me.

"It was right down here," Ronnie insists.

More scuffling and dislodged mud. Someone slides down the embankment. "Too dark to see," Zeke says, his voice so close I could probably reach out and touch him.

"We've got his gold," Emmett says. "Let's head back to Dalton, find a doc to look at my arm."

"You mean my face!"

"That too."

Boots stomp within inches of my nose. If he steps on me, I'm done for. Or maybe, if I'm quick, I can wrench him down by the leg and put my own boot in his face before he can say howdy.

I hold my breath, sure it's a trick, but the boots step away, and the underbrush thrashes as Zeke scrambles up the slope. I'm quiet as a rabbit in a burrow with a fox nearby, and I stay that way long after their footsteps fade, listening desperately to the silence.

I feel more than hear the soft swoop of wings as a screech owl shadows down from the trees and lands in front of my face. His head twists as he calls out, like a crying baby. His eyes are huge and wide and golden, just like mine.

After a moment, the owl's silhouette launches back into the sky, and I'm a little sad to see him go, like I've lost the night's one beautiful thing.

He never would have left his tree if the brothers were still around. Still, I don't move from my pile of leaves until morning quickens with the rising sun.

Chapter Twelve

$\mathcal{I}$ crawl out from under my leaf pile and creep back up the hill, where I pause at the camp's edge. The brothers could be watching this very spot, waiting for me. But everything I owned in the world was here, and I have to see if anything can be salvaged.

I glance around for Peony, as if the brothers wouldn't take such a perfect, beautiful mare. Tears prick at my eyes. She saved my life with her cantankerous ways. I don't know how I'll carry on without her.

If Mama were here, she'd remind me that things could always be worse, and she'd be right. The night was freezing cold, and I was afraid, so I left all my clothes on, including my coat and Daddy's boots. I've got a full outfit, even if it's filthy from hiding under rotting leaves. I still have Mama's locket around my neck and nearly ten dollars in my pocket, so I won't starve for a while yet.

But I'd give it all up to know Peony got away. I hope

she's halfway home to Dahlonega by now.

The camp is a trampled mess. The fire pit is wrecked, and ochre bits of broken jug lay scattered about. My saddlebags are gone, and along with them my knife, the roll of extra shirts, my hat, all my food, even my guns.

My throat tightens to think of Daddy's Hawken rifle. I loved that gun.

The cut end of Peony's lead is still hitched to a tree, so I undo it and coil it up. That's one piece of rescued gear.

I explore the clearing, toeing at leaves and mud with my boots. My bedroll is intact, though it's thoroughly stomped. I start to roll it up and discover the most wonderful surprise underneath: the cap-and-ball revolver, sitting there, nice as you please. I hardly have time to celebrate before I realize the back of my throat itches, making itself known even through my jangled nerves.

Gold.

I drop to my knees and crawl through the leaves, brushing cold ash and half-burned sticks aside, following the pull. I find them lodged under a small log—four coins total; two tens and two fives. *Thirty dollars.* They must have gotten kicked aside in the scuffle.

My heart pounds. Can I make it all the way to California with a total of forty dollars? Maybe with a bit of luck. I'm Lucky Westfall's daughter. If anyone can do it, it's me.

After shoving the coins into my pocket, I continue circling through the trees. I let out a little yelp. My saddle lies lodged against a trunk at the bottom of the hill. They sliced the straps and tossed it, and I suddenly regret cutting the straps to Hiram's saddle. *The harm we do others always comes back around,* Daddy used to say.

I skid down and retrieve the saddle, hefting it over my shoulder. Strange that the brothers didn't take it. It's beautiful, and worth a decent price, with diamond patterns punched into the well-oiled leather. Daddy liked his tools and said a smart man always bought the best and took good care of them. Peony's saddle was another tool to him, and he spared no expense.

Making the climb back to camp with a heavy saddle over my shoulder nearly proves too much. My feet keep slipping, and Daddy's enormous boots are rubbing a painful blister onto my right heel. The pain evaporates with a sudden thought: They never would have left the saddle behind if they'd caught Peony.

I open my mouth to holler her name, but close it just as quick. Those brothers could still lurking about. Then again, they left the saddle and pistol and coins right where they dropped them. Which means they were hurt bad and needed to see the doc quick. If I were a gambling kind of girl, and I most certainly am not, I'd wager they'll return to loot the camp in the light of day, just as soon as they're tended to.

So I take a deep breath and shout it with my whole lungs until I hear it echo back through the rugged hills: "Peony!"

I don't expect her to come running down the hill like a dog, but . . . I don't know what I expect.

After calling her name a few more times, I resume the

trudge uphill. With luck, she'll find her way to a good family. One that will pamper her with brushing and treats. One that understands how sometimes even an ornery horse can be the best horse in the world.

When I top the rise, Peony is right there, ears and tail twitching with irritation that I took so long. I drop the saddle and throw my arms around her neck. Her head tosses, as if she's not sure what all the fuss is about.

I check her over from head to tail, even pull up her hooves and check the frogs of her feet. One shoe might be a bit loose, but other than that she seems perfectly sound. Still I linger, finger-combing her mane, rubbing my hands down her neck, planting kisses on her nose.

She snuffles at my coat, looking for a treat. Poor girl is probably starving, so I set about figuring how to saddle her up again and getting us out of this place. I consider using the length of lead-rope I rescued to rig a temporary fix. But without a blanket to pad it, the rub would give her a sore. I'll have to ride bareback, the saddle in my lap.

I use a log to mount up. Holding the huge saddle makes my weight awkward and sloppy, but Peony doesn't fight it. It's her way of saying she's as happy to see me as I am to see her.

When we find our way back to the road, I pause.

I look toward Dalton with half a mind to ride right over and tell the sheriff about those brothers. No, that's a broken notion. I can't afford one more delay. Besides, Emmett said they know everyone for miles. Who would take the word of a stranger over theirs?

Even if someone heard me out, they'd have questions about my family, my home, my destination. I'd have to tell a heap of lies. Then once they figured out I'm a girl, they'd tie me up and drag me back to Dahlonega faster than I could sneeze. Back to my no-good viper of an uncle, because he's my guardian, and a fine-looking, well-spoken gentleman besides.

I turn Peony north, toward Tunnelsville and Chattanooga. We keep to the side of the road so we can hide in the woods at a moment's notice.

Tunnelsville cozies up to the mountain, a whole town built just to support the work of digging a hole. The houses are bare and crooked, most not even whitewashed, some barely more than lean-tos. The railroad tracks I've been following end abruptly at a wide, dark tunnel. From its base, a steep trail climbs up and over the peak. It's as thick as ants, with people and horses and mules, all laden with packs.

The town has one saddler. He's a squinty-eyed man with a wisp-thin beard and calloused hands. I ask him about fixing Peony's saddle while he's bent over an awl and a strip of cowhide. He mumbles something about taking a couple days because of his other orders.

"No! I mean, no, thank you. Can you refer me to someone else?"

"Nearest saddler is in Dalton, which is more than a day's . . ." His words freeze halfway out of his mouth when he finally looks up and notices Daddy's saddle.

He grabs it out of my hands, squints at it closely, turns

it over. Then he squints at me and my admittedly ragged condition.

"I'll make you an offer, son," he says. "You trade me this saddle for one that's already fixed."

While I hesitate, he retrieves it from a wooden saddle rack and hands it to me.

It's plainer than my daddy's saddle, smaller and worn. But all the straps are new, and it seems sturdy enough.

"That'll carry you all the way to California, no lie," he says, and I recoil. How did he know? But no, gold fever is in the air, and he's only talking in a general way.

"Well. Maybe. I . . ."

"Tell you what, you leave your name, and if you decide to come back this way again, I'll trade you back my saddle for yours, plus the cost of my supplies and labor."

"That seems fair." Not that I ever expect to come back this way again, but knowing I could makes it easier to let go. "My name's Lee . . ."

"Lee?" he says, scratching it into a ledger.

Jefferson's last name is the first one that comes to mind. "Lee McCauley."

"All right Mr. McCauley, it's a deal."

I don't have to spend any money, which makes it a bargain for me. Even so, giving it up leaves me hollow and empty. First Daddy's rifle, and now his saddle.

"Sir," I say, remembering one more thing. My remaining coins are going to disappear so fast.

"Yes, son?"

"Do you have any saddlebags for sale? Just something small, maybe."

He gives me another studied look, and I'm suddenly glad to be covered in filth. Hopefully, I look more like a beggar boy than a runaway girl.

He rummages through a pile of leather on his workbench. "Here," he says, handing me a bag. "I was going to cut this up for scraps, but you might get some use out of it yet."

I swallow, choked up by his kindness. It's worn, the leather cracking, but with a good oiling it should last awhile. He grabs a hat from a peg on the wall and plops it onto my head. There's a small tear in the brim, but it'll do.

"That makes the set complete," he says. "Good luck to you, wherever you're headed."

"Thank you," I gulp out, and turn and flee.

Peony regards the new saddle with disdain. I let her give it a good sniff, and she stops fussing when I tighten the buckles.

The portage trail over the mountain is steep and rocky and ugly as sin, because the whole mountainside is stripped of lumber and trampled. There are so many people traveling it that no one gives us a second look, which suits me just fine. The plodding, heavy-laden mules keep everyone at an agonizingly slow pace, and it's hours before we crest the ridge and start down.

Halfway to the bottom, Peony stumbles. Her gait takes on a slight lurch.

I hop off. People stuck behind me grumble, but they go silent when I pull up Peony's left front foot and reveal that she's thrown a shoe, the same one that I thought might have loosened during our scuffle with the brothers.

I check her hoof thoroughly. No cracking or wear that I can see. Still, there's no galloping in our near future, even if I see Hiram himself striding toward me.

My heart is heavy as I lead her down the awful, rocky trail, every step a slow agony that puts Peony at risk. Another crowded settlement clusters at the bottom, where the railroad starts right back up again. I wander around, looking for a farrier or at least a blacksmith, but there is only a small boardinghouse, a tavern, and a handful of shanties.

As much as I'd love a soft bed and a watertight roof at the boardinghouse, I don't dare show my face in town, or part with any precious coins, so we make camp in a clump of bare trees. I spend an hour searching for dry wood this time; can't risk the smoke giving me away again. I check Peony's feet, cleaning the bare one of excess mud. Finally, I'm warm, and my eyes are heavy with sleep. Still, I lie awake a long time.

I picture that creased map spread across Free Jim's counter. Getting out of Georgia was always going to be the hardest part, I tell myself. But I'm almost there. I imagine the colored county squares marching all the way to the Mississippi. Maybe I can chop wood, do chores for food, like I did the other morning. There's got to be a way.

Horses clop by, and I hear bursts of conversation, and once, even though it's dark, the echoing ring of a hammer and nails. Gold seekers and merchants, tunnel workers and families—people like me—are all only yards away, but it feels like miles.

Peony and I cross into Tennessee and reach Chattanooga by late afternoon the next day. It's such a pretty place, with a wide sparkling river winding through rolling hills that are stubbornly green, even in winter. It puts me in mind of Jefferson, who always appreciates a pretty view. I hope I'm following in his footsteps; that he traveled this exact road, looked down on this exact bend in the river. He was only three days ahead of me. Maybe I'll run into him here.

No sense getting my hopes up. This is a mighty big country, and Peony throwing a shoe has put me behind.

Chattanooga is the first town I've seen to rival Dahlonega. It's big enough that folks don't look twice as we walk by; they just go about their business along the riverbank. The first blacksmith I find has a farrier's horseshoe hanging over his door. I lead Peony into the stable area and ask a young man with an apprentice's apron about getting her shod.

"Pretty girl you've got here," he says, checking her over. "A dollar will get you two new shoes. So her front hooves have even wear."

Five other horses already crowd his stable, waiting to be shod. "I'm in a hurry. I'll give you two dollars if you do it right away." I can't afford two dollars. Neither can I afford another delay.

"Deal. Come back around suppertime."

It feels awful to leave her in the care of a stranger, even

if it's only a few hours. But once she's shod, we can gallop right out of here and north to Kentucky, just like Free Jim suggested. In the meantime I'll work up my courage to get some supplies.

I find the feed store first. My heart is aflutter the whole time, even though all I do is buy a small sack of grain. But the transaction goes smoothly enough that by the time I reach the general store, my nerves have calmed. This time, I remember to remove my hat.

Inside, I head toward an iron rack hung with pots and pans. If I buy a small skillet and some flour, I can make flapjacks. I'd planned to supplement my supplies with hunting, before the brothers stole my Hawken. I'm grateful to have the five-shooter, but I'm not well practiced with a revolver, and I'd be lucky to bag even a rabbit or a squirrel. So, flapjacks it is. Flour weighs a lot, but it won't cost much, and I can make better time if I don't have to stop for supplies.

Another customer is already at the counter—a tall, handsome young man with magnificent sideburns and a fine coat. He puffs on a cigar while a clerk peruses a list he just handed over.

The clerk frowns. "These are overland supplies, Andrew. Please tell me you didn't get the fool notion to go gold hunting."

"It's just lying on the ground," the gentleman says around his cigar, "waiting for a man of action to pick it up. But you have to be an early bird, or it'll be too late. Just like the gold rush in Georgia."

I inch closer, ears pricked like a cat's.

"You're taking everyone? Mrs. Joyner and the little ones too?"

He nods. "I aim to stay on. A prosperous man in California can live like a king."

"If he's prosperous enough, he can live like a king wherever he is. The railroad'll be bringing a lot of opportunities for a smart fellow with connections in these parts."

"A smart fellow with connections makes his own opportunities wherever he is."

The clerk laughs and gives up. They dicker over a few items on the list, like shovels and pans and coffee.

"Excuse me! Sirs!" comes a familiar voice. My mouth goes dry.

I catch the barest glimpse of Abel Topper—ragged hat in hand, left suspender strap busted and dangling at his side—before I melt into the shadowy corner.

"Can I help you?" the clerk asks in an annoyed voice.

Topper is between me and the door. If I tried to sneak out now, he'd see me for sure and certain. I keep my back turned and pretend to study a bolt of canvas.

"I'm looking for a horse. Well, a horse thief. I expect—"

"Do you mind?" the fine gentleman interrupts. "We are in the middle of a business transaction."

"Your pardon. It's just that time is precious—"

"I assure you, there are no horse thieves in Chattanooga. They stay to the back roads."

"Yes, but—"

"I'd lay odds your thief fled north into Kentucky. That's the quickest way to lawless lands, where folks like him would feel right at home. Now, please allow me to conclude my affairs."

"North into Kentucky, eh?" Topper says.

"You a sheriff?" the clerk asks. "A marshal?"

"Naw. Just trying to get in good with the horse's fancy owner, if you know what I mean."

"I'm sure I don't," the gentleman says.

"Do you have a leaflet?" the clerk asks. "I'd be happy to post it at my door."

My heart races like a thousand galloping hooves.

"Naw. Never got a good look at the fellow."

If he doesn't know I'm the one who took Peony, then he struck off on his own. My uncle didn't send him. But my relief is short-lived; Abel Topper could describe my horse to anyone, easy as pie.

The gentleman loudly clears his throat.

"Fine!" Topper snaps. "I'm leaving." Boots tromp away as he mutters something about uppity rich folks under his breath.

"Uncouth fellow," the clerk says.

"Can't trust a man with only half his teeth," the gentleman agrees.

They continue to dicker over supplies, but I pay no attention. I have to get out of here. I have to retrieve Peony from the blacksmith and flee before Abel Topper sees her. And maybe I shouldn't take the road north like I'd planned. Not if that's the way Topper aims to go.

"So who's your captain?" the clerk says.

"Rodney Chisholm."

"I heard he's crewing with Fiddle Joe and Red Jack," the clerk says.

"I don't know any gentlemen graced by those sobriquets. But perhaps they have Christian names with which I would be more familiar?"

"Perhaps they do," the clerk says. "But those are the only names I know. Great musicians both, fiddle and guitar."

"Thank the good Lord you said guitar— I thought I might have to suffer a banjo."

"Whatever you say. Is this everything?"

"Yes. Put it on my father's tab and have your boys carry it down to the landing."

"When do you need it?"

"At once. The river's high, good for passage over the shoals."

Free Jim warned me against taking a flatboat, but it might be my best option. If this Andrew Joyner fellow and his family are heading west, maybe I can follow. Or better yet, join up. It'd be a whole heap safer; those brothers would never have robbed me if I'd been traveling in a group, and it's the last thing my uncle would expect.

I need to wrangle an introduction; it's not proper to just go over and announce myself.

No, it wouldn't be proper if I was a girl. Maybe I should walk right up and offer my hand. I take a few steps in his direction, but remembering his reaction to Abel Topper's interruption gives me pause. If he considered Topper *uncouth*, then he certainly doesn't have time for me, with my bad haircut, mud-smeared shirt, and ill-fitting trousers. I pretend to examine the hats on a nearby stand while I try to figure out what to do.

"Say hello to Captain Chisholm for me," the clerk says.

"I certainly will," Mr. Joyner says.

Captain Chisholm. That's who I need to talk to. I dash from the store, looking right and left to make sure Topper is not around. *Captain Chisholm, Captain Chisholm,* I repeat silently.

The blacksmith is only a few blocks away. I walk fast, but not too fast, hat brim low, hands shoved into my pockets. I glance around one last time before heading into the stable, and I nearly trip over my own feet because Abel Topper is just down the street, broken suspender swinging at his side. I hold my breath as he mounts the steps to a tavern door and disappears inside.

Now is my chance. If Peony isn't shod yet, we're leaving anyway.

"You're in luck, lad," says the blacksmith's apprentice, coming toward me. "Just finished with your pretty mare."

My relief is so great I nearly stumble. "So fast!"

He shrugs. "You're paying for it."

I fumble for my money and hand him two dollars. "Thank you."

"Heading west like everyone else?" he says.

I almost deny it, but I get a better idea. "Sure thing. Heading to Kentucky on the Federal Road tomorrow."

"Well, good luck."

Peony nickers in greeting, and I drag her from the stables. I ask the first person I bump into: "Which way to the landing?"

"You're close enough to smell it," he snaps, and he walks off.

I sniff the air; he's not wrong. Following the fishy, rotten vegetable scent of slow water, I head toward the riverbank and see it at once. I stare, mouth agape.

A line of flatboats hugs the river's edge. They seem as rickety as rafts, but they're eighty to a hundred feet long and covered with low roofs. One is full of cattle; others are stacked with barrels, which men are rolling down the riverbank. In the middle of the river, a small, rocky island serves as anchor for a swing ferry. A thick line of people stretches along the landing as they wait their turns to cross.

"Where can I find Captain Chisholm?" I ask one of the men rolling barrels.

He wipes sweat from his brow with the back of his glove and points me to a flatboat that sits high in the water on account of not having cargo.

I stare at the boat, hesitating. If Mama is watching, she'll probably toss in her grave to see me walk over to a bunch of strange men and ask a favor. But I'm Lee McCauley now, I remind myself. It shouldn't be a big deal.

I leave Peony tied to a dock post, then I hitch my suspenders the way I've seen Jefferson do a hundred times and swagger across to the boat like I've every right. "Captain!" I stand at the dock's edge and holler down under the roof. "Hey, Captain."

A short fellow with a sunburned nose and carroty hair pokes his face out. "Who's asking?" he says.

"I am."

"Who're you?"

"Who're *you?*"

He grins. "Red Jack."

"Are you going to California, Red Jack?"

He steps into the cold sunshine. His feet are bare, and his belly hangs over the waist of his trousers. His suspenders strain to keep them up.

"Lord, no, we're just heading over to the Mississippi."

"But you're taking folks west, right?"

"Are you a friend of Mr. Joyner's?"

"Never met him. Just heard you were taking people west, and I'm looking for a ride in that direction."

Red Jack studies me, running a hand through his hair like he's trying to stir loose some thoughts. "We're taking Mr. Joyner's family as far as Missouri. They'll have to walk the rest of the way on their own."

"How much for passage to Missouri?"

"Rates are up to the captain, who ain't here right now." He looks me up and down, taking in my filthy clothes, my second- or thirdhand hat. "But if you ain't with the Joyners, you ought to know they've hired the whole boat for themselves."

My shoulders slump. "All right," I say, gazing down the length of the river at all the other flatboats. It'll mean talking to an awful lot of people, but surely I can find someone willing to take us aboard.

"Ah, don't go looking all forlorn," he says.

Another fellow pokes his head out. He's so tall he can't stand up straight inside the cabin. His skin is as wrinkled and brown as tree bark, and his twiglike fingers are long and thin. He sees me and smiles, and it's such a friendly, craggy grin that I can't help grinning back.

"Are you the captain?" I ask.

"No, name's Joe."

Fiddle Joe. He turns away and starts up a fire in the little cookstove perched on the edge of the boat. His back is still turned when Joe says, "You like chicory coffee?"

A cup of warm anything would taste heavenly at the moment. "Yes, sir."

"Then come aboard."

I glance toward Peony to make sure she'll stay in view, and I step onto the deck, which looked solid enough from shore but is actually in a constant state of sway. As my legs adjust, Joe hands me a tin cup steaming with coffee. It's hot enough to scald my tongue, but no bitter liquid has ever tasted so sweet.

Red Jack returns carrying three small chairs and a table, which they set up on the open deck. "Well, don't stand there like a begging dog, sit down for supper," Red Jack says.

I can't believe my luck. I pull up a seat, and Joe slaps down three bowls of grits mixed with runny eggs. The other two start eating, but I hesitate to dig in.

"Don't be shy, boy," Joe says to me. "Eggs and grits make as fine a supper as they do a breakfast."

It's the "boy" that does it. I shovel the mess into my mouth like a starving stray. Joe sure likes his salt, more than Mama ever put on our food, but I don't mind one bit. "Thank you," I say around a huge mouthful.

"So, you're an argonaut, eh?" Red asks. "Heading to California with the rest?"

I swallow and say, "I've got a friend—well, practically family—who's going west, and I said I'd meet up with him in Independence, like we read about in the paper."

Joe nods knowingly. "Lots of folks meeting up there. But Mr. Joyner is the only one who can decide on passengers."

I frown. Guess I'll have to work up the courage to introduce myself to that fine and proper man after all. Might be worth it to spend the money for a shoeshine first. Maybe even a barber to fix my sawed-off hair. If I can work up the courage to go to a barber.

No, doing anything in town puts me and Peony at risk of being discovered.

"But he doesn't have any say over the crew," says a voice behind me.

I look over my shoulder. He's the roughest of the bunch so far, with a square jaw, uneven stubble that makes him look like he shaves with a spoon, and red-rimmed eyes from either exhaustion or drink. Joe slaps another bowl of grits down on the table and gives up his chair for the newcomer.

"I don't know anything about crewing boats," I say, eyeing him warily. He looks too much like the brothers who robbed me, with his unkempt hair and ratty shirt. "To be completely honest, this is the first time I ever set foot on one."

The newcomer swallows his coffee. "If you want to hire a flatboat to carry you over to the Mississippi, I can recommend some to you."

"I just want to get there, whatever way I can. I've been walking overland so far." But I don't want to keep on that way, and the sullen tone of my voice gives me away.

Red says, "It's much nicer on the river. And faster. The current does all the work."

Faster. I desperately need faster.

"Not *all* the work," the rough man says. "I have to do a bit of it too, while the two of you are busy plucking strings and scaring off the fish."

"Singing lullabies, making 'em easier to catch, you mean," Red says.

"We could use another hand," the rough one says. "Someone to do the unskilled labor on board."

"For God's sake, just don't tell him you sing," Red Jack mutters.

"I don't sing at all, sir," I hurry to say. I love singing, truth be told, but my singing voice would give me away as a girl faster than you could say *Open your hymnals*.

"That's too bad," the newcomer says. "So, if we give you victuals and transport—"

"For me and my horse?"

"For you *and* your horse, you do whatever work we need on the way."

I don't know what unskilled labor is, and I don't care.

There's no way my uncle or Abel Topper or those brothers could follow me on a boat. And even though I can't walk on water like the Lord, as Free Jim suggested, Peony and I can swim just fine. "That's a wonderful idea, sir. I'll ask the captain."

Red and Joe share a chuckle. Joe picks up the empty plate and mug. "This *is* the captain," he says to me in a low voice.

My face warms.

"Rodney Chisholm," the captain says.

"Lee," I reply. "Lee McCauley."

"Pleased to meet you, and welcome aboard, Mr. McCauley." He stands up. "This is just a trial, boy. A week from now, if you haven't proved trustworthy and able, we'll put you ashore."

"Understood, sir."

"This table and chairs get stacked in that nook."

Seconds pass before I catch on. I jump up. "Yes, sir!"

I try to tuck all three chairs under one arm, but they slip from my grip and clatter to the deck. So I pick up two and run to put them away, then come back for the last.

The crew stands at the bow, smoking their pipes, watching me.

"Please tell me I was never that green," Joe says.

"Ha," the captain says. "Don't let Joe fool you, boy. I signed him on to do unskilled labor too."

"Thirty-four years old before I ever set foot on a flatboat," Joe says. "If an old dog like me can learn it, you'll do fine."

My face feels hot under their scrutiny as I stack the last

chair. Beneath the roof, the boat is divided into stalls. Some are filled with straw; others are fitted with cots or hammocks. It feels like a barn—a barn on water!—which makes it feel a little like home. I guess it is home for some. I bet the crew spends the whole year on this boat.

These fellows don't know anything about me, and yet they've taken me into their home. I know I'll be working for my keep, but it still feels like an act of angels when I sorely need one. It's a second kindness in almost as many days. Not everyone is like the brothers or Uncle Hiram. I'd do well to remember that.

Chapter Thirteen

$\mathcal{T}$he flatboat is long and low and dark. It takes a bit of tugging to convince Peony to come aboard. She prances in place in response to the boat's gentle sway, but she settles upon seeing her stall. It's dry and has fresh straw and plenty of feed, which seems to be all that matters.

Once she's out of sight and happily eating, a weight drops from my shoulders, and I can breathe easy for the first time in days.

A slave boy from the general store brings the supplies down about an hour later. I help him unload the cart and carry everything into the empty stalls. I can't figure what some of the items have to do with gold prospecting—like the two full bottles of laudanum or the Oldridge's Balm of Columbia for hair and whiskers—but it's possible Mr. Joyner knows something that I don't.

The surface of the river is burnished red gold with late-afternoon sunshine when two men roll a huge wagon down to the dock. I stare agape at it, wondering how in the world we'll get everything aboard. It's full to bursting with flour, grains, barrels of salted pork, and a whole heap of fancy furniture. There's a sideboard table, and four high-back chairs. A bed frame and a feather mattress. A lady's dresser with a gilded mirror. Mr. Joyner said he was moving his whole household, but I didn't figure that meant his whole house.

We unload it all, every single piece, and it's a good thing Mama's shawl is wrapped so tight around my chest because sweat pours down the front of my shirt, making it stick to any available skin.

By the time we finish, it feels like my aching back won't bear another burden, which is when the captain directs us to disassemble the wagon. I don't dare complain or show even a hint of weakness, so I go at it like I'm as fresh as the morning.

After taking the wagon apart, we heft and slide the wagon box onto the boat. Then we fill the box with all the other pieces—the wheels, the tongue, the bonnet. Next, we bring the oxen aboard. There are four teams of two, which seems like a lot for one wagon, but when you're moving a whole household, I guess that's how many you need. The huge beasts don't care for their stalls, and they have a lot to say on the matter, but once they're settled in and we spread some straw, they seem resigned.

"Where's the rest of it?" Captain Chisholm asks once the wagon and oxen are all safely aboard.

"There's more?" I gasp.

"You have a problem, son?"

"Course not."

He grins.

Suddenly my plan to go all the way to California with nothing but Peony and a saddlebag seems like the height of tomfoolery.

By evening, more supplies and more animals have arrived, including a pair of fine horses and a hound dog with white patches and drooping ears, who licks my hands and face as if we're long-lost friends. I scratch his ears and rub his scruff, thinking about Nugget. I hope she's a comfort to Jefferson on the road, the same way Peony is a comfort to me.

"Coney, get over here before I whip your hide."

It's Mr. Joyner, dressed in a fine black suit with a yellow silk cravat. Standing prim beside him is a pretty blond woman in a blue calico dress and a lace shawl. One hand clutches an embroidered satchel, full to bursting; the other grips the shoulder of a girl in blond braids who can't be more than six years old. Another child, a towheaded boy of about four, stands half hidden in her voluminous skirt, though he dares to peek out at me. I wink at him, and he turns away fast, burying his face in his mama's skirt.

Even the two children carry bulging satchels. At the family's feet is a huge luggage trunk, which will probably take all four of us to haul inside and which Coney the dog is now giving a thorough sniffing.

Red Jack shares an amused look with me before grabbing

a couple of satchels. "That's a fine rocking chair we just loaded," he says by way of conversation.

Mr. Joyner nods solemnly. "I'm having my whole house disassembled and floated downriver on another flatboat," he explains as we work. "When it reaches New Orleans, it'll be loaded onto a ship and sent down to Panama, where it will be trucked across the isthmus and then loaded onto another ship and transported up the coast to California. We'll have our own familiar home waiting for us—walls and all—when we get to San Francisco. We're only bringing with us those things essential to our overland journey."

I had no idea packing up a whole house was possible— or that a dressing table could be considered *essential*. "Why didn't you go the same way?" I ask.

He seems startled that I would dare speak to him, but he answers nonetheless. "And expose my wife and children to the harsh climates and rough heathen of Panama? Or the relentless waves of the Pacific? Never. Besides, the trip across the continent will be an adventure, something they'll remember for the rest of their lives. Isn't that right, Andy?" He tousles the boy's near-white hair.

"Yes, Pa," Andy says, but he gazes wide-eyed at the decking before him. The river is choppy with activity, which makes the boat pitch and sway. He slips a hand into his mother's.

Mrs. Joyner is stiff beside her husband, and I'm put in mind of an egret, the way the woman's senses are attuned to everything around her, the way she stands so pale and frozen, but perhaps ready to launch into graceful flight if startled. She squeezes her son's tiny hand, saying, "It's God's will for America to cover the continent from sea to sea." Her voice is soft, and it seems to have a question in it. "We'll be part of something grand, helping spread civilization into the wilderness."

"That's exactly right, dear," Mr. Joyner says.

I imagine civilization as a bag of seeds that she'll be scattering along the roadside as we go. Like Johnny Appleseed. The thought makes me smile, but she glares at my grin like I've done something wrong.

"Come along, children," she says, pointedly turning her back on me.

"Yes, Ma," they chorus as she herds them aboard. I stare after them, wondering at "Pa" and "Ma." I've never heard anyone call their parents that before.

"Hello," someone says in my ear, and I whirl. It's a gray-haired lady in sensible navy wool, with a straw hat and a patched satchel.

"I'm Matilda Dudley," she says. "The Joyners' cook. But you can call me Aunt Tildy."

I tip my hat. "Pleased to meet you, ma'am. I'm Lee."

She chatters at me while I continue to load cargo, explaining all the ways in which she has served the Joyner family over the years, from tending their herb garden to caring for the children.

I don't discourage her from talking, but her friendly prattle sets me on edge because the flatboat, which originally seemed huge, is shrinking rapidly. I don't know how I'll keep my identity a secret aboard this floating homestead, with all of us crammed in like sheep in a pen. How does anyone attend to their private business on a boat like this? What if I need to launder my shirt?

"That's enough, Aunt Tildy," Mr. Joyner interrupts finally. "No need to bore these gentlemen with ancient history."

"Yes, sir!" she says. Then she continues, unabashed, "You know, it'll be a wonderful thing to see the wild frontier. They say it's summer all the time in California."

If a sweet dumpling took human form, it would look just like Aunt Tildy, right down to the flour-dusting of her gray hair. When she starts to argue with Joe about who's going to do the cooking, I dare to hope I won't be eating runny, oversalted eggs again.

Mr. Joyner gestures to the captain. "Everything's aboard. Why aren't we under way? California's not getting any closer while we tarry."

"Soon enough, sir," Chisholm calls out.

He calls the crew over and says to us in a low voice, "We'll just push off and float a few miles until dark. Make our passengers happy."

It'll make me happy too. Once we're under way, it'll be harder for Uncle Hiram to find me, either by accident or on purpose. Almost everyone in Chattanooga who might remember me—or Peony—is aboard this boat.

"We won't try to pass the rapids today, will we?" Red asks.

"Not on your life," says the captain. "Or mine." Then he

turns around, and the size of his voice turns from pistol shot to cannon fire: "Get ready to push off!"

Red and Joe untie the ropes tethering us to shore. The animals, crowded inside their swaying barn, start lowing and kicking. Coney launches onto the roof and barks at nothing in particular. Mrs. Joyner brings the children to the open bow of the boat and says something about beginning a great journey.

I glance around, feeling useless. "What should I do?" I ask.

"Grab a pole and push off," says Joe, lifting his pole high with both hands to show me. Red and the captain already have theirs in hand, and the three men space themselves along the side of the boat.

I see where the poles are stored and grab one. It's heavy and at least twice my height. It thumps and scrapes along the deck as I hop onto the roof, dragging it up behind me. I maneuver it around, whacking Joe in the back of the knees.

"Hey!"

"Sorry!"

He glares at me while I jab the end into the shore and push.

"Your grip is too far back," Joe warns.

The pole sticks. Our boat slides away, but my pole won't come free. I yank harder. The pole starts to slide through my hands. I'm leaning over the edge, tipped precariously over the water.

"Joe!" I holler.

Joe darts over and grabs the back of my trousers. "Let go."

"I'll lose the pole!"

"Then go with it," he says.

I let go, and the pole sticks out of the mud a moment before slowly drooping down and sinking into the water.

Red Jack snorts. "Off to a good start, boy," he says, motioning me toward the middle of the roof where I can't make any trouble.

The captain regards me with a cool eye.

"I'm really sorry, sir," I say.

"I'd take it out of your pay," he says. "Only I'm not paying you. So go ashore when we tie up for the night and cut a new one."

"Make sure it's one you can handle," Red Jack says. I don't hear any meanness in his voice, only practicality.

I have no idea how to cut a long, sturdy pole from the twisting trees that hug the riverbank. "Yes, sir."

We drift downriver until it's past dark, so he doesn't send me ashore tonight. Aunt Tildy lets Joe cook dinner one last time. She vows to take over the boat's kitchen tomorrow, and no one argues. After the plates are cleaned up, Joe gets out his fiddle and Red Jack fetches his guitar. They sit on the roof and play while the captain sings in a startlingly beautiful tenor. Joe dances while he fiddles, slapping his boots on the thick planks of the roof. Mrs. Joyner holds tight to her children, refusing to clap along or even smile, but when Aunt Tildy and the little ones start clapping, she doesn't protest.

It's not the best music I've heard, but it fills the cold night sky with energy and warmth. I gaze up at the stars and find the bright cluster of the Pleiades. My throat tightens with the memory: Jefferson and me lying on our backs in the hayloft last winter, straw poking out of our mouths, the loft shutter propped open to the sparkling crystal sky. The Cherokee don't call it the Pleiades, he told me, but the Ani'tsutsa, which means "the Seven Boys." His mother told him the story, how eight boys got so mad at their mama they decided to run away, but as they leaped into the sky, she grabbed the eighth boy by the heel and dragged him back to earth, leaving his seven brothers to shine in the night.

Jefferson liked to imagine he was the eighth boy, the one who stayed. Staying is important, he said. And he liked the idea that he had brothers somewhere, maybe looking after him. Jeff was embarrassed afterward, and he made me swear never to tell that he had such fanciful notions. I swallowed the lump in my throat and said that having a brother would be the very best thing.

I hope Jefferson's all right; I hate to think what might happen if he ran afoul of those freebooter brothers or their ilk. I wish I could have caught up with him on the road, but now I find myself hoping he's still three days ahead. Because anyone sent after me would recognize him just as easily. With luck, he's practically to Independence by now.

The final note from Joe's fiddle echoes over the water, dying slow and sweet. The wind on the river is icy cold, colder even than on the road, so everyone gets up and turns in. No one has indicated where I should sleep, so I head back to Peony's stall and prop myself in the corner. It's been a long day of hard work, and this is the first time I've had a roof over my head at night since leaving home. I'm cold, but I feel safer than I have in weeks, with a full belly to boot. My eyes drift shut.

I startle awake. It's Fiddle Joe. He hangs a blanket over the side of the stall and walks off without saying a word. I snatch it up. It's old and threadbare, but after losing everything else, it seems finer than gold.

Morning on the river is one of the prettiest I've ever seen, with golden sunshine gleaming on water as smooth as a mirror. Red Jack pokes his head out moments after I do. He yawns and stretches, and he's untying his pants to relieve himself into the water when he spots me.

"Holy—" he says, jumping in alarm. "You're up early. Been sitting there the whole night?"

I'm blushing like the girl I am. "I'm an early riser," I say, turning my back and giving him his privacy.

Joe stumbles out a while later and starts bacon sizzling on the box stove. At the breakfast table I try to return his blanket.

"Naw," he says. "Everybody ought to have their own blanket."

I can't squeeze out my thanks through the tightness in my throat. I have a blanket again, and I didn't even have to buy it.

The Joyners rise late. While they eat breakfast, I learn what the captain meant by "unskilled labor." It's my job to muck stalls every morning, which is no different from my chores back home. At least I go after it with a sure hand.

"Just toss it overboard," the captain says. "The current washes everything away." I do as he says, but it gives my belly a squirm to think of drawing our cooking water from the same river.

Water laps gently against the boat as we get under way, morning mist rises from the banks, and great white herons swoop low for leaping fish. No wonder some people spend their whole lives here. Just like Joe said, it's a pleasant way to travel, with the lovely river to do most of the work.

Or maybe saying so was all for show, because we haven't drifted far before Joe and Red and the captain become thin lipped, and wound tight as rattlers. About ten miles downriver from Chattanooga, I discover why.

We reach a narrow gorge. Walls of rock rise up on either side as the water flows fast and white, like it's being pushed through a mill chute. The wind picks up, whipping at my short hair. Spray coats my skin, making me shiver. The walls of the gorge sweep by faster and faster.

The captain orders the Joyner family inside, and Mrs. Joyner can't comply fast enough. Her husband lingers beneath the overhang. "Chisholm!" he booms. "Our contract stipulates *safe passage* to Missouri. If we don't arrive safely, you don't get paid."

"You've nothing to worry about, sir," the captain returns.

But once Mr. Joyner ducks inside, Captain Chisholm and Joe Fiddle exchange a dark look. The captain takes the steerboard while Joe and Red grab their poles and take up position to either side of the boat.

I still don't have a pole of my own. I look around for something useful to do, but the boat dips violently, and my legs fly out from under me. I hit the deck hard, pain shooting up my tailbone. The boat lurches again as I scramble for the edge, for anything to hold on to.

The captain stands on the roof, yelling out hazards, riding the waves like a duck in a storm, while I cling for dear life. We veer left, toward the wall. It looms over me, getting closer and closer. The wall is slick with tiny waterfalls, and dotted with clumps of stubborn vegetation that I could reach out and touch if I wanted.

The captain strains at the steerage, but our course won't correct. What happens if we hit the wall? I imagine the boat splintering apart, wood and water flying everywhere. Peony can swim in a pinch. I hope the Joyners can too.

Red Jack jams his pole all the way down to the bottom of the river. He strains until every vein in his neck stands out as though painted in blue ink. The water froths between the boat and the cliff side, geysering up and soaking me to the skin. I hold my breath.

Slowly, the boat turns on Red's pivot.

We break free, and the boat shoots down the center of the gorge like an arrow. Red Jack lets out a whoop of joy.

The gorge opens up, wider and wider. The cliffs give way to gentle hills. Our flatboat slows until it lazes along like it's out for a Sunday buggy drive.

"Any damage?" calls the captain.

"We never hit!" Joe calls back. "Not even once."

"Nice work, men," the captain says, and his glance includes me, even though my only accomplishment was not getting washed overboard.

Red Jack stashes his pole and helps me to my feet. "So, how did you like your first trip down the Suck?" he asks.

It takes a moment to find my voice, but when I do, I surprise myself by blurting, "Very much, sir!"

He grins and slaps me on the back.

I'm alone in my sudden affection for white water, though, because now that things have quieted, I can hear the oxen lowing mournfully. Something crashes inside the cabin, followed by a long wail.

Aunt Tildy charges out, her face white and her hands shaking. "No, Lordy, Lordy, no, I'm not going one mile farther. You put me ashore! You put me ashore this second, or I'll tell your mother."

The rest of the family tumbles out after her.

Mr. Joyner's cravat is askew, and he mops his forehead with a handkerchief. The children cling to Mrs. Joyner's skirts, who is just as wide-eyed and white-knuckled as Tildy.

"Please don't go, Auntie," Mrs. Joyner says. "Who will feed the children?"

"Get Fiddle Joe over there to do it," Aunt Tildy says with a wave of her hand. "Or learn to do it yourself, I don't care. But Lord have mercy, I am not fit for this mode of travel."

Captain Chisholm hops down from the roof. "Don't worry,

ma'am," he says. "Most of the river is as calm as a sleeping babe. We're through the worst already."

Aunt Tildy shakes her head. "I'm going ashore at the first landing, and I'll make my own way back home if I have to crawl."

"We should have brought one of the slaves," Mrs. Joyner says to her husband. "Polly, or maybe Sukey. Surely your father would let us have Sukey? We can put ashore here, and the children and I will wait while you go overland to fetch her."

My heart lodges in my throat. Waiting here on the riverbank, possibly for days, is the very last thing I want to do. We're only a day's ride from Chattanooga, where I saw Abel Topper. I hope he's on his way to Kentucky by now, but I can't be certain.

"Nonsense," Mr. Joyner says. "I've read about these pioneers. They're rugged, hardy types who solve their own problems, and we shall do the same."

"Darling, you know I don't cook! I am mother to your children, not some . . . not some . . ."

"There's really nothing to it, ma'am," Joe says.

Mrs. Joyner looks back and forth between Joe and her husband, her face shifting from panic to horror.

"Then it's settled," Mr. Joyner says. "We'll put off Aunt Tildy as she requests, and you shall use the remainder of our waterborne voyage to practice your culinary skills for our principal journey west."

The ensuing silence is long.

In a near whisper, Mrs. Joyner says, "If you think it's best." I almost feel bad for her. Almost. I've never heard of anyone who couldn't cook a blessed thing. Even my daddy could make coffee or fry up bacon or spit a rabbit.

After many tearful farewells, the family puts Aunt Tildy ashore at the next settlement. I hang back, because it's none of my business, but I can't stop staring after her. Tildy was the only one of the Joyner party to show me any kindness, and now she's gone.

Chapter Fourteen

We drift for days down the meandering Tennessee River, first through Alabama, and it feels strange to head south after I spent so much time trying to go north. But soon enough the river twists up through Tennessee toward Kentucky, ultimately aiming for the Ohio. Our journey is cold and wet, and at mealtimes, we huddle by the stove while Mrs. Joyner tries her hand at cooking. She pretends to ignore us, but our hovering must make her nervous because we end up with burned flapjacks and runny grits every time.

Occasionally, we land to get supplies and stretch the horses' legs. I'm glad for the opportunity to care for my personal needs in privacy, but I don't breathe easy until we're back on the river. More often than not, we go days without stopping, and I'm forced to duck down in Peony's stall and use a slop bucket. I don't dare remove my clothing to launder it. My shirt becomes stiff and stained.

The nights we do put to shore, Mr. Joyner always tries

to find other gentlemen for a game of cards, even though Mrs. Joyner prevails upon him not to go. I think about the brothers and their plan to rob card players along the river, about Uncle Hiram and Abel Topper, and I sit on the roof unable to sleep because I'm keeping watch. The fact that I never see them is no reassurance. I didn't see the brothers coming the last time.

Each morning, I muck stalls. During the afternoons, Joe teaches me to pole, using a piece he helped me cut from a long, skinny spruce. The work is no harder than what I'm used to, and indeed, some of it is a good deal easier. With so much feed and so little exercise, Peony fattens up, and her winter coat grows in thick and lovely. I don't begrudge her one bit; she'll need a store of strength for what's ahead.

After a week, I screw up my courage to approach Captain Chisholm, who stands at the back of the boat, one hand on the rudder, the other shading his eyes.

"Captain?"

"Son?"

"It's been a week."

He stares at me a moment as if confused. "Oh. Right. Well, I reckon I can give you another week's trial."

A twitch of his lips indicates he might be having a bit of fun at my expense, but I don't dare put it to the test. I mutter a quick "Thank you, sir" and get right back to work.

One of the oddest things about this boat ride is the utter lack of gold. I'm the only one who carries gold coins. The mirror we loaded on board must be gilded with brass, or maybe even paint, and I hope the Joyners didn't pay good money for it. I know the captain carries some money, and surely a wealthy man like Mr. Joyner does too, but if so, it's in small denominations; Seated Liberty dollars and quarters and dimes never give me the smallest niggle. Back home, and even on the road, gold was always poking at my senses. But not now. Now, there's a hollowness inside me, like I'm missing a part of myself.

I find myself reaching for Mama's locket more and more. I pinch it between thumb and forefinger, trace the hinged edge and the lacelike filigree on the front, letting the gold sing sweet until I'm filled up again.

Weeks pass. Captain Chisholm does not put me to shore. The flatboat winds through rolling blue mountains and deep valleys like I've never seen. Small towns and lone farms hug the riverbank every bend or so. We pass flatboats heading down the river, and rowboats coming up. Even this far west, the river is the busiest highway I've ever seen, full of energy and purpose.

We're halfway through Kentucky one sunny morning, and I'm in the stalls mucking. My belly has been feeling hot and tight for hours; I hope I'm not getting sick. Suddenly, wet warmth blossoms between my legs.

I freeze, pitchfork half raised.

No need to look at my drawers to know I'm in a heap of trouble. Mama told me all about it, and once she made me wash her monthly rags so I'd understand. She said my time would come when I was seventeen or so, that since I wasn't planning on having babies anytime soon, it would be a regular visitor. With another start, I realize we've passed well into February, which means that sometime in the last couple of weeks, I turned sixteen years old.

"It came early, Mama," I whisper, touching the lump of locket beneath my shirt.

I'm a woman now. A woman with a big problem.

I dash into Peony's stall, where I hunker down and rip off Daddy's pants. I check them over and am hugely relieved that they seem untouched. My drawers are ruined, though. I whip them off and use them to wipe myself down, then I put on my one spare. Using my teeth, I rip a strip from the blanket Joe gave me, then I fold it up and shove it between my legs. I re-don the pants, and I bury the stained drawers under a pile of straw. Tonight, when it's dark, I'll rinse them in the river, then lay them out to dry where no one can see. They'll be spare rags now, though not nearly as many as I need.

There's no doubt the crew has accepted me for a boy; Joe and Red and the captain relieve themselves around me without a thought, though I avert my gaze every single time. When Red teased me about it once, I told him my mama raised me to be modest.

Stained rags are a different business entirely. There's no way I can explain them away. I'll have to be very careful and very smart.

At night after dinner, I offer to help Mrs. Joyner clean up. While we're scraping dishes and rinsing them in the river away from everyone else, I say, "Your pardon, ma'am, but I was wondering. Do you have a spare blanket I could buy?"

Her hands freeze over the cook pot. "You don't have a blanket?"

"An old one. It's small and . . . ripped."

"I'm sure I can manage something."

"Thank you."

We finish the dishes in silence. Mrs. Joyner avoids me the rest of the night, refusing even to meet my eye. Maybe she's taken offense at my request. But after I quietly wash up in the dark, I return to Peony's stall and find a small quilt hanging over the low wall. It's faded and patched, and one end is a bit ragged, but it's a whole heap better than the blanket Joe gave me.

I'm not one for praying much, but I can't help the bit of gratitude that slips heavenward. Then I get to work ripping strips from Joe's blanket, which I hide in my saddlebag. Now I have all the rags I need.

The next night, while Joe is fiddling away and Red is strumming his guitar and the captain is singing to the stars, I try to slip Mrs. Joyner a dime. She closes my hand into a fist and pushes it away. She turns her back and takes little Andy onto her knee to bounce in time to the music.

I slink away. Mrs. Joyner did me a kindness, and I don't understand why she won't take my dime or even glance my way, but I'm grateful to her just the same.

In fact, all the Joyners have proved amazingly adept at ignoring me, even on this tiny boat. Just this morning I caught little Olive, their daughter, staring at me as I stacked poles. But the moment her mother noticed, her gaze darted away. I suppose it's for the best. Wouldn't do to have little ones milling about, pestering me with questions I'm not willing to answer.

In the end, I'll never be fully crew or pioneer. The men are friendly enough, but they know I'm leaving when we reach the Missouri shore, and they have a whole history together before this trip that I'll never be a part of.

The crew's music is still going strong as I curl up in Peony's stall, Mrs. Joyner's blanket around my shoulders and Mama's locket clutched in my fist. The tightness in my belly spreads to my lower back and sets it to aching. I remind myself that Jefferson will be waiting for me in Independence. He's the closest thing I have to family now.

The morning sun hasn't yet peeked over the hills, and the air is clammy with fog. We push off from shore, and I congratulate myself at being an old hand with the poles now. We slide past the sleepy, low-lying city of Cairo, and suddenly, impossibly, the river breaks wide.

I gape, my pole dangling uselessly. We've reached the massive, muddy confluence of the Ohio and the Mississippi Rivers, and never have I seen so much water. With the fog clinging thick to the surface, and the shores a distant blur, I can almost imagine we're poling through the calmest ocean.

A bell echoes behind us, chased by the sound of churning water. Captain Chisholm orders us to the sweeps and runs forward to the gouger. Together we steer the boat out of the main channel.

A giant paddleboat materializes in the fog. It's two hundred feet long if it's a yard, with a pair of giant chimneys belching black smoke. *The Western Hope* is painted in gold letters on the side, surrounded by the yellow rays of a rising sun. I've never been superstitious, despite being a girl with witchy powers, but the coincidence of this moment and our intentions could make me reconsider my notions.

"That's a good omen," Mrs. Joyner says in a wistful voice.

Maybe she's wishing she were on that steamboat, and I don't blame her. The decks are lined with clean, white railings. Crowds of people stand at the upper levels, packed as tight as cattle in a flatboat. I take off my hat and wave to them, and they wave back. A few cheer at us. Their captain stands outside of what passes for a crow's nest but looks like a gingerbread house. Beside it is a big bell, which he gives a yank and sets to ringing. Olive looses a rare grin, and little Andy runs around in a circle yelling "Ding, ding, ding!" until he suddenly falls down, giggling.

Mr. Joyner frowns through the whole thing, and I can't imagine what's in that man's head. I've never seen such luxury in my life— That steamboat must be as fine as the finest hotel in Savannah, and if that's not worth getting excited about, I don't know what is.

It glides beyond us as quickly as it arrived, and we steer our humbler craft into the middle of the river and aim for a shore I can't see.

"Pa, I want to ride a boat like that one," Olive says.

Mr. Joyner removes the cigar from his mouth and blows

out a cloud of smoke. "It's a fine sight, isn't it, darling?"

The girl's mother brightens. "Mr. Joyner, perhaps we should pass the next part of our journey on a steamboat. It will make a wonderful memory for the children."

Andy and Olive regard their parents with wide, hopeful eyes.

"I wouldn't advise it." The captain jumps in. "The accommodations are fine, for them that can afford it, but all the paddlers are overbooked and crowded."

"But the cabins are nice?" Mrs. Joyner asks.

"Some of them, yes. Another word of warning: Lots of gambling takes place on those boats. If you go for a ride, hold on to your coin purses."

Mr. Joyner brightens at "gambling," but when he sees everyone staring at him, he frowns again. He takes a puff on his cigar and says, "I've read about this. It's a swindle. They take you all the way up the Missouri, but in the end you have to walk south again to get back on track. We're better off putting ashore here."

Mrs. Joyner stares at him.

He hastily adds, "We'll place our trust in my original plan. I see no reason to change our course before we've even reached the starting line. No, we'll head overland for Independence as intended." He gazes after the steamboat, though, his mustache twitching.

As we cross, the rising suns burns through the last of the gauzy clouds, finally revealing the far shore. The water between here and there is busier than the busiest town. I count three more steamboats, with smoke from still more rising around the river bend. We steer among flatboats—too many to count—and tiny rowboats that are clustered like gnats between them. We even pass a tiny raft containing two boys with straw hats and fishing poles.

As we approach the mud-churned riverbank, Captain Chisholm leans over and says, "You'll want to go north along the river until you reach Cape Girardeau. You can go west from there, but the most popular route is to continue north to St. Louis and then head westerly."

I picture it like Free Jim's map and try to memorize it, but I'm not sure it will do any good. The Mississippi River is so much broader and murkier than the twisting blue line I saw. Turns out, the great wide world doesn't look anything like a flat little map.

I reach under my shirt and grab the locket, but instead of thinking of Mama like I usually do, Jefferson springs to mind, and it's a punch to the gut how quick and easy and clear I imagine those keen dark eyes and that wide, serious mouth. I wish I could poke at his quiet ways and get a quick grin out of him, just like always. Tell him about my journey so far and hear about his.

Ask what exactly he meant by that mealymouthed proposal. Marrying for the sake of traveling convenience seemed like a fool-headed notion at the time, but now I can't get it out of my mind.

Trust someone, Mama said. *Not good to be as alone as we've been. Your daddy and I were wrong. . . .*

Floating down the river has given me plenty of time to ponder, and I'm not sure Mama was right. I wouldn't be in this heap of hurt if Daddy hadn't been so trusting. Still, I can't help thinking about Jefferson and about how, in California, we could start all over; maybe even build up something great.

What if Jefferson didn't make it? What if he's not waiting for me in Independence after all? Suddenly, it feels as though I'm falling into a mining pit, with no gold and nothing at the bottom but dark forever.

By midday my back and shoulders ache from unloading the Joyners' wagon and furniture. The wagon must be reassembled and reloaded, but Captain Chisholm's contract with them has officially ended, and Mr. Joyner plans to hire respectable workers to help with the journey to Independence. In the meantime, Fiddle Joe calls out from the roof of the boat: "Victuals is ready, for them that's hungry."

My stomach rumbles as I soak my kerchief in the river and wash up. Joe has made a chowder from a big catfish he caught this morning, mixed with salt pork and onions. Beside the pot of chowder is a steaming cornmeal cake. Thank the stars Mrs. Joyner didn't bake it, or it would be burned to a crisp.

We crewmen grab our bowls and run to be served. Mrs. Joyner retrieves a checkerboard tablecloth from a trunk and spreads it out over a walnut table with shiny polish. It's an odd sight, all that fancy furniture sitting on the riverbank, surrounded by mud and grass, water and trees. People stare as they pass, but Mrs. Joyner goes about smoothing that cloth just so and setting a perfect table like she's preparing for Sunday after-church visitors.

I sit on the edge of the flatboat's roof and dangle my feet, watching the Joyners eat their formal meal together. That's what civilization looks like out west, I suppose. Like a round peg in a square hole. As I use the cornbread to soak up the chowder, I find myself itching to put all that furniture away and out of sight.

"You sure you don't want to travel down river and see New Orleans?" Captain Chisholm says at my shoulder.

I jump. "No, sir, I'm set on heading west." If he could find gold the way I can, he'd head west too. Anyone would.

"Thought as much." He reaches out to shake my hand, and presses some coins into my palm. "Here's wishing you luck along the way."

Before I can force out a thanks, I notice Joe packing left-over cornmeal cake into my saddlebag. "It's going to go bad with no one here to eat it," he says.

"Please stay," Red Jack says. "But only so I don't get demoted back to unskilled labor."

"We emptied the whole boat," I protest. "There're no more stalls to muck. You'll sleep in every morning like the lazy cat you are."

He frowns at me, just like he did that first day, but now I know he means it kindly.

That's about all the good-byes I can take, so I pull my hat brim low to hide my watery eyes and head ashore. Peony paws the ground, itching to stretch her legs, but I hang around, pretending to check my gear while Mr. Joyner haggles with some longshoremen about pay.

"Need help loading everything?" I ask Mr. Joyner.

"I'm not paying you," he says.

"I didn't ask for pay."

He hesitates, but he nods. "I'd be much obliged."

As I heft a trunk toward the wagon, he says, "You might as well go north with us, at least as far as Cape Girardeau."

My relief is short-lived. Mrs. Joyner, who sits on the wagon bench, jumps in with, "Now, darling, don't impose yourself on the lad. I'm certain he has plans of his own."

I angrily heave the trunk over the side, and it lands with a too-loud clunk.

"There's only one direction to go," Mr. Joyner says, "and the lad might as well travel with us. It's too late to send him scouting ahead, and there's no point in making him wait behind when he's traveling light—he'll simply overtake us. He can help load and carry, and I don't even have to pay him."

"That's fine by me," I'm quick to add. It's not fine. It's highway robbery, is what it is. But it's also better than being alone.

Mrs. Joyner folds her hands into her lap and frowns.

We wait while Mr. Joyner hires two men who are relatively clean and able to provide references. Even so, we're another hour getting all the furniture loaded. Mr. Joyner climbs onto the bench, snaps the reins over the oxen, and the wagon lurches forward. Peony and I follow, Coney running circles at her heels.

● ◆ ●

We glimpse the Mississippi River through breaks in the trees as we ride along. I keep Peony behind the wagon and out of Mrs. Joyner's sights, which ensures that I inhale buckets of dirt and mud flecks. Andy and Olive peek at me through the bonnet, their cherub faces jerking up and down with each rut in the road.

We travel less than five miles before night begins to fall. The wagon slows and pulls over to the side. I steer Peony around and discover that we've reached a small farmhouse.

A small slave girl, no more than ten years old, answers the door and runs to fetch her master. He's a lean older man, with skin like weathered hickory.

"Hello, good sir," Mr. Joyner says. "My family and I—"

"What state are you from?" the old man asks.

"Tennessee," says Mr. Joyner.

He grunts. "As long as you aren't from Illinois or Ohio or any of them places."

I gape at him, realizing he means free states. Maybe things are different near the frontier, but no one in Georgia ever refused to help my father because of his Yankee ways.

The old man steps inside to have a brief conversation with his wife, and they reach an agreement. "We can provide accommodations and provisions. Supper and breakfast. You'll have to share the beds."

Mr. Joyner offers many expressions of gratitude, as well as a few coins. After taking care of the animals, we go inside and find a cozy, warm cabin that smells of dried apples and wet soot. We sit around a plank table beside a stone hearth. The table's centerpiece is a wooden vase, filled with wrapping-paper flowers dyed yellow, and I swallow against the sudden sting in my throat.

The tiny slave girl brings a tray of salt pork and onions, which isn't nearly as tasty as Fiddle Joe's cooking but still hits the spot. The men trade news, most of it focused on the gold in California and the settlement in Oregon territory. When the table is cleared, the old man and his slave drag a feather mattress out from the bedroom and place it before the hearth.

"I reckon you and your family can sleep here tonight. Your hired hands can have the back porch, and your boy can make do in the barn."

Mrs. Joyner bristles. "He is not our boy. He's traveling with us temporarily."

I don't understand how that woman can be so hot and cold, so kind one moment and so uppish the next. But I know better than to stay where I'm not wanted, so I excuse myself and slip into the barn.

"Looks like I'm sleeping with you tonight, girl," I say to Peony. "Just like always."

I'm so tired it's only a few minutes until I drift off. A whisper startles me awake.

"Mr. McCauley?" Mrs. Joyner's voice.

Lantern light pools around me, and I tense up in my bed of straw, but I don't turn over. "What?" Maybe she wants her blanket back.

"I . . . um . . ." She falls silent.

"Spit it out, ma'am. I've very tired."

She gasps a little, then says all in a rush: "Mr. Joyner says he wants you gone by morning."

"What?" I flip around to face her. "Why? I haven't been any trouble. I work hard."

Her face is even more prim by lantern light, her features sharp and mean. "We face a grave challenge, Mr. McCauley, as we head into the godforsaken wilderness. I must shelter my children, give them a chance at a good life. That means protecting them from . . ." She falls silent again, and a muscle in her cheek twitches.

"From people like me?"

"I am a *mother*, and a mother knows a runaway when she sees one. I'm sure you understand. Perhaps if you had references . . ."

"Does Mr. Joyner really know you're here?"

Her lips press into a thin line.

"Pardon my saying, ma'am, but this is hardly the Christian thing to do."

"I gave you that quilt!"

"And I suppose it made you feel good about yourself. Here, take it back." I start to untangle myself from it.

She hesitates. Then: "No. It's yours. But, please . . ."

I let her plea hang in the cold night air for a spell, until she shifts on her feet and drops her gaze. Finally, I say, "I'll be gone by morning."

She slumps in relief.

I say, "I wish you and your family the very best of luck, ma'am. Maybe I'll see you in California." I don't really mean it, but it gives me a nasty twist of pleasure to see her startle at my words.

"To you as well, Mr. McCauley." She turns and walks away fast, lantern light bobbing with each step.

I lean into Peony's shoulder. "How do you feel about leaving right now?" I whisper, and she nuzzles my hair in response. It's not like I could sleep after that, anyway.

I pull on Daddy's boots. My feet have gotten used to them, big size and all. I don't even get blisters anymore.

My hands shake as I throw Peony's saddle over her back, and I realize I'm crying. I wipe at my cheeks with the back of my hand. I grab Mama's locket and squeeze a moment, giving it a chance to refill my well of resolve.

I tighten the cinch, check my saddlebag, and mount up. Outside, a light mist is falling on a world that's so cold and wet it feels like a tub filled with misery. The Joyners plan to head north, either to Port Girardeau or St. Louis, so I'll take the first left I find and head north later.

Coney is curled up on the porch of the house. He lifts his head and stares quizzically. He stands, shakes himself, and follows us down the road a ways before whining and turning back. Of everyone in the Joyner family, I'll miss him the most.

I nudge Peony forward. "It's just you and me now, girl."

Again. It's just you and me *again*, is what I should say. But I know she understands.

Chapter Fifteen

The first person I meet on the road as the sun rises is a grinning huckster with a beard as stiff as a whisk broom. Patches cover his elbows, and a striped feather juts from his hat's band. His mule cart is loaded with pots and pans, bolts of fabric and plaster dolls, pickaxes and even wishbone-shaped divining rods that he claims will lead a fellow to gold.

"No, thank you," I tell him. If the divining rods worked at all, my uncle wouldn't have killed my folks to claim my magic.

His smile is fierce and determined. "I have it on the best authority that these rods—"

"I don't have any money."

His smile disappears like fog in the sun. "Good day, then."

He snaps the reins, the mules protest, and the cart rattles forward. I turn Peony around and walk beside him.

"Can you tell me if this is the road to Independence?" I ask.

He waves his hand dismissively. "Every road will take you

to Independence if you choose the right direction and keep on going till you get there."

"But which direction is the right direction?"

He points ahead. "If you go down to the river and turn north—"

"I don't want to go that way."

"If I had any maps, I'd sell you one. Huh." He rubs his whisk-broom beard. "Maybe I should load up on maps."

"Can I go that way?" I point in the direction he's just come from.

He pulls up short and twists in his seat. "Head west and ask folks for the road to Charleston. You can make it there by lunchtime. Go to Mrs. Moore's boardinghouse on Market Street if you need a place to stay, and tell her that—"

"Where do I go from there?"

He sighs. "From there, you'll head west to Sikeston, Poplar Bluff, and then Springfield. There are a lot of towns along the way, but if you remember those, it'll get you in the right direction."

"Sikeston, Poplar Bluff, Springfield."

"When you get to Springfield, you make a quarter turn to the right and head north. That'll get you to Independence."

"Thank you, mister. I sure appreciate it." *Charleston, Sikeston, Poplar Bluff, Springfield, Independence.* I tip my hat to him and turn Peony back around. I almost feel hopeful again.

"It's more than four hundred miles!" he shouts at me.

"Then I better get started!" I shout back.

"Good luck."

"Good luck to you too, mister!"

Four hundred miles is nothing. I've traveled farther than that already. I'll reach Independence by early March, find Jefferson, and leave with one of the first wagon trains of the season. If everything goes well, we'll be in the gold fields of California by the end of summer.

An hour later, clouds roll in, and a cold rain falls, soaking me to the bone. Peony slogs through fetlock-deep mud. By the time we reach Charleston, my head feels thick, and it hurts to swallow. I'm far away from Georgia now, and more than willing to spend the twenty cents I can't afford to pass the night in Mrs. Moore's public boardinghouse, but it's already full up with folks heading west.

I keep going until nightfall, when I find a farmer willing to let me sleep on the floor in front of his hearth.

I make it as far as Sikeston before coming down with a fever, and I spend an anxious week burning up in a farmhouse near a place called Gray's Ridge. Despite the family's kind care, I rave something awful, fighting them constantly—first because I'm afraid they'll find out my secret, and later because, in my feverish state, I mistake the father for Uncle Hiram. Even after my fever breaks, I find him hard to look at, with his long, fine nose and keen gaze. When I'm well enough to travel again, they're glad to see me go, but not as glad as I am to leave. I give them two precious dollars for all the trouble.

It's a cold, wet spring, with day after day of weather that can't decide if it wants to be rain or snow. Many of the roads are quagmires, trapping wagons and blocking passage. It's slow going, and I can't make up lost time no matter how hard I try.

These hills are chock-full of pioneers who are making an enterprise of boarding westbound travelers. I almost always find a bed, a meal, or unasked-for advice in exchange for mucking a few stalls or splitting some firewood or—if I'm desperate—parting with a few pennies. When I get back on the road, I sometimes find a napkin full of cookies, or a little grain for Peony. Once, I even discover a tiny ball of lavender-scented soap tucked into my saddlebag.

In spite of the goodness all around me, the low clouds feel like a yoke about my shoulders, and the sky drizzles sorrow down on Peony and me as I slump over her withers. It gets harder and harder to smile at strangers, and each morning, I'm clumsy and slow about packing up and getting back on the road. One night, when I'm camped in a small glen after having shot a squirrel with my pistol, I'm finally able to put words to my misery.

I miss Daddy.

With the thought comes a flood of memory. The winter I was nine years old, Daddy announced that he would teach me how to hunt. Mama bundled us both up and packed all the jerky and hardtack we could carry and sent us on our way without wringing her hands once. Daddy and I hiked horse-less into the woods and were gone six days.

He showed me how to test the wind, to read tracks and scat, and to be as patient and ghostly as winter itself. He taught me to field dress an animal when it was too big to carry, to shoot a rifle without toppling over, and to find dry wood in the snow. At night, we scraped hides in front of our tent while the fire crackled and our clothes steeped in wood smoke, and he regaled me with tales of his own father, who headed west and spent years on the Ohio frontier in search of adventure and fortune.

Sure, I was little, but I was smart enough to understand the wistfulness in my daddy's voice. That's why Mama let him do wild things without complaint—like take his nine-year-old daughter on a hunting trip. Because the kind of man who fled Boston to make a new life in Indian country was the kind of man who might just keep on going. If Mama didn't let him sow some wild oats, maybe he'd do something wilder. Maybe he'd go west.

So it's now, with my own fire crackling, my lips greasy with the squirrel I just ate, and the night echoing with the distant yip of a coyote that I miss Daddy most. He should be here with me. We should have been on this adventure together.

On April 1, 1849, I reach Independence. I crest a rise, and there she is, stretching wide and strange below me.

My first impression is of mud. It spatters off horse hooves and wagon wheels, stains the base of every building and the legs of every pair of trousers, mixes with half-melted snow to create a soup of gray and brown. The few buildings making up the town proper are painted muddy white or muddy red. Centered before the largest of these is the one bright spot: an American flag, whipping proudly from a high pole. It's the new one, with a full thirty stars.

Surrounding the town are acres of tents and wagons, thousands of oxen and horses; even a few hasty shacks, spread over a vast, flat landscape of mud and snow. And beyond it all is a slow, muddy river, curving gently into the horizon and shimmering like gray silk in the early spring sun.

I'm not sure what I expected. A neat town square like Dahlonega's. An empty corner with no one in sight but Jefferson McCauley, standing there with his hands in his pockets and a welcoming grin on his face.

I spend all day wandering, getting to know the lay of the land. I've never seen so many people all in one place. I'm bumped and jostled everywhere I go, and it's a peculiar thing to be so crowded and so alone at the same time.

The general store is a small, cluttered building with a floor made from poorly joined wood planks, all covered with muddy boot prints. I open my mouth to ask the clerk if he's met anyone named Jefferson McCauley, but words fail me.

A gleaming Hawken rifle is mounted on the wall behind him. It's Daddy's. Which means the brothers who robbed me are here in Independence. The scent of rotting forest trash suddenly fills my nose, as if I'm still hiding in that pile of musty leaves.

"Sir? Can I help you?"

My hands are clammy cold, and my legs twitch, as if to run.

Don't panic, Lee. The brothers could have traded it to someone bound for Independence. They're probably still plunder-
ing the back roads of Georgia or robbing flatboatmen along
the river.

"Sir?"

"I . . . How much for that rifle?" I ask, pointing. Maybe it's
not Daddy's gun. The wood grain is different, the polish a bit
worn near the trigger guard.

"Sixty dollars."

I gasp. "Why so much?"

He shrugs. "People need guns to go west, and they're willing to pay for 'em. Tell you what. You come back in a week,
and if this gun hasn't sold by then, I'll let it go for fifty."

"Sure. Thanks." I stare at it, thinking of the twenty-four
dollars I have left. The gun isn't Daddy's; I'm sure of it now.
My fright made me stupid.

Even so, I can't bear to be in this store a moment longer. I
ought to pick up some hardtack and a new whetstone for my
knife, but I don my hat and turn to go.

"I knew a man who had a gun just like that," says a voice at
my shoulder. A familiar voice.

I whirl, my hand flying to my five-shooter.

A tall Negro grins down at me. Though a graying beard
sprouts on his jaw, and his eyes are crinkled with new lines, I
recognize him at once. "Free Jim!"

He looks me over. "Well, hello, uh, Mr. . . . ?"

"McCauley," I whisper.

"Mr. McCauley! Aren't you a sight for sore eyes."

It's like God dropped a little piece of home right in front of me, and it's all I can do to resist throwing my arms around him. Instead, I hold out my hand, which he clasps. "Nice to see you too, Mr. Boisclair."

"Long way from Dahlonega," he observes as his eyes continue to search my face.

"I'm not the only one who's come a long way." Though it's only been a couple of months, Free Jim looks as though he's aged years. A thousand questions dance around in my head. *Why did you leave? Where is Jefferson? Is my uncle looking for me? Is he here?* I manage, "Rough trip?"

His smile drops away, leaving only fatigue. "Maybe I'll tell you about it sometime."

"Maybe we'll swap stories."

"Hey, you there," the store clerk interjects. "You going to buy anything? Because if not, I'd rather you didn't clutter my doorway."

We're nowhere near the doorway. "Show some respect," I snap. "Mr. Boisclair is a free Negro and a respected businessman, and his shop is about ten times bigger and cleaner than this godfor—"

"Let's go, Lee," Free Jim says, tugging my arm. I let him drag me out the door, even though I'm seething. The street is bustling. A buggy rolls by, spattering mud onto my legs.

"Guess I'll have to do business elsewhere," I tell him as we walk toward Peony. "There's another store a few streets over by—"

"I didn't need your help in there."

"I wasn't trying to help. It's just . . . He had *no* right to talk to you that way."

He sighs and changes the subject. "Glad to see Reuben's palomino in good health. I thought that was her, but I wasn't sure until I saw you inside."

"Jim, I have to ask." I drop my gaze and shuffle my feet, gathering my words and my pluck. "Did you travel with anyone? I mean . . . Is anybody from Dahlonega here with you?"

"I came alone."

"Oh." It feels like I can breathe again. "That's good."

"Your uncle Hiram left a few weeks after you did," he adds gently, "when it was clear you'd run off."

My gaze darts around the busy street, even as I grab for Peony's reins. "Is he here? Did he—"

"Hiram sold the Westfall land to Mr. Gilmore and went to catch a boat in Charleston. He's sailing to California by way of Panama."

My knees go watery with relief, and I lean against Peony for support.

"He sent some men west after you, just in case. But no one caught even a hint of you." His eyes twinkle. "They were looking for a young lady, after all."

My plan worked. I can hardly believe it.

"Well, except that good-for-nothing Abel Topper," he continues. "He rode back into town more than a week after you left, insisting he chanced upon your mare. By then it was too late; you were too far ahead."

"Where's Topper now?"

"He left for California with your uncle, once it was clear no one would hire him for the railroad." In a dropped voice he adds, "They aim to reach the gold fields ahead of you."

I nod. I've always known I'll have to face Hiram again someday. "At least I won't see him on the trail. Is anyone still looking for me? Did he post a reward or something?"

"Not as far as I know."

But there's an agitation about him. He opens his mouth to say something, closes it. He runs a hand through his tight beard, clears his throat, tries again. Finally, he asks: "Did Hiram kill Reuben and Elizabeth?"

I can hardly force the word past the lump in my throat. "Yes."

He nods, as if he'd already worked out the answer. "I expected he'd do something foolish someday."

"Why?" Tears sting my eyes, and my hands clench so hard that my nails dig into my palms. "What are you talking about? I don't understand!"

Free Jim settles a giant hand on my shoulder and clasps it. "Do you have a place to stay?"

"Sure," I lie. I can't bring myself to tell him I lost most of his money and all of his shirts.

"I have some things to do. Meet me tomorrow at the Hawthorn Inn. It's two blocks north of the square. Noon. We'll talk."

"Okay." I almost beg him not to go. I'm not ready to be alone again.

He tips his hat to me. "Until tomorrow, then."

I watch his back as he walks away, and I'm unhitching Peony before I realize I forgot to ask him about Jefferson.

Noon tomorrow can't come soon enough. I spend the next hours meandering through town, searching the face of every stranger, hoping to find Jefferson, worrying I'll run into the brothers instead. Evening falls, and I head out of town as the clouds break open, a coral sunset lighting up the western horizon.

The first empty spot suitable for camping is nearly a mile from the town proper. Tree stumps are everywhere, jutting out of the muddy ground like grave markers. But there are no trees; everything has been chopped down for firewood and wagons. I lie down in the open beneath the stars, and I let the sound of chirruping crickets and the scent of a hundred campfires lull me to sleep.

The next morning I make a circuit of all the groups forming up to head west. There are at least a dozen companies, each larger and more sprawling than the last.

I pass a woman bent over an honest-to-goodness box stove, and something about her makes me pause. She turns to grab a wooden ladle, and I glimpse her face. It's Mrs. Joyner!

Somehow, she convinced someone to unload that stove for her. Certainly not Mr. Joyner, who I've never seen carry anything heavier than a cigar. I raise my hand to wave, surprised at how glad I am to see her safely arrived, but I flash back to her prim mouth and hard eyes as she gave me the good riddance. I let my hand drop and slink away before she can spot me. That's one wagon train where I won't be welcome.

I resume my search for Jefferson. Time and again I see someone with his lanky form and dark hair, but then he turns around, or moves in a way that Jefferson would never move, or calls out in a voice I've never heard.

Finally, the sun is high enough that I head into town for my meeting with Free Jim. The Hawthorn Inn is easy to find, though calling it an "inn" is generous and optimistic. It's little more than a giant shack, with wax-paper windows, sleeping cubbies curtained off with sheets, and a huge, canvas awning pretending to be the roof of a busy dining area.

Free Jim is already sitting at one of the long benches, a mug before him on the table. Though the inn is crowded, there's a bubble of space around him, so I climb over and plunk down beside him.

"I ordered us up some fried catfish," he says by way of greeting. "Hope you don't mind."

My mouth waters. "Thanks, Free Jim!"

"It's just Jim now."

I peer at his profile. "But Missouri is a slave state. It would be better if—"

"Do you have to go around introducing yourself as 'Free Lee'?"

"No, of course not."

"Then why should I?"

Because I couldn't stand it if something happened to him, but I take his point.

A serving girl not much older than me sweeps by and plops our plates down before us.

"Eat up," Jim says.

The fish is a bit rubbery, like it sat out a day or two before getting cooked, but I can't afford to turn down a meal. I'm halfway through when Jim says, "What are your plans?"

I swallow my mouthful. "Find Jefferson. He said he'd meet me here. Then we'll figure out how to get to California."

He nods. "Some folks thought the two of you ran off together."

"I wish we had." If Jefferson had been around, those brothers wouldn't have dared rob me. Then again, maybe his Cherokee blood would have made him a tempting target. The thought turns my stomach. "Have you seen him? He left a few days before I did, so I really thought he'd be here by now."

"I haven't, no." At the look on my face, he adds, "Sorry. Some companies have left already, even though the grass isn't growing in yet."

It's an awful possibility, that we could come all this way and not find each other.

"The reason I ask about your plans," Jim says, "is that I'm heading out tomorrow. Found a good company willing to have a Negro along. You're welcome to join me."

I stare at him. "But . . . Jeff . . ."

His smile is sympathetic. "I figured you'd say that. But in honor of your daddy, I had to offer."

"You could wait! Just a few days. We could look for Jefferson together."

He stabs at his catfish. Puts down his fork. "I may not

get another opportunity. I have two wagons full of goods. Plenty of money from liquidating the store. But it doesn't seem to matter. Only one company will have me along, and I have to go."

I mash the fish on my plate with my fork, my appetite gone. I guess I don't blame Free Jim—*Jim*—one bit for wanting to head off with a big outfit. It's what I'd do, if not for Jefferson.

"Well, good luck, Jim," I say wistfully. "I hope you find mountains of gold."

His eyes flash. "I hope so too."

Everyone gets the fever. Even rich men. "Jim, you said something in the store. About Hiram."

Jim dabs his mouth with his kerchief and twists to face me. "How much do you know about him?"

I shrug. "Not much. That he's Daddy's older brother, a college-educated man. He came south from Boston with my mama and daddy; they were all great friends. But when Daddy won a parcel in the land lottery and he didn't, Hiram left for the big city to practice law. We didn't see him much, not for years at a time."

"Did you know that Hiram and Elizabeth were going together?"

I nearly choke. "No, Mama never said."

"They were planning to marry."

I gape at him.

"She was running away from something in Boston, something awful. So when the Westfall brothers decided to head south during the gold rush, she asked to come along. She and

Hiram fell in love. They were going to get married when they reached Georgia."

My meal rolls around in my belly. "But she married my daddy."

Jim nods. "She changed her mind at the very last moment. That's about the time your daddy and I were getting on as friends. Reuben comes to me one day and says, 'Jim, I'm going to marry Elizabeth, and my brother is going to be heaping mad, and I don't know if she'll ever love me or if Hiram will ever forgive me, but it's something I got to do.'"

I stare down at my plate, trying to take in his words. Conversation hums around us, like buzzing insects. A breeze gusts through the dining area, flapping the awning.

"He never told me why," Jim adds. "But he was wrong about one thing and right about the other: Yes, Elizabeth did love him, and no, Hiram didn't forgive him. Especially after the lottery, when your daddy got a nice piece of acreage and he came up with nothing. And a few years later, when Reuben and Elizabeth had a daughter, a beautiful baby girl they named Leah, Hiram left Dahlonega for good, and I only saw him but once or twice after that."

"So he murdered them out of *revenge?*"

"I can't say what's in that man's head, but maybe so."

The serving girl sweeps by and collects our plates. I realize I'm squeezing the golden locket with my hands, twisting, twisting, twisting at the chain. I force my fingers to let go. "Hiram paid us visits, when I was little. And Daddy went to Milledgeville a few times, before he got sick."

Jim nods. "Reuben told me they'd reconciled, years later. But your uncle has a politician's face. Never can tell what that man is thinking. He lies slicker than a huckster with a love potion."

I'm still not convinced Hiram wanted revenge. He was after *me*, what I can do.

It's on the tip of my tongue to tell Jim everything—about the gold dust that used to be hidden beneath our floorboards, about Hiram tricking my daddy into leaving the estate to him. It's even on my mind to tell Jim that the gold coins in his pocket are singing to me like a hymn, that I know for sure and certain he's carrying at least twenty dollars.

But I say nothing.

"Did you ever hear tell why your mama left Boston?" Jim asks.

"No. She hinted that something bad happened when she was a girl. Why did she?"

Jim frowns. "I don't know. I was hoping you did."

"Daddy never told you?"

"I don't think Reuben ever knew."

"Oh."

A sudden thought almost makes me jump out of my seat: Maybe Mama had witchy powers too. Maybe that's why she was so prickly whenever I found gold. That's why she never let me use the word "witch" in the house.

I sigh. I'm full up on heartache and ire, on frustration at not knowing enough, and it's making me fanciful.

"You're sure you can't come with me?" Jim says as he rises from the bench.

I stand up too, even though I'm not ready to say good-bye. "I'm sure."

"Will you be all right if Hiram finds you in California?"

I swallow hard. "I guess we'll find out."

He reaches out and grasps my shoulder. "I wish I could tell you more."

My eyes feel hot, and my throat constricts. "It's more than I knew before." *Please don't go,* I want to cry out. *You and Jeff are all I've got.*

He gives me a sad smile, then thrusts out his hand. It swallows mine when we shake. I hold on longer than I should.

"I have a lot to do before sunup tomorrow, so I have to go," he says, gently pulling his hand away from mine. "Take care of yourself, Lee. I surely hope to see you in the gold fields."

My cheek twitches with the effort to not cry. "I surely hope so too. Thanks for dinner. For everything."

Watching him walk away is like losing home and Daddy and friends all over again. I don't have it in me to talk with anyone else today. Not even to search for Jefferson. I loose Peony from the hitching post and ride her out of town to our camp on the muddy rise.

I sit there a long time, knees to chest and locket in hand, watching busy Independence go about its day while the shadows grow long, thinking about Mama and Daddy and Hiram and gold-witching and questions that will never have answers now that the only people who know them are gone.

Chapter Sixteen

Morning brings a new day, and I take up the search with renewed determination. I have to find Jefferson. If I don't, I have nothing. No one.

I'm methodical, picturing the town and its surroundings like checks on Mrs. Joyner's tablecloth. I explore each check at a time, corner to corner, and move on to the next. I learn the town forward and backward—every alley, every lean-to, every wagon. Faces become familiar. Some even call out as I pass by: "Hey, Lee! Found your friend, yet?"

And so it goes, day after day, for more than two weeks, past the full moon and Easter Sunday. I haunt the town and the staging areas like a ghost, searching for the one familiar face in the whole world that still means something to me.

By the middle of April, grass shoots start poking up through the prairie mud. Every couple of days, usually on a morning without rain, a wagon company heads west. As soon as it's gone, a new one sprouts in its place. My supplies run low. An egg that cost me a penny in Georgia costs a dime here. There's no grazing to be had, and grain for Peony is even more expensive. I spend futile hours looking for a rabbit or squirrel that has somehow managed to evade everyone, but I just end up discharging my revolver and wasting ammunition. At night, I sleep outside wherever I can find a dry place to spread my blanket, usually on the rise a mile outside of town. Most nights I settle for "almost dry."

As my store of coins dwindles, so does my hope.

Three weeks into April, I'm forced to consider leaving without Jefferson. My heart is heavy as I make one more circuit of the staging area. I wander among the few companies that remain, even peeking toward the one with the Joyners. There's no sign of Jeff. Reluctantly, I turn away and head back to the town, unsure what else to do.

"Hey, Lee!"

The voice comes faintly over the muddy fields. A man on horseback waves his hat at me—one of the cattle drivers. I don't remember his name, but I've passed him at least twenty times, watching his herd dwindle from hundreds of cattle to dozens as he sold them off. This is the first time he's called out to me. At my urging, Peony trots toward him. Maybe he remembers that I was looking for someone.

"Did you find your friend?" he asks as I pull up.

It's hard to keep the disappointment from my face. "Not yet. Guess I'll give him another day."

"There aren't many more days to give." A wad of chewing tobacco puffs out his cheek, and he shifts it to the other side.

Brown juice stains his graying beard. "I'll be taking the rest of the herd out soon."

I repeat the same thing I've said a hundred times the past few weeks: "Well, good luck. Maybe I'll see you in California."

"I could use an extra hand. The rest of my crew ran off with other companies when the weather turned. I've only got about sixty head left. Too much work for one man, but not quite enough for two. So one and a half seems about right. I've seen you on that pony. You ride well, and a sturdy little lady like that should do fine on the trek. You interested?"

My head spins. I haven't given much thought to working my way west. When I had the Hawken, I figured I'd buy as many supplies as I could and hunt for the rest. "What's the pay?"

He turns his head to squirt out a line of tobacco juice, then he squints at the horizon. "Board, if that'll suit you. All the way to California, or wherever you hop off. Course, a fair bit of it'll be beef."

It's a good offer. Still, I hesitate.

"And two dollar and two bits a week, to be paid whenever we decide to part ways," he adds in response to my silence. "If any of the cattle make it as far as San Francisco, I figure I can sell them for five to ten times what I can get here. So there might be a bonus."

I do the arithmetic in my head. I'd end up with around fifty dollars. More than enough to buy pickaxes and lumber and food to get me started. "Sir, I don't recall your name."

"It's Jacob, Jacob Jones."

"Mr. Jones, it sounds like a fair offer. But I still need to look for my friend. We planned to meet here and go together."

"Could be gone with another train already. Could be waiting for you there."

"Could be." It feels like no matter what I decide, it'll be a mistake.

Jacob says, "Have you checked the post office lately?"

"He's not going to mail me a letter."

"Sure. But folks leave messages for one another at the post office. Maybe he left a note, saying where he went."

My heart leaps. Why didn't I think of that? Of course there would be a place where folks could leave messages. I turn Peony toward the bluff, then pause in my saddle to look back. "Thank you, Mr. Jones!"

"Leave him a message too, in case he comes looking for you."

"I will."

"Then come back and ride west with me!" he shouts. "I'll be leaving tomorrow or the day after. Good luck!"

I almost ask if he's willing to hire two hands. Maybe I can find Jefferson and bring him back here. For the first time in weeks, I feel a spark of hope.

I wait in line for the postmaster, who has all the hurry of a cow chewing cud. His pocket watch gives the back of my throat a slight tingle. I bet he thinks it's a fine piece, and I'm irritated enough from waiting, waiting, waiting that I've half a mind to tell him it's less than forty percent pure.

When it's finally my turn, I lean on the counter and say,

"Did Jefferson McCauley leave anything for me?"

"I don't know. Who would the letters be addressed to?"

"Lee Westfall. Or maybe Leah Westfall."

He peers at me.

"My sister," I add quickly.

"Let me check." He steps away from the counter and flips through a box of letters. Every time he lifts one up to get a better look, my heart pounds a little harder. His hands are empty when he returns to the counter. "No, sir, Mr. Westfall, I'm sorry, but there's nothing for you or your sister."

"Oh." I was so sure this was the bit of luck I'd been waiting for. "How can I leave a message, in case . . . our friend shows up?"

"You write a letter, pay the postage, and I hold it for him."

"All right," I say, fishing in my pocket for pennies. "Do you have pen and paper?"

He's already reaching for them. "It costs extra."

Of course it does, but I gladly pay.

It's been months since I've had reason to write anything, more than a year since I've used stationery, and my penmanship is a disgrace. Best to keep things simple.

April 20

Dear Jeff,

Hope you are safe well. I am here in Independence waiting for you. I can be found in that clump Grove of Hickory stumps about a mile north of Town. If you don't

come soon I will wait as long as I can. Please leave a
Message with the Post Man. Where can we meet? Address
to Lee McCauley. I'll explain later. ~~Sincerely, Yours,~~ Lee

I blow it dry, fold it shut, and hand it back to the postmaster, who has been helping other customers while I wrote. I watch as he drops it in the box, and when Jefferson does not appear instantly to claim it, I head outside.

The general store draws me like a moth to a flame because two pretty blue-gingham dresses are now displayed in the window. The more I stare at them, the more I consider the possibility that I miss skirts even more than I miss my daddy's rifle. For some reason, the thought of meeting Jefferson while looking like a boy makes me feel funny inside.

Then I see the prices. Twenty dollars each!

Someday, I'll be rich. I'll use my magic to find so much gold in California that I'll be able to buy all the dresses and rifles a girl could ever want. I'll buy carrots and sugar cubes for Peony too. White sugar cubes just because I can afford them. And I'll have a tidy house with an oak bannister and a bright dormer—

"Hiram!" comes a voice.

I flatten myself against the wall like a rat trapped in the pantry corner. My eyes frantically search the crowd. Maybe Jim was wrong about Hiram taking the sea route. He probably turned around and came up the Mississippi in a steamer. Caught up to me when I was down with fever.

"Hey, Hiram, over here!"

The man shouting and waving is no one I recognize. He has a curly beard and an army issue jacket. His gaze leads my attention across the street and—

"Lemuel!"

A little sob escapes my lips. It's not my uncle. Just someone who shares his name.

But Uncle Hiram will surely be waiting for me in California. It's a big territory, I tell myself. Big enough to disappear in, maybe. Especially if he's looking for a girl.

My hands don't get the message though, and they refuse to stop trembling as I untie Peony from the hitching post. She nuzzles my fingers, looking for a treat.

"Sorry, girl. We don't have enough money left for—"

"Lee McCauley!"

There's nothing but jump left in me. I whip my head around, half ready to run, and find Mr. Joyner bearing down on me. His suit is as pristine as always, and I don't have a single notion as to how he's not as mud-spackled as the rest of us. "Sir," I say, surprised. "Glad to see you." I'm even more surprised that I mean it. It's good to see a familiar face, even if it's someone I don't care for much.

"I can't believe my good luck. Have you signed on with a wagon company yet?"

"No, sir," I say, and immediately regret it. I don't fancy being chased off by his wife again.

"Our hired hands took off. Thought they could make more money with another company. They'll regret it, though."

"Oh. I'm real sorry to hear that." Though not at all

surprised. "Must be hard on Mrs. Joyner."

"It is, thank you. The thing is, now I need a couple hands to help manage the wagon and cattle. I found one fellow already, but I need another."

"You offering me a job, Mr. Joyner?"

"You've proven yourself reliable and of decent moral character."

"I don't think your wife agrees, pardon my saying."

He has the grace to seem confused. "Mrs. Joyner accepts my judgment in these matters. I remember that day, Mr. McCauley, when you helped us load the wagon without asking for pay. I was going to offer you a job the next day, but you disappeared."

I don't like the Joyners, and I'll probably never like the Joyners. But this might be my last chance to travel in a big company. Might be my last chance to head west this season at all.

I've done all I can. I came here to meet Jefferson, just as I said I would. I've looked for him. I've left a message for him. If I wait any longer, it'll be too late. It's time for me to give up the search and hope our paths cross somewhere else.

My heart is a stone in my chest as I say, "Board as long as I'm with you. And two dollars and fifty cents a week until we get to California or part ways."

He hesitates.

"I've got another offer," I say. "Heading out tomorrow." He doesn't need to know that my other offer is with a single soul, when I'd rather travel with a big outfit.

"Done!"

He spits into his palm and holds out his hand. I stare at it.

I've never entered into a contract before. Not formally, like this. And I still wouldn't, if he knew I was a girl.

I spit into my own palm, and we clasp hands, shaking firmly.

Chapter Seventeen

Mr. Joyner jabbers incessantly as we ride toward the wagons, which suits me fine because I don't care for talking just now. I know I've made the right decision, but I feel like a shell of a girl, all hollow and aching at the possibility that I've missed Jefferson for good. What if I never see him again?

The Joyners had several delays on their journey, he tells me, including an inauspicious layover in St. Louis that involved riverboat gambling, where Mr. Joyner tried to increase their stake and would have, if not for that cheating Ohioan. But the good Lord watched over him, and he managed to come out even, more or less, by which I gather he means "less." But wonderful memories were made, and now they're here and ready to go, and all's well that ends well and every other phrase he can think of to make things sound good when they're not.

"We've had terrible luck finding a wagon train that would take us," he says.

"Oh?" Peony's ears twitch; Mr. Joyner's gelding has veered too close for her comfort. I pat her neck to soothe her.

"Many of the so-called leaders of these expeditions are puffed-up martinets," he explains. "Uncouth men who feel that the miles on their boot soles entitle them to pass judgment on their betters."

"I see."

"I saw right through them, of course, and they resented a man who could so easily smash their pretensions."

"I'm sure." I've been wandering the staging area for weeks, so I know full well that no one wants to take on an overloaded wagon.

"We finally found a small company of God-fearing men," he continues. "Mostly from Missouri, with a few other families besides. The group is led by an excellent man, Major Wally Craven, a veteran of the Black Hawk War, who knows how to deal with Indians."

We near the camp, which is a tight bundle of wagons and campfires and small tents. He says, "I'm off to tell Major Craven the news. He's eager to depart."

"What should I do?"

"Familiarize yourself with the company and then come find my wagon. It's the big one."

"I remember your wagon."

"I've hired one other young man. He came west with a German family from Ohio. They're part of our company too, though he works for me now. He's congenial and hardworking, so don't you worry about his deficiencies."

I have no idea what he means by "deficiencies," and I'm making up my mind whether it would be impolite to ask when he says, "Speak of the devil, and he appears."

He points to a rider coming across the field. "There's the fellow now. Go on, introduce yourself and ask him to perambulate the camp and familiarize you with our traveling compatriots, as well as the procedures we've agreed to follow. I'll meet you at the wagon later."

Mr. Joyner leaves my side, and the distant rider approaches. Two dogs dash forward to greet me, tails wagging. One is the Joyners' floppy-eared hound dog, my old friend Coney.

The other is Nugget.

I snap the reins, and Peony surges forward. "Jefferson!" I shout.

"Hello!" he shouts back, pulling up on the sorrel mare. "You must be the new fellow. . . . Lee?"

I rein in Peony so that we're sitting in our saddles face-to-face. Tears brim in my eyes, but I don't care. If we weren't mounted up, I'd throw my arms around him right in front of everybody.

He's taller now. Even leaner than before, with sun-darkened skin and a hard line to his jaw that makes him seem years older. He's staring at my face, not smiling, not talking. His near-black eyes are wide with something I don't understand.

His gloved hand comes up and cups my chin. His thumb is so near my lips I could almost kiss it. "Leah," he whispers at last.

"Hello, Jeff," I whisper back.

He peers closer, his hand dropping away. "What happened to your hair?"

"I cut it."

"Why on earth would . . . Oh."

"I'd appreciate it if you kept my secret."

He frowns. "I don't see how anyone with half a mind would mistake you for a boy."

"It's worked so far. I'm strong and I work hard and I ride well."

"Also, you can spit farther than any boy I know."

"And shoot straighter!"

He nods solemnly. "And opine louder."

I'm grinning big enough to burst. "Sure is good to see you, Jeff. I was afraid you'd left Independence already. Worse afraid you didn't make it here at all."

Nugget nuzzles my boot in its stirrup. Jefferson is wearing boots too, now. They're years old if they're a day, but they're probably brand-new to him. "Good to see you too, girl," I tell Nugget, still staring at Jeff's boots.

My skin buzzes as he looks me over, from head to toe and back again. In a dropped voice, he says, "I have a secret too."

"Oh?" I lean closer.

"Been going by my mother's name—Kingfisher—since I crossed the river."

"Oh." It makes me sad, though I'm not sure why. "Jefferson Kingfisher," I say, trying it out. "How come?"

A shadow passes over his face. "I don't want anything to do with my old man."

"Can't say I blame you."

By silent agreement, we've drifted to the edge of camp, away from prying ears. He says, "My mother's people came out this way, you know. The Cherokee crossed the border here, went up to St. Louis to trade. Figure if someone hears my name, and they know her, word might get back."

I open my mouth to remind him that it was more than ten years ago, but the look on his face makes me say, "Good thinking. Any luck?"

"Not yet."

"I'm riding under a different name too. I put this on"—I indicate my clothes with a gesture of my hand—"and when people asked my name, I didn't want to say Westfall. So . . . I said McCauley."

"You gave them my name!"

"I remember someone saying we ought to get married." I say it like it's a joke, but I watch him carefully for his response.

His cheek twitches. "I . . . Well . . ."

I blurt, "My uncle killed my folks."

His mouth drops open, and there's something gratifying about the horror on his face. He collects himself quickly and says, "You're *sure* it was him?"

"Sure as the sunrise in the east." I can't stop staring at him. He's so comforting, so familiar. But he's different too, in ways that give my chest an ache. "Hiram showed up right after you left," I tell him. "He was covered in gold dust. Couldn't stop talking about how the place was all his now. How *I* was all his now."

"That's . . . I'm so sorry, Lee. Why'd he do such a thing?" He scans the horizon, as if expecting him to appear. "Where is he now? And where's your rifle? You ought to keep it handy. I'll keep mine loaded as we ride—"

"Jeff, can we talk about that a little later, maybe?"

He gives me a dark look. "Sure. Whatever you want."

I feel his gaze on me as we aim our mounts back into camp and weave them through the cluster of wagons. Come departure day, they'll leave one by one, forming a neat and lovely line. I've seen it happen a dozen times.

"Anyway, I had to get away," I whisper. "Become someone else. Yours was the first name that came to mind."

"Well, you can have it, Lee McCauley. I don't need it anymore."

"No, you don't, Jefferson Kingfisher." He aims the sorrel mare toward a huge flock of sheep, and I turn Peony to follow him. "You give that horse a name yet?"

"What's wrong with 'the sorrel mare'?"

"'Sore old mare' is more like it."

"Don't listen to her, girl," he says, reaching down to pat her neck.

But he keeps staring at me, the same way I'm staring at him, like I can't believe he's really here. After a long silence, we suddenly crack grins at the exact same time.

"Sure is good to see you, Lee," he says in an abashed voice.

To distract from the warmth in my face, I gesture toward the wagons. "Which of these did you come with? Mr. Joyner said you were with a German family from Ohio."

"The Hoffmans. They're good people."

"How'd you end up with them?"

"Not a lot to tell," he says. "After I crossed the Ohio River, I joined some folks headed north along the Mississippi. Families, mostly. The Hoffmans were with them. When it was time to cross, everyone hired passage on a steamboat, but I hardly had any money left."

I can sympathize.

"So I kept going upstream a few days until I found an old raft, lodged on shore after high water, and I wrangled it into the river. I drifted across—mostly downriver with the current—pulling the sorrel mare behind. Didn't know if she'd make it, but she's a dab at swimming, that girl. Landed near St. Louis, where I met the Hoffmans again. We decided it must be providence."

We're still meandering aimlessly, and I'm not taking everything in the way Mr. Joyner wanted. "So you and the Hoffmans decided to travel together?" I ask.

"I helped out a little in exchange for meals. It's a big family; father, mother, six kids, and the oldest only fifteen. The little ones are hard to keep track of sometimes. We've been trying to join a company since we got here, but no one would have us."

He pauses, frowning. Then he adds, "The Hoffmans' English is a little funny, and apparently I look too much like my mother's people. Finally, Major Craven let the Hoffmans join his outfit. Then Mr. Joyner offered me a job, and the Major didn't object, so I stayed on. How about you? How'd you get here?"

For months I imagined telling Jefferson everything that happened to me, imagined the sympathy on his face, maybe the quick hug that would ensue. Now, though, I just want it all behind me, so it comes out in a rush: "I left a few days after you did. Sold Chestnut and Hemlock to pay my way here, but I got robbed along the way. In Chattanooga, I found work on a flatboat, which brought me all the way to Missouri, but I got sick for a bit, and that slowed me down. I arrived weeks ago."

"Wait. You got robbed?"

If I tell him I lost Daddy's gun, the hurt might be too much, so I say, "I've been looking everywhere for you."

"I figured if I stayed in one spot, it would be easier for you to find me."

"I have the worst luck," I say, shaking my head. The only place I avoided was the place Jefferson had been the whole time.

"Hey, we're going to change our luck, right? As soon as we get to California." His grin is so easy now, like the weight of the world has fallen away. Maybe it's being away from his da that's done the trick.

"Sure, Jeff."

"Mr. Joyner ordered me to tell you about our company," he says. He points out a group of twenty or so wagons and twice that many men, all set apart from everyone else. "That lot from southern Missouri decided to head out at the last minute. We've been waiting for them to pull their gear together."

"A rough-looking bunch."

"Maybe so. But there aren't enough for them to feel safe from Indians, so they needed to merge with another group. It's all men, no families. And, Lee, they don't know a lick about gold mining. You and I have more experience than the whole group put together."

Jefferson doesn't know the half of what I can do. "They good folk?"

"The opposite of good folk. Their leader is a fellow named Frank Dilley. You don't want to cross him."

"I'll keep that in mind. Is that the group Major Craven came with?"

"No, Craven is a guide, hired by Mr. Bledsoe, who's a sheep farmer from Arkansas." Jefferson waves toward a smaller group of wagons, all filled to bursting and sunken deep in the mud. "He owns all ten of those wagons. He's a late arrival too, just like the Missouri group. All the other wagons belong to families. The families don't trust the bachelors, and the bachelors don't like the families, but everyone seems to get on with the Major."

"The families?"

"You'll see. That wagon over there? That's the Hoffmans."

Three small children chase one another around the wagon wheels. An older girl with blond hair spilling out from under her bonnet keeps an eye on them. She sits on a stool, knitting a stocking and whipping through her stitches without looking down once. When she sees Jefferson, a huge smile lights her face.

"Who's that?" I ask. She's a lovely girl, with a tiny nose and rose-flushed cheeks and eyes the color of an indigo bunting. Even Annabelle Smith back home couldn't hold a candle to her.

"That's Therese," Jefferson says, tipping his hat to the girl. "She's nice. You'll like her."

"I see." My gut is suddenly in knots. Therese is the real reason he followed the German family from Ohio. It's written all over his moony face. Maybe Jefferson wasn't waiting in one spot in Independence so I could find him. Maybe he wasn't even looking for me.

"Hallo," she says as we approach.

"Therese, this is my old friend Lee. Lee, this is my friend Therese."

"Pleased to meet you," she says, her consonants soft and clipped.

"Nice to meet you too," I reply, and I mean it. If Jefferson says she's good people, then that will have to be enough for me. At the last second, I remember to tip my hat like a proper young man.

"Lee is going to help the Joyners wrangle their gear." Jefferson straightens in his saddle. A sweep of his arm encompasses all the wagons. "I'm supposed to show her—"

I glare at him, but he's already caught himself.

"Er, I'm supposed to show him the wagons and the camp, describe the work, and . . ."

Jefferson has always been a terrible liar.

"Better get back to it," I say. "Be seeing you around, miss."

"Be seeing you around," she says, mimicking the cadence

of my phrase perfectly. To Jefferson, she says, "Come by after dinner; I'll save some."

"Sure," he says, grinning. His eyes follow Therese as she rounds up her siblings and herds them toward the back of the wagon.

"So that's the family you followed west," I say, wondering if Therese's dinner invitation included me. Probably not.

"I don't know how I'm supposed to do this, Lee."

"Do what?"

"Pretend you're someone you're not."

"What do you think you're doing, Mr. Jefferson Kingfisher?"

"That's different."

"It's no different at all. Those of us going west aren't just seeking fortunes, you know. It's a chance to start over. Be whoever we want to be."

He grins.

"What?"

"I've missed y— your opining."

"You've got to keep my secret, Jeff. All the way to California. If you don't, they'll leave me behind, or make me go back. And I can't go back. I've got nobody to go back to, unless you count the uncle who killed my folks and took over my whole life."

The grin disappears.

"Hiram said he had a *plan* for me. I have no idea what he meant, but I'm sure it was nothing good. Jefferson, you're the only person left who I trust. You have to keep my secret. You *have* to."

"Okay. I'll do it."

I exhale relief. "Thank you. You can start by helping me cut my hair. It's getting too long."

"Keeping your hair short isn't going to make you look like a boy. At least not to me."

"Please?"

He scowls. "If you say so."

The scent of beans boiling in molasses tickles my nose, makes me realize how hungry I am.

"Here, I'll show you the rest," he says. "That's the Joyners' wagon—"

"I know them well enough." For better or worse. "We came west on the same flatboat."

"None of the other companies wanted them. They're hauling too much. Major Craven keeps telling them to leave something behind, like that dining table."

"But Mrs. Joyner won't hear of it."

"Indeed she won't. Believe it or not, she hauls out that table and sets it with a checked cloth every single night. It's like she thinks she's still in Chattanooga."

"You don't say."

"I can't imagine all their stuff will make it over the mountains. Not unless we carry it."

"That's probably what they hired us for."

He points to a single, neat wagon. "That's Mr. and Mrs. Robichaud from Canada." A cheerful red-and-blue quilt hangs over the sideboard, as if on display. "They arrived last week. His wife speaks mostly French, but she's practicing her

English every day. She'll weary you with questions if you get too close. They've got twin boys, five or six years old. It's a sturdy wagon, well organized, and Mr. Robichaud knows a bit of blacksmithing. So they're welcome."

His gaze shifts to three young men crouching around a cook fire. Easy laughter rolls from their mouths.

"Those are the college men—Jasper Clapp, Thomas Bigler, and Henry Meek. From Illinois. Jasper says they left college before they graduated."

We steer our horses into a flock of sheep, who bleat as they scatter. Nugget and Coney run to meet the herding dogs, and everyone gets in a good sniff. A short Negro with arms as thick as tree trunks waves to Jefferson as we pass.

"Those sheep belong to Mr. Bledsoe, and that's Hampton, his shepherd."

"Mr. Bledsoe is the one from Arkansas, with ten wagons?"

"That's right. He's got about a thousand head. He says sheep are smaller and more sure-footed than cattle, so they're more likely to survive the trek across the mountains. Plans to get rich establishing a herd in the gold fields. It's causing problems with the Missouri men because the sheep foul the grass, and the cattle won't eat it. Right now the plan is to let the cattle go first and have the sheep bring up the rear." He points. "That wagon over there is Reverend Lowrey and his wife."

"Just the two of them?"

"And one more on the way."

My face must register surprise that he would mention such

a thing, because he quickly adds, "You'll know it as soon as you see her. The reverend says God called him west to minister to the miners in the gold fields. To be honest, Lee, it's a pretty misfit bunch. We're the leftovers. People the other companies wouldn't take, mixed with a few who arrived too late to set off with the rest."

He's about to say more, but we come to the end of the line.

"That's Major Craven over there," he says. The tent he points to is military style—plain and exacting.

"I heard he was a major in some kind of Indian war."

Jefferson's face darkens. "The Black Hawk War. An ugly bit of business. More than a thousand Indians killed. Craven was a sergeant. Only reason everyone here calls him Major is because of Mr. Joyner."

"How's that?"

"The other companies were appointing captains, and Mr. Joyner said that since ours was so distinguished, it needed a guide with a more distinguished title."

"That's . . ."

"I know!"

I shake my head. "We'd be lucky to make it to California if Mr. Joyner was in charge. He doesn't know a rabbit from a raccoon."

"He doesn't need to know anything. Haven't you read the papers, Lee?"

"Read what in the papers?"

His eyes twinkle. "It's the easiest thing in the world to get to California—you just aim yourself west and start walking."

Chapter Eighteen

The sun sets over the western horizon, and it's like an omen, the way it lights up the plain in fiery gold. Major Craven makes a circuit of the camp. He's a middle-aged man with a huge scar across his top lip that almost disappears in the brightness of his easy smile. He announces to all that our company is now complete and that we'll be leaving on the morrow.

When Mrs. Joyner sees that her husband has hired me, her eyes widen and she draws in a little breath. I brace myself for her protestations, but they never come, not even when Mr. Joyner offers to let Jefferson and me sleep beneath their wagon bed. It's the first time I don't leave town and go off on my own to spend the night.

We flip out our bedrolls so that they're almost-but-not-quite touching. I spent so much time looking for him that it's a delight to lie down side by side, to face each other in the dark. I'm not the least bit tired. I want to stay awake all night talking, soaking up the fact that he's finally here.

"So," he says in a low whisper. "Tell me about this uncle of yours."

He's the easiest person in the world to talk to, and now that we're alone in the dark I don't hesitate. "Hiram. Daddy's brother. He . . . Well, I ran into Free Jim here in Independence."

"You don't say! What was he doing?"

"He sold his store. Now he's on his way to California. You know he was great friends with Daddy, right?"

"Sure. Always thought that's why your daddy stopped going to church after the Methodists split."

"That's right. Well, Jim knew a few things." In as soft a voice as I can manage, I tell Jefferson everything: about Hiram being sweet on my mother, about how he lost both Mama and the land lottery to his brother, about how no one—not even my daddy—knows what happened to Mama in Boston that made her run away from her fine house and wealthy family to hack out a living in Indian country. I tell Jefferson every single thing, except the one thing I should never tell a soul: that of everything Hiram thought life had cheated him of, the witchy girl who could find gold might be the one that rankles him most.

"So," Jefferson says after a long pause. "You think you're rid of him?"

"Maybe." Dread curls in my belly. "No. I'm not rid of him. But I don't think Hiram wants to kill me. He wants . . . something else. He wouldn't say what. After I ran away, he headed west by sea. He might reach California ahead of us."

"You think he'll be looking for you?"

"I know he will."

"Huh." He's silent a moment. Then: "I don't like it one bit."

"Me neither."

"And I don't understand how a man could kill his own brother. Lucky Westfall of all people! Everyone liked him. Even my da."

I choke a little on my next breath.

"Lee?"

"I miss him bad, Jeff."

"I know."

The wagon bed above us groans as one of the Joyners turns over. "Long day ahead," Jefferson says. The weight of his hand descends onto my shoulder. He gives me a squeeze, and the gesture fills me up even better than Mrs. Joyner's badly baked beans. "Lee, I'm glad you got away. Even gladder that you're here."

I smile into the dark. "Me too."

"I won't let that uncle of yours near you. I promise."

"Thanks, Jeff."

We say our good nights, and Jefferson turns his back to me and falls right asleep. I lie awake awhile, listening to the sounds of our camp—crackling fires and creaking wagons, shuffling oxen and bleating sheep, and my best friend breathing easy beside me.

When the bustle of morning rouses me, Jefferson is already gone. I shove on Daddy's boots and scoot out from under the wagon to find our camp in a flurry. Everything is half loaded, and most of the oxen stand yoked before their wagons. It must have drizzled last night, because the ground is muddy and churned from all the goings-on. Mist chills the air, and gray hazes the sky, but everyone waves and smiles like it's the Fourth of July. And maybe it is, in a way. Today begins a new life for many of us.

While Mrs. Joyner industriously burns flapjacks over the cook fire, a huckster with a coonskin cap weaves through the wagons, a wheelbarrow squelching through the mud before him, calling out, "Pickaxes, pans, and pickles for the argonauts!" He sells two pickaxes to a man in the wagon next to us, then he approaches Mrs. Joyner.

"Pickaxes, pans, and pickles for the argonauts! Surely you'd like a jar of pickles, ma'am? Argonauts are a notoriously hungry bunch."

She recoils, bristling. "I'm no argonaut. I am a *Methodist*."

The smile goes clean off his face. "Of course, ma'am. Your pardon, ma'am." He tips his cap to her and moves on to the next wagon.

Major Craven makes rounds to check that everything is in order and to assign a line number. Jefferson returns with crumbs on his shirt—I assume he got breakfast with the Hoffmans—and together we hurry to load the Joyners' many possessions before the Major reaches us.

Less than an hour later, Major Craven gives the call. My heart leaps. This is it. I'm going to California.

As the first wagon pulls out, I'm grinning like a cat who

got into the cream. One by one the others fall into place until our company is a line stretching across the plain. The Joyners' wagon is one of the last to go. Mr. Joyner drives the oxen, with Mrs. Joyner and the little ones walking beside it. Jefferson and I ride behind and slightly off to the left to avoid the mud kicked up by the rear wheels.

The sun breaks through the clouds as we leave Independence, sending streamers of bright yellow to cut the mist. I take off my hat and lift my face to the sun, feeling its warmth on my skin.

The first few days are pleasant enough, though I work as hard as I've ever worked. Every morning, Jefferson and I are the first to rise. Before the sun comes up, we check on the oxen and start the cook fire. When the sky brightens, the Joyner family climbs out of the wagon. Mrs. Joyner cooks breakfast, careful to ignore me, while Jefferson and I reload everything back into the wagon—a dresser and chairs, sacks of flour and coffee and bacon, traveling trunks—everything except the table with the checked cloth, which the family will have breakfast on. After the furniture is loaded, we roll the water barrel down to the river to refill it. Jefferson does that by himself some mornings so I can slip away from camp to take care of my personal needs.

When I return, Jefferson and I lift the heavy water barrel onto the sideboard. If we're lucky, breakfast is ready, along with something hot to drink. Frost still covers the ground some mornings, and I'm cold down to my bones, so I don't care whether it's real coffee, or chicory root, or tea, though I always hope for coffee. Coffee is the one thing Mrs. Joyner gets right.

We only have a few minutes to eat, so I gobble my flapjacks, even though they're burned on the outside and mushy in the middle. I always thank Mrs. Joyner and tell her they're delicious. On the third day, she gives me a quick nod in response, which I take as progress.

After breakfast, we load the dining table, yoke the oxen, and hook them up to the wagons, which is a lot easier than working with mules, apparently; Frank Dilley cusses at his mules and his Missouri men alike until he's red in the face. I'm happy to have the ox team instead, no matter how slow they plod.

Then it's my turn to let Jefferson off to do his business, which as far as I can tell means swinging by the Hoffmans' wagon to say good morning to Therese and get a second meal. He's eating better than anyone else in our company.

While he's gone, I take the grease bucket from the back axle and climb under the wagon to grease the wheels. I nail down any boards jarred loose by the rough road and make sure the spare tongue and axles are lashed firmly in place. I store the tools in the box up front, latch it tight, and announce that we're ready to roll out.

Then we wait. I always make sure we're done early, because you don't want to be the wagon everybody's waiting for. Most mornings we end up waiting on Reverend Lowrey. He can't do the work alone, and he expects the rest of us to help out in exchange for a prayer and a bit of preaching. Everybody takes a turn, even me. Some do it out of the goodness of their hearts. I do it to get us on the road.

Jefferson shows up again about the time the wagons pull out, and we ride side by side. The road is barely more than ruts in the ground, pushing through an endless muddy plain filled with the budding tips of yellow-green grass. The rising sun steams the land dry as we go while meadowlarks trill in greeting. It's the best part of my day.

Sometimes, though, Mr. Joyner rides his gelding, and Jefferson and I take turns driving the team. It is the most god-awful, bone-rattling, thankless job you could ever hope to have. Each rut is a kick to the seat of my trousers; some days it kicks me down the road from morning till night. Mrs. Joyner and the children always walk behind the wagon, out of sight, when one of us drives.

At noon, we break for an hour to feed and rest the animals and to eat lunch. Jefferson and I unload the dining table and spread the tablecloth. Mrs. Joyner adjusts it to her satisfaction, making sure the corners drape just right. Honest to God, sometimes she even unpacks the china and arranges place settings. I'm glad to take my tin plate and sit elsewhere.

Mr. Joyner has a clever device called a "road-o-meter." It's attached to the rear wheel of the wagon, and through a set of cogs and levels, it records the miles traveled. He checks it after lunch each day—we've usually made five or six miles by then.

It's my job to clean up afterward and store everything

away—including the china, which I must wrap in paper and pack up tight, so it doesn't break. Someday, inevitably, the wagon will hit a particularly big rut, smashing the china all to pieces, and I know just who Mrs. Joyner will blame.

We go all afternoon until we find a spot with the three necessities—water, grass, and timber. Frank Dilley's Missouri men and Mr. Bledsoe, the Arkansas sheep farmer, always get there first because the horses and mules travel faster. By the time our oxen teams bring up the rear and close off the circle, they've had their pick of the best grazing, cleanest water, and driest spots to sleep.

We let the cattle out to graze, feed the horses some oats if they haven't found themselves enough grass, and get everything set up for the night. Then we eat supper, and people gather around one of the campfires to tell stories or sing songs or share dreams of what we're going to do when we're all rich with gold. I don't go in for all that, because my singing voice would surely reveal my secret, and because it's a good time for me to sneak away to take care of my personal necessities.

The college men have a brown milk cow named Athena, who has the longest eyelashes I've ever seen on a cow. They milk her each morning and put the cream in a churn inside their wagon. The rough road does all the work. By the end of the day, they have a nice fat roll of butter, which they are happy to share with the families. They make the rounds every night to pass it out.

Jasper always has a twinkle in his eye when he sees me.

One night he chucks me under the chin, which makes me flinch away.

"That's a terrible haircut," he says cheerfully.

"It's Jefferson's fault!" I blurt.

He rubs a hand through his own curly brown hair. "Next time it needs trimming, you come to us." Jasper's friend Henry has a neatly manicured beard that's as pale and thin as the rest of him, and Tom keeps his chin clean but waxes his mustaches into sharp points. It's like they have a barber stashed in their wagon.

"I'll do that," I say. "Somebody's got to keep up the standards of civilization around here."

He laughs. "You sound like Mrs. Joyner. Here's some fresh butter for you and Jefferson. That's about as much civilization as we can manage tonight."

Mrs. Joyner has made a loaf of bread in the Dutch oven. I tear off a piece and let a clump of butter melt into the hot, almost-cooked dough. Jasper's butter makes even Mrs. Joyner's bread taste good.

"This is harder than I thought it would be," Jefferson says that night as we lie beneath the wagon.

We're both used to hard work, so that isn't what he means. Maybe it's the hard work and no place to go home at night. No family to welcome you, even if they are sickly, like my daddy, or mean drunk, like Jefferson's. I miss having people familiar and dear—so familiar and dear that being with them is easy. Never worrying what they're thinking or if they care about you or what will happen if they find out who you really are.

"It'll be worth it once we get to California," I say.

"It's already worth it!" he says. "But sleeping on wet ground, waking up cold, jumping every time Mr. Joyner says so . . ."

"Keep your voices down," booms Mr. Joyner from the box right above our heads. "People need their rest."

"You hear that?" Jefferson whispers to me, his breath tickling my cheek. "I need my rest."

He pulls the blanket up to his chin and rolls over, turning his back to me. Within moments, his breathing slows and lightens, like someone shedding a heavy load.

Not me. My head spins, and I lie awake for what feels like a long time, listening to Jefferson's breaths mingling with the patter of the rain on the wagon covers, smelling the rich scent of wet dirt. I've got some happiness in me, I realize with a start, where there used to be only loneliness and grief. I've found Jefferson. I'm earning a wage. I'm on my way to the Promised Land and mountains of shining gold.

This thought is still in my head, as if I've only just drifted off to sleep, when Jefferson shakes me awake in the predawn chill.

"It's another day," he says.

"You don't have to sound so cheerful," I grumble.

"I know!" he says. "But it vexes you."

We make twelve to fourteen miles a day for a week, through land so lovely it's a pain in my chest. Thoughts of Uncle Hiram niggle at me like impure gold in a distant stream—faint and far, but always there. Each day is both a curse and blessing, bringing me closer to him, but also to the gold I was born to find.

So I push away thoughts of Hiram. For now, I want to enjoy the burn of hard work, the company of my best friend, and the prettiest sky I've ever seen. Hiram has taken so much from me. I'm not going to let him take this too.

One morning, it starts pouring rain and doesn't stop. We cross one creek, then a second. After lunch, we come to yet another, and by now the water is high and fast; the path, churned and muddy; the banks, steep.

The wagons squish through the mud, creeping forward at a pace that makes a tortoise look like a hare. When it's finally our turn to cross, the right front wheel drops into a sinkhole and sticks tight, and no whipping and yelling at the oxen can make it budge.

Jefferson and I unload everything, and the college men and Mr. Robichaud help lift and lever it free. Reverend Lowrey stands off to one side with his Bible and prays for us.

After the wagon is across and on dry ground, we load it back up. Mr. Joyner whips the team to hurry them, but they pay him no mind. By the time we overtake the rest of the company, the wagons are circled for the night, their camp-fires glowing.

As we ride up, Jefferson leans over and says, "Those mules move fast. Mark my words: One of these days the Missouri wagons are going to leave the rest of us behind."

I'm afraid he might be right.

◆   ◆   ◆

One Saturday, after a couple of weeks on the trail, Reverend Lowrey makes his wife drive the wagon so he can ride up and down the line exhorting everyone to spend the Sabbath as a day of rest. We've been neglecting the Lord, he says, and our travels are sure to go better when we remember Him as we ought. There's not much enthusiasm for the idea, but Major Craven decides we could use the extra day to fatten up the cattle before crossing the Kansas River. He says there's not much forage to be had between the Kansas and the Platte.

The next morning, everyone unloads what chairs they've brought along. The college boys fashion a quick pew from a split log and a pair of sawhorses. I sit on the Joyners' wagon bench, which is close enough to look like I'm participating. Reverend Lowrey drones on about fearing God and the dangers of hellfire. I allow my eyes to drift closed and my chin to hit my chest, because if it's a day of rest, then I'm going to rest. By the time services are over, I decide I like the Sabbath very much.

We set off the next day feeling restored. I gaze about as we ride, admiring the wild green fields and their copses of tall woods, stretching as far as the eye can see. The world has exploded with wildflowers—black-eyed Susans and blue chicory and yellow mustard—and the sun lounges heavy in the sky, casting the world in a golden haze.

I admit, it's even prettier than Georgia. Mama and Daddy would have loved it.

◆   ◆   ◆

The Kansas River fattens as we reach its confluence with the Big Blue, which is an odd name because it's as muddy brown with spring rain as all the rest. Major Craven says we must ferry across the Kansas and follow the Big Blue north for a while.

I think longingly of Captain Chisholm's flatboat, because these ferries are nothing but overgrown rafts made of weathered wood that looks near to splintering apart. I can't imagine them carrying wagons and oxen and horses.

Just like we did for the flatboat, we unload the wagon, then lift off the box and fill it with the wheels. It's too heavy for Jefferson and me alone, so all the families help one another— the college men and Mr. Robichaud help us, then we help them right back, which sets my back to aching and shoves a splinter into my left thumb.

Athena, the milk cow, rides across the ferry with us. She lows pitifully. Her pupils are huge and her muscles twitch, like her skin is covered with flies. Twice, she empties her bladder onto the deck.

Mrs. Joyner gathers up Andy and Olive and flees to the far end of the raft.

"What's wrong with her?" I ask Jasper.

"I don't know," Jasper says. He kisses Athena's muzzle, but she flinches away. "I hope she didn't eat something disagreeable."

The ferryman at the tiller says, "She been ettin' a foul smelling weed, about eh high?" He holds his hand midthigh. "Leaves are toothy, dark green on top, light on bottom?"

"Maybe," Jasper says. "I haven't been paying attention. Fellows?"

Henry gazes back toward the dwindling shore. "There was something like that where we stopped for lunch."

Tom nods. "She was eating it, all right. There wasn't much else. The whole trail has been grazed over by the argonauts who preceded us."

The ferryman chortles. "That's jimsonweed she et. Devil's snare. Make sure she gets fresh grass, and she'll be fine in a few days."

"Poor girl," I say, starting toward her. I have some grass in the pocket of my trousers that I pulled for Peony—a habit I picked up while riding the flatboat—but Athena is welcome to it. Tom and Henry have the same impulse, and her eyes go buggy as the three of us close in on her. She shakes her head, lowing mournfully. Quicker than I can blink, she stumbles off the ferry and plops gracelessly into the river.

We stagger over to the side as the ensuing wave sets us to rocking. Athena's head breaks the surface, and she flounders, blowing water from her nostrils.

Mr. Joyner laughs. "She's going to drown if she doesn't get herself aimed toward shore," he says.

"The children will miss the butter," Mrs. Joyner says.

I gape at them both. "We've got to do something to help her!" But I have no idea what.

The ferry glides past, and Athena falls behind. The college men run to the back of the raft. "This way, Athena!" Jasper calls. "You can do it, sweetheart. Just keep swimming."

"Pardon, pardon me, if you please, let me help," Mr. Robichaud says, brushing past me and pushing Jasper aside. He has a rope in one hand, a looped noose in the other.

Mr. Robichaud swings the noose into the air above his head and tosses it out. It arcs unnaturally, but somehow lands right over her head and settles around her neck. He tugs the rope gently to tighten the noose, giving it one firm yank, which gets her swimming toward the boat.

"That was something else!" Jasper says to him. "Never seen that done on water before. Thank you, sir."

"When did you learn that?" I ask.

"I wrangled cattle back in Ottawa Valley."

"On a plantation? Or did you drive them?"

"I'll make a deal with you," Mr. Robichaud says. "I'll tell you about it if you practice English with Lucie."

Jefferson warned me that Mrs. Robichaud is a chatterbox, but it would be nice to talk to another woman, which is something I can't do without an invitation, not dressed as a boy. "I'll do it," I say.

When the ferry bumps onto shore, Jasper and Henry splash through the water to aid Athena. Her legs are wobbly, and she shakes with exhaustion and misery, but she manages to scramble up the riverbank with help and coaxing.

She's just a cow, but I'm so glad she made it, and I look for Jefferson, wanting to share the feeling with someone. He's already over by the Hoffmans' wagon, helping them reattach the wheels.

I run to assist; it's easier if we all pitch in. I'm loading a trunk when I freeze, nearly dropping it on my toes.

My throat buzzes and my knees tremble. Gold is some-where nearby. A lot of it. In one of the Hoffmans' trunks, maybe.

"Lee? You all right?" Jefferson peers into my face. A sack of flour is balanced over one shoulder.

I jump, startled. "Sorry. Yes. I . . ." Therese and her tiny sister, Doreen, are giving me a strange look, which sets my heart to pounding. "I thought I heard a coyote," I finish lamely. "But I was mistaken."

I turn away and get back to work, as if nothing is amiss. The presence of gold fades, first with familiarity, then with distance, as one by one we lift the wagons, slide the wheels back on, and yoke up the oxen. With all of us working together, the ferry empties quickly, and we roll off, glad to be on solid ground. Jefferson leaves me behind to ride off with the Hoffmans. I stare after him, my sense of gold fading even more.

I've no desire to ride alone with the Joyners, where I'm barely welcome, so I steer Peony toward the college men instead. Athena rests on the ground, her sides heaving. Tom paces with his hands in his pockets. Henry picks his teeth with a bit of straw. Jasper crouches over the cow, rubbing her with a blanket.

"Is she going to be all right?"

"I think so."

"I could stay—"

"Don't trouble yourself," he says.

"You'd better catch up with your family," Henry says.

I open my mouth to snap that the Joyners are not my family, but I stop myself in the nick of time. He's just trying to be helpful.

"Go on," he says, gesturing me away. So I turn Peony and start her after the wagons again. As I ride away, the college men and the ferry landing grow distant, but I don't feel like I'm getting any closer to the folks ahead.

Chapter Nineteen

The country north of the Kansas River is wide and flat and treeless. Stumps are scattered here and there, left over from earlier wagon trains. The prairie will be abundant with grass again in another month or two, but huge swaths of trail are grazed out and fouled with manure. The good watering places are much the same—churned up and dirtied with the waste of the folks ahead of us. We often veer far from the path to make camp.

At least there's less mud. The rain is tapering off, and the air is pleasantly warm.

One morning, after I rise early and venture far to take care of my necessities, I return to find Major Craven with a scowl on his face. "There's no need for you to go off. We're getting to Indian country, and you can never tell what those savages will do."

If he forbids me to wander off, I'll be in a heap of trouble. "Maybe the Indians just want to trade," I say, trying not to sound quarrelsome. I have vague memories of Daddy trading with the Cherokee, before the government chased them out of Georgia.

"Possibly, possibly," he says. "Still, be careful. Take a dog with you."

"I will, sir. Thank you, sir." I'm grinning ear to ear. I should have realized he wouldn't forbid me to go off on my own occasionally; I'm a boy now.

Coney is delighted to follow me the next time. I give him lots of belly rubs, something he's always begging of Mr. Joyner but never gets. He and Peony have always been easy with each other, but before long, they're fast friends; he walks beside her every day and curls up at her feet at night.

I make good on my word to Mr. Robichaud and take some time each day to ride alongside their wagon. It's smaller and lighter than any of the others, and packed so neatly that the twins have room to sit in the back and play when the trail is smooth enough for it. They are good-natured children who get along well, often referring to each other as "_frère_," which their mother immediately corrects to "brother."

"We are going to live in America, we must learn to speak a little of American," she says.

"A little American," I say, because she has asked me to correct her. Her husband sits on the bench, eyes ahead, acting as if he doesn't overhear. "And you speak it very well," I add.

"Mrs. Lowrey says I speak it _good_," she says.

"You can say it that way. 'Speak it good.' But it's better to say 'Speak it well.'"

"I speak it very well," she intones, then she smiles in triumph. Her English is passing fair, much better than she seems to think. She's a young woman, younger even than Mrs. Joyner, with a cheerful and chatty disposition, dancing brown eyes, and a dusting of freckles. She often stays up late, talking and singing around the campfire, and I suspect this makes her learning go faster.

The Robichauds have matching gold wedding bands— probably the most precious things they own. Those rings are never far apart, and the closer they are to each other, the more they call to me.

They're not the only ones with a bit of gold. I don't go near the Hoffmans' wagons often, but I still get a strong sense from them, and for the life of me I can't figure out what they're carrying. A treasure chest of coins, maybe. Or a hundred lockets like the one I wear. If they park too close to the Joyner wagon, it's like a beacon burning all night long. One night, I take my blanket and move farther off just so I can sleep.

Major Craven has some too. Gold pricks at me every time he stops by for a chat. Finally, I spy the pair of gold buttons at the cuffs of his shirt.

Mr. Joyner, on the other hand, makes quite a big deal about the gold cuff buttons and shirt studs he wears every day. They are shiny and pearl-studded, and while I can't speak to the authenticity of the pearls, that "gold" is barely more than a moth brushing up against my skin in the dark. He doesn't even have a decent stash of coins. I sure hope he has a plan for paying Jefferson and me when we finally part ways.

I suspect he's not rich at all, not on his own merits, anyway. More and more, I gather that his father funded this expedition for him. Maybe Mr. Joyner is pretending to be something he's not. Pretending he's wealthy, when he has no money to his name. Pretending he knows what he's doing, when he couldn't find the end of his own nose out here on the open plain.

Pretending is exhausting. I know it better than anyone. But I hope I never go so far as to pretend to myself, like Mr. Joyner does.

One night, after a record-setting nineteen-mile day, Major Craven stops by Mrs. Joyner's dining table, which is laid out with its usual tablecloth and china. Tonight she's even put out a vase full of black-eyed Susans, plucked while she walked during the day. She and her family sit around the table. Jefferson and I eat on the wagon bench.

She offers the Major a plate of pork and beans, and the quickest look of panic flits across his face before he gently changes the subject. "Be alert," he says. "If the alarm sounds, the men must grab their guns and set up a defense."

Mr. Joyner pats his rifle. "Ready, willing, and able."

"And the women and children should stay low in the wagons until danger has passed. Can you do that for me?"

Andrew and Olive nod solemnly, but Mrs. Joyner says, "Is that wise? The wagon circle is so exposed. The women and children should run to the middle, where we'll be safe."

Major Craven shakes his head. "If the horses and cattle get

stirred up, you'll be trampled. Best if you stay put."

She bristles. "Better that than being captured! I'd rather risk trampling than allow myself or my children to abandon civilization and become savages."

Andy and Olive stare wide-eyed at their mother.

"I don't know about that," Major Craven says. "They seem more interested in cattle and horses and anything else that's not nailed down."

"Oh. Well, I find that reassuring," Mrs. Joyner says.

He smiles and tips his hat. "I'm glad, ma'am. Sir."

"It's utter rubbish," Mr. Joyner says when Craven is out of earshot.

"What's that, darling?"

"The part about not taking women or children. He only said it to make you feel better. Those savages would steal a comely lady like you in a heartbeat and make your life a misery of servitude. And they'll grab the children fast as a Gypsy." He makes a grabbing motion at the children. Olive squeals and shrinks away, then dashes back to her father and squirrels into the safety of his arms. "That's what they are," Mr. Joyner adds. "Gypsies. Gypsies on the plains. The best thing to do would be to exterminate the whole race."

Jefferson freezes beside me, a spoonful of beans halfway to his mouth.

"Unless they turn from their savage ways," Mrs. Joyner amends, and her voice has a note of discomfort in it.

"Of course," Mr. Joyner agrees quickly.

I lean over to Jefferson and whisper, "Are you all right?"

"The Joyners know nothing," he snaps, turning away.

Jefferson refuses to help clean up after dinner, and I don't try to make him. As the campfires burn low, the animals are all herded inside the circle for the night. The weather's nice enough that Jefferson and I take our blankets and find a spot in the grass just outside.

He's silent the whole time. I search for something to say that will get him to talk to me. I settle for: "Mr. Joyner is a fool. God forgive me for saying so, but it's true."

"It's not just him," Jefferson mumbles. "I mean, he's one of the worst. But everyone talks about the Indians that way. At least a little."

It's a warm, clear night. The stars burn overhead like sparks from a fire, and the grass around us smells fresh and alive. "Hey, look," I say. "It's the Seven Boys."

When he doesn't say anything, I add, "You know, I think the stars are even brighter out here. No trees, no lanterns, sometimes not even clouds."

"I'm not the eighth brother anymore," he says softly.

"Huh?"

"I didn't stay behind."

"Oh. Well, that's a good thing, right?"

"I guess," he says, and he rolls over, pulling his blanket up to his shoulder.

I stare at his back, wondering if I said something wrong. Sleep comes harder for me, as it always does. I'm just starting to drift off when gold tickles the back of my throat.

It's Major Craven. He always takes a turn at watch, which

means walking the perimeter. But he's awful quiet this time, creeping along like a hunter after a spooked deer.

He peeks inside all the family wagons, though I'm not sure what he's looking for. After peering in on the sleeping Joyners, he steps back and lets out a whooping cry. "Indians! It's Indians!" He waves his arms and starts running.

Maybe it's a test; Major Craven watches the wagons, instead of focusing his attention outward. Still, I leap to my feet, grab my five-shooter, and start loading.

Jefferson startles from a deep sleep and stumbles to his feet. He hops on one foot, trying to pull on his boot. "What is it? What's happening?"

"Grab your gun and gear. Let's get inside the wagon circle." I've got nothing but a blanket and the saddlebag I use for a pillow. I throw them over my shoulder and cut between the Joyners' and the Robichauds' wagons.

The camp is in an uproar, just as Major Craven intended. The animals churn in confusion. The Missouri men have formed a credible line of defense just inside the wagon circle, guns held at the ready. Mr. Bledsoe has done the same with his Arkansas men. Even his slave, Hampton, grips a long shepherd's staff, ready to thrash somebody on the head.

Our side of the circle has performed poorly. The college men stand outside in their long underwear, scratching their heads and yawning. The reverend wanders around, Bible in hand, as though looking for someone to preach at. The Hoffman children huddle around Therese and her mother, with the littlest ones clutching their skirts.

The Joyners are the worst. Little Andy wails, tears run-ning down his cheeks, while Olive cries softly in her mother's arms. Mrs. Joyner snaps at Mr. Joyner to get his gun, and Mr. Joyner curses at the Major, demanding to know that all the women and children are accounted for.

The Major ignores him, instead climbing up onto a trunk and ringing a bell. Silence gradually descends on our com-pany. Even Andy's wailing turns to quiet sniffles.

"When I was in the militia, this is what we called a drill," Major Craven says. The Missouri men nod knowingly.

Jefferson hobbles over with only one boot on. His blanket is in one hand, and his rifle is in the other. "Wait— None of this is for real?"

"It's real enough," I say, thinking of the sleep we've lost.

The Major says, "But next time it could be Indians! So you have to be ready."

"I must have kicked away my other boot," Jefferson whis-pers, looking around. "Blast it, I'll never be able to find it in the dark."

"We are now deep in Indian territory," Craven says. "We'll be going deeper, all the way to California. In my experience, we've nothing to fear by day. They'll come to trade, and they may have food and other valuable information. For our part, it's a chance to resupply and lighten our loads."

He looks pointedly at those of us standing by the Joyner wagon. But my conscience is clear. I can hold everything I own in my hands.

"But if they come at night, it'll be to rob us. They'll steal our horses and our cattle if they can. So be on guard and be ready to defend yourselves!"

"Hey, Wally!" someone calls. One of the Missouri men. "How many Induns you kill in the Black Hawk War?"

The Major's face blanches.

"Ten? A hundred?" the caller persists.

In a voice almost too low to hear, the Major says, "Too many. And hopefully not a soul more. Now get back to sleep." He hops down from the trunk.

"As if anyone could sleep after that alarm," Mrs. Joyner grumbles.

"The man's just doing the job we elected him to do," Mr. Joyner says. "Back into the wagon."

Jefferson glares after Major Craven. "That was a lot of ruckus about nothing," he says.

"Guess we better sleep under the wagons or inside the circle from now on," I say.

"It's not true, what he said."

"He's not talking about the Cherokee."

"But back home they said all that about the Cherokee— that we were thieves and worse—and it's not true. You remember when Dan Hutchings killed his brother-in-law?"

"Sure." It was a big scandal in Dahlonega. They'd been arguing over a piece of land that Dan said was his, through his wife. He hung for it.

Jefferson stares off at nothing. "Dan was a white man, as white as they come," he says. "And nobody ever said he did it because white men are savages. But one Indian does something bad, and suddenly all of them are bad."

In the moonlight, his profile looks more Cherokee than ever. Mama used to say that Jefferson had a noble dignity about him, which was her way of pointing out his Indian blood while pretending to be polite. He doesn't seem noble to me. He's just Jeff.

"No one thinks you're bad," I say softly.

He turns on me, eyes flashing. "That's not . . . I mean . . ."

"I knew a lot of Indians back when I was a little girl, and not a one of them was bad. And I know you, and you're the best person I know. Do you want me to walk on over to Major Craven and spit in his eye?"

"Course not," he says, but I've coaxed a little smile out of him.

"I could probably hit it at five paces."

He says nothing, but his eyes rove my face, and he gets a strange expression.

My cheeks warm. "Come on," I say, tossing my saddlebags and blanket under the Joyners' wagon. "Let's go find your boot."

Chapter Twenty

$\mathcal{L}$ate the next morning, we spot a mound of dirt ringed with rocks, staring down at us from high on a hill. A small wooden cross made of not-quite-straight branches stands guard over it. The grave can't be more than a week old, but already the cross lists to the side. There's no headstone that I can see—no name, nothing to mark who this person was, who they left behind, or who carries on without them.

Major Craven and some of the Missouri men climb the hill to investigate. Moments later, they gesture wildly at one another, their angry voices carrying on the wind.

Mrs. Joyner leans over from the wagon seat. "What's going on?"

"I don't know, ma'am."

"Well, go find out."

So Peony and I climb the hill and discover that the grave has been scraped open. I catch a glimpse of pale, gray skin before Major Craven and his men shovel dirt to quickly cover it up.

"What happened?" I asked.

Major Craven shakes his head sadly. "The grave was desecrated."

I'm about to ask about the person buried here, but Mr. Joyner crests the rise. "Go back to the wagon and make sure Mrs. Joyner keeps it rolling," he orders.

"Yes, sir." I turn Peony around and go right back the way I came.

"So, what was it?" Mrs. Joyner asks.

"Something dug up the grave," I tell her. "Maybe wolves or wild dogs. They're covering it up again."

"But who was in it?"

I shake my head. "Don't know, ma'am."

She frowns.

As we ride on, she cranes her neck, keeping the hill in view for as long as possible.

I can't stop thinking about my glimpse of dead flesh. Maybe it was a girl like me. I've got no family, no friends besides Jefferson. If I die, I'll end up in a shallow grave like that one, unnamed and unremembered.

About an hour later, the wagons stop for a short break, and Mr. Joyner catches up with us.

"It was Indians," he announces.

"Oh, how terrible," Mrs. Joyner says, covering her mouth.

"Indians killed him?" Jefferson asks. He's tight and coiled on the sorrel mare, like a thunderstorm about to let loose.

"It was a her, not a him. And no, looks like natural causes did it," Mr. Joyner says. "But Indians dug up the grave. They stole the girl's clothes. Even the blanket she was wrapped in."

Mrs. Joyner shakes her head in vigorous denial.

I'm about to point out that we can't know what they stole if we didn't see what the poor girl was buried with in the first place, but I decide it won't do any good.

Mr. Joyner says, "Truly, these savages have no fear of God nor love of the white man."

Jefferson rides off on the sorrel mare.

I almost ride after him, but I'm not sure he wants company. I'm not sure I want company either.

I don't know what to think about the Indians. Seems to me we don't really know anything about them. We don't even know what we don't know.

I avoid the Joyners when we stop for lunch. My appetite is gone, anyway. I keep thinking of that poor girl, with no family, out here all alone and even her grave dug up.

By the time we're moving again, I'm regretting my decision to skip lunch, and hunger makes me even grumpier. When I see Jefferson riding toward me, I almost steer Peony away. A strange look on his face makes me pull her up instead.

"What is it?" I ask

"They're saying it's cholera," he whispers.

A chill rolls down my spine. Mama told me about cholera. "Where?" I ask. "Here?"

"It's what killed that girl we found. Cholera morbus. There was a sign on the grave."

I didn't see any sign. They must have moved it before I got there. "Morbus? What does that mean?"

He shrugs. "I think it means they're dead."

Cholera usually springs up in big cities. A wagon train isn't a big city, but it's definitely dirty and crowded. We're all jammed together, treading over the same ground and cooking and sleeping, hour after hour, day after day, in the same tracks as the wagons before us. It's not like a barn that I can muck out and clean up. It's just muck.

"Are you sure?"

"They were trying to keep it quiet, but some of the Arkansas men already have it. They've moved away from the rest of the wagons, but they're afraid to go too far because of Indians."

"Too weak to go too far either, I reckon."

"I reckon."

I don't know who is buried in that grave we left behind this morning, but now I know why they put the body up high, where everyone could see it. Not as a memorial, but as a warning.

Mr. Bledsoe, the Arkansas sheep farmer, catches the cholera and sickens fast. So fast that Jasper says he was probably sick already—maybe even in the early stages of consumption. Whatever the reason, within a day he's flat on his back and must be tended by his men.

I suspect Mr. Joyner is also sick. When the wagon train starts up the next morning, he seems more irritable than usual and frequently excuses himself, disappears for a while, then rushes to catch up.

My stomach is in knots, partly from worry, because anyone could catch the cholera. Anyone. And partly because it's my monthly time. I have to slip away constantly to rinse my rags and change them for fresh ones. By evening, Jefferson has noticed. "You aren't sick, are you?" He looks me all over, up and down, as if checking for ticks.

"Not like that," I say.

"You'd tell me if you were, right?"

"Of course."

"You shouldn't go off alone."

"I have to."

"Take me with you, at least."

"No."

"I'm not worried about Indians, but it's easy to get lost out—"

"Jeff!" I whisper frantically. "It's my monthly time!"

He gives me a blank look. Then understanding dawns. "Oh." I swear, if not for his swarthy skin, he'd be blushing down to the roots of his black hair.

As soon as the wagon train stops for the night, I ride off on Peony to take care of things. It's too late; I've got a bloodstain on my pants. I find a muddy stream and scrub it out as best I can, glad it wasn't worse.

The sound of moaning reaches me long before I've made it back to camp. It's Mr. Joyner. As I near the wagon, I realize he's not alone in his vocal misery. The Arkansas men are a regular choir of retching and grunting and begging for clean water. The air is starting to smell peculiar.

Mrs. Joyner hands a cup of water through the bonnet opening, then leans wearily against the back of the box. Her skin is pale, and strands of blond hair stick to her sweaty forehead. I hope she isn't sick too. If she is, then taking care of the children will surely fall to me. I know what my mama would tell me to do right now.

"Excuse me, ma'am," I say, intending to offer help.

"Where have you been?" she snaps.

"Had my own business to take care of."

"From now on your only business is Mr. Joyner. Do you understand me?"

I glare at her.

"I asked you a question, you—"

"Ma'am!" I interrupt, because if she calls me names, it'll go too far to make better. "I've done all my assigned work. If you're unhappy with it, then you can pay me seven dollars per our agreement, and we can part ways."

Her mouth opens. Closes. Then: "You can't do that."

"If you want to call me names, then it's time for me to go. I'll head back to Independence if I need to."

Once the words leave my mouth, I realize they're not true at all. I'm for California or bust, regardless of loathsome uncles and uppity employers. I suppose I could ride on, catch up with the next wagon train, see if they wanted to hire me. Maybe Jefferson would come too. We might have to leave, anyway, if Mr. Joyner doesn't get well.

My threat has the desired effect; it takes the spine right out of her so that she seems to shrink into herself. "That's not necessary. I just . . . With Mr. Joyner under the weather for a bit, I could use some extra help."

"I have to take care of myself occasionally, but the rest of the time I'm happy to do what I can."

"Mr. Kingfisher doesn't go off nearly as often as you do," she points out.

"I . . . prefer privacy and modesty. Way my mama raised me."

Her eyes narrow, but she nods. "Do you mind setting up the table for lunch? As close to the wagon as possible. If Mr. Joyner feels better, he may attempt to share our company."

"Yes, ma'am," I say.

"I want that tablecloth perfectly straight. Mr. Joyner does love a tidy tablecloth."

"Yes, ma'am."

"And could you pick some flowers for the table? In times of sickness and trouble, it's more important than ever to hold to the tenets of civilized living."

I sigh. "Yes, ma'am."

The table is harder to wrangle by myself than I expected. I could use Jefferson's help, but he's nowhere to be seen. I can't rightly complain after disappearing myself.

Once the table is on solid footing, the wings extended, and the braces in place, I spread out her checked tablecloth. I unpack their box of fine china plates and silver and put out four place settings. I wander far afield to find a few clumps of violet prairie clover, and I pick the best ones for the vase.

When I return, Mrs. Joyner is crouched over the cook fire.

The Dutch oven sits nestled in the coals. The lid rattles, loosing bits of steam.

"What's cooking?" I ask.

She looks up, startled, and her eyes are wet and her cheeks blotchy. She seems as helpless as a babe, and I feel sixteen different kinds of sorry for her and for every harsh thing I ever thought about her.

After a sniffle, she takes a rag and lifts the edge of the pot. "Water, I think."

"No one can mess up water," I say, and I realize it sounds like an insult, but she just smiles in response.

"Where are Andrew and Olive?" she asks with a start.

I spied them earlier, playing with the Robichaud twins. "They're fine, perfectly safe, over with our Canadian friends."

She starts to rise but doesn't seem to have enough energy for it. She sags back down to her knees, her hand on her belly. "I should fetch them. The Robichauds are very kind, but they don't want to be bothered."

"I'm sure it's no bother."

"You know, I'm not even sure they're *Christian.* Mrs. Robichaud says they never put much stock in religion. Can you imagine?"

"How about I check on them? In the meantime, if you toss some oats in that water, they ought to be ready enough before we load up again. Mr. Joyner might like something plain." My daddy always liked plain food best when he was feeling sick.

"That's an excellent idea. I'll get started on it."

I turn to go after the children, but Mrs. Joyner calls out. "Mr. McCauley?"

I stop. "Yes, ma'am."

"I don't mean to drive you away."

"We're fine, ma'am."

"Are you sure?"

"Perfectly."

Nothing out here is really fine or perfect. We just have to do the best we can.

Mrs. Robichaud sees me coming and waves.

She's seated on a trunk, sipping tea, wearing a light yellow calico with lace trim. She was smart to bring a warm-weather dress. "It feels already like a summer of Canada," she says. "I don't know what it is I am to do when it makes hot."

"When it gets hot."

"'When it gets hot,'" she intones.

"I'm sure you'll be fine," I say. "Thank you for watching Andrew and Olive." I don't see them anywhere. Maybe they're playing nearby.

She flips her hand as if it's nothing. "How are Mr. and Mrs. Joyner?"

"They'll be fine," I say. I sound just like Mama, assuring everyone about Daddy. "It will pass."

"Poor Mrs. Joyner," she says. "Her and Mrs. Lowrey."

"What's that?" I can't imagine what Mrs. Joyner and the preacher's wife have in common. Maybe the reverend is sick too. Then I remember that Mrs. Lowrey is hugely pregnant.

"Ah," I say, recalling how often I've seen Mrs. Joyner with a hand on her belly. No wonder she's so tired and troubled.

Mrs. Robichaud smiles sadly. "She has much to worry herself, yes? It is to be very bad if she gets sick."

"I'll do what I can to help."

"I know. I gave the *enfants* some food for lunch," she says. "I hope that is good."

"Very good," I say. "I'm sure the Joyner *children* were pleased."

"My own *children* are not feeling so well. I think they have, I don't know the word, *la rougeole*."

I have no idea what she means, but her face is grave. "Sorry to hear that."

"I hope Andy and Olive do not catch it. I sent them back to their mother a few minutes ago, for to be safe."

"Thank you," I say. They probably returned by way of the generous Hoffmans, hoping for a treat. "I hope the twins feel better soon."

I make my good-byes and wander away, my mind still churning over the news of Mrs. Joyner's pregnancy.

Mrs. Lowrey, the preacher's wife, is alone on her wagon bench, mending a bonnet.

"Beg your pardon, ma'am," I say.

Mrs. Lowrey jumps, startled. She's a small woman, mousy and plain, with a belly as big as a barn. She almost never leaves the wagon; her husband keeps her under tight rein. He would probably loathe what I'm about to suggest.

"I know you're busy, Mrs. Lowrey, but with Mr. Joyner sick

and all, Mrs. Joyner could use . . . well, not a hand, maybe, so much as an ear. It'd be a blessing if you could check in on her, and maybe offer to pray with her."

It's like my words are magic. "Well, no one could have an objection to that!" she says.

No, they couldn't. As she pries herself up from her bench, I hope it'll be good for both of them.

I check in with the Major, and let him know that some of our folks are sick—Mr. Joyner, the Robichaud children. I don't say anything about Mrs. Joyner's condition, because I'm supposed to be a man now. Soon enough, it'll be visible for all to see, and there won't be any point saying something now.

I take some jerky and bread with the college men, who are always unstinting with their butter and glad for company. We chat for a long time. Jasper tells me that some of the Missouri men have fallen ill too. "Stay away from them," he warns. "And from Mr. Joyner, if you can. I expect we'll lose a few people to the sickness before it's done."

I recoil a little. "Like who?"

He shrugs. "People who have eaten unripe fruit, maybe. Or those who drink too many spirits."

I need to warn Jefferson. I thank the college men for dinner and make my way back to the Joyners' wagon. Jeff isn't here, but I find Mrs. Joyner in a much better temper.

"That was a kindness to send Mrs. Lowrey over," she says.

"She looked like she could use the company."

"We prayed together," Mrs. Joyner says. "She prays

with sincerity and sound doctrine, even though she is a Presbyterian. I may invite the Lowreys over to our wagon for supper sometime." After a pause she adds, "She could fall sick any day now."

"Any of us could. But I don't think she has the cholera," I say.

Mrs. Joyner turns her face away. "No, woman-sick. Forget I said anything. You wouldn't understand."

Frustration boils up inside me, because I do understand. Mrs. Lowrey's birthing time could be upon her any moment. And every child on the way is like a roll of the dice with fate. You never know if you'll deliver easy or if the pains will kill you. Or if your baby brother won't even draw breath long enough to earn his name.

But men don't talk about these things, much less hired help to genteel ladies. I start to walk away, boots scuffing the dirt, thinking about evenings on the porch with Mama, when we watched fireflies and drank sweet tea and talked about all the things that men don't talk about.

Mrs. Joyner says, "Can you run over to Mrs. Robichaud's wagon and fetch Andy for me?"

I whirl back around. "Andy's not here?"

"No." Her voice is steady, but her eyes are alarmed.

"What about Olive?"

"She returned more than an hour ago."

"Mrs. Robichaud sent them both back. Her own boys are unwell."

Mrs. Joyner sheds her malaise like it's a second skin. She

jumps to her feet, picks up her skirts, and jogs through the camp yelling her son's name. When Andy doesn't immediately appear, I dash over to the Hoffmans' wagons to find Jefferson.

He and Therese are sitting side by side on a bench. Therese's hands are folded neatly in her lap, her shoulders not quite touching his. "Andy junior wandered off," I say breathlessly.

"Wandered off where?" Jefferson says.

"I don't know. No one has seen him for at least an hour."

He rises, plopping his hat back on. "I'll have a look around."

Therese says, "I will too."

"Thank you," I tell her.

She hollers for her siblings' attention and starts organizing them to search.

My belly is in a tangle. Bad men like the brothers are out there. And quicksand along some of the streams. Subtle changes in the flat landscape that you don't notice until suddenly you can't see the wagons any more. And even though I'd never say it aloud to Jefferson, Andy could have been kidnapped by Indians. He might already be miles away.

I can cover more territory with Peony. I've only taken three steps toward her when a glad cry rings out from the far end of camp, where the sheep are grazing away from the cattle.

A silhouette manifests in the firelit darkness. It's Hampton the shepherd, Mr. Bledsoe's slave, carrying a boy on his shoulders.

Someone reaches for Andy, but he flinches away, clinging to poor Hampton's head.

"Unhand that boy!" someone else shouts.

I push through the growing crowd, Mrs. Joyner on my heels. Andy starts to wail in panic. He's covered in dirt or worse, and tears streak muddy trails down his cheeks. Hampton tries to lever the boy's arms away from his face, but without success.

"Hey there, Andy," I say, arriving a few steps ahead of his mother. "It's Lee. Want to come back to the wagon and get something to eat?"

His wailing stills. I offer my arms, and all at once he releases Hampton and tumbles right into them. His tiny hands go around my neck, and he rests his cheek on my shoulder. "I'm thirsty, Lee," he whispers.

"He's not hurt," Hampton says. "Just scared is all."

"What were you doing with him?" Mrs. Joyner cries.

"For God's sake, he was bringing him _back_ to _you_," I say.

She stiffens, but then the fight melts out of her. She reaches with a finger and brushes a bit of blond hair from Andy's head.

"I suppose I should thank you," Mrs. Joyner says to Hampton.

"You're welcome, ma'am," he says. "I better get back to the herd, or Mr. Bledsoe will be displeased."

"I should tell him of your good deed," Mrs. Joyner says.

"That's not necessary, ma'am."

The commotion is over as fast as it started. Hampton

returns to the sheep, the crowd disperses, and Andy, Mrs. Joyner, and I walk back to our wagon.

"I can carry him," she says.

"If you don't mind me saying, you look tuckered out."

She gives a little harrumph of assent, but she reaches over and strokes his forehead again.

Andy has grabbed the chain around my neck, pulling Mama's locket out from under my shirt. He opens it and closes it, opens and closes. He has the softest brown eyes, not like his mother's at all. My baby brother would have brown eyes if he'd lived, for sure and certain.

I get an idea.

Before I can think twice about it, I give Andy over to his mother and reach under my collar to unclasp my locket. I drape it around Andy's neck and hook it closed. It feels strange not having it tingling against my skin. Like emptiness. Like wind where there should be water.

"This locket has given me strength and courage," I tell him. "You can wear it now, if you want."

"All right." His chubby fingers deftly open it. "What's this?"

"A lock of hair."

Mrs. Joyner perks up. "A sweetheart?"

"From my baby brother," I explain quickly. "He's gone now."

"Oh, I'm sorry," Mrs. Joyner says.

"So am I."

"It's soft," Andy says.

It's not, glued in like it is, but I'm glad he likes it. "This is a treasure to me, Andy," I say. "Do you understand what a treasure is?"

He nods, his eyes big.

When I was his age, Mama would hand me things—mixing spoons or bits of fabric or a whisk broom—depending on the task she was working on. She said that children were happiest when they felt useful. "I'm busy all day and I have to do lots of work," I say to Andy. "If I let you keep it, will you guard it for me? Maybe it will give you strength and courage too."

He nods again.

"It's an important job."

"I'm big."

"I know you are, or I wouldn't have asked. So, will you do it?"

"Okay, Lee."

We reach the wagon. Mrs. Joyner clutches him to her chest for a moment, but he squirms away and runs to the water barrel to drink and wash up. Olive hops down, and though she stares after her baby brother, she throws her arms around Mrs. Joyner's waist, who squeezes back.

"You didn't have to do that," Mrs. Joyner tells me over her daughter's head. "That's a family heirloom."

"Well, I don't have any family out here," I say.

"He might lose it."

"He's a good boy. I trust him."

I do not trust him to keep my locket. Not one bit. But the locket is doing its work, and even now, I feel it close by. So long as he wears it, I'll know exactly where he is.

"Darling?" comes Mr. Joyner's plaintive cry. "What's going on?" He sounds even weaker than yesterday.

"I better go see to him," Mrs. Joyner says.

As I watch her clamber into the wagon, my hand comes up to clutch the locket, but of course it's not there.

Chapter Twenty-One

At dawn two days later, the Arkansas crew finds Mr. Bledsoe, the sheep farmer, dead in his wagon.

Major Craven calls off travel for the morning. Mr. Bledsoe's men dig a grave, and after we all view his earthly body, they wrap him in the bed comforter he died in, which is noticeably fouled anyway, binding him up with strips of cloth.

I barely spoke two words to Mr. Bledsoe, but my heart is heavy. He did nothing at all to get himself killed. Just pointed his boots west. It could have happened to any of us.

Reverend Lowrey reads from his Bible about death and resurrection and follows up with a prayer. We all think he's done, and Mr. Bledsoe's men stoop to roll him into the hole. Mr. Joyner, whose health has improved enough to attend, excuses himself and dashes away to take care of his personal business.

But then the reverend launches into a lengthy and effusive eulogy, enumerating the many outstanding Christian virtues of Mr. Bledsoe, which ought to serve as an inspiration to us all. I can't imagine he knew the man any better than the rest of us, but he sounds sincere enough, and more than a few people are moved to tears.

The only people not present are the Robichauds.

It turns out *la rougeole* means the measles. Major Craven broke the news last night that the Robichaud twins were exposed at a trading post a couple weeks ago. He assured everyone that even though the measles spreads rapidly, it's less likely to prove deadly than cholera. The Robichauds have agreed to quarantine themselves until the sickness passes, and anyone who shows symptoms is to tell Major Craven at once.

The sun is high and heat is rolling off the plains by the time they lower Mr. Bledsoe into his final resting place. They're about to shovel dirt on top of him when Mr. Joyner returns and says, "Stop. Hold your horses."

Everyone looks at him expectantly.

"Can it wait?" Reverend Lowrey asks. "This is a Christian burial."

Mr. Joyner looks to Major Craven. "The Indians are going to dig up this grave, aren't they?"

This sets everyone to mumbling among themselves. "I don't think we can stop 'em," Major Craven admits.

"Maybe we can leave them a gift." He turns to me. "Run to the Frenchman's wagon and get the blankets from their children."

"But they've got measles," I say.

"That's the general idea. Rub those blankets all over the boys first."

"No, sir."

"I'll give them new blankets," he says, misunderstanding my refusal. "Fine, I'll do it myself. Wait until I get back before you fill in that grave."

I turn to look for Jefferson, but he's gone.

Though weak from the cholera, Mr. Joyner strides away with purpose. Someone calls out, "Don't do this, Joyner!" Henry, maybe.

But he ignores the voice, disappearing behind the Robichauds' wagon. A moment later comes the sound of Mrs. Robichaud yelling in French.

He returns with his arms full of blankets.

I glance around at everyone else. Surely someone will put a stop to this? A few of the men shift uncomfortably on their feet. Major Craven looks down at the ground.

"This is a terrible notion," I say.

"It's none of your business, boy," he says. His eyes are red-rimmed, and his face is gaunt and pale under days of beard growth.

I step forward, but a hand grips my upper arm. "Let him be," says Frank Dilley.

Mr. Joyner staggers to the grave and throws the blankets over Mr. Bledsoe's body. "You can finish covering him up now," he says. "If anybody disturbs this burial, I hope they get exactly what they deserve."

I don't hear a word of complaint. A few murmur agreement. Frank says, "I like the way you think."

Mr. Joyner slumps over, exhausted now. He staggers back

to the wagon, Mrs. Joyner and the children in tow.

"Let's sing a hymn," Reverend Lowrey says in a shaky voice. He demonstrates, and we repeat it, except I just move my mouth, pretending.

Come, Thou Fount of every blessing,
Tune my heart to sing Thy grace:
Streams of mercy, never ceasing,
Call for songs of ceaseless praise:

Rescued thus from sin and danger,
Purchased by the Savior's blood,
May I walk on earth a stranger,
As a son and heir of God.

The last shovelful of dirt patters down onto Mr. Bledsoe's body. They tamp it down, mound it up, and step back. It's less than any person deserves, but there's nothing more we can do.

"Let's roll out," Major Craven says, and everyone flows away from the graveside and back to their own wagons.

The hymn echoes in my head while I ready our wagon to leave. I've never felt so far from God's grace. I suppose I am a stranger walking on earth, but I'm no son of God. I'm no son at all.

The wagon train is markedly shorter than before. A glance eastward reveals a handful of wagons going back the way we came. Major Craven comes by to explain things to Mr. Joyner.

"Mr. Bledsoe's group feel they have neither the authority nor motivation to carry on to California without him," he says. "Seeing as how we've haven't yet reached the divide, they've decided to go back."

"They're fools," Mr. Joyner says.

"Maybe," Craven says.

"You aren't leaving with them?" I ask. Major Craven was hired by Bledsoe's group.

"I reckon I'll stick around until we get to California. I've got my gear, and Bledsoe's men paid off my wages in food. Frank Dilley will carry it for me in one of his wagons."

"Sounds like you've got it well in hand, then," Mr. Joyner says.

"Probably." He turns to go and then stops. "Oh, and you'll want to keep an eye out for Bledsoe's slave."

"The shepherd?" Mr. Joyner asks.

"Hampton," I say. "The one who found Andy."

Craven frowns. "He ran off last night."

"You don't think he had anything to do with Bledsoe's death, do you?" Mr. Joyner asked.

"Not unless he could do witchcraft," Craven says.

I jump a little at the word.

"No," Craven continues. "Bledsoe died from the cholera. But his slave was gone when Bledsoe's men got up this morning."

"Maybe the Indians'll find him," Mr. Joyner says.

"Yeah, and then they can give him measles," I say, and I don't regret it, even with Mr. Joyner glaring at me.

There's no reason to antagonize people, Mama always said.

But sometimes there's no reason not to, is how I would reply.

"He'll likely make for Iowa or one of the free states," Craven says. "So I don't expect him to be a problem." His face becomes stern. "Some of the Missouri men, former pattyrollers, are talking about organizing a party to go after him, but you should know that this company won't wait around. If you leave, it's at your own peril."

"We'll keep an eye out," I say. But I make no guarantees about how hard I'll look or what I'll do if I see him. With any luck, Hampton is already half a day's journey to Iowa. I wish him luck.

The next day the temperature drops, and the rains return. The wagons get stuck in the mud over and over. By evening, Mr. Joyner's road-o-meter measures only six miles. We make camp, and everyone gathers water and relieves themselves nearby, because it's too miserable and dark to wander any distance.

With everyone remaining close, I don't have to stray far for my own privacy. Even in the rain, I linger to enjoy the time alone, taking time to clean my clothes and gear and fill my canteen and take care of my other needs.

Night has fallen when I return, and Jefferson has already spread his blanket under the wagon and stretched out to sleep.

"Aren't you afraid of Indians?" he says, and his voice has a mocking edge.

"No," I say, not wanting to get drawn into an argument.

"Why do you spend so much time out there?" he says.

"I don't know." I settle my head down onto the saddlebag. I whisper, "Maybe because it's the only time I don't have to lie to anyone."

"You don't *have* to lie to anyone."

"Yes, I really do."

"Well, you don't have to lie to me," he whispers back.

I open my mouth to tell him I know that, and maybe thank him, but two hard thumps sound on the bed of the wagon just above our head.

Jefferson sighs.

Please don't roll over again, I think.

He rolls over.

I stare at his back a long time.

When we reach the Platte River, my heart sinks, because it's as wide as the Missouri. But it turns out to be as shallow as a puddle. It's less of a river, and more of a muddy, rolling ribbon of slurry water and quicksand.

"It's a mile wide and an inch deep," Major Craven tells us when the wagons stop.

"Too bad it's not the other way around," I say to Jefferson. "Then we could step across it without getting our feet wet."

He smiles, his first in a long time, and it does my heart good.

We come to Fort Kearny two days later, which isn't how I imagined a fort to look like at all. It's no more than a small scattering of low buildings made of sod blocks. But the rooftops are bright green with grass, and they sit beside the lazy Platte as pretty as a painting. The soldiers stationed here are indistinguishable in clothes or character from the Missouri men in our own wagon train. Mrs. Joyner and several others drop off letters for family back home. We refresh our supplies, and the blacksmith shoes our animals and mends our wagon wheels. Peony's shoes are worn thin, and it costs four dollars to get new ones. I make the mistake of counting what's left: eleven dollars and forty-two cents. Staying a long time in Independence cost me dear.

"How's the sorrel mare holding up?" I ask Jefferson the evening before we depart.

He shrugs.

Something in his face makes me peer closer. "Jeff? Does she need shoes?"

"She's fine."

"Our trail gets steep and rocky, and—"

"I said she's fine!"

I reach into my pocket and fish out four dollars. "Get her shod. I know she's not a barefoot horse, so don't you dare say no. We need her sound."

He stares at the coins in my hand. Sighs. Grabs them before he can change his mind. "Thanks, Lee."

"You'd do it for me."

I stare after him as he leads the sorrel mare toward the blacksmith's stable, my pockets feeling light as air.

In the morning, we leave Fort Kearny behind, and it feels

as though we're stepping off the edge of civilization. The trail starts to incline, and the weather warms. I'm thirsty all the time. Still, we push on as hard as we can because the general word at Fort Kearny is that the cholera clears up past Fort Laramie.

Our train rolls by more shallow graves, most of them dug up. We make graves of our own when two of the Missouri men pass on in the night. I didn't know them well, but I stand a long moment at their graveside, hat off, just like everyone else. Unlike everyone else, I stare at Jefferson the whole time, assuring myself that he seems as hale as always.

Mr. Joyner continues to improve, much to his family's great relief, though he moves more slowly than before. The mood is better around our wagon, and at night, when we set up camp, I play hide-and-seek with Andy junior. He still wears my locket, like a good luck charm, and each time he hides, I pretend for a few minutes that I don't know exactly where he is.

"You don't have a rifle?" Mr. Joyner says, blinking against the afternoon sun. Major Craven has called an early halt today on account of us already making sixteen miles and coming to a spot rich with grass.

"No, sir," I say, thinking longingly of Daddy's Hawken.

"Lee's the best shot in Lumpkin County back home," Jefferson says as he lifts a chair from the wagon.

Mr. Joyner snorts, as if hearing a tall tale. "Well, the Missouri boys say this is buffalo country. I'll lend you my rifle until I'm back in fighting form. You and Jefferson head out, try to find one of the beasts. If you do, shoot it and bring it back."

His rifle is a beautiful Springfield with a single trigger, made of shining chestnut wood, or at least stained to look just like it. The barrel is nearly three feet long. I've never shot one before, but I like its easy weight and elegant balance.

Jefferson is as thrilled as I am to get away from camp chores for a bit. We ride out, rifles in hand, into rolling wild pasture.

"What you said a few nights ago," Jefferson says once we're out of earshot.

"What did I say? 'Shut up and sleep'?"

"No, about not having to lie to anyone. You don't have to lie to me. You know that, right?"

"It's not lying with words," I explain. "Everything I do is a lie. My clothes, my name, who people think I am."

"Yeah, but it's great, isn't it?"

"Great?" I peer closer, trying to figure him.

"This is the best we've ever had it." At my expression, he quickly adds, "It's the best I've ever had it in *my* life. Plenty of food. The work is easier than mining and farming."

"Oh. Yeah, great." Jefferson doesn't feel the same sense of loss that I do. My mama and daddy are a constant ache in me, even months later. But Jefferson is glad to be rid of his da, and I don't blame him. Therese looks at him in a way none of the girls back home did. He's stronger than he's ever been.

"I mean, no one likes me," he amends. "Or trusts me much. But that's no different from back home."

"Therese likes you."

His face turns thoughtful. "She does. And maybe I'm winning some of the others over too. Don't you think?"

I stare down at Peony's mane. "I think you could win over anyone in the world, if you wanted."

We plod on, keeping an eye out for game. Bees flit around the wildflowers, and sleepy crickets leap through the grass to avoid our horses.

"You're not lying to me about anything, are you, Lee?" he says, and his voice has a strange quality to it.

Words congeal in my throat. What do I say? Yes, Jefferson, I haven't told you that I can find gold the way a hound finds foxes. I haven't said that seeing you with Therese makes me sad. That on the way to Independence I started getting used to the idea of marrying my best friend, and that sometimes when you turn your back on me at night, it feels like the world is cracking open.

I find my voice. "No. I'm not lying. It's just . . ."

He reins in the sorrel mare. "Lee?"

"It's just that maybe I'm not telling you everything."

"Oh." He looks down at his hands clutching the reins. "I might not be telling you everything either."

I startle a little, and Peony dances in response. But if I'm keeping secrets, it's only fair that he does too. "I reckon that's all right," I tell him.

"Yeah."

We ride on. With Jefferson, silence is sometimes as comforting as talking.

Chapter Twenty-Two

Jefferson and I ride out every afternoon, but we never see buffalo. Our company keeps rolling, fifteen miles a day, give or take, with half a day on Sunday to make up for lost time.

Weather announces itself from far away now, low dark clouds that are more green than gray. The Platte River valley is the hugest I've ever seen, and it looks flat as a flapjack, though my sore legs tell me otherwise. I walk often, Peony by my side, to give her a break.

When a steady rumble of thunder wakes me one dark morning, I rise from my blanket, resigned to a day of soaking rain.

Jefferson is already up. He stands with his suspenders hanging at his hips, his face lifted toward the eastern horizon, which is just now brightening from black to the dark blue of a bruise.

"It's clear," he says. "See all the stars?"

"I do."

The air tastes dusty and dry, not like rain at all. The winds have been relentless lately, which is why we've camped in this shallow bowl of land. For once, it's possible that a storm is on the way, and we just can't see it.

Our wagon circle has shrunk since Bledsoe's men left, and now it feels like the animals and the people are all on top of one another. Maybe that's why the oxen are so fidgety this morning, milling about and snorting. Nugget and Coney trot over to greet us, and Coney stretches up to lick my fingers.

The thunder grows louder. The ground twitches beneath my feet.

"An earthquake?" Jefferson says.

The rest of the camp is beginning to stir. Major Craven hurries toward us, rifle in hand. "I'm heading to the top of that ridge to get the lay of the land," he says to us. "Want to come?"

"Sure," we say in unison, and duck between the wagons and follow him up the gentle slope.

The prairie stretches endlessly before us, an expanse of black that is gradually brightening to green before the rising sun. About half a mile away is the strangest storm cloud I've ever seen. It hugs the earth, a rolling mass sweeping across the horizon.

"That's no storm," Jefferson says.

"Buffalo!" Craven shouts. "Run back and warn everyone. They *must* stay in the wagons!"

Jefferson reacts instantly, sprinting away with his long legs, hollering as he goes.

But I'm frozen by the sight. It's not possible. How can there be so many of one animal in the world? They are a frothing sea of heads bowed low and whipping tails and flying mud.

Craven grabs my arm. "C'mon, you fool—unless you want to get trampled."

His words unstick my legs. We turn and run.

Jefferson's warning cries have drawn everyone out. They linger about the wagons, sleepily curious. Jeff grabs Henry and forces him toward his wagon, then does the same to Jasper. No one is moving fast enough.

"Hide!" I scream as we run down the slope. "Hide!"

I know the exact moment the buffalo crest the rise behind me, because curiosity turns to terror. Men blunder over their rifles and ramrods while mothers grab their children and run for cover. Jefferson hefts Andy under one arm and drags Olive by the hand, toward Mrs. Joyner. Thunder vibrates all around me. I expect hooves to impale me at any moment.

Yards short of safety, my toe catches on a hole in the cattle-churned sod. I fly out, hit the ground hard. My lungs won't draw air. My head spins. I'm scrambling to my feet when I feel the first hard impact on my back.

I scream, but it's only Jefferson's hands. He grabs me by my suspenders and the waist of my pants and heaves me up onto the wagon bench. I turn to pull him to safety beside me, but he has already rolled between the wheels to the other side. He glances back, just quick enough to make sure I'm secure, then he starts herding families toward the shelter of their wagons.

A rifle booms a few feet away, and I duck. Buffalo pour down the slope like a muddy brown flood. More gunshots crack the air, though I barely hear them through the roar of hooves. A few buffalo drop and tumble, but there are so many it makes no difference. Major Craven rips off his shirt and stands before the lead wagon. He whips it through the air and hollers, as if the buffalo are nothing but giant cows, easily herded by a little yelling and waving.

They are not cows. A great horned creature with a giant black head is nearly upon him. Finally, he turns to run.

"Major!" I scream.

He makes it three steps before he drops and disappears beneath a cloud of dust and hooves.

"Major!"

A buffalo slams into my wagon. It teeters violently, and I slide across the bench, grabbing the footboard to keep from falling off. Their wet noses and glossy eyes are close enough to touch as they twist aside.

The herd breaks on the wagon circle like a river flowing around an island. I clutch the footboard with all my might for a minute or ten or maybe twenty. Dust clogs the air, filling it with a heavy, musty-fur scent, choking me. Buffalo snort and pound. Wagons rattle and shake. Oxen scream.

My arms tremble from clinging to the footboard. I raise my head, praying that I will see Jefferson, sheltered somewhere safe. He's nowhere to be found, but I watch, heart in my throat, as two wagons topple over. Buffalo get tangled in the hoops of one. They stomp and knock it about with their heads until it's in splinters, dusted over with white flour and sprinkled with feathers from someone's pillow.

I can't tell if there are bodies in the wreckage.

Suddenly, the buffalo are a trickle. And then they're gone, disappeared as quickly as they came. The thunder of their hooves fades; the dust settles. I cling to the footboard a few seconds more, unable to make my limbs move.

Finally, I slide from the bench seat. Oxen and horses mill about in panic. People call out to one another. Mrs. Joyner climbs shakily from their wagon bed, Andy in her arms. The college men are whooping and slapping one another on the backs, like they've just seen the greatest wonder of their lives. Mrs. Hoffman's brood is gathered around, like a clutch of chicks. I suck in a breath when I spot Jefferson safe among them.

"Peony!" I call out frantically. "Peo—" There she is, right by the Joyner wagon. Her sides heave, but she seems unharmed. The other animals seem unharmed too. Except for the two toppled wagons and one trampled cook fire, our camp is mostly untouched.

I stagger toward the area where I saw Major Craven go down, afraid of what I'll find. A weak voice drifts toward me.

"Help . . ."

I'm trembling, like wheat in the wind, and my knees are so wobbly I can barely run.

"Oh, Lord, help me. . . ."

An ox lies on its side in the dirt, its ribs caved in, blood pooling around it. Rope from a clothesline is twisted around its neck. I leap over it. "Major! Where are you?"

"Here . . ." He's crumpled in the dust, at least twenty yards from the spot where he went down. Everything about him is the gray-brown color of dirt, except for the leg of his trousers, which shows a splash of red and a snow-white splinter of bone.

"Hold tight, Major." I turn toward the wagons and wave my arms, hollering, "Help! Somebody help over here."

Everyone is busy looking to others or cleaning up. I yell again, and this time Jasper sees me. I beckon urgently. He grabs hold of Tom and Henry, and all three college men come running.

"Don't worry, Major," I tell him. "Help is coming."

"Son," he starts, but his breath is choked off with pain. He tries again. "Not much help for this."

The college men fall to their knees around him. Henry blanches. Tom averts his eyes.

Jasper grabs the Major's hand and leans close. He says, "Is anything else hurt, Major Craven?"

"A couple ribs . . . Hard to breathe."

"Can you move your toes?"

"Do I have to try?"

Jasper looks at me. "Get a blanket roll or something we can use to prop his leg."

I sprint over to the smashed wagon, noting with relief the absence of bodies, and I grab a roll of canvas from the ground. A voice hollers behind me. "Hey, where are you going with that?"

But I'm already gone, dashing back to the Major's side.

Jasper nods approval. "When I lift his leg, you slide that underneath." To the Major, he says, "This is going to hurt."

"I already hurt—" He gasps as Jasper lifts his leg with both hands. I jam the canvas batten underneath and follow Jasper's directions until it's situated exactly where he wants it. Only then does he lower the broken limb.

"I need clean water," Jasper says. He looks up at his companions, but they've stepped away, faces averted. I jump up again, and soon find a kettle sitting on a campfire, still hot. The water inside is pristine, just like the fire pit itself, which is a wonder. There's no one at hand to give me permission, so I take the whole pot.

Water sloshes over the side as I run. I slow down just enough to keep from wasting it.

Jasper accepts the kettle with a nod. "All right, Major, I need to wash out the wound. I'll go easy on you, but no lie, this is going to be awful."

"Do it," he gasps.

"Hold his leg steady here," Jasper says. "No sudden movements."

I drop to my knees and brace the leg. Jasper pours the water over the wound. Major Craven screams and jerks hard, but I've got a tight grip on him. I push down with all my might, and after that first horrible twitch, he doesn't move.

"That's good," Jasper says, and I'm not sure whether he's talking to the Major or to me. "Now loosen up so I can turn it."

He rolls the leg to the side. Water flows over the wound, washing away the dust and blood and even bits of skin. The Major kicks out with his good leg; his boot heel catches me in the thigh, and pain explodes through my leg. But I refuse to let go.

"Tom, Henry," Jasper says. "Can you grab . . . ?" Both men have fled.

"I'm sorry," the Major gasps at me. Tears pool in his eyes.

"It's nothing," I say, though my leg throbs something fierce.

"How are you doing so far, Major?" Jasper asks.

"Ready to start walking," the Major says, and we laugh, because it's unexpected, but then he laughs, and the effort sends pain like a cloud across his face.

"And you?" Jasper says to me in a low voice.

I'm going to be bruised, no question. "What next?"

"Run to my wagon," Jasper says. "There are splints and clean bandages in the medical chest. It's the small one, up front, right behind the seat."

We've loaded and unloaded the wagons enough times by now that I know just the one, so I take off running. Neither Tom nor Henry is at the wagon to help. Still, Jasper will be wanting medicines next, so I lift the whole heavy chest. It bangs hard against my bruised thigh as I climb out of the wagon and run all the way back to Major Craven.

A crowd has gathered. Mr. Joyner stands with the Missouri men. Henry hangs back by Reverend Lowrey's side. Jefferson and Mr. Hoffman are crouched at the Major's feet. I catch Jefferson's eyes. He gives me a quick relieved smile; he's as glad to see me as I am to see him.

"The sorrel mare?" I ask Jeff, plopping the chest down beside Jasper.

"Fine. Nugget and Coney too. The Missouri men lost a few cattle; they got trampled when they broke out of the circle. One horse ran off."

Jasper has wrestled off the Major's boot. The leg is already swollen and misshapen. Another minute more, and we would have had to cut away the boot.

"Thanks, Lee," Jasper says, flipping open the lid. It's jampacked with bandages and tinctures and things I don't care to think of as medical equipment, like saws and knives.

"So much!" And I thought the Joyner chest was well stocked.

"I was studying to be a doctor," Jasper says. He grabs some shears and snips along the leg of Major Craven's trousers. "Sorry about your pants there, Major."

"Judas pants . . . tripped me . . . when I was running." His words come in short bursts, between pained breaths.

"What about Tom and Henry?" I ask, mostly to distract myself from the sight of a mangled leg.

"Huh?" Jasper says. "No, Tom wants to be a lawyer. Henry's a poet."

"I mean, they should be the ones helping you."

"You're doing fine. Just do what I tell you."

The fabric makes a sticky sound as Jasper peels it away. I hold the Major's leg down while Jasper uses the last of the water to rinse the wound again. The skin has a jagged tear, pushed apart by the snapped ends of bone. Beside it is a deep gash. Someone whistles, high and sharp. Frank Dilley. He holds a shotgun.

"Wally," Frank says in a low voice.

"I know how bad it looks," the Major says between gasps for breath.

"We're out here in the middle of nowhere," Frank says. "You can't stay here; the savages'll get you. And you can't keep going."

"I'll be right as rain," he says.

"We'll make it work," Jasper says.

"Maybe," Frank says. "But you'd be better off if you'd left with the rest of Bledsoe's men."

"Little late for that now," the Major says. I'm glad to hear the fight in his voice.

"Guess so," Frank says. "But if you decide you want me to put you down, keep you from being a burden, and end your misery . . ." He holds up his shotgun.

"Get out of here," Jasper snaps.

"Ain't no crime to say the truth," Frank says. "When that leg goes gangrene, you come find me."

"I'll walk over, get you myself," the Major says. I haven't cared for him much, not since he stood by and let Mr. Joyner put diseased blankets in Mr. Bledsoe's grave. But maybe I haven't given him enough of a chance. I like him a fair sight better than Frank Dilley, that's for sure.

"See you then," Frank says. He and the other Missouri men turn and walk away.

Reverend Lowrey steps forward to kneel by the Major's

side. "If you take my hand, we'll pray together," he says. "Or maybe there's something you'd like to say to your loved ones back east?"

"Pray somewhere else," Jasper says, waving dismissively with his hand. "At least five to ten feet away."

The preacher stares wide-eyed, as if wounded, and he opens his mouth to protest, but Jasper cuts him off.

"You're blocking my light," Jasper says. "I need to see what I'm doing."

The preacher doesn't move.

"Give him the light!" Jefferson snaps, and Lowrey jumps back. Jasper shoots Jeff a grateful look.

"This next part's gonna hurt the worst," Jasper says.

The Major looks faint, with sweat beaded on his forehead and the pulse in his leg pounding as fast as a steam engine. "Pretty sure the part that hurt the worst . . . when . . . the buffalo stomped me . . ."

Jasper grins. "I'm going to align the bones now."

A sudden jerk. The bones scrape. The Major's eyes roll back, and he goes limp.

I gasp. "Jasper—I think he's dead!"

"He just passed out, which is a mercy. See? His chest is still moving. Brace him now."

I hold tight as he sticks his fingers right into the wound and adjusts the bones until he's satisfied with how they align. His fingers come out slippery with blood, and he looks for something to wipe them on.

"Grab my neckerchief," I say, pointing with my chin. It's

tucked into my shirt, which makes it as clean as we're going to get at the moment.

I lift my chin so Jasper can grab the kerchief. He wipes his hands and pulls a glass bottle labeled "Hawes' Healing Extract" from his medicine chest. He pours it liberally over the leg, which makes the Major jerk around in spite of being passed out. Jasper packs the wound with a clean bandage and wraps the whole thing up with what he calls a Liston splint. As he ties it down, the Major's eyes flutter open.

"Lord, I hurt," he moans.

"That's to be expected," Jasper tells him.

"Was hoping it was all a dream," he says.

"Then close your eyes and keep on dreaming," I tell him.

"Thanks for finding me," he says. "You saved me."

I didn't do anything. Just waved for Jasper. But I duck my head to give him a quiet "You're welcome."

Jasper gets to his feet and stretches his lower back. "Henry, go find Tom. We'll need his help to carry the Major back to our wagon."

Jefferson steps forward. "I can carry him."

As his eyes meet mine, I realize Jefferson was right; the trail is good for him, with all its wide-open space and no da to slap him down. He's the one we ought to be thanking— for picking me up when I fell, for getting everyone to safety. I open my mouth to tell him so, but Jasper steps between us and leans down over the Major.

"I'm not putting you out of your wagon," Craven says.

"Nonsense," Jasper says. He pauses long enough to give my

shoulder a squeeze. "I want to keep an eye on that leg the next few days, and I can do it easier if you're close."

While Jefferson and the college men get the Major settled, I wander back toward the Joyners' wagon. My limbs tremble, and my mind is a haze as the memory repeats itself over and over: Major Craven trying to wave off the buffalo, and then disappearing so fast it was like the very earth sucked him away.

A large group of men huddles beside the smashed wagon. I approach their circle to see what the fuss is, and a couple Missouri men step aside to make room.

"With Wally dying, I've got the most experience," Frank says. "I've been as far as Fort Laramie twice, taking supplies. I already lead the biggest group of wagons. Wouldn't be any trouble to lead everyone else."

The last thing we need is a good-for-nothing pattyroller in charge. I step forward to protest, but Mr. Robichaud speaks up first: "Dilley's right. He has the most experience." But he says it with a furrowed brow, as if it's grave news. Half a dozen others nod and murmur agreement.

I clamp my mouth shut.

Mr. Joyner says, "Major Craven was an officer in the militia. He led a *disciplined* outfit. It's no aspersion cast upon your character, Frank, to acknowledge him as your better."

Frank spits tobacco juice at Mr. Joyner's feet. "How's that for casting a 'spersion?" The mob of men behind him chuckle like it's the funniest thing. "Sounds like they know who their leader is."

I can't keep quiet any longer. "Jasper's a doctor. He cleaned the Major's wound and splinted it. The Major's going to be fine."

"And if that works out, we'll all hold hands and sing hosanna," Frank says. "In the meantime, I'll take care of things."

"We ought to pray together," Reverend Lowrey says. "Ask for God's guidance in our hour of need."

Everyone nods, but no one drops their head to pray.

"All I'm saying is we ought to choose a natural leader," Mr. Joyner says. "Someone with the proper background, with command experience."

"Just because you've bossed slaves doesn't mean you're qualified to boss me," Frank says. Some of the men shift uncomfortably.

"Gentlemen, gentlemen," Reverend Lowrey says. "Let us come together in Christian accord and ask for God's guidance. All of this is part of His plan for us—"

I've heard enough. I return to the college men's wagon, wanting to assure myself that I told the truth, that the Major will be fine.

Jefferson is gone, and the Major is settled in. Jasper crouches over him, holding a cup of water to his lips. The stains on the Major's bandages are darkening to brown instead of continuing to bloom with bright red. I take that as a good sign.

Jasper notices me. "What are they doing?"

"I don't know," I say. "But I feel confident they're going to be blockheaded about it."

"We're lucky no one else was seriously hurt," he says in an exhausted voice. "Just a few cattle."

"I suppose so." I glance at his medicine chest. It seemed so heavy when I carried it out to Major Craven, but it's already half empty. If anyone else is badly injured, Jasper won't have anything left.

I watch him tend to the Major for a little while, but he doesn't have anything more to say, and I realize I don't either.

I drift through camp, looking for Jefferson so I can thank him for saving me, maybe even just sit down and talk for a spell. But I find him with the Hoffmans, helping Mr. Hoffman and the two oldest boys as they make repairs. Mrs. Hoffman and Therese are picking up a trunk that had burst open, spilling clothes and linens. Therese steals a glance at Jefferson.

"You working two wagons now?" I say.

"Just helping out," he answers. "Mrs. Joyner is looking for you."

"Of course she is." I don't want to talk to him after all. I turn away, knowing I'm irritable and not fit for company, and I have no idea why, except the memory of the Major getting trampled keeps flashing in my mind's eye. If not for Jefferson, the same would have happened to me.

I'm halfway to the Joyners' wagon when I hear the cry: "Indians!"

Chapter Twenty-Three

The Indians follow the herd of buffalo, and we are in their path. Our men are still arguing over who should lead the company as the first few stride calmly into our camp.

Frank Dilley's hand moves to his gun holster. "They incited that stampede on purpose, mark my words," he says.

"We should tell them of the blood of Christ," Reverend Lowrey says, eyes bright with the same fever that always took my daddy when he talked of gold. "If we hold services now, they'll stop out of curiosity. I'll fetch my Bible—"

"Hold on now," Mr. Joyner says, grabbing his arm. "We're not doing anything until we know our belongings are safe."

I study the Indians as they drift among us, looking for people interested in trade. The men wear buckskin suits decorated with quills and colored beads. Some have cloth blankets thrown over their shoulders; others have buffalo hides. Most have feathers sticking out of their glossy black hair. There are a dozen or so, and by the way they whisper to one another while eyeing Frank and Mr. Joyner, I figure they understand English just fine. Many of their faces are pocked with scars. One has blue eyes; another, freckles.

The thought hits me like a raindrop out of the clear sky: Put Jefferson in different clothes, and he would blend right in with this group. The same thick black hair and sharp cheekbones, the same broad mouth and dark skin. I glimpse him watching the Indians from behind a wagon. He catches me looking at him, and I swear he knows what I'm thinking. He frowns and ducks away.

A handful of women follow after the men. Some carry babies in baskets that hang down their backs, held in place by nothing but bands around the mothers' foreheads. My neck hurts just looking at them. One of the babies starts crying. The mother lifts it from her head, basket and all, and affixes the babe to her breast, as if it's the most natural thing in the world.

A girl, probably a few years younger than me, spies the gold locket around Andy's neck and gestures that she wants it.

I dash forward to interpose myself between the curious little boy and the Indian girl. "No, absolutely not."

She cries as if I've wounded her, reaching around me to get at Andy. Several of her companions come to her aid. I scoop up Andy and bundle him to my chest, but he tries to squirm free, as interested in the girl as she is in my locket.

"What's going on here?" Mrs. Joyner says.

"Just friendly introductions," I tell Mrs. Joyner. The girl's wailing grows louder. Andy squirms harder. I look toward the men for help, but they're still busy arguing. "You can't give them my locket."

"I would never . . ." She pauses. "Is that what they want?"

"They just want to trade. I think."

"I . . . have some things."

She runs to her wagon and returns with a silver hairbrush. I cling to a wriggling little boy while she engages in some quick negotiations, coming away with a buffalo hide. The Indian girl's wailing evaporates. She and her friends take turns touching the shiny silver handle. Then she unravels her left braid and starts brushing her hair.

Others, perhaps sensing the angry mood of the camp, gesture southward toward the herd of buffalo. Moments later, all the Indians melt away much as they arrived. The girl follows slowly, brushing, brushing, brushing as she goes.

Mrs. Joyner stares after her, beaming. "Maybe next time I can trade some salt pork for fresh buffalo meat," she says.

She'd be better off trading away some of that big furniture before we get to the mountains.

"Ma'am?"

"You don't like buffalo meat?"

"I don't know— Never had any. Jefferson said you wanted to see me? Before the Indians arrived."

The joy vanishes from her face. "Ah, yes. I'd like a favor."

"Anything."

"I'm worried about Mrs. Lowrey."

"How come?"

Her brow knits. "She should be . . . Forgive me for speaking indelicately, I hope I don't offend you."

"Not at all."

Everything comes out in a rush. "She ought to have delivered that baby by now. She's long past due, but she won't ask for help. Mrs. Robichaud can't go to her because of the twins' measles. Mrs. Hoffman is already overburdened with her six children. Six births, can you imagine! And Reverend Lowrey . . . Well, the reverend puts all his faith in God, as he should. He's a good man and a loving husband, and I'm sure he just wants to protect his wife, and I'd go myself, but you see . . ." She leans forward and whispers, "They're *Presbyterians.* It doesn't foster casual relations, you understand? I asked them to dinner, but the reverend . . . Anyway, I'd like to do what I can to help her."

This is the kind of conversation you have with another woman. I can't help glancing down at my chest to make sure Mama's shawl is in place beneath my shirt. It's been harder and harder to tuck in every day; the material is ragged and stained now, the edges unraveling. But everything seems to be secure. "I . . . What do you want me to do?"

Mrs. Joyner's hand goes to her own belly, a gesture I'm not sure she's aware of. "Just make an excuse to stop by her wagon, like you did before. I have to stay and help Mr. Joyner—he wears himself out so quickly. Find out how she's doing, perhaps? Maybe if the Lowreys ask for help . . ." Her quivering voice trails off.

I haven't seen her so frightened and white-faced since we

shot through the Suck on the flatboat, and I'm not sure why Mrs. Lowrey's situation has her in such a state. "I'm glad to do it," I say, even though it's something a boy would probably never agree to.

"Hey, Lee!" Jefferson rides over on the sorrel mare. "Do you still have Mr. Joyner's rifle? A few of the men are heading out to hunt some buffalo. The ones we downed here are all trampled and useless."

"What about the wagons?"

"A few of them need repairs. They'll take all day."

I look to Mrs. Joyner. "I could bring you that meat you wanted."

"Go on," she says. "You can do that other favor when you get back."

We ride out with a group of Missouri men, following a huge swath of mud and dirt that cuts through the prairie like a river. There's some discussion about which band of Indians visited us, with the men generally settling on Omaha. Who ought to be removed, they say, so white men can settle the Nebraska territory.

The small band is also following the herd, and we pass them about a quarter mile out. Frank aims his rifle at the leader and holds it to his shoulder until the Indians notice. "Bang," he says. Then he laughs, lowers his weapon, and waves to the Indians all friendly-like.

They don't wave back.

"Suspicious beasts," he says. "We could shoot all of them

from here before an arrow ever reached us."

"They're sneaky," offers one of his companions. "Come up and slit your throat in the night."

"That's why you shoot them first."

Their talk puts my belly in a bad way. I glance over at Jefferson, whose lips are pressed tight.

"The Missouri men are snakes," I whisper to Jeff. "The lot of them."

"Men are men," he says with a shrug. "It's men thinking other men are snakes that's the problem."

Shame clenches my throat. He's right.

The buffalo ended their stampede a mile or so beyond our camp, where a few small hills rise from the flat prairie. There are thousands and thousands of bison, as far as the eye can see. I've never seen that many of anything in all my life. Even ants on an anthill can't compete.

Under Frank's direction, we spread out to either side. He explains that we'll shoot at stragglers to drive the herd back together and start them moving again, away from the Indians.

My first shot is good, even with the unfamiliar rifle, and the animal crumples. The nearest buffalo trot away, but the herd doesn't spook.

"Nice shooting, Georgia," Frank says.

"Show-off," Jefferson whispers.

"Let's go get it," I say, grinning.

"Not yet," Frank says. "We don't stop until we're done hunting."

Maybe it's not safe to dismount with so many buffalo nearby. I look to Jefferson for an explanation, but he shrugs, equally confused.

While I reload my rifle, the others start shooting. Gunfire cracks all around me, and burned powder fills the air. The buffalo take off running.

The men shoot indiscriminately and laugh at the cries of agony. They ignore wounded animals to shoot at others. All Jefferson and I do is follow behind and put down animals too injured to run.

It's a slaughter. We kill more animals than our entire company can possibly eat, and then we kill some more. Finally, after driving the herd for miles, the men get bored, and Frank gives the command to pull up.

We gather around a dead buffalo, and I dismount to get there first. My daddy field-dressed a bear once, so I know it's possible to handle something so large. I put my knifepoint to the buffalo's hide. Frank grabs my shoulder.

"Like this," he says. He pushes me out of the way, reaches into the buffalo's mouth, and yanks out the giant tongue. He hacks it off with a knife. "Tongues and humps, that's all we're taking," he says. "The delicacies."

"What about the rest?" I ask, astonished.

"Leave 'em out here to rot. We can kill 'em all, far as I'm concerned. If the Indians can't find anything to eat, maybe they'll go live somewhere else."

Even taking only the simplest cuts, we've killed far too many buffalo to take them all. The sun climbs past noon, so we stop and cook up dinner. Someone unhooks a pot from his saddle and sets a tongue to boil. It must steep a while, he explains, so the men stretch out on the grass and trade stories and joke about lingering until the mess is cleaned up back at camp.

Jefferson and I sit off to one side. His face is dark, his eyes troubled.

Softly, he says, "This is one of the worst things I've ever done."

"At least we put some out of their misery," I reply.

"I can't wait to get to California. Then we can be rid of Frank Dilley and his boys."

"That would be nice," I say.

"You sound doubtful."

I pick at a blade of grass, pulling it apart. "It's just that I've learned a few things on the road. About bad people. And good ones."

"Like what?"

A few yards away, someone slaps Frank on the back, laughing over something he said.

"That bad people are everywhere," I say. I think about the brothers who waylaid me and stole my gold and gear. They'd be right at home with some of these folks heading west. "Every place there's people, there's badness."

"There's goodness too."

"Sure. When we get to California, there'll be plenty of good people. Like the Hoffmans and the Robichauds and the college men. But there'll be Frank Dilleys all over the place."

"And your uncle."

I try to toss the blade of grass away, but the breeze flips it right back into my lap. "Yeah. Him too."

Jefferson brings his knees to his chest and wraps his arms around them. Staring out at the Missouri men, he says, "Are you scared?"

I say nothing. Behind us, Peony's bridle rattles as she tosses her head.

"Because I'm scared for you," he says. "If he really killed your folks—"

"California is a big place."

"Seems like he wants you for a daughter. Believes you ought be his. So, maybe he won't hurt you?"

He says that like it's a good thing, but the thought turns my stomach. "Parents hurt their kids all the time."

He stiffens.

"Sorry, Jeff. I didn't mean to—"

"Looks like lunch is ready," he says, rising.

"Wait, Jeff," I say, tugging on his pants' leg.

He stares down at me.

"I just . . . Thank you. For saving me. The buffalo would have gotten me if not for you."

"You'd do it for me," he says, and he yanks his pants leg away.

Everyone gathers around the pot. We peel off the outer skin and eat the meat underneath. It tastes like beef, I guess, but it's as tender as butter. Not that I have much appetite for it.

After eating, we retrace our steps. Along the way we pass dozens of buffalo corpses, a trail of brown and crimson breadcrumbs leading back to camp. Vultures circle in the sky like a cloud of blowflies. I used to feel proud when I'd shot something I could take home and feed to my family.

Near the end of the breadcrumb trail we find the group of Indian women and children clustered around the remains of a buffalo. The hide hangs on a makeshift frame. Most of the meat is cut into strips and smoking over a fire. I hope it's the one I shot.

Frank and a few others kick their horses into a gallop, as if to run down the women and children.

Jefferson looks at me, and I shake my head. "Not going to do it," I say.

"Good."

I want to yell at them to stop, but I'm a coward and I say nothing. The women and children scream and scatter. Frank and his men turn aside at the last second. When Jefferson and I catch up, they're still laughing about it.

Evening is falling by the time we return. Jefferson takes all his meat to the Hoffmans, saying they've been feeding him all along, and this is his chance to repay them a little.

I drop off some of mine with the Robichauds, who are grateful. Their little boys are nearly over the measles, and their appetites are coming back. I take more to the college men and Major Craven. Jasper says things are looking good so far, but his expression contradicts his words. The

Major forces a grin and tells me he'll eat every bite to get his strength back.

My next-to-the-last stop is the preacher's wagon. I stand outside near the back curtain, nerving myself up to inquire about Mrs. Lowrey on behalf of Mrs. Joyner. Maybe I should ask Therese to do it. She would be a more appropriate choice.

A movement to my left catches my eye. It's Reverend Lowrey, huddled in the shadowed lee of the wagon. He's on his knees in prayer.

The wagon's curtain is whisked aside. "Ma'am?" I say, expecting to see Mrs. Lowrey.

It's Mrs. Joyner. Her sleeves are rolled up to her elbows, and her hands are bloody. It's the first time I've seen her without a cap on her head, and her wet blond hair is plastered to her face. Her own belly swells as she stands on the back of the wagon bed, wearing the grimmest expression.

"I'm s-sorry," I stutter, not knowing what I'm sorry for just yet.

She rubs sweat from her forehead with her upper sleeve. My gaze jumps between her bloodied hands and the wagon bed, which is silent and still.

"Not your fault," she says softly. "Reverend came to get me right after you left. Mrs. Lowrey . . ."

I want to tell her it's all right, that I understand, that she can speak plain to me, woman to woman. *Her water broke. Her laboring came.*

". . . she fell sick last night, I gather. She strained all alone for hours. Reverend didn't get help at first because he said the outcome would be God's will."

"*What?*"

The reverend jumps up at my voice. The Bible dangles from his arm like a piece of overripe fruit. Fingers jammed between the pages mark the passage he was reading. His face is a swirl of worry and hope. I don't know how he can hope. Surely he hears the silence.

Mrs. Joyner shakes her head.

The reverend opens his mouth to say something, but nothing comes out.

"I came too late," she says. "I'll tell the others. See if there's someone who can come stay with you."

"The babe?" he squeaks out.

"I'm sorry."

He doesn't respond, just stands frozen. For the briefest moment, his features twist with gut-wrenching pain.

Then he hefts his Bible and stalks off. "Blessing be to God!" he shouts at the top of his lungs. "Even the father of our Lord Jesus Christ, the father of mercies and the God of all comforts, who comforteth us in all our tribulation . . ."

"Can you help me down?" Mrs. Joyner says in a quiet voice.

"Yes, ma'am."

I offer her my hand, and she practically falls into my arms. I'm lucky I don't topple under her weight.

She steps away from me as soon as she's steady on her feet and wipes her hands on her skirt, as if wiping away my touch. "I need to get back to Mr. Joyner," she says, her voice trembling. "He still hasn't recovered. This morning's exertions nearly undid him."

She staggers, and I move to steady her, wrapping an arm around her shoulder. "Let me help you."

She stiffens, as if to fight me, but common sense prevails. "Thank you."

I spare one more glance at the preacher's wagon. There's a dead woman inside. Not much older than I am. And she's all alone. Her husband is off stomping around the camp. Mrs. Joyner has to take care of her own family. There's no one to keep Mrs. Lowrey company until she can be prepared for burial. Not that she needs company. She's dead; I know that. But someone should do something.

This has been a terrible day right from the moment I woke, from Major Craven's injury to Mrs. Lowrey's death, and I didn't do a thing to make it better. I froze in panic instead of running from the buffalo. I didn't check on Mrs. Lowrey right away, even though Mrs. Joyner was terrified for her. I didn't say anything to Frank Dilley and his gang of ruffians during the buffalo hunt.

Leah Westfall was never like that. Only Lee McCauley is so scared and useless.

We reach the wagon. Mr. Joyner is propped up on his mattress, looking wan and tired. Olive sits at his feet, playing with a doll.

I'm about to leave when Mrs. Joyner says, "Where's Andy?"

"I thought he was with you," Mr. Joyner says. "He was bored and whining. I couldn't sleep. So I told him to go find you."

Mrs. Joyner looks gut-punched. "I was . . . I couldn't . . . When did you see him last?"

"Hours ago," he says. "Around lunchtime."

It's like her chest cracks open and all the air rushes out as she cries in anguish.

"He's got to be around here somewhere, ma'am," I say. I know it's rude to interrupt their conversation, but I can't abide one more bad thing happening today. "I'll go find him."

She turns around. "Help me down. I'm coming with you."

There's no point arguing, so I help her down again. This time she practically jumps into my arms and hits the ground running.

She scurries around the circle of the camp so fast I can barely keep up, checking every wagon, asking people if they've seen her little boy. I follow after her, reaching out with the gold sense for my mother's locket. But after one complete circuit of the wagons, I have to admit the worst: The locket is not nearby.

A crowd has gathered around the Reverend Lowrey, who is sermonizing about the many virtues of his late wife, but they shift their attention when Mrs. Joyner comes running up. "Has anyone seen Andy?"

Reverend Lowrey immediately offers to pray for the boy.

"We will turn the whole camp outside in," Mrs. Robichaud promises. "Where he is hiding, we go to find him."

I close my eyes and stretch my gold sense out to its limits. The hidden treasure in the Hoffmans' wagon shines like daylight, and Major Craven's cuff buttons tickle the back of my throat. But the familiar tug of Mama's locket is definitely nowhere near. "We need search parties," I say, opening my eyes. "In case he wandered away. I'm going out with whoever wants to go with me."

Frank shares a meaningful glance with another fellow. "We know where he is," he says.

"Where?" cries Mrs. Joyner.

"The Indians were eyeing him and his pretty blond hair. They wanted that boy of yours. We find the Indians, we'll find your son."

"We don't *know* that," I say.

"Well, you look wherever you want," Franks says. "We'll be the ones to find him." He and several others grab their powder horns and start loading.

The Indians didn't take Andy. We passed them on our way back from hunting buffalo, and I didn't sense the locket once. But there's no way I'm saying so to Frank Dilley, a man who raised a shotgun to his own leader just for getting hurt. How much worse would it be for me if he found out I had witchy powers?

I grit my teeth as I watch the Missouri men ride out in a pointless pursuit. Jasper must stay behind and tend to Major Craven. That leaves me, Jefferson, Mr. Hoffman, Mr. Robichaud, Tom, and Henry to search. I ask Jefferson, "Think Nugget or Coney could track him?"

"With all the people and animals that have muddled through here, they'd be lucky to track him if they could see him."

He's right. "So we spread out and think like a little boy and try to figure out which way he went."

"We need a signal," Mr. Robichaud says. "If anyone finds him, fire two shots into the air."

We all agree, and we split up and spread out from camp.

The land grows shadowed with dusk. Tiny bugs rise from the grass, fogging my path, while frogs chirrup endlessly. My throat is hoarse from shouting Andy's name, but there has been no sign of the boy, not even the faintest tickle of gold sense.

A gunshot rings out from the direction of camp. In its echoing aftermath, I can't tell if another shot follows. I turn Peony around and breeze her all the way back.

The campfires are burning bright when I arrive. I dismount and walk Peony between wagons into the circle. Everyone else is there—Frank and his men, Tom and Henry, Mr. Robichaud, Mr. Hoffman and his two oldest sons, Jefferson.

"Who found him?" I ask. "Where was he?"

Jefferson shakes his head. "No one found him."

"I heard a gunshot."

"Rattlesnake."

"Is anyone bit?" My heart will burst if one more person gets hurt today.

Jefferson's face is grave.

"Who? Who was it?"

"Athena. Jasper's milk cow. Tom shot once to kill the snake and then once to put her down."

Tears spill out of the corners of my eyes, and I scrub at them with the back of my hand. It's too much. Everything that could go wrong since I woke up this morning has gone wrong. And now sweet Athena, with her soft brown eyes and fine lady lashes.

"Grab some dinner, Lee," Jefferson says. "You'll feel better after you get something to eat."

"I'm going back out. I won't let today end this way."

"Lee—"

"I won't."

Chapter Twenty-Four

*E*veryone is staring at me. "I'll welcome anyone who wants to help," I call out.

No one volunteers.

Frank says, "You go back out there in the dark, you're asking to get yourself killed. The Indians'll put an arrow through you. You won't even hear it coming."

I look him dead in the eye. "A brave man would offer to come with me."

"I forbid it. You ain't going out there."

"Try to stop me." I whirl and head toward Peony.

"If you're not back in the morning, don't bother!" he shouts after me. "We'll leave without you."

My hands are shaking and my eyes are blurry with tears that won't fall. Footsteps pound after me. I brace myself, but it's Jeff.

"Lee?"

"Don't you start," I snap. "And don't you dare try to change my mind."

"I'm coming with you."

"Oh."

I unhitch Peony. She nips at my arm, but her teeth don't touch me, so I know she's not serious. I stroke her neck by way of apology, but her skin twitches under my palm. She needs a good rubdown. I've worked her hard all day.

"Thanks," I say softly. To her and to Jefferson.

"You're a McCauley, right? Lee McCauley. That makes us family."

I choke out a laugh, and then the tears dribble down my cheeks and I'm rubbing my sleeve across my face. "I don't know what you're talking about, Jefferson Kingfisher."

"I knew you'd throw that back at me," he says.

"Too bad you can't pick your family." It's what Daddy always said about his mother-in-law, my Boston grandma who refused to return my mama's letters after she ran away to Georgia.

"Maybe you can."

I stare at him, not sure what to say. I'd pick him for family, for sure and certain, if I could.

"I'll get the sorrel mare and the dogs," he says.

The contents of the Joyners' wagon are stacked outside. I'm quiet as a mouse as I get some feed for Peony and refill my canteen. But the canvas flap whips open, revealing a red-eyed Mrs. Joyner.

"Just restocking," I say. "Then Jeff and I are going back out."

"Promise me you'll bring him back," she says.

My shoulders tense. Daddy taught me never to make promises I couldn't keep. "We'll look all night."

She reaches out her arms and begs me to come close. When I do, she bends down and wraps her arms around my neck. "We're lucky to have you with us, Lee McCauley. You're a good man."

I extricate myself awkwardly, duck my head, and tug my brim at her. My heart is in a tangle, and I don't know what to say. I've lost everything—my parents, my home, my gold, my daddy's Hawken rifle, his saddle. I even lost my name. Leah Westfall, the girl who took care of Lucky Westfall's farm for him and panned for gold—she doesn't exist anymore. But maybe Lee McCauley isn't so bad after all. I stood up to Frank Dilley a few minutes ago, and now I'm going to go search for a little boy, because it's what *I* want to do.

"I should get going," I say.

As Jefferson and I climb into our saddles, Therese comes running up, her skirts in one hand, a bundled kerchief in the other. "Here!" she says breathlessly, handing the bundle up to Jefferson. "For you and Lee. Might be a long night."

"What is it?" I ask.

"Cornbread! We used the last of our cornmeal today. Thought everyone could use a treat after that stampede and Major Craven and . . ." She looks down at her feet.

"Thank you, Therese," I say.

"I . . . I wish I could go with you." She straightens, forces a grin. "Anyway, good luck!" She dashes off, and Jefferson stares after her.

I lean over and rap my knuckles on his leg. "Let's go."

He snaps out of his thoughts. "Let's go," he agrees.

I cluck to Peony, and we ride into the wide black night, lit only by a giant prickly sky and a low, menacing moon. The grass muffles the horses' steps. Insects buzz against a whipping breeze, and a coyote yips in the distance, coaxing a growl from Nugget.

"So what's the plan?" Jefferson asks. "How are we going to find him?"

I can't tell Jefferson my real plan, which is to crisscross the land until I feel the tug of gold. So I say, "Andy knows us. He'll answer to our voices. So we head down every trail, every path that a four-year-old might take, and we call his name until we find him."

"That's it?"

"That's it. Think like a four-year-old boy."

He says nothing.

"You've had more practice thinking like a four-year-old boy than I have," I point out.

He frowns. "You already searched downriver?"

"Yep." I sensed a tiny bit of gold dust, the same trifling amount found in almost any river or stream, but nothing as big as a locket. "I'm confident he did not go in that direction."

"So we head upriver," he says. "He's a smart boy. At four, I would have known to avoid the river and quicksand. After we go far enough, we'll turn inland until we find another trail or wash and then make our way back to camp. Like cutting slices out of a pie."

That makes sense to me. "How big a pie?"

"As far as a four-year-old can walk. Did I ever tell you about the time, after my mama left, when I decided to walk into town to find her?"

"Never heard that one."

"I was only five, but I made it more than halfway to town, all the way past the old sawmill. I was sitting there, by the side of the road, when your daddy found me and took me home."

"Daddy came looking for you?" Hearing something about him that I didn't know before is like a drop of water in the desert.

"I don't remember if he was looking for me on purpose or if he found me by accident. All I'm saying is that a little boy with single-mindedness of purpose will make it farther than you might think."

I nod. "Upriver it is, then."

The dogs dart ahead, tails wagging, even though I know they're as exhausted as I am. That's what I like about dogs. They're always happy to help out and be with their people.

"Andy!" Jefferson's shout makes me jump.

I add, "It's Lee and Jeff! Come home!"

"What if he's hurt and can't answer us?"

"We need to make our path twisty, make sure we look in every crack and crevice."

"We can go faster if we split up," he says, and guides the sorrel mare away from me.

"No!"

He startles at the strength of my answer. Jefferson could pass within ten feet of Andy, and if he's tucked into a holler or huddled under a bush, he'd never notice him. But not me. I'll sense him in the dark, clear as a meadowlark's song, as long as I get close enough.

"Two sets of eyes are better than one," I tell him, knowing it's a weak argument. I think of a better one, which I almost don't say, but the words come tumbling out anyway. "Also, Jeff, I couldn't stand it if something happened to you. I'm not letting you out of my sight this far from camp."

"I . . . All right."

For the next hour or so, we zigzag back and forth along the bank of the Platte. The air cools. Coyote silhouettes skim the land in the distance. Twice, the dogs take off after something rattling in the grass, but they return when we call. Once, we startle a small herd of antelope drinking at the river's edge. But Andy never answers our cries, and when we come to a tributary stream that's too deep for him to have crossed, we turn inland and start cutting the pie.

We make it all the way back in sight of the wagons with no luck. The only gold nearby is the Hoffmans' hidden treasure, and I'm used to the weight of it in my head now. The dogs dash past us to return to camp, and we have to call them when we turn and head out again.

"Tom searched this direction already," Jefferson says, stifling a yawn.

"We checked every direction once," I say. "Now we're checking again."

His shoulders slump, and his face is wan. If he says he wants to grab some shut-eye and start again in the morning, I'll let him go.

Instead he takes a bite of Therese's cornbread and a swig from his canteen, rolls his shoulders, and leads us back into the night.

We follow a dry creek that cuts into the hills. It's just low enough that we can't see our campfires from the creek bed. I have a good feeling about it, like it's a place that might feel cozy and interesting to a child. We follow it for miles, long after I think we must have gone too far. I sniff the air, detecting a zing of moisture. If a storm comes up, a wash like this could flood in minutes.

"What's your problem with the Hoffmans?" Jefferson says all of a sudden.

"What? I don't have any problem with them."

"They're the only family you never visit. You've made friends with everyone else."

"Well, there are so many of them, it seems like they don't need friends." That sounds ridiculous the moment I say it. "I didn't mean that."

"Therese thinks you hate her."

"I don't even know her."

"That's why she thinks you hate her. You avoid their wagon. She's convinced it's because she talks funny or because you don't like Germans. I told her that's nonsense. It *is* nonsense, right?"

"I . . ." It's not her I've been avoiding. It's the two of them, *together*—something I'm not sure I can bear. "I'll keep company with whomever I choose. I don't have to explain it to anyone."

He's silent a long moment. Then: "That's not like you, Lee. You're a better person than that."

"There isn't any good or bad about it. I just—"

"The Missouri men don't keep company with me because I'm half-Cherokee. Reverend Lowrey never let his wife keep company with Mrs. Joyner because she's a Methodist. And Mrs. Joyner didn't want to keep company with you for a long time because she thought you were a runaway scamp and a bad influence. So what's *your* rotten excuse for not keeping company with Therese?"

"I don't . . . I didn't . . ." I sigh. Sometimes, having a best friend with uncanny clarity is the most irritating thing in the world.

"Therese is nice. You'd like her."

I'm a worse person than Frank Dilley. "I'm sorry, Jeff. I thought I was giving you . . . freedom, I guess. To be with her. I know you're sweet on her."

He doesn't say anything.

"You're right," I add. "I know you are. She *is* nice. Bringing us that cornbread was a kindness."

"Thanks, Lee. But—"

"Shh," I say, holding up my hand. "I heard something."

He whispers, "What is it? What do you hear?"

It's not what I hear; it's what I sense. A tickle in the back of my throat. "I'm not sure. Let's keep going."

Other wagon trains have traveled down this gulch. We pass a broken wheel, half-buried in the dirt. A little farther on, an empty barrel. Cold campfires.

"I don't hear a thing," he says.

"It's close." I dismount and lead Peony by the reins.

"What's close?" Frustration tinges his voice.

"I'm looking for tracks," I say, bent over. "Footprints, anything he may have dropped." Gold buzzes between my ears now, just like a cat's purr.

Ahead, an abandoned wagon lies toppled over. The wood is white in the night, like the bones of a skeleton. A rib cage of hoops curls up from the spine of a wagon bed. My sense pulls me toward it, toward Andy . . .

I stop a hundred feet shy.

The locket is so, so close. But I see no place big enough for a boy to hide. I slow down, moving cautiously. Ten feet away. Five.

I fall to my knees.

The locket is smashed into the dirt, the chain broken. There's no sign of Andy anywhere.

"Is that—?" Jefferson half asks.

"Yeah."

"You and your big owl eyes! I wouldn't have seen that in the dark if it was dangling from my nose."

"Got lucky, I guess." I don't feel lucky at all. Andy's not here. I didn't have a second plan. Despair washes over me.

"He has to be close," Jefferson says.

A rustling in the grass alerts me. Three rangy silhouettes

materialize around the broken wagon. Coyotes. They must have a den here. The dogs lay back their ears and growl.

"Nugget, Coney, stay."

"There's something under that wagon," Jefferson says.

"A coyote den."

"Maybe. Something moved." He hurries forward.

Probably just spring pups, but I grab my rifle from Peony's saddle holster and jog toward the wagon on Jefferson's heels. The coyotes mark our approach with ears pricked forward, but they don't move. "Andy!"

There's a small cry in response.

"I'm going to fire my gun, sweet pea. Don't panic." I lift the butt to my shoulder and put a round in the dirt beside the nearest skulking coyote. They scatter. The dogs take off after them, and I let them. I rip off the ramrod and start reloading, just in case.

"I can't believe you missed that shot," Jefferson says.

"Who says I missed?" I tell him. "I'm tired of killing things today."

A bare foot protrudes from under the wagon bed. Jefferson nods to me, creeping forward.

Please be okay. "Andy, it's us, Lee and Jeff," I say. "We're here to help you."

That's all the warning we give before Jefferson grabs Andy's ankle and drags him out. He screams, pounding Jefferson's arms with his tiny fists. Jeff gathers him tight to his chest and whispers reassurances as the boy wails, raking lines into his shoulders with his fingernails.

"Grab my canteen," Jefferson says.

Andy is covered in mud, and he stinks of urine. I hold the canteen to his mouth, and he stops wailing in favor of gulping water like a wild dog.

Too much too soon could make him sick, so I pull the canteen away. "Lee," he whispers. All the fight goes out of him, and he wilts against Jefferson's chest. "Why'd you leave without me?"

"We didn't leave," Jefferson says. "We're right here." Jefferson strokes the boy's head, which makes my chest feel funny.

"Where's Ma?" Andy says.

Poor boy must have gotten so lost that he thought this wagon was part of our company. He crawled out of sight and stayed because he didn't know where else to go.

"I've got something for you." I pull the locket from my pocket and show him.

Tears fill his eyes. "I broke it."

"It's just a chain. We can fix that."

He blinks up at me, as though the possibility that things can be fixed is the greatest wonder of the world.

"You did a good job taking care of it for me. We'll fix it together in the morning, how's that? In the meantime, keep it buttoned in your pocket." I shove it into his chubby fist.

"Okay, Lee."

Jefferson is staring at me, eyes narrowed. He looks to the locket clutched in Andy's hand. Back at me.

"Let's go find your ma," I say quickly.

I call the dogs until they come loping back, tongues lolling through wide grins, like they're on holiday. I climb into my saddle, and Jefferson starts to hand the boy up to me, but Andy clings to him. "I wanna ride with Jefferson," he says.

Jefferson says, "No problem, little man." He hitches the boy high and manages to mount the sorrel mare with Andy in hand.

Even though it's the middle of the night, fresh fires are burning, and half the men are up drinking coffee. The sentry raises his gun when we approach, then lowers it.

"Well, I'll be cussed," he says. "They found him! They found the boy!"

The whole camp comes running, and we're surrounded before we have a chance to dismount. Mrs. Joyner shoves her way through the crowd like Moses parting the Red Sea. Andy lurches for her, toppling out of Jefferson's lap and into her arms. They cling to each other like a pair of burrs. Even Mr. Joyner hobbles over, Olive at his side. A dozen questions fly at us at once, mixed with hearty congratulations.

"Don't thank me," Jefferson says when most of the questions are directed at him. "Lee's the one who found him."

He doesn't know how close I was to giving up when I found the locket lying broken in the dirt. "We did it together."

"She . . . oot," he says, glancing at me. "Shoot! Lee kept on going long after I wanted to quit. Said we wouldn't stop until we found him."

We answer more questions, describing the gulch, the wagon, the coyotes. Before we're done, every man in camp has come by to shake our hands, slap us on the shoulders, and say something kind. Everyone except the college men, but I don't have time to wonder about them because Frank Dilley approaches, frowning.

"You got lucky," he says.

"Bible says you got to seek in order to find," I answer, only because I'm not about to let him have the last word. "Seems to me we made our own luck."

He looks fit to say something pointed, but Mr. Joyner pushes past him. He puts one hand on my shoulder and the other on Jeff's. "I can't thank you men enough. What you've done for my family, not just today, but through this whole journey . . ."

Mrs. Joyner appears at his side, Andy in her arms and Olive at her hem. "It's impossible not to see the hand of divine providence, from the moment we met you on the flatboat in Chattanooga." She stares straight at me. Her lips tremble. "I am sorry for . . ."

I can't bring myself to tell her it's all right, that everything is fixed between us. "I'm glad we could help out today. Andy's a good boy."

Mr. Joyner wraps a companionable arm across his wife's shoulders. It might be the first time I've seen him show her kindness. "If there's ever anything we can do for either of you, all you have to do is ask."

"Sure," I say.

"Thank you, sir," Jefferson adds.

As they head back to their wagon, Reverend Lowrey is the

last to approach. He clasps my hand and grips it tight. His own hand is bumpy with blisters. "I heard what you said to Mr. Dilley. I had no idea your own faith was so strong, Lee."

I try to pull my hand free, but he won't let go. "It's really not."

"Seek and ye shall find," he says with a wan smile. "'What man, having a hundred sheep, if he lose one, doth not leave the ninety and nine in the wilderness, and go after that which is lost, until he find it? And when he hath found it, he layeth it on his shoulders, rejoicing.' Tonight we all rejoice with you."

His eyes are dark circles. His shoes are covered with wet dirt, and his sleeves are rolled up to the elbows. He's been up all night digging his wife's grave. My joy at finding Andy dissolves like a drop of water on a hot frying pan. Instead of yanking away my hand, I give his a reassuring squeeze. "I'm so sorry, Reverend Lowrey."

"Don't be," he says earnestly. "The Lord taketh away, but He also giveth. Finding that boy was a blessing."

He turns away, and finally, Jefferson and I can take the saddles off our horses and rub them down. Dawn bruises the horizon. It's been twenty-four hours since the stampede woke us up. I could use a hot meal, though I don't know that I could stay awake long enough for someone to cook it.

"It's like we're heroes," Jefferson says. "Did you see the way everyone looked at us?"

I certainly saw the way Therese looked at him. I suppose he earned it. "Thanks for coming with me."

"Of course. You'd have done the same, if I had asked."

Yes, I would have.

He tosses his saddle under the wagon, and he pauses, thinking. "Mr. Joyner says if we ever need *anything*, all we have to do is ask. I bet he forgets by tomorrow."

"I bet you're right."

We give our horses some oats and fresh water and lay out our bedrolls. For the first time since we set off from Independence, I'm asleep so fast I don't even see Jefferson's head hit the pillow.

"Hey, Lee."

I jump awake from the deepest sleep, heart hammering.

It's Henry Meek, leaning down toward me. His eyes are red-rimmed, his beard ungroomed, for once. "So sorry to wake you, Lee," he says. "But can you come to our wagon? Jasper needs some help, and he says it's got to be you."

Chapter Twenty-Five

Jefferson mutters something, rolling over. I clamber to my feet, yawning, and follow Henry. The angle of the sun indicates late morning. At least I got in a couple hours of shut-eye. I'm not the only one late abed—the camp is silent and still as a graveyard as Henry and I wade through cold campfires toward their wagon.

Tom stands outside, hat twisted in his hands.

"I'm really sorry about Athena," I say. "She was a good cow. Everyone liked her."

A muscle in his jaw twitches. "Everyone liked her butter," he says, not meeting my gaze. He indicates the wagon with a tip of his chin. "Jasper needs you in there."

I push aside the flap. It's warm and bright inside. An Argand lamp hangs from one of the bows, and two candles rest on the front edge of the box. It's a fire waiting to happen, and I'm about to say so, but speech leaves me.

Jasper leans over Major Craven. The Major is in a bad

way. He's pale and dry with fever. His trousers have been removed, leaving flannel drawers that are cut off at the knee. The bandages wrapping his broken leg are yellowish brown with pus and blood.

I flash back to Frank Dilley offering to put him down.

"I . . . I can't do anything here," I say before he even asks.

Jasper reaches over to clasp my wrist. "His leg has to come off if we want to save his life. I need your help to amputate it."

"Get Tom or Henry."

"Absolutely not," says Henry. "The one time my father tried to show me how to butcher a hog, I passed out cold."

Tom shakes his head. "I tried, but I vomit every time I get close enough to smell it."

I yank my hand free of Jasper's grip. "Get Jefferson. Or Mr. Robichaud. Or any of the other men."

Major Craven raises a cadaverous hand toward me. His voice sounds far away. "I . . . want . . . you."

"He says you're good luck," Jasper says. "You got help for him right away after the stampede. You went out and found that missing Joyner boy."

"You're . . . blessed . . ." the Major says.

Right about now, I feel a little cursed.

Jasper whispers so low I must strain to hear. "Doesn't matter if it's true or not. He wants you here, and a hopeful, cooperative patient is about a hundred times more likely to pull through."

"Oh." It's hard to say no to a man who wants you to help save his life.

"We have to do it soon," Jasper adds. "So the Major can spend his fuel healing up his broken ribs and other wounds. He can't move his toes anymore. The wound hasn't stopped seeping blood, not even after I stitched it up. And now it's infected."

"The shock could kill him," I whisper.

". . . heard that . . ."

"He's going to die anyway—slowly, and in a lot of pain. If we amputate the leg, he has a chance."

"I'll take it. . . . Even a small . . ."

A knot of fear is forming beneath my breastbone, and I swallow against it. "What do you need me to do?"

"Be my assistant. Hand me the tools I need, when I ask for them. Do what I tell you."

"All right."

"Thank you. Now, go wash up—scrub with soap and hot water. Tom'll show you. Do you have a clean shirt to put on?"

"I'm going to get all bloody! Why would I ruin a clean shirt?"

"Dr. Liston—the man who invented that splint I used— he's shown conclusively that clean hands and clean clothes mean clean wounds, and that means less infection."

It's been weeks since I did laundry. "I don't have any clean shirts."

"You can use one of mine," Henry says from outside the wagon. "Put it on over the other one. I'll wash it when you're done."

"Thanks," I say, relieved he doesn't expect me to change in front of them.

"I've boiled some water for you to scrub with," Tom says. "And I've got a fresh bar of soap."

Jasper turns to the Major. "I don't have any ether. It's going to hurt bad."

The Major closes his eyes tight. "Just . . . do it."

I pause at the edge of the wagon. "The Joyners," I say. "They have laudanum. Would that help?"

Jasper's eyes widen. "That would ease things considerably."

"I'll be right back."

I hop down and dash across the circle to the Joyners' wagon. Jefferson is still curled up beneath it, snoring softly. I peek inside the bonnet. "Mrs. Joyner?" I whisper.

"Lee?" she responds blearily. "Everything all right?" Someone murmurs beside her, and she says, "Go back to sleep, darling."

"We're about to amputate the Major's leg," I tell her. "Jasper says it's the only way to save his life. Could you spare some of the laudanum?"

She hesitates before saying, "Mr. Joyner needs it."

Mr. Joyner must be sicker than I realized. "It would be a real blessing to the Major right now."

A soft sigh. I hear rustling, the sound of a trunk opening, a slight *thunk* when it shuts again. "Here." Her hand thrusts from the bonnet, holding a small glass jar with a cork. "Bring back whatever's left."

"Thank you so much." I grab the jar. The skull-and-crossbones label gives the recommended dosage: only one drop for a three-month-old baby. Surely something suitable for babies isn't truly poisonous?

I jog back to the college men and hand the bottle to Jasper.

"Hallelujah," he says, popping the cork. "All right, Major, two full swallows, but no more, or that leg will be the least of your worries." He holds the bottle to the Major's mouth, so he can sip it. "That's good. I need to scrub my hands again. We'll be back in a minute, and it will be over before you know it."

We climb down and find that Tom has set up a wash area with towels and soap and fresh water. I take off my hat and splash hot water on my face to wake up my eyes. Jasper starts scrubbing, and I follow his example.

"You ought to think about coming to San Francisco with us, Lee," he says, rubbing suds all up and down his arms.

"Why's that?"

"Gold mining is hard work."

I laugh. If only he knew.

He grins. "Seriously. People work hard for gold, but they spend it easy. They might as well spend it buying services from the likes of us. Plus, I've seen how you look at Jefferson sometimes . . . You're one of us. Scrub under your nails. That's where the worst dirt hides."

"You sound like my mama," I say, but I clean under my nails, one at a time, making each one gleam. "What do you mean I'm one of you?"

"A confirmed bachelor. San Francisco is a new world, with more money than laws. There's a place for us out there. To live the way we want to live, without interference."

He looks up to gauge my reaction.

"I . . ." Tom and Henry are staring at me too, waiting to see what I'll say.

Jasper must trust me completely to be so frank. Or maybe secrets have a way of making people so lonely that they eventually take a risk on someone.

"Do you want to get married someday?" he persists.

And never have anything of my own? "Lord, no. But . . ."

I shut my mouth. I *have* thought about marrying Jefferson. All because of that fool-headed proposal, which he probably wishes he could take back.

"So you're a confirmed bachelor?" he says.

My breath feels tight in my chest. Jasper is on to the fact that I have a secret or two; he just hasn't figured out what they are. Maybe I could trust him. Maybe I'm lonely enough to take a risk on someone.

The Major groans in the wagon, and I realize Jasper has been distracting me from the unpleasant task at hand.

"We must work quickly," Jasper says. "Dr. Liston can amputate a leg in two and a half minutes. I won't be that swift, but speed is of the essence. The faster we cut, the better his chances."

It's a good thing I didn't stop for a bite of breakfast.

Henry returns with his best shirt. At Jasper's instruction, I lift up my arms, and Henry pulls it on over my head, so I don't have to touch it. Henry is much taller than I am, and his shirt hangs on me like a dress.

He steps back to check me over, and his eyebrows go up.

Jasper is also studying me; a tiny grin quirks the edges of his mouth.

My heart is suddenly pounding like a herd of buffalo. I resist the urge to check whether Mama's shawl wrapped around my chest has come loose. "Um . . . into the wagon now, right?" I say.

"Yes, of course." Jasper climbs inside, with me on his heels. Tom helps us up by the elbows, so we don't have to touch anything. There's hardly room for the three of us, not with the Major stretched out.

"Stay on my right, near the Major's head," Jasper says. "I've got all my tools laid out. Knife, saw, towels, needle. Hand me whatever I ask for, but don't touch anything I don't tell you to. If the Major tries to jump up, you hold him down."

"Ain't gonna jump," the Major slurs. His voice is less pained, thanks to the laudanum. I hope that's a good sign.

"First, we tie down his wrists," Jasper says, looping a rope around the Major's wrist and tying it to a bolt in the floor. He indicates that I should do the same on the other side.

"How tight?" I ask.

"Loose enough that he still has blood flow, tight enough that he doesn't punch me in the nose when I'm cutting through the bone. Sure wish we had leather buckles. His wrists are going to be a mite sore afterward."

I do as Jasper asks, while he quickly ties down the Major's good leg. He props the broken one up on a wooden box. My heart is racing, like I'm the one who's going to be cut.

"Bite down on this," Jasper says, reaching a

leather-wrapped bit toward the Major's mouth.

Craven turns away his head. "Just be careful how high you cut," he says. "I might want to use some of those parts later."

"I won't cut any higher than your knee," Jasper says. He fits the bit into the Major's mouth. "I'm tying a tourniquet around your leg. This is going to pinch, but it's got to be tight."

The Major nods.

Jasper works quickly and efficiently. "Are you ready?"

The Major squeezes his eyes shut and nods again.

"God be with you—with us all," Jasper says. "Knife."

I hand him the hunting knife, handle first, then I concentrate on the Major's face, so I don't have to see what else is going on. I've butchered deer, sure, but the Major is a man, and alive.

I wince at the sound of the blade biting into flesh. The Major clamps down on the bit and grunts. His shoulders curl, and he starts to rise up.

"Hold him!" Jasper snaps.

I press his shoulders back down until he stills.

"Saw," Jasper says, and puts the handle of the bloody knife in his mouth, between his teeth. I hand him the hacksaw. The scrape of metal on bone makes the hair on my neck stand on end.

The Major's nostrils flare as he pants through his nose. Tears leak from the corners of squeezed-shut eyes. "You're doing fine," I tell him, though I have no idea if it's true.

The sawing goes on and on, and bone dust fills the wagon,

making the air smell like a wet dog. The Major shakes his head back and forth. He cries through the bit, jerking his bad leg.

Jasper spits out the knife. "Hold it down," he says. "Hold it down so I can finish!"

I grab the Major's thigh with both hands and press hard. Jasper goes at it again with the saw. I turn my head away as a strange squealing leaks from the Major's lungs. Jasper picks up the knife to make a few last cuts, but I refuse to watch. With a heavy thump, the leg falls off the box and onto the bed.

"Needle," he says. I hold the leg down with one hand, even though the Major isn't kicking anymore, and grab the needle. It's already threaded with gut. "Be ready to cut the thread when I tell you."

I pick up the shears and wait while he sews. The tiny wagon smells of fresh blood now, which is a vast improvement on bone dust and sour flesh. The Major is as still as death. I peer close and am relieved to see his chest rise with a breath.

"Cut," Jasper says.

I snip where he indicates.

"Towels."

I hand him the clean towels, which he packs at the base of the Major's stump. He wipes his hand on the last clean towel, and he pulls the bit from the Major's mouth and checks his pulse.

"Well, he's alive for now," Jasper says. "You did good work."

"Thanks." I hardly did anything. Just held the man down and tried not to be sick.

We climb from the wagon to find Henry offering another pot of clean water. Tom stands beside him with a stopwatch. "Five minutes, twenty-seven seconds," he says. "Nowhere near Liston's record."

Henry's smile is squeamish. "But not bad for your first time."

"Your first time?" I say. "I thought you said you were a doctor!"

"I said I *want* to be a doctor." Jasper scrubs his hands again. Triumph fills his face. A man lies near death in his wagon, but Jasper is grinning from ear to ear. "That's the exciting thing about California—we can all go there and be whatever we want to be."

I peel off the white shirt and toss it back to Henry. "Well, if he lives, then I guess you really are a doctor."

"What do you want to be, Lee?" Jasper says. His face is euphoric enough to make me wonder if he snuck some laudanum, but the look he's giving me is pointed and strange, like he's searching for a specific answer, one I'm not ready to give voice to.

"Right now? I want to be asleep."

All three laugh at that. Jasper says, "You know, you helped save two lives today."

"And if I don't lie down right now, I'm going to die."

I can tell Jasper wants to talk more—he's all wound up from what he's just done, and I don't blame him—but I can hardly stay on my feet. I make my good-byes and stumble away.

Jefferson is still asleep under the Joyners' wagon. I flop down beside him, exhausted, but I can't sleep for thinking about the preacher's wife and little Andy wandering around lost and my own baby brother and the Major and even Athena the cow. Above it all rises the possibility, both wondrous and frightful, that the college men have realized I'm a girl. And they didn't seem even a little bit angry.

When I wake, the Major is still alive. He does not die that day. Or the next.

Chapter Twenty-Six

Summer brings blazing sun and hot winds. The horizon shimmers gold with long, waving grass all dried out and gone to seed. Above it is a sea of sky, crystal blue and stretching forever. The Missouri men insist we're near the mountains, and indeed, our trail has a slope to it, so gentle you'd never know until you stop the wagons without braking them and watch them roll back a piece. For several weeks, we make excellent time, and on July 3, we make twenty whole miles in one day.

Frank Dilley is so pleased with our progress that he announces a half day's rest to celebrate Independence Day. We roll out before the sun rises.

"I'm going to go ride with the Hoffmans," Jefferson says after we've mounted up.

"Oh." It's such a pretty day, and I was looking forward to riding together. "All right."

"Do you want to come?"

"I . . . Okay."

My stomach is in a tangle as we approach the wagon. I know I've done the Hoffmans wrong, and I'm not sure how to make right. But when Therese sees me coming, she grins ear to ear and says, "Hallo, Lee!" And that's that.

She chatters our ears off the whole time, about her brother Otto, who got his arm stuck in a hole while trying to catch a prairie dog; about one of the Missouri men, who whistles at her every time he walks by; and about the tiny mouse that got into Doreen's bedroll last night and made her squeal like a baby pig.

Seeing the two of them together puts a sting in my chest—the way they laugh so easily, the way she walks beside the sorrel mare with a hand resting on the stirrup or possibly Jefferson's boot. But Jeff was right; Therese is as warmhearted as she is pretty, and she gives no indication that she ever thought me unfriendly. Despite the way she gazes at Jeff all the time, I'm sorry I avoided her so long. Friends are hard to come by, and I wasted too much time on the trail being blockheaded.

By noon we've traveled eight miles and reached a small creek. It's barely more than a trickle. Another week of dry weather will turn it into an empty, graveled ditch. The mud on either bank is plowed into long ruts and dried solid—monuments to the wagon wheels that have gone before us.

We make camp with the sun still high. We're to have a feast tonight, and everyone contributes. Jefferson tickles a couple of trout from the creek. The Missouri men share some coffee—they're the only ones with any real coffee left—and Mrs. Hoffman makes a mountain of flapjacks and serves them with honest-to-God black-currant jam that she said she was saving for a special occasion. When the college men reveal a bottle of whiskey they're willing to share, I expect Reverend Lowrey to launch into a sermon about drunkenness and debauchery. Instead, a rare smile splits his face, and he extols the many virtues of partaking in moderation, as exemplified by God's own Son, who turned water into wine.

Only the Joyners hold back, and Mrs. Joyner goes through her usual ritual of setting out the checked tablecloth with impeccable linens and fine china. She is heavy with child now, her movements slow, her rests frequent. But she lines up those checks perfectly with the table's corners, and she smoothens out the tablecloth like the world might come to an end on account of a single wrinkle.

She bakes a loaf of lumpy bread in the Dutch oven and sets some dried peas to soaking over the fire. Jefferson and I take one look at each other, and by silent mutual agreement decide to take supper with the Hoffmans. Maybe we can trade for Jefferson's trout.

We're heading away when she calls out to us. "Wait!"

She disappears inside the wagon, rustles around, bangs hard against something. She mumbles to Mr. Joyner, who has not come out of the wagon in two days, though no one will say why. I hope the cholera hasn't returned.

When she climbs out, she's holding two wax-sealed jars filled with a yellow-orange substance. "Peach preserves," she explains. She puts one on the table and hands the other to me. "Please share them with the Hoffmans, with my compliments."

My mouth waters and my eyes sting, because the thought of peach preserves gives me such a pang for Mama that it's an actual hurt in my chest. I tip my hat at Mrs. Joyner and manage a thank-you.

No one in the company has pie or dumplings, milk or butter. We haven't had a fresh fruit or vegetable in months. Still, we have a regular potluck, everyone wandering from wagon to wagon to see what's been cooked up, and we eat until we're fit to burst.

As the sun sets, we clear a space in the middle of our wagon corral. Two of the Missouri men bring out their fiddles. Then Mr. Robichaud surprises us by fetching his own instrument—a glossy walnut violin that soars over them all. He plays "Hail Columbia" and "My Country 'Tis of Thee," even though he's from Canada. Mrs. Robichaud beams with pride as everyone sings along, even me, though I sing softly, so my girl's voice doesn't carry.

Then we start dancing, and though I've never been one for dancing, there doesn't seem much to it except twirling a lot and kicking up your heels. I dance with Andy in my arms, then with Olive, and when Jefferson asks me for a spin I almost say no, but the Missouri men are dancing together, and no one is paying them any mind, so away we go.

Jefferson knows as much about dancing as I do. We bump into each other and step on each other's feet and laugh so hard our guts hurt. Then he asks Therese to dance. Then *I* ask Therese to dance. Then Jasper asks me, but halfway through our dance, the fiddles suddenly cease, and we go shock-still.

Major Craven has climbed out of the wagon all by himself and is limping toward us, using a thick branch wrapped in rags for a crutch. His shortened leg swings oddly as he hobbles along, and sweat beads on his forehead, but he's grinning like it's the best day of his life.

He's been bedridden since his amputation and hasn't left the wagon except to relieve himself, and then only with Jasper's help. He sees us staring at him, frowns, then bellows, "I can't believe you started the celebration without me!"

I let out a whoop of joy. Someone else follows. Then everyone is yelping and laughing and clapping him on the back. Mr. Robichaud starts fiddling "For He's a Jolly Good Fellow," and everyone sings at the tops of their lungs.

Only Frank Dilley holds back.

Major Craven spots Frank, extricates himself from his congratulators, and hobbles over.

"Good to see you up and about, Wally," Frank says, but his arms are crossed and his eyes are hard.

The Major braces himself on the crutch while lifting a hand to clasp Frank's shoulder. "Thanks for leading the company, Frank. You've done a fine job."

Frank nods but says nothing.

"I'd take it as a personal favor if you kept at it," the Major adds. "I'm still stove up."

Frank unclasps his arms and offers the Major a hand to shake. "Sure thing, Wally."

Everyone breathes a little easier, and the fiddles start up again.

As the sun sets over tomorrow's road, our singing winds down, and the dishes are cleared and scraped. I head off into the darkness to take care of my personal necessities, thinking that this has been the best Fourth of July ever. I'm a quarter mile up the creek when I sense it—a tingle in my throat that intensifies until it's buzzing like mosquitos at the base of my skull. I hone in on the source and drop to my knees, right in the middle of the creek. A water bug skitters away as I sift through the gravel of the creek bed. I can hardly see what I'm doing, but I don't have to.

Warmth washes through me when I touch it. To my fingertips, it feels like any other pebble, but my soul knows it's anything but. I lift it from the water and hold it up to the stars. The tiny gold nugget is no larger than the nail of my pinky finger. Probably worth about ten dollars.

I smile. I can't wait to get to California.

Jefferson and I have ridden out ahead with our rifles, hoping to spot some game. My eyes hurt from squinting against the sun, even though I wear a hat all day long.

"See that mountain up ahead?" Jefferson points to a low, rounded mound on the horizon. "I think that's it."

"It's called Independence *Rock*, not Independence Mountain," I say.

"Everything is bigger out here. Just look at *me*." He straightens in his saddle and puffs out his chest and fails to keep a straight face.

"Your head is bigger, that's for sure." But he's right. Jefferson has grown at least an inch. His neck has thickened, his shoulders broadened. He's hardly the lanky boy with giant knees I knew back in Georgia. I've grown too, but not in height. I shift uncomfortably, resisting the urge to check on the shawl hidden beneath my shirt. It's getting harder to keep my chest wrapped tight.

Jefferson urges the sorrel mare on, and I wish I could feel as cheerful as he does. Things have gone well for us. Major Craven continues to improve. We resupplied at Fort Laramie. We've traded with Indians along the way and haven't had any problems except for minor bits of theft—a blanket, some food, a single gun.

Frank Dilley has kept the wagon train moving seven days a week. Which is how we've come to reach Independence Rock only a week after the Fourth of July. We're almost on schedule, in spite of starting out so late.

But I can't shake this mood, like something's going to happen and I ought to see it coming.

"That's the rock, Lee," Jefferson says. "I'm sure of it. Doesn't it look like a piece of the moon fell down from the sky?"

"Yeah, it kind of does."

It's a big gray dome, big enough that you could fit the entire town of Dahlonega inside, rising from the flat golden plain, like God dropped a giant ball in the mud and left it half-buried. Everything *is* bigger out here in the west. I suppose I should feel smaller by comparison, but it makes me feel bigger too, like the whole world is growing inside me.

We reach the rock and dismount, then hobble our horses to graze. "Oh!" Jefferson exclaims, brushing the rock with his fingertips. Names and dates are scratched into the stone, and some of the lettering is as fine as anything you'd see in Mr. Anders's schoolhouse back home. There are hundreds of names. No, thousands.

"Look at all these people," Jefferson says. "You think they were going to California for the gold?"

"Nah, look at this one—'Wm. Shunn, 1846.'"

"Here's one from just two weeks ago."

"The Mormons came this way. And folks going to Oregon. People have been passing by this rock for a long time."

Jefferson pulls out his knife and starts carving letters. I peer over his shoulder. He's picked a small spot for such a big name, squeezed between other etchings.

"Wait," I say. "I want . . . Our names should be together."

He freezes, like a rabbit who just heard the cry of a hawk. "Okay." He lowers his knife, and his gaze shifts to my face, lingers on my lips, and I'd give all the gold in California to know what he's thinking.

I swallow hard. "Right there?" I say, pointing to an untouched area.

"Sure."

I pull out my own knife and start scoring the rock. He goes

to work beside me, and we have a comfortable silence with nothing but the *scritch-scritch*ing of our knives and the wind in the grass.

"Lee, I'm sorry I left."

"What?"

"It's been eating at me. Your parents had just been killed. You were my best friend, and you were in a bad way, and I abandoned you."

I dig in harder and blunt the tip of my knife. It will need a good sharpening tonight. "You were in a bad way yourself. I didn't blame you for leaving. Not one bit."

"Truly?"

Well, maybe for a moment or two. "Truly."

"It's just . . . I did the thing I swore I'd never do."

"I don't understand." But my knife stills as suddenly I do. Jefferson was abandoned too. "You swore you'd never leave someone, same way your mama . . . You were the eighth brother. The one who stayed."

"And maybe I was a little mad. From when I asked you to . . . you know."

"Marry you?" At his silence, I can't help but add a stinging, "Or the part about pretending to be brother and sister?"

He winces. "I figured you were done with me."

"I wasn't done with you. I was just getting started with me."

He snorts. "And have you finished with you yet?"

I clear gravel and dust from my lettering with a fingertip. "I don't know, Jeff. People here actually like me and respect me, and that's nice. But they don't know who I really am, and truth be told, I'm not sure either." For some reason, my stomach is tied up in knots. "Look, about that time, I'm sorry if I—"

"Stop saying that," he says. "You don't have to be sorry for anything."

"Well, you don't have to be sorry neither."

I've got *LE* carved into the stone. I pause a moment, deciding.

I reach for Mama's locket before remembering it's not there anymore. I think of the afternoons we spent on my new Sunday dress. I think of Jefferson asking me to marry him, back when I was a girl. I lean forward and add an *AH*.

LEAH WESTFALL.

That name won't mean anything to anyone in our wagon train, but it means something to me.

Jefferson pauses his own efforts to stare at my name. A tiny grin tugs at his mouth.

I ask, "You going to be Jefferson McCauley or Jefferson Kingfisher?"

"Jefferson McCauley Kingfisher," he says brightly.

I sigh in mock despair. "We're going to be here until the middle of the night."

"Good thing this rock is big enough to be a mountain."

We climb to the top and look back over the country we've traveled. The trail is a wide depression in the grass, stretching like a river into the eastern horizon. To the south and west are mountains. At this distance, they are no more than blue blurs on the horizon, soft and gentle and cool.

Our wagons approach, headed by the Missouri men. We wave wildly, and they wave right back. There's a short break while people carve their own names or initials, then we get underway again.

I aim Peony for the college men's wagon. Jasper drives, and Major Craven sits on the bench beside him, an awl in one hand and the sole of a boot in the other. I didn't know he was a cobbler, and I can't imagine how he's getting any work done, being jounced around as he is.

"Hey, Major," I say.

He looks up from his work. "That was a brevet promotion, and I'm no longer commander of this expedition. Call me Wally."

"Sorry, sir. You'll always be Major to me."

He laughs. Then he points to my stirrups. "Are your feet really that big? If not, I could fix those boots for you. Trim 'em down to size. Least I could do."

The skin of my feet have grown so accustomed to getting rubbed every which way that Daddy's boots hardly bother me at all anymore. "They're fine. Anyway, I don't want anyone cutting into them. Thanks, though."

"Let me know if you change your mind."

"The mountains don't look so bad from here," I say to change the subject.

"We ought to reach the Devil's Gate around noon. You'll know it when you see it. It's a narrow gap between two cliffs, like a doorway in a garden wall."

"Why such a gloomy name?"

"Because once we pass through it, the rest of the road is a bloody hell. Sulfur springs with boiling water. Hills so steep that wagons roll right back down. Mountains so high you can't breathe on top. Rivers without water. And deserts in every direction that take three or four days to cross."

Jefferson has ridden up beside me. "Can't we go another way?"

"Nope. Only way to reach the green grass of Oregon or the sweet gold of California is through hell itself."

I roll my eyes. The Major has been especially colorful since his amputation, cussing and exaggerating and telling tall tales. He reminds me of Daddy, except not fit for female company.

"You think we can climb to the top and take a look around?" I ask.

The Major pats his stump. "As long as you don't mind going without me."

"That's a great idea, Lee," Jefferson says. I turn to smile at him, but he's already heading away. "I'll see if anyone wants to come with us."

I want to shout no, to explain that I want it to be just him and me, but he's already asking Tom and Henry, so I steer Peony toward the Joyners' wagon.

Mrs. Joyner drives the team, something she never would have done when we started out. She wears a pinafore over her skirts, and the oxen's reins are pinched between her knees. In her hands is a small walnut clock with brass trim, which she is polishing with a cloth.

There is no sign of her husband.

"Lee," she acknowledges, rubbing at that clock like her life depends on it.

"Ma'am." I tip my hat. "Came by to see if you or Mr. Joyner were interested in climbing up Devil's Gate with us. It's right on the river. Should be a sight."

"Mr. Joyner is not interested," she says.

I'm not sure how long it's been since I've laid eyes on him, except to see a vague shadow in the wagon bed whenever Jeff and I load and unload. I've worried that the cholera has returned, but the wagon definitely does not smell of cholera.

"Maybe Andy and Olive would like to come? I won't let them out of my sight." I expect her to agree at once. Lately, Mrs. Joyner has been trying to keep them away from the wagon—to give Mr. Joyner his rest, she says—jumping at every opportunity to let them play with the Robichaud twins or the Hoffman children.

Olive has been walking beside the wagon, a rag doll in one hand, her baby brother's hand in the other. "Please, Ma?" she says.

"Me too!" Andy says.

Mrs. Joyner rests her hand on her enormous belly. If it gets any bigger, she can throw a tablecloth over it and serve tea. "Certainly. As long as you both mind Lee."

I spy Jefferson talking to the Robichauds, so I head over to the Hoffmans, Olive and Andy in tow.

Mr. and Mrs. Hoffman sit side by side on the bench of the

first wagon. Mrs. Hoffman holds a needle and an embroidery hoop. I'm surprised her fingers don't look like she picked up a porcupine.

"*Guten Morgen*, Herr Hoffman," I say.

"Good morning to you," he replies in a thick accent.

Therese sticks her head out from the wagon and peers at me from between her parents' shoulders. "Hallo, Lee!"

"Want to climb up to Devil's Gate with Jeff and me? We're taking some of the children."

"I would like very much to go with you. *Bitte?*"

"*Ja, ja,*" her father says.

"*Danke,*" Therese says, kissing her mother's cheek. She climbs onto the jockey box and hops down.

"Hey, always jump from the back of the wagon, away from the wheels," Jefferson says, riding up.

"Yes, I will," Therese says, looking chagrined for all of a split second before brightening. "I'll ask my brothers if they want to come."

She walks beside Andy and Olive as we all catch up to the Hoffmans' second wagon, which is being driven by Martin and Luther, the two oldest boys at thirteen and twelve, respectively. They're already taller than me, with broad shoulders and sandy hair like their father's. A thump from the back of the wagon indicates that Carl and Otto, the youngest boys, might be playing inside.

There's no sign of Doreen, who's usually out walking. She's the youngest at five years, close in age to Olive, and the two have become playmates, even though Mrs. Joyner thinks

Doreen is not well-groomed. "Not a proper lady" is how she puts it, though how anyone can be a proper lady at the age of five is beyond me.

As I steer Peony alongside the wagon, Doreen comes into view, and my stomach drops into my toes.

She rides on the tongue behind the oxen, her bonnet hanging down her back. Luther and Martin shout encouragement while she bounces up and down, laughing like she's on a hobbyhorse. Nothing keeps her there but the grip of her own tiny hands. The wagon hits a rut, and she teeters precariously a moment before straightening.

"Doreen!" Therese cries out. "What are you doing?"

Doreen turns at her sister's voice. She swings her leg over the tongue to hop down, but her ankle snags, and she starts to list.

"Yaw!" I shout, spurring Peony on.

"Stop the wagon!" Jefferson yells. "Now!"

Peony trusts me and leaps toward the oxen. We pull parallel to Doreen. I stand in my stirrups and reach between the wagon and the oxen for Doreen's dress. It brushes my fingertips. She falls, and I fall after her. My shoulder bashes against the wagon's tongue as I finally grasp her skirt. The ground knocks the air out of me, but I wrap my arms around the girl, curl up to protect her, and roll us both to the side. Dirt fills my mouth as I press us flat. The wagon's axle passes over my head. The sharp iron edge of the wheel snags the flap of my coat and pulls it halfway over my head. The coat catches on my armpit, drags us forward. Gravel grinds into my side.

"Whoa!" yells Jefferson. The wheels slow. Finally, the wagon creaks to a stop.

Doreen and I are both breathless. "Are you all right?" I gasp.

She looks at me with big blue eyes and nods.

Hubbub is all around us. People come running; boots kick up dust at my nose. Jefferson is shouting my name. Therese is shouting for Doreen.

"Can you roll the wagon off my coat?" I ask. My voice feels funny in my head, like it's coming from far away.

Pairs of boots line up behind the wagon. It inches forward, and the constriction under my arms releases. Doreen and I crawl out. She darts over to her daddy, who sweeps her up. A raw scrape covers her cheekbone, but otherwise she seems unharmed.

A dozen questions fly at once, and I have trouble parsing them.

"She's fine," I say to the frightened faces around me. "I don't think she was hurt at all."

"Not her. You," Jefferson says, terror in his eyes.

I follow his gaze, and that of everyone else, and look down. Shame floods me like water through a millrace. My monthly bleeding has started. My trousers are soaked with red, mixed with dirt.

No, that's not it. I stagger, and Jefferson leaps forward to catch me. I'm hurt, somehow. I don't remember exactly when, but my right leg doesn't feel right, and the edges of the world are suddenly blurred.

"Jeff," I whisper. "What's wrong with me?"

"Get Jasper!" he yells. "Do it! Now!"

I can't get enough air, and neither leg will hold my weight. Jefferson lowers me to the earth, saying, "You're okay, Lee. You're okay, you hear me?"

I vaguely note several people are standing over me. Therese, Mrs. Robichaud, Luther, a couple of the Missouri men. They part to make way for Jasper, who drops to his knees and reaches for the waist of my trousers.

"No!" I cry. He can't strip me here, right in front of everyone.

"I need to stitch you up, Lee. You've got a bad gash on your hip, I think. And your ankle is already swelling, so we're going to cut off your boot. Just hold still."

"He has to do it, Lee," says Jefferson. "He *has* to. No matter what, you understand?"

They'll see I'm a girl. Everyone will. I reach down with useless hands to bat him away. "Please . . ." My lips struggle to find the words. *Don't take off my trousers. Don't tell them. Don't . . .*

What comes out is: "Don't cut Daddy's boots."

My vision goes fuzzy-red, and the world is snuffed like a candle flame.

Chapter Twenty-Seven

$\mathcal{I}$ open my eyes to gentle lantern light. I'm sunken into a feather mattress. The bows of a wagon curve above me.

"You wake yourself!" says Mrs. Robichaud. She looms over me with a canteen. "Drink," she orders.

I lift my head. The moment the cool water slides down my throat, I start gulping.

She laughs. "Jasper will be glad to know you drink so much."

Jasper. My last memory is of him readying to strip my clothes in front of everybody.

"What happened?" I ask tremulously. "Did I . . . Does everybody know . . ."

"That you are a young lady?" She waves her hand as waving it off. "*Bien sûr.* But you will be glad to know that Jasper fixed you. You had a bad slicing. From hip to knee. Never have I seen so much blood! The wagon wheel, I think. And you twisted your ankle, but it is not broken."

I reach for my thigh and find thick bandages there. I'm wearing a long white shirt. Henry's, I'd wager. My legs and feet are bare but for the bandages.

"How long?" I ask.

"Just a day. Jasper forced some laudanum into you, so you'd sleep. And so you'd stop bleating about your boots."

I lurch up.

She puts a hand on my chest and pushes me back. "Don't worry yourself. Jefferson wouldn't let Jasper cut them. He insisted."

"Oh. All right."

"Mr. Robichaud and me, we take good care of you."

It's odd that I'm here instead of with the Joyners, who are my employers. Or maybe not so odd. They probably refused to help, once they knew.

"*Merci,*" I tell her. *Merci. Danke. Thank you.* It's a good thing there are lots of ways to say such an important thing.

"I sent Therese to bring you some undergarments. It will be nice to see you in skirts, finally."

I gape at her. "You knew?"

"*Bien sûr.*"

Her smile is kind, which does not reassure me. "How long have you known I'm a girl?"

"A woman. You're a woman." She pauses. "Since the first time I saw you, I think."

"Oh, no." I pinch the bridge of my nose between thumb and forefinger. "Who else?"

"My husband noticed too. The college men—"

I wince. "I thought they might have figured it out. Back when we took off the Major's leg. Did *everybody* know?"

"No, that's all." She frowns. "Reverend Lowrey says he knew all along, but I think he does not tell the truth." She sits across from me in the tiny space and folds her hands on her lap. "And of course, Jefferson."

"We grew up together."

"Yes. It is obvious. You do things together without words. Like the way you went for Doreen while he went for the oxen. You would have much worse than a gash if not for that young man." She reaches forward and strokes my cheek with a forefinger. "Poor *chérie*."

A thump on the back of the wagon makes me jump. Therese's head pops over the edge, and she tosses a bundle of frilly fabric into the wagon. She sees me awake and gives me a relieved smile.

Mrs. Robichaud grabs the bundle and shakes it out, revealing white drawers with lace trim and a ribbon tie of yellow silk. They don't have a speck of dirt or the slightest wear at the hem. Therese must have been saving them.

"Therese, I couldn't."

"Oh, yes, you could. You saved my sister, and you will wear them or I will feel bad."

Still, I hesitate.

"Jasper cut yours off," she adds. "You really need to take them."

"I have something for you too," Mrs. Robichaud says, pulling another bundle from an open trunk beside her. It's a yellow calico skirt with a ruffled hem and enough pleats that I could ride Peony while wearing it.

"I'm sorry I don't have petticoats to go with it," Mrs. Robichaud says.

"That's perfect for you," Therese says. "You have those pretty golden eyes. Like tiger's-eye gemstones, Jefferson always says."

Jefferson says that about my eyes? "Well . . ." I swallow hard. "Danke, Therese. Merci, Mrs. Robichaud."

"Call me Lucie."

Therese ties the canvas tightly shut at the rear of the wagon, then she clambers over me and does the same at the front. "I'll help you change," she says. "We need to be careful of those bandages."

I sit up, wincing at the sharp pain in my thigh.

"Jasper says no walking for you for a few days," Mrs. Robichaud says. "You must ride in the wagon or on your horse."

Therese holds up the drawers while I put my first leg through. "Why did you do it?" she asks. "Wear men's clothes?"

"Uh . . ." I'm not sure how to answer.

Mrs. Robichaud—Lucie—says, "My sister married a voyageur, a trapper. They trapped along the Hudson Bay. She didn't want to stay home while he went out hunting, so she sometimes dressed like a man and went with him. When he died from a *hernie rupture*—"

"A ruptured hernia?"

"That's it, a ruptured hernia. She continued his work for

several years. Lived with his sister."

"It's not like that," I say.

"What happened?"

I open my mouth to spin a tall tale. With a start, I realize I don't have to lie anymore. The truth is the perfect explanation. It's a relief to say: "My mama and daddy were murdered."

Therese gasps.

Saying it out loud brings back the images: Daddy lying dead on the doorstep, Mama propped against the woodpile, trying to breathe. "My uncle Hiram, Daddy's brother, did it. He as much as admitted it to me, but he's such a fine gentleman— rich, handsome, educated. No one would have believed me. And then suddenly he was my guardian and our whole farm belonged to him, and I didn't know what he was going to do with me. . . ."

"*Quelle horreur,*" Lucie murmurs.

I take a deep breath and slow down. "Truth is, I wanted to go west. My daddy was a gold miner. I grew up knowing everything about gold. So did Jeff. He was the only person I trusted, and he was going to California. I needed to leave town, quick and quiet. My uncle was—is—looking for me, you see. And then I got robbed—my daddy's Hawken rifle, almost all my money . . ."

"No wonder you chose a disguise," Lucie says.

"I didn't mean to become a liar." Tears well up in my eyes.

Therese's hands tying the ribbons of my drawers have stilled. "I would have been so scared," she says.

I consider pretending to be brave for all of two seconds, but I'm done lying. "I was afraid the whole time. Afraid I was going to be found out, afraid of the men who robbed me, afraid that I was going to be alone forever. And then once I started pretending, I was scared to let . . ."

My teeth are suddenly chattering. I cross my arms around my waist and squeeze, like something terrible will come out if I let go.

Lucie puts an arm around me. I lean my head on her shoulder, and I feel such a pang for Mama it's hard to breathe.

She squeezes me tight. "Is Lee your real name?"

I nod against her shoulder. "Well, it's Leah. Leah Westfall. But everyone always called me Lee."

"Then I will call you Lee. But if you want to change it, all you have to do is say so."

I look up at her, confused. "What else would it be?"

Therese sighs dreamily. "I've always liked the name Anneliese. If I could change my name, I'd be Anneliese."

"Who do you want to be, Lee?" Lucie says.

It sounds like something Jasper said to me. I didn't understand then, and I don't understand now. "What do you mean?"

"We'll get you some clean trousers, if you want. And when you leave this wagon, everyone here will go on looking the other way. What you do when you get to California is your business."

"Oh, the Missouri men will not look the other way," Therese says. "Trust me on that."

"But they'll behave," Lucie says.

Therese and I exchange a look.

"That's very optimistic, ma'am," I say. "Also, I can't imagine Mr. Joyner—"

"Mr. Joyner has no business judging anyone," Lucie snaps.

I recoil, startled at her burst of anger. "Why do you say that?"

"That man, he was hiding in his wagon for weeks because he had *la rougeole*. Can you believe?"

I blink. "Wait. He had the measles?"

Therese rolls her eyes. "He says he was hiding so no one else would catch it."

"Such a spirit of kindness," Lucie says dryly.

"And he's lucky his wife and children didn't," Therese adds. "Especially with Mrs. Joyner in the family way. But *I* think he was ashamed."

"And rightly so," Lucie says. "Anyway, he should not judge. You have done your share, it is the truth. You've worked as hard as anybody, and harder than some. What do *you* want?"

What do I want? To stop lying, for sure and certain. But I also want to keep greasing the axles and riding Peony and hunting game and earning my own way. "I don't mind working. I mucked stalls and found . . .er, panned for gold and went hunting on our homestead while growing up. But I did it as *me*." As a girl with gold-witching magic. "As a girl."

"A woman," Lucie insists.

Therese helps me to my feet. My leg throbs, but it bears my weight. Holding Therese's shoulders, I step into Lucie's skirt. My man's shirt tucks in nicely, and Lucie helps me tie the skirt in back. I twist in place, letting it swish around.

I take a deep breath, the first really deep breath I can remember in a long time. It feels like I'm back in my own skin, after six months of wearing someone else's.

"Here are your boots," Therese says, pushing them forward. "I got out most of the blood, but they have a few stains now."

I slide them on, gratitude clogging my throat.

"It's all right if you want to hide in here a bit," Lucie says.

"No use putting it off," I say, but I stare at the canvas opening, unable to reach for it.

Lucie loosens it, and light pours in. "Be careful with that leg," she says.

I blink into the sunshine, bracing myself for rifles and pitchforks and angry glares. Except for Peony, the wagon circle is empty, the cook fires cold. A cloud of dust rises in the distance, back the way we came.

I climb over, using the toolbox as a step, so I don't have to jump far with my bad leg. Therese and Lucie climb out behind me.

"Where is everyone?"

"The men spotted a herd of pronghorn," Lucie says. She holds her hand over her eyes and stares into the distance.

"Antelope?" I slam my hat onto my head, gingerly lower myself down, and hobble over to Peony. I grab the saddle; Mr. Joyner's rifle is gone.

"Where are you going?" Lucie asks, voice full of concern.

"To make sure we get one." Really, I just want to be riding Peony again because I'm never uncomfortable on her back, no matter what I'm wearing. "We haven't had fresh meat for more than a week."

I saddle her quick, mount up, and adjust the skirt to drape comfortably. The fabric flaps in the wind, but Peony doesn't seem to mind. The ankles of my boots show, but it's nothing everyone hasn't been seeing for months.

"Watch the leg," Lucie says, but she's grinning ear to ear.

"Good luck, Lee!" Therese says, and her gaze has a bit of longing in it as she watches me ride off.

Outside the wagon circle, Mrs. Joyner, Mrs. Hoffman, and the Major are watching the children play. I wave as I ride by, and after a moment's pause, the women wave back. Major Craven stares longest, but eventually he waves too.

Peony sees the other horses ahead and pulls at the bit. I let her loose as gunshots crack the air. A small herd of antelope leaps away. The men give chase, but the herd is too quick, and they pull up after only a few strides.

"Did we get any?" I say, riding into the group. I am going to brazen it out, even if my skirt feels like a giant flag.

"Hey, Lee," Jefferson says, all business. Like there's nothing different about me at all.

The bachelors tip their caps, wearing small, secretive smiles. Mr. Robichaud nods to me. Mr. Joyner's face is mottled with scabs, his eyes red-rimmed, his brows furrowed, but he nods too. Mr. Hoffman says, "Lee, I want to thank you—"

"Nice skirt, Georgia," says Jonas Waters, Frank Dilley's second-in-command.

I frown. "Never mind that. Did we get any?"

"Tom winged one," Jefferson says. "But it didn't go down. The others leaped away too fast."

Once pronghorns spook, lightning can't catch them. The herd is disappearing over a low hill, but a few stragglers lag behind.

"They'll stop at the river. Let's cut around that way, stay downwind, see if we can get a second shot." I head off as soon as I say it, like I have on a dozen other hunts. I glance back over my shoulder. Everyone is right behind me except Mr. Joyner, who hesitates before deciding to follow.

Just as I suspected, we round the bend and find the small herd at the water's edge. Only half of them drink. The rest hold their heads high, ears twitching, ready to bolt at the slightest alarm.

"It's a long shot," I say softly. "But I don't think we can get any closer. Can I have the rifle?"

Mr. Joyner shakes his head.

"Why not?"

"You're . . . you're . . ."

"I was a woman the last time I shot something for you."

"Take my gun," Jefferson says. When Mr. Joyner glares at him, Jeff says, "She's a good shot. And I'm hungry."

"We can do this ourselves," Mr. Joyner says. He lifts his rifle and aims it. "Let's all pick an animal and fire on the count of three. One . . . two . . ."

"No!" I shout, but my voice is drowned out by the ragged volley. Not a single animal falls, but they all spring away.

I lift Jefferson's rifle, and though it isn't nearly as sound as Mr. Joyner's, its heft is familiar. I've shot it plenty of times, and I know just how it handles. I sight the last animal in the herd. It struggles to keep up; probably the one Tom winged. I aim just ahead, in the direction of its flight, note the westward breeze. It's getting too far, too fast.

I am patient. I am a ghost.

Rear trigger, soft breath, hair trigger, *crack!* Smoke puffs up as the butt kicks into my shoulder. Almost two hundred yards away, the poor animal's rear legs fly out sideways, and it goes down in a cloud of dust.

Jefferson whistles as I hand the gun back to him.

"Not bad for a girl," says Jonas Waters.

"It's not bad for *anyone*," Jefferson snaps.

"I slowed it down for you," Tom says, but he's grinning.

"Don't worry, we'll share it." I realize, belatedly, that this isn't my promise to make. "Isn't that right, Mr. Joyner?"

But he's already heading back to camp alone. The hollow pit in my stomach has nothing to do with hunger.

Chapter Twenty-Eight

$\mathcal{A}$ week later, the pitiful lowing of thirsty oxen echoes through the camp. Mr. Joyner is scouting ahead for water with the other men while Mrs. Joyner prepares breakfast. Everyone else in camp makes do with items that are dusty, broken, and makeshift. But come hell or high water, she has that dining table set up with the tablecloth over it. The wind ruffles it, and she rushes to smooth it flat and square all the china.

I lick my cracked lips and say, "Mrs. Joyner, ma'am, good morning."

The furtive glance she casts my way is toward my clothes, not my face. My chest is wrapped beneath my shirt again, though for comfort rather than disguise, and not nearly as tightly as before. I wear trousers today, which I got from Tom in exchange for two sage hens I bagged with my five-shooter. I love the skirt Lucie gave me, but it needs laundering already, and I've a strange notion to preserve it as much as possible.

"Good morning, Leah."

"I'm ready to go back to work," I tell her. "My leg is much better. Jasper says it's fine for me to do some lifting."

"That's Mr. Joyner's decision. You'll need to speak to him." She turns her back and crouches beside the cook fire. Batter sizzles and pops as she pours it on the griddle.

"I've tried, ma'am. He won't hardly talk to me. He won't pay me parting wages, because he says I can't enter into contracts, so as far as I'm concerned that means I'm still working for him. But he won't let me work, neither. He says it's not right. But I've been doing the work for months, same as Jefferson. You've seen me."

Her shoulders sag. "That's not the point."

"Well, what is?"

She pauses to flip the flapjacks. They're burned, as usual. "You'll have to talk to Mr. Joyner. He's the head of this family, and his decision is final."

"Ma'am, can't you talk to him? He's still not hale after the cholera and the measles. Him doing all the work I used to— It's tiring him out something awful."

"He knows best."

Wind sweeps through camp and blows over one of the high-back chairs. Mrs. Joyner jumps as it hits the ground. I dash over and prop it again, making sure it's square at the table like the others.

Her eyes meet mine. Her face is drawn and strained. "Don't worry. I'll still feed you, like we agreed. It wouldn't be Christian to let you starve. Though, truth be told, we're a little short." At my perplexed look, she adds, "Someone's been skimming our food stores."

"I would never—"

She holds up a hand. "I know it's not you. Mr. Joyner says Indians. Anyway, you're welcome to whatever we have; just keep in mind that we're short."

"Thank you, ma'am," I say, more concerned than I let on. She needs all the food she can get right now. "But honestly, I just want to be useful."

She considers. Brightens. "I'm almost out of buffalo chips," she says. The dried patties of half-digested grass are all we've been able to find for fuel lately. "That Hoffman girl is out gathering some."

"I'll see what I can round up."

I find Therese swinging a big tin bucket while Carl, Otto, and Doreen run around looking for chips to toss inside. Doreen barely pretends to look. She has both arms out like windmill blades as she runs through the dry grass, her bonnet dangling behind her as usual.

"Guten Morgen," I say to Therese.

"Good morning," she says. "We are in America, we should speak American now."

"You sound just like Lucie. Though, I think we left the United States a long time ago." I peer inside her near-empty bucket. "No luck?"

She shakes her head.

Not as many buffalo pass through this arid place, and the

wagon trains ahead have gathered up the easy pickings. "We might find more over there," I say, pointing down a slope.

"How do you know?"

It's the first thing you learn about hunting, how to spot a watering place. "That dry creek leads toward water, at least some of the year. They're likely to gather there and do their business."

She calls to the children and indicates that they should head toward the creek.

"Here, let me carry that," I say.

"No!" she snaps. "I can do it."

"I didn't mean—"

"You have a horse, you ride wherever you want, you shoot things with your gun, you go out in the night and find lost children and jump under wagons to save little girls." Her face is fierce, her blue eyes bright.

"Well, I *did*. I don't know that Mr. Joyner will let—"

It's like talking to the wind, because her words just keep coming. "I'm always watching little ones or helping Mutti cook or washing clothes. Lee, I have washed so many clothes I have lost track. I might be the only person who is glad to be going into the desert. No water means no washing. Maybe my hands will heal a little."

"Washing is important too."

She shrugs. "But not very heroic. And not much fun." Ahead of us, Doreen takes a tumble, then she bounces back to her feet, laughing. Gazing at her sister, Therese adds, "I miss fun."

"Well!" I put an arm through hers, and we continue down the slope, our elbows joined. "When we get to California, I'll teach you everything I know about the fun, fun job of panning for gold. Squatting for hours on end is really fun."

She nods solemnly. "I'm sure getting your skirts soaked to the knees is fun."

"Oh, yes. And all the mud and gravel getting lodged under your nails? No church social was so much fun."

She is silent a long moment, watching her siblings disappear down the slope. Then: "Lee? I'm glad you turned out to be a girl."

From the base of the South Pass, a twisty road leads up the Rocky Mountains. It's a well-earned name, because the steep slopes are covered in giant rocks split open and turned on edge every which way, like God started a quarry and got distracted. Major Craven calls it the backbone of America. I tell him it looks more like a backbone breaker.

Our oxen and mules strain to pull the wagons uphill, which turns out to be the easy part. The first downhill slope is so steep that we unhitch the animals and lower the wagons on ropes. We're lucky to make four miles all day.

We repeat the process the next day and the next. The Missouri men lead the way each morning—first out, first up the slope, first down into camp. Their mules move so much faster than our oxen, and I worry that Jefferson was right, that they'll leave us behind someday.

I tell myself that I'm glad they're so far ahead. I hate the way they stare at me now, especially that Jonas Waters.

On the fifth day into the Rockies, the Missouri men are well out of sight by the time we top the first rise. The downward slope is the steepest yet, and mostly gravel, interspersed with dry brush and stunted pines. Peony balks at the path, and I don't blame her. I don't know how we'll get our wagons down safely.

Mr. Joyner and the men all confer, deciding on wagon order. I stand off to the side with the women, too far away to hear what's being said. I kick at pebbles with the toe of my boot, glaring at them as they skitter away.

Finally, the men gather their ropes and gloves and get to work. They tackle the Robichauds' wagon first. Though it's the lightest, it still takes all the men braced together against the ropes to lower it. Reverend Lowrey's wagon goes next. The men pour sweat, and gravel clatters down the slope ahead of the wheels, but the lowering goes smoothly. The dogs sport around at the bottom of the incline while Olive plays tag with Carl and Otto, as if it's a holiday and not the most dangerous part of our journey so far.

Mrs. Hoffman and Therese roll two barrels from the back of one wagon and toss a trunk out of the other. The abandoned goods of previous wagon trains litter the slope too: a box stove toppled onto its side, several broken barrels, spare wagon parts, a dressing table with a cracked mirror. Mrs. Joyner runs a finger over the wooden frame of the discarded mirror. I'm suddenly terrified she'll see everything as a treasure, needing to be rescued.

"You ought to think about doing the same thing," I say quickly. "That big carved headboard, the table and chairs."

She looks back and forth between the dressing table and her own wagon. "I . . . We will not live like savages," she says, but her voice lacks its usual conviction. "It's up to us to bring civilization to California."

"They're just things."

"It's Mr. Joyner's decision."

I hold back a retort. I never know if she says this because she truly believes it, or if she just wants to end the discussion. I stare after her as she gathers her children and waddles down the steep slope to wait.

The Hoffmans' wagons bounce down a little faster but reach the bottom safely. As does the college men's wagon. Morning turns to afternoon. I catch Jefferson staring at his hands. They've become raw from the rope sliding through sweat-slippery palms.

"I have an idea!" Therese says. She runs back to her abandoned trunk and lifts out some linens, which she distributes to everyone who has thin gloves or no gloves at all. Jefferson gives her a grateful smile.

The remaining women and children skid to the bottom. I let Major Craven ride Peony down, on the promise that he'll watch her for me. I remain at the top of the ridge, ready to jump in. Jefferson wipes sweat from his forehead and gives me a nod. But when I look to Mr. Joyner for permission to help, he ignores me.

"C'mon," he says, clapping his hands. "One more wagon to

go. Let's get this done and get back on the road." He whips off his gloves to study his hands. Scabs have ripped off, and when he wipes his palms on one of Therese's linens, they come away bloody.

He re-dons the gloves and lashes the rope around the wagon's tongue so it can be lowered backward. His hands tremble as he knots it, but his face has a fierce determination I've never seen before. This is probably the hardest he's ever worked in his life.

They push the wagon over the lip of the ridge and let it start rolling. It slips forward and then jerks to a stop, slips and then jerks. Jefferson shoots me a worried look.

Permission be damned. I run to the end of the rope, behind Mr. Hoffman, who's the biggest member of our group, and loop it around my waist and brace my legs.

The rope slips again and nearly pulls me off my feet.

"We have to slow it down," Mr. Joyner yells.

Nobody answers. We just grit our teeth and strain as more rope slides through our hands.

Something crashes, splinters apart.

"No!" Mr. Joyner says. The wagon blocks my view, and I don't dare let go to have a look, but I assume some bit of precious furniture has tumbled from the wagon bed.

"Hold on, hold on," Mr. Joyner says. "I'm going to push that dresser out of the way so we can keep lowering it."

"Andrew, no!" Mr. Hoffman yells. I grip the rope with all my strength. My heels start to slide. The veins in Mr. Hoffman's neck bulge.

Jefferson yells, "Hurry!"

"Be careful, darling!" Mrs. Joyner shouts from the bottom of the slope, but she's wasting her breath. She might as well tell a dog not to lick up its own mess.

"Almost got it," Mr. Joyner calls out.

The rope slips again. "Get everyone out of the way *now!*" Jefferson hollers.

The wheels hit a dip. Reverend Lowrey is jerked off his feet. He slams into Jasper, and both of them tumble to their knees. My shoulders wrench, like they're about to pop out of their sockets, and the rope around my waist squeezes the breath from my body. Jefferson and Martin squat low for leverage, but the weight of the wagon drags them to their bottoms. All of us slide slowly, inescapably, dragged by the wagon's weight.

"Get out of the way," I yell at Mr. Joyner.

"Almost got it," he yells back.

Another rut, another lurch. The rope burns through my palms. I roll on the ground, twisting away before it can strangle me. Gravel fills my mouth and scrapes my cheek.

I'm flat on my stomach as I watch, horrified, while the wagon bounces down to the bottom, rope trailing behind. It crashes into a rock, and topples over. The headboard flies out and splinters.

Shakily, I get to my feet, looking for Mr. Joyner. I see the dresser first, a shamble of busted wood and dirtied shirts. Beside it is a man's boot, empty and alone.

"Daddy?" I whisper.

I slide down the hillside, Jasper right behind me. I'm heedless of the gravel imbedding itself into my palms or the tears blurring my vision. I know it's not Daddy, of course it's not, but I'm going to be too late again. I already know what I'll find.

I round the dresser's remains. Mr. Joyner is a broken and bloody mess, lying mashed into the gravel where the wheels rolled over him. He doesn't even look like a person anymore, and I have to turn away.

"Damn fool," Jasper says at my shoulder just as Therese rushes up.

"*Mein Gott,*" she says breathlessly. She must have started sprinting the moment she saw him go down.

My stomach is roiling, but I find my voice. "We have to take him down to Mrs. Joyner."

Jasper wipes sweat from his brow. "You don't have to do this."

"I still work for him," I say.

"I will help you," Therese says in a voice nearer to a squeak.

Jasper gets a grip beneath Mr. Joyner's shoulders. Therese and I each pick up a leg. Slowly, we half carry, half drag what's left of him to the bottom of the hill, preserving as much dignity as we can muster. In my care to avoid looking at the area of his chest and abdomen, I notice the trail of blood that scars the slope behind us.

We reach the bottom, and I look to Mrs. Joyner, expecting to find her inconsolable.

Andy and Olive have disappeared, already ushered away

by some kind soul. Mrs. Joyner just stands there, her hands neatly clasped above her enormous belly, her face as stony as the mountain her husband died on.

There's no digging in this soil, but there are plenty of rocks, so we bury him in a hastily made cairn. Jefferson finds some crooked pine boughs, which he strips and lashes together into a rickety cross. Reverend Lowrey says a few words, but when he starts to sing a psalm, he chokes up and falls silent. We all stare at the pile of rocks, not sure what to do next.

A small voice rises, high and lovely. It's Therese, singing "All Creatures of Our God and King."

Everyone joins in, softly at first, and then with conviction. I hang back as I always do, letting the hymn wash over me. Then I remember that I'm a girl again, and there's no shame in it, so I pick up a verse and let my voice soar above everyone's:

"And thou most kind and gentle Death,
Waiting to hush our latest breath,
Oh praise Him! Alleluia!"

After the last note fades, I glance up to see Reverend Lowrey staring at me, looking a little stunned. Maybe I was too loud, like Annabelle Smith back home.

I turn away from him, my neck prickling, as everyone drifts toward their respective wagons. The college men help Jefferson and me tip the Joyners' wagon upright. Miraculously, nothing's broken that can't be fixed. Even more miraculously, Mrs. Joyner's dining table, the one she always covers with fine china and a checked tablecloth, does not have a single scratch on it, even though it tumbled out of the wagon and landed upside down.

I'm shaking with exhaustion, and I could use something to eat, but I would rather keep busy to avoid the images in my head. "Jefferson, can you help me with the furniture?" The sooner we get loaded, the sooner we can leave this place.

"Leave it behind."

Mrs. Joyner stands there, holding the hands of her children, one on either side. Olive is carefully matching her mother's grim expression. Andy's face is red from crying, and his bottom lip trembles. His chubby hand is fisted at his chest. He's clutching my locket like his life depends on it.

"Beg your pardon?" Jefferson says.

"It's junk. Worthless. Take what we need to finish the journey and dump the rest."

I'm careful to keep the surprise off my face. "Yes, ma'am."

She pries her children's hands from her own and strides over to the wagon, where everything lies scattered and spilled. She picks up Mr. Joyner's rifle and shoves it into my hands.

"Your contract is with me now," she says. Looking at Jefferson, she adds: "Both of your contracts. Same conditions as before."

"With back wages to Independence?" I ask.

"To the start of the journey, with no interruption of service."

"That'll do." I pause. "Do we need to . . . shake on it?"

"Please," she says brusquely. "We ladies can manage an agreement without spitting into our palms." She turns away and crouches to comfort Andy.

"Well, I'll be," Jefferson whispers.

"I wouldn't mind rescuing that one table for her," I say. "And the tablecloth."

He nods. "I'll help."

Chapter Twenty-Nine

$\mathcal{I}$t's nighttime, with a waning moon to light my view. It took us three days to catch up to the Missouri men, but catch up we did, and we are now camped in a beautiful grove between the Soda Springs, which bubbles gently with soda water, and Steamboat Spring, which shoots steam high into the air. Reverend Lowrey has been telling the little ones that demons' work engines are hidden underground. But I think anything so wondrous must be the work of angels.

The springs whoosh and spout while I lie hidden beneath a cottonwood tree, my rifle aimed at our wagon. I'm covered with brush, which makes me itch, and I fight the temptation to scratch the back of my neck. At least the itching keeps me awake. I've been lying here for hours, watching, seeing nothing. But that's all right. I am patient.

The regular theft of supplies has continued. Since Mr. Joyner died, we've twice awakened to discover that the loaf of bread Widow Joyner cooked overnight in the Dutch oven is gone. Last night, Widow Joyner prepared another loaf and left it sitting by the coals. I could never shoot an Indian, or any man, but I plan to catch someone in the act and be as frightful as possible.

Jefferson sleeps beneath the Joyner wagon. He promised to jump up at my warning cry and help me make a dreadful racket. If the thief doesn't come tonight, we'll swap places tomorrow; Jefferson will keep watch while I sleep with my rifle beside me.

Yawning, I break off another piece of chicory root and put it my mouth. Chewing it floods my tongue with invigorating bitterness.

I expect our thieves to approach from outside the camp, so I almost miss two dark shapes creeping among the animals inside our wagon corral. I shift my rifle in their direction.

They're not Indians; I can tell even in the dark. Their silhouettes are rumpled and bulky, like argonauts. One wears a broad-brimmed straw hat, just like the one worn by Henry Meek.

Coney is curled up in his usual spot between Peony's front legs. He lifts his head as the shapes approach. The man with the hat crouches to scratch his ears, and Coney thumps his tail before lowering his heads back to his paws. My low opinion of the dogs' guarding abilities is somewhat mitigated. At least they know friend from foe.

The men glance around and tiptoe over to the cook fire. The one in the hat bends to remove the Dutch oven's lid.

I rise from my hiding place. The loose brush and sage

drop away like a dead skin. "Stop right there, Henry Meek, or I will shoot you and your companion." My voice is clear but soft; I don't want to wake Jefferson or alert anyone else before I hear Henry's explanation.

They turn to face me, and I'm the one who jumps in surprise.

With Henry is Hampton, the slave who belonged to Mr. Bledsoe from Arkansas.

"I thought you ran away," I whisper.

"I'm still running away," he whispers back.

Henry puts a finger to his lips and gestures for Hampton and me to follow. He grabs Widow Joyner's bread loaf and leads us away.

I follow warily, past the Soda Springs and down an incline. Once we're out of sight, we huddle in a small grove of birch trees. The stolen blanket is wrapped around Hampton's shoulders.

"What's going on?" I ask. "And talk fast before I decide to rouse the camp."

Henry offers a chunk of bread to Hampton, who grabs it and shoves it into his mouth. He gulps it down without chewing. After a long sigh, he says, "I'm going to California to find gold, same as you."

"But . . ." I close my mouth. I'm not exactly sure what my protestation is.

Hampton continues, "I'll send every speck of it back to Arkansas. Buy my freedom, clear and legal. Maybe I can buy freedom for my wife too."

Can't blame him for that. If I still had folks back home, I'd do everything in my power to have them with me again.

"No man should have to pay for his freedom," Henry says. "It's a natural right—'life, liberty, and the pursuit of happiness.' So we've been helping him as much as we can." He tears off another piece and offers the loaf to me. "Go on," he says. "Take a bite. In the spirit of true Christian communion."

I'm not sure what makes me take it. The bread is still warm when I put it in my mouth. "I wish you fellows still had Athena. Some butter would make even Widow Joyner's bread taste good." But I feel wrong. I'm eating stolen bread.

Henry smiles at me. I don't return his smile as I pass the loaf back to Hampton. "I guess the rest is yours."

"I'm sorry we took from you," Henry says. "But our rations are running low. We've been helping Wally since his leg came off. Frank Dilley 'lost' most of Wally's supplies right after his leg was broken. We've used every persuasion at our disposal, but he remains unmoved."

"But Widow Joyner's eating for two, and . . ." Even in the dark, I can see how much thinner Hampton has become since he left us.

"I wanted to tell you," Henry says. "But you being from Georgia, I just didn't know how—"

"I love Georgia, but I've never held with slavery." I scuff my boots in the dirt. "My daddy raised me right."

"Sounds like a good man," Henry says.

"He was."

"My congressman spoke several times at Illinois College,"

Henry says. "Made an abolitionist of me, that's for sure. He says we'll have to end slavery if we want to keep the country together. Not a lot I can do about that, way out west, but I figure I can help one man."

Hampton is hanging his head. I hope his thieving ways don't set well with him. "I'd rather take from Frank Dilley and his people," he says. "But they pack everything up tight and keep an extra guard."

"We're lucky they never caught you trying," Henry says.

Hampton nods. "Some of them—like Waters, Dilley's foreman—well, they're slave catchers. They get hold of me, I'm done for."

"And we don't want that," Henry adds.

Hampton stretches out his bare feet, and I wince. His thick calluses are cracked and dry.

"We've a long way to go," I say. "The Major says the hardest part is still ahead. Hundreds and hundreds of miles, some of it through desert, with no water and no fuel."

"I'll follow behind like a ghost," Hampton says. "You won't even know I'm here."

"But now I do," I say.

"Now you do," Hampton agrees. He and Henry stare at me, waiting to see what I'll do.

"You've done wrong, Hampton."

He doesn't argue, but his face screws up tight.

"No man should be a slave, but no man should be a thief either."

I think I've spoken fairly, but it makes him angry. "Can't

steal my labor from me my whole life and then accuse me of theft."

I open my mouth to protest but think better of it. Was I stealing from Uncle Hiram when I took my own possessions and Daddy's colts besides? No one could convince me so. And while I can dress up like a boy and earn my way on a wagon train, there's no way for Hampton to dress up like a free man.

"I never thought of it that way before," I say finally.

Henry leans forward. "So are we all in accord here?"

I nod, even though I don't like it one bit.

After a pause, Hampton meets my eye and nods too. For better or worse, I'm now part of their conspiracy.

"I have an idea," I say. "Why don't you send Major Craven over to help the Widow Joyner? He can drive the wagon, watch the little ones, repair the shoes they've outgrown—"

"Cook," suggests Henry.

"And cook. We'll feed him, and it won't be a such a burden on your supplies." I glance at Hampton. "This stealing has her afraid for her life. She thinks she'll be murdered in her sleep and her children stolen from her. She's got enough trouble and doesn't need the extra strain." I know it for falseness as soon as it leaves my mouth. Widow Joyner's strain is nothing compared to Hampton's, and it never will be. Quickly, I add, "If people catch you following along, there might be mercy. If they catch you stealing, you'll be sold at best, strung up at worst. You know it as well as I do."

"I'll talk to Wally," Henry says.

"Good." I slip my canteen strap over my head, open the lid, and take a drink. Then I hand it to Hampton. A peace offering. "It's not communion if there's no wine."

Hampton tips it to his lips and swallows long and hard. He wipes his mouth when he's done. "Well, darn. The Savior got confused and turned this wine into water."

"The Lord works in mysterious ways," Henry says, taking the canteen from Hampton. He sips and offers it to me.

I put my hands up in refusal and look at Hampton. "Do you have something to carry water in?"

"No, sir," he says.

"No, ma'am," Henry corrects him.

"I know," Hampton says. "I mean, sorry, ma'am. He told me about your situation. It's just that you act like a sir."

"It's fine," I say. "I'd rather be treated with respect than treated like a lady."

Hampton presses his lips together into a firm line, like I've said something stupid and bothersome again, though I don't know what.

"Keep the canteen," I say. "Otherwise, you'll never make it across the desert ahead."

I get to my feet and shake dry grass from my trousers. "I would have given you something to eat if I'd known," I say.

He nods acknowledgment.

Henry and I decide to walk back to camp separately. When I get there, Jefferson is awake and hunkered over the cook pot. He looks up as I approach. "They got it again!"

"I know," I say. "I must have dozed off. Maybe next time,

we'll . . ." Jefferson's gaze on me is open and honest and trusting and the very last thing I deserve. "Blast."

"What?"

I tug on his sleeve, pulling him away from the wagon circle. Once we're out of earshot, I whisper: "The truth is, it was Hampton. The runaway slave. He's been following us."

Jefferson's eyes widen.

"The college men will take care of him from now on, in secret. In return, we have to coax Major Craven to join our wagon. He could be a big help to Mrs. Joyner."

Jefferson mulls that over for a moment. He glances eastward, as if expecting Hampton to materialize on the horizon.

I brace myself for his protest. Instead, he says, "So much for that bread. I guess we'll have burned flapjacks for breakfast. Again."

I smile gratefully. "I reckon we'll survive. Let's go see if the Major wants to come help with the cooking."

We stop to resupply at Fort Hall, which is less of a fort and more of a trading post consisting of two rickety blockhouses and a small stable. A constant stream of humanity flows through: trappers, Indians, argonauts, and settlers. It's too many people. After being in the wilderness so long, I can hardly breathe.

California is bound to feel crowded too. Maybe that's a good thing. With Hiram looking for me, the last thing I want to be is uncommon or noteworthy.

The meadows nearby are dotted with tents and wagons

and even a few teepees, but otherwise, filled with lush, fast-growing grass. We let the cattle and mules graze freely to regain their strength. Meanwhile, we take our laundry down to the hot springs. I wear Lucie Robichaud's skirt again while I scrub the rest of my clothes against Mrs. Joyner's washboard.

Now that Mrs. Joyner knows I'm a girl, she has no problem assigning everyone's laundry to me, and I spend the whole day scrubbing and scrubbing, until my hands are red and chapped and I can't feel my fingertips. I almost never did laundry back home in Georgia. While I was out helping Daddy, Mama must have done a lot of work that I took for granted. Now I understand what Therese meant by wanting to give her hands a chance to heal.

Near the trading post is a military encampment made up of low tents. On our second day at Fort Hall, their leader, General Loring, rides out to speak with the wagon companies. He's younger than I would expect for a general, despite his long beard. One of his sleeves swings empty at his side; someone whispers that he lost an arm in the Mexican War. He dismounts from his giant roan gelding and walks among us, making conversation. His uniform shows the same dirt and wear as the common soldiers'.

"You ought to go to Oregon," he tells Frank Dilley. "California is filled with bad men—runaways and thieves. The gold will be gone in a year or two, but good rich soil lasts forever. You can pass that down to your children."

Their conversation attracts attention. The rest of the Missouri men gather around. A few Mormons bound for Salt

Lake trickle over from another company. Even Reverend Lowrey and Mr. Robichaud creep closer, ears pricked.

"Any saloon is happy to take my gold," Frank says. "But I always get the boot when I try to pay with buckets of soil."

His men laugh, and even I can't help cracking a grin.

The general turns toward Lowrey and Robichaud. "What about it? Some of you look like farmers. There's wonderful farming in the Willamette Valley. It's good country for raising families."

A few women have gathered too—me, Mrs. Hoffman, Lucie, some Mormons. His eyes skim over us like we're not even here, which is fine by me. I'm bound for California or bust, no matter what he says.

But Frank Dilley jerks a thumb at me. "Better aim your sermon at that one," he says. "I reckon Georgia there wears the pants in that company."

Jonas Waters chortles like it's the funniest thing. "And never have I seen pants worn so finely!" he adds.

The general gives me a puzzled look. My face flushes hot, but I keep my peace.

"I can see you're all set in your ways," the general says. "But since you're a mixed company, with women present, let me warn you: We had a situation here a few weeks ago, where an Indian offered a man three horses in exchange for one of his daughters. The settler joked that if the Indian gave him six, it was a deal. This joke, as it were, at his daughter's expense, nearly led to bloodshed, when the Indian came back with the horses."

"That must be how the half-breed got hold of *her*," Frank says, loud enough for everyone to hear. Jefferson leaps forward, but I grab his arm and yank him back.

"Ignore him," I tell him. "Dilley's a toad."

Jefferson's jaw is clenched tight, and his eyes flash darkly. For the briefest moment, he looks just like his da.

"He'll get his in time," Jasper says.

"I think the time is right now," Jefferson says, but the fight trickles out of him, and he backs down.

"See what I said about wearing the pants?" Frank haws.

The general goes on for a fair bit, and all the men pay close attention. Except Reverend Lowrey, who keeps glancing my way.

As evening falls, we pack up our gear to depart in the morning. Therese and I are taking clothes down from the laundry line stretched between the Joyner and Hoffman wagons.

"Look at this!" she says in disgust, waving a dark gray stocking at me. "Luther put a hole in it again. Too big to be darned. If he trimmed his toenails once in a while, I wouldn't have to do so much knitting."

"I don't know how to knit," I admit.

She gapes at me, but she schools her expression quickly. "Well, I would be happy to teach you. No, on second thought . . ." She leans forward and drops her voice. "If you learned, Mrs. Joyner would make you knit your way to California."

I giggle, glancing Mrs. Joyner's way to make sure she didn't overhear. "I bet you're right." I grab a table napkin from the clothesline and shake it out. If I fold it now, while it's still sun-warmed, Mrs. Joyner might not insist it be pressed. "But will you teach me to knit later?" I ask. "When we get to California?"

Therese smiles. "Of course."

Someone clears his throat, and I turn to find Reverend Lowery bearing down on us.

"Miss McCollin," he says, not even knowing my name. "If I could have a private word with you?"

Therese's eyebrows rise. She turns away quickly, but not before I notice how hard she is trying not to laugh. I stare at her back, puzzled.

"Go on, Lee," Mrs. Joyner calls from her place by the cook fire. Her tone is smug. Like she knows something I don't.

"All right," I say to the preacher. "But let's be quick about it. I've got work to do."

We step away from the wagons as the sun is dipping below the horizon. The damp summer breeze has a bite of sulfur, thanks to the hot springs. We're nearly to the river before we stop. Reverend Lowrey stands quietly a moment in his best black suit, like a crow. He clutches his Bible in one hand.

"Leah," he says, eyes lowered. "Today's admonitions from General Loring brought to mind my own serious neglect of duty, and I wanted to apologize to you."

"Huh?"

"Long have I indulged in grief at the loss of Mrs. Lowrey,

and thus failed to see God's plan and purpose. I deeply regret the hurt I've done you, in your condition."

I recoil a step, even though I have no idea what he means. "What exactly is my condition?"

His gaze is earnest. "That of a young woman, alone in the world, with no man for protection."

"I've done a fair job of protecting myself."

He waves his hand like a teacher erasing a chalkboard. "Everyone knows how diligently you toil. You are, in fact, an exemplary worker, and when you apply those exertions to duties more befitting your gender, to housekeeping and raising children, you'll make a fine wife."

"I guess."

"What I'm trying to say is, I see our Father's hand at work. You, all alone in the world—"

"I'm not alone." I didn't realize it until this very moment, but it's true. "I've got Jefferson, and Jasper and Tom and Henry. I've got Widow Joyner and her children. The Robichauds and the Hoffmans. I am"—a touch of wonder fills my voice—"blessed with friends."

The reverend scowls—he's not a man used to being contradicted. "God took my beloved Mary because he has a purpose in mind for you. Our Heavenly Father, and myself—all of us—want what's best for you. God has cultivated within me a miraculous affection for your spirited ways and comely eyes. He wants you to find the right man to marry. That man is standing before you this very moment."

My jaw drops open. This is even worse than Jefferson's

proposal, and Jefferson had the excuse of no experience. A *miraculous affection?*

Finally, I find words: "Oh, hell no."

He steps closer, looms over me. "I know you . . . carry on . . . with Jefferson. Under the wagon at night."

I hold my ground. "*What?*"

"But I forgive you, my Gomer. I am your Hosea, and I will redeem you. Surely you see how unsuitable Jefferson—"

"What about Jefferson?"

"I don't wish to allude to his parentage, as that is something over which he has no control."

I lean forward so that I'm right in his face. "If you don't wish to allude, then you'd better stop talking."

He retreats a step. "I'm neither impugning his good qualities nor denigrating his character."

"You are! You are definitely impugning and denigrating."

He holds up his Bible with both hands, like it's a shield. "Let me start over again. What I'm trying to say is, Leah, it's not our place to question God's will, and it is clearly God's will that the two of us become man and wife."

It's a testament to my fine character that I don't smash that Bible right into his nose. "You wouldn't know God's will if it tipped its hat and said howdy. My answer to you now is *no* and will always be *no*." I turn to walk away but pause. "Because you've been grieving, I'm going to forget you said anything to me tonight. But I don't want you to bring it up again. Ever."

I stomp back to the wagons hard enough to shake the ground.

Widow Joyner is repacking a trunk with clean clothes when I return. She looks up as I approach, and her expectant smile instantly disappears. "What happened?"

"The reverend and I had a theological disagreement that ended in a permanent schism."

"So . . . no congratulations are in order?"

In answer, I lift the toolbox and slam it onto the wagon. I have too much to do to let that preacher waste any more of my time.

Jefferson is returning from the meadow where he's been keeping an eye on the oxen. "Hey, Lee, will you—"

"I don't want to talk right now." I grab the grease bucket and crawl under the wagon to check the wheels.

Men. And their no-good, fool-headed proposals.

Chapter Thirty

The next morning, Fort Hall shrinks rapidly behind us. The animals have eaten their fill for the first time in weeks, if not months. The size of our company has doubled, because it now includes a group of settlers headed for Oregon, who will travel with us for a short while.

Major Craven tips his hat to me from the jockey box of the Joyners' wagon. He took Henry's suggestion, and Widow Joyner eagerly embraced it. That leaves me and Peony free to make our own way. I'm wearing Lucie's skirt, but I have trousers on underneath so I can ride without raising too many eyebrows. Everyone I pass is cheerful and energized, waving and smiling.

Everyone but me. My return smiles are forced, and I find myself drifting farther and farther from the line of wagons, wanting a little open air to myself.

Jefferson and the sorrel mare come up beside us, and it's fine as long as he's quiet. Then he says, "Hey, Lee—"

"I don't feel like talking or listening."

"All right."

I'm being unkind, but I can't help it. I stare after him as he rides over to the Hoffmans' wagon, and I'm screwing up my courage to apologize and explain, when he turns around and rides back, wearing a scowl as big as the western sky.

"They didn't want to listen either," he says.

I say nothing. I'm not sure I made the right choice in the Robichauds' wagon. Now that I'm a girl, I'm treated like I'm nobody again, to be owned or herded or strung along, so helpless and awful that I must be redeemed or married off because it's convenient for someone. And it doesn't matter whether their intentions are wicked, like my uncle Hiram's, or good—more or less—like Reverend Lowrey's. It doesn't even matter if it's my best friend in the whole world.

It's possible the person I'm most steamed at is Mrs. Joyner. She knew the reverend was going to propose. It didn't matter that she desperately needs my help. It didn't even matter that we have a contract. She was ready to hand me right over to that self-righteous son of a goat.

Just like the folks back home in Dahlonega. They were relieved when Uncle Hiram showed up to take charge of me and my homestead.

There's not a place in the whole world where everyone isn't willing—no, *eager*—to give a girl up to a man. I don't want to be a boy again. I hate lying. But when I get to California, I might not have a choice—not if I want to belong only to myself.

At noon we cross Ford Creek. The grass is still good, and we let the animals graze for an extra half hour before continuing. By nightfall we reach the bluff above the Raft River and make camp. I spend extra time with Peony, making sure she's fed and watered and thoroughly brushed. Since the Major joined our wagon, the families have started taking meals together. I'm still in no mood for company, so I put off joining them until I see the Robichauds seated around the fire. The Robichauds have always treated me well, no matter what I'm wearing. Lucie is the one who said I could be whoever I want.

"Saved some for you," the Major says, handing me a tin cup with beef and onion soup.

"Thanks," I mumble, and go sit beside Lucie.

"I'm glad you came back," she says to me.

"There's nowhere else to go out there," I say.

"No, I mean, tonight. Tomorrow morning is our parting of the ways."

I choke on my food. "What?"

"We've decided to head north for Oregon."

"But why?"

Mr. Robichaud wipes his mouth with a kerchief. "General Loring made some good points yesterday. We're looking for a better country to raise our sons. California sounds lawless and dangerous."

"The world is dangerous," I say, my voice shrill. Lucie puts a gentle hand on my knee, which makes me feel worse.

"It is," Mr. Robichaud says. "Our family has made it this

far without any losses." He nods toward the Major, or maybe the Joyners. "Things are going to get worse before they get better for this group. With the cruelest part of the road ahead, we don't want to push our luck."

"But what about the gold?"

He puts an arm around his wife. "Family is more important than gold."

But you're my *family,* I want to say. They showed me kindness when no one else did. They kept my secret without a second thought.

I get to my feet and start undoing the buttons of Lucie's yellow calico skirt. Several of the men avert their gazes. From the direction of the Missouri wagons comes a high whistle.

"Stop, please," Lucie says.

"I've got on trousers," I say.

"No, I want you to keep it. You're so pretty in it."

"I can't!" I say. "It'll just remind me of you and make me sad every time I see it." I kick my way out of it, yank it up off the ground, fold it messily, and shove it into her hands. "Sorry I don't have time to wash it."

"It's fine," Lucie says.

There are tears in her eyes, and then there are tears in mine. She throws her arms around me and gives me such a hug. Not like Mama. I was my mama's little girl, and she always held me gently, like I was precious and fragile. Lucie's hug is fierce, as if I can't be broken, and I hug her back just as tight.

She lets go, pushing the skirt into my hands. "Even if you never wear it again. Just so you remember me."

"I . . . *Merci*," I whisper, and hope she knows I'm not just saying it about the skirt.

Her husband stands, saying, "Guess we ought to be going."

Everybody says good-bye and shakes hands and makes promises to visit one another when they make it to Oregon or California, but nobody expects to keep those promises, and it's writ all over everyone's faces that we'll never see one another again.

When I roll out my blanket outside the wagon circle, I take Lucie's skirt and fold it up under my knapsack pillow. I lie on my back, and I don't acknowledge Jefferson when he settles down next to me. I stare at the clear sky and all the cold stars and think about how far away they are.

Jefferson says, "I'm sad to see them go."

He sounds so lonesome that my impulse to tell him to shut his trap dribbles away. "Yeah."

"Mr. Hoffman has forbidden me from talking to Therese."

"What?" I flip over. "Why?"

Jefferson is lying on his back, his head toward the Joyner wagon. I glance over too, my shout echoing in my head as I brace for Mr. Joyner's thump—which, of course, doesn't come.

I lower my voice anyway. "Why?"

"Frank Dilley told them I'd been the one stealing. He said I was giving it all to my red-skinned brothers."

"No one who knows you would believe that."

"Mr. Hoffman said he couldn't ignore the accusation. He said he needed to think on it a bit."

I roll onto my back to stare at the sky again, because my heart aches too much when I look at Jefferson's face, even in the dark. "I should have let you bust Frank Dilley's nose," I say.

"That would have made things worse," he says.

"But it would have been a pleasure to watch."

Major Craven's tent is only about ten feet away. He coughs and rustles around inside. The wagon creaks beside us as Mrs. Joyner shifts her weight. Muted laughter comes from the bachelors' wagon.

Jefferson whispers, "Why've you been so mad, Lee?"

I sigh, not sure what to say. A cricket chirrups nearby. Such a cheerful sound, which makes me even grumpier. "Reverend Lowrey proposed marriage to me."

"What?" It's his turn to shout.

"It was the most unromantic proposal a girl could have. Which was good. Because until it happened, I thought *yours* was the most unromantic."

"I—"

"Hey, Lee, maybe we can pretend we're brother and sister," I mock.

"Yes, but—"

"Is it wrong to want to be wanted?"

"No, but—"

"You wanted me to help you escape and go west. Uncle Hiram wanted me—*wants* me—because of . . . because he's greedy. Reverend Lowrey wanted to pat himself on the back for rescuing a soul. It's like I'm not really a person. Just a thing to be tossed around to make men feel good about themselves."

I hear him breathing softly beside me. Finally, he says, "That's not why I asked you."

"Doesn't matter anymore, does it?" I say. "You're sweet on Therese now, even if you can't talk to her. I don't blame you one bit. She's wonderful."

Jefferson shifts beneath his blanket. Suddenly, his warm fingers slip between my own, and it's like lightning zipping up my arm.

"I do like Therese," he admits. "But she's not you. No one is you, Leah."

My next words get lost trying to find their way from my head to my mouth.

Jefferson's thumb makes little circles on the back of my hand. My throat tightens, and all my limbs tingle, like I've just struck the purest, brightest vein of gold. Neither of us lets go.

The Major starts snoring in his tent. The dogs trot by, panting, as they return from whatever mischief they've been in.

I reach with my other hand for Lucie's skirt. I finger the fabric, telling myself that the family we find can still be family, even when they're far away. With one hand in Jefferson's, the other clinging to Lucie's skirt, I finally drift to sleep.

In the morning, when the wagon trains split and go their separate ways, I wait alongside the trail, so Lucie can see what I'm wearing.

Chapter Thirty-One

The hot sun beats down on me. It's at least a hundred degrees. There's no shade, no cool breeze, no escape. Sweat wicks off my skin faster than it forms, leaving everything caked with salt. My lips are cracked, my tongue swollen and dry. The sun is so bright it bleaches the color out of everything. I've never felt this hot, not even standing over Mama's stove in my winter dress with the fire fully stoked.

All I can think about is that cold day last January when Jefferson stood behind the schoolhouse, surrounded by melting snow, holding a copy of the paper announcing gold in California.

The article made it seem like we were called to some great national purpose, a destiny so manifest that it was inevitable we should pack up and cross the continent. The discussion of travel routes, by sea and land, made us feel a part of some greater strategy. The instructions, the lists of supplies—they all felt like foolproof plans that would protect us and deliver us safely.

But the strategy does not matter, and our plans will not protect us.

In the end, it's nothing complicated, or grand, or beautiful. It's no more than the simple act of aiming in a direction and putting one aching foot in front of another across a baking desert until we either reach our destination or falter and quit.

Or die. We've lost too many people already. I look around at the families nearby, all trudging along with the same heat-glazed determination—the Hoffmans, the Joyners, the college men. My heart would break if we lost even one more soul.

"Another ox down!" comes the cry ahead of me.

This time it's the bachelors' wagon. Jefferson, Therese, and I run to help. Jeff reaches the exhausted animal first and unyokes it. The ox staggers free, barely able to stay on its feet.

Jefferson pulls down the bandanna that protects his mouth and nose from the relentless dust. "What do we do with it?" he asks Jasper. "Do you want me to put it on a lead?"

"No," he says. "Let it follow the wagons if it can. If it can't, then good luck to it."

Jefferson and Jasper stare at each other a moment. Jefferson's face has a hardness to it, like that of a man twice his age. At last he says, "I'm going to butcher it."

Jasper nods once and turns away.

"Jeff, no!" Therese says, putting a hand on his arm. It's the closest they've been since Mr. Hoffman forbade them to speak to each other. "I can't eat one of the oxen. I just can't."

The look he turns on her is fierce. "You can and you will, if it comes to that. But it's not for us. Not yet."

"Then . . ."

"Nugget and Coney," I explain. "We have no water to spare. There's no fresh game. If we keep sneaking pieces of flapjack to them, letting them drink from our own canteens, Dilley will put them down."

"Oh," she says, her face blanching with the realization that it's not the meat Jefferson wants to save so much as the blood. She stares at the poor creature. Its ribs are stark and sharp, its sides heaving. "Just make it quick."

"Of course." He pulls his knife from his belt.

We resume our plodding journey. Jefferson stands beside the ox, waiting for us to get out of sight before doing the deed.

All the animals are struggling. For the last three hundred miles, the ground has been hard and rocky, wearing out joints and splitting hooves. Jefferson and I walk all the time now, to spare our horses. He might be sneaking his water rations to the dogs, but most of mine are going to Peony. I won't lose her, no matter what.

Dust coats our trail, sometimes gravelly and coarse, sometimes fine as flour. We wear kerchiefs over our noses, but I still chew grit all day. My eyes crust over every night, and I wake each morning to find them blurry and swollen. The back of my throat is a patch of desert. My lungs burn. Andy started coughing a few days ago and hasn't stopped. And all day long the sun pours fire on our heads.

The occasional grass is rough and sparse, and the mules ahead of us eat the best of it. Whenever I find a missed clump, I yank it up for Peony or the sorrel mare. We burn sagebrush for fuel, but it turns to ash too fast for proper cooking. My belly aches from eating little more than prickly pear.

Our trail follows the lazy Humboldt River, which was lovely and clear at first, but the water has slowed and thickened until it's little more than a marsh, and too brackish to drink. We soak our kerchiefs in it to keep out more dust, but that's all it's good for. The poor oxen drink it until they fall down sick. Soon enough, we'll start drinking it too.

"Wagon train ahead," calls Major Craven from the bench. I crane my neck. The Missouri wagons are taking a short break, circled near a wide puddle. Men and animals alike stand knee-deep in the water to cool off. With a start, I realize we've come to the end of the river.

"This godforsaken trickle of a river just ends," Therese says. "It turns into *nothing*."

"Know what we'll find when we get there?" Craven says.

"All the good grass eaten and all the best water drunk or gone?" she says.

"Besides that."

"I don't know."

"We'll find them packing up to leave without us," he says.

Therese mutters a few words under her breath that I'm pretty sure she learned from Frank Dilley.

As our weary group of five wagons—two for the Hoffmans, one for Reverend Lowrey, one for the college men, and one for the Joyners—rolls into the camp, Dilley steps up onto an abandoned trunk to address everyone.

"Fifteen minutes until we roll out again," he calls out.

"Fifteen minutes?" I can't believe my ears. "We need longer than that."

"We can't afford to wait. That's fifty-four miles of waterless desert ahead of us. We're going to go straight through, day and night, until we reach the other side."

"Which is why we need more than fifteen minutes," I insist.

"Don't get your skirts in a twist, Georgia. Just take it or leave it. We've cut most of the grass already, but there's a bit left on the other side of the sink."

I lead Peony through the water, muttering curse words that would make my mama ashamed. Peony snorts and kicks up her knees to splash water onto her baking hide. On the other side, we find an abandoned wagon, its wood splintering from the heat. Its shade has allowed a large clump of grass to thrive unnoticed. I let Peony free to graze.

Major Craven gestures for everyone to gather round, so I hurry back to the wagons. "We need to figure out what to do next," he says. Jefferson and the dogs catch up just then. Nugget and Coney are bouncing with their recent meal, tails wagging and ears pricked.

"Our oxen are weak," Mr. Hoffman says gravely. "We're going to put everything in one wagon, leave the other behind. They should be able to pull us through. Maybe we'll have enough to start over, once we get to California."

The Hoffmans definitely have enough to start over, if the gold I've sensed is any indication.

"That's smart," Major Craven says. He looks at the college men, and they look at me. They've got something planned.

"Therese took the boys downstream to cut and bundle any grass they find," Mr. Hoffman says. "But we don't mean to take it all. We'll share."

We nod in thanks. It saves time to have his children do the work.

Reverend Lowrey says, "This is the last water we'll see for days. The Missouri men have fires already going. We should mix dough now, cook all our flour into bread, so we can feed it to the animals while we cross."

It's the most sensible thing I've ever heard him say. "Can we do it in fifteen minutes?" I ask.

"I've got baking soda left—I can make quick bread if I get started now," he says.

"That's a good plan," Jasper says.

The reverend runs off to his wagon.

"I'll go mix up whatever we have left," Henry says. "It's not a lot."

"What about the Widow Joyner?" the Major asks.

I shake my head. He knows the answer. "She's as big as a house that's about to give birth to a woodshed," I say. "The road's been shaking her hard for days. She's in no shape to cook."

"I know that," the Major says. "What I'm asking is, her

being a particular sort of lady, do you think she'll mind if I interrupt her to get the flour out of the wagon?"

How should I know? I say, "I'm sure she'll understand."

He looks unconvinced. Major Craven has been considerate and respectful around Mrs. Joyner, but I've no doubt that dealing with a sharp-tongued widow is a lot harder than he expected.

"I'll help carry the barrel," Tom says.

They head off together.

Jefferson says, "I'll go find . . . something to burn, I guess."

"I'll help you," I say, but Jasper grabs my arm before I can turn away.

"How are your oxen?" His voice is urgent.

"Down to six. Two are weak. All in all, holding up better than I expected. Mr. Joyner had a good eye for animals, and he bought the hardiest stock he could find."

"We've got four left, and they're almost played out."

I nod. He's not telling me anything I haven't seen.

"You've got the strongest oxen," he says. "We've got the lighter wagon. Our chances are better for getting across the desert in one shot if we combine them. Ten animals, one light wagon."

He's right. Except . . . "But the Widow Joyner, she's going to come down sick anytime now."

"She can have the back of the wagon when she needs it. We'll just have to make space. Major Craven says he can walk with his crutch. The rest of us are already walking."

"Why are you asking *me* about this?" I say.

"Because you can talk to her, woman to woman, and explain things."

I frown. Seems to me that men only say things like this when they want to get out of doing something unpleasant. "I'll tell her the plan, but it's up to her. I won't make her do anything she doesn't want to do."

"Fair enough," Jasper says.

I circle around to the rear of Widow Joyner's wagon and knock on the board like I'm calling at a fancy house.

"Yes" comes her voice.

I pull open the flap. She sits propped up on her mattress, hands wrapped around her belly as if to protect it. Her blond bun is skewed, and her hair is sweat-plastered to her head. Andy and Olive huddle at her feet, looking frightened but too listless from the heat to do anything about it.

"Jasper wants to combine our efforts to cross the desert. Our oxen, his wagon," I say. "I told him I can't make any promises, but—"

"Do it," Widow Joyner says. She takes a deep breath and closes her eyes. "The Major and Tom came by for our baking supplies. They hinted at the plan. It makes sense."

"All right. We're going to make the shift quickly."

"Speed is of the essence," she says with a wan smile.

"We'll be back to move you shortly." It's odd; Mrs. Lowrey was walking alongside her wagon right up until the day she died in childbirth. Widow Joyner hasn't walked in a week.

I hop down from the back of the wagon, turn around,

and jump five feet in the air—Jefferson is standing right in front of me.

"I thought you were looking for something to burn."

"And I found it. Right here. This wood's so dry it ought to burn hot and clean."

I can't argue with that. "Let's get the oxen into the water before we move them to the other wagon."

All we do is unyoke them, and they rush into the water of their own accord. Once they taste it, they low pitifully enough to break your heart into a thousand pieces, but they drink up.

Therese and her little brothers return carrying three large bundles of cut grass. "Vati says these are for your animals." She and Jefferson exchange a furtive look. The three of us walk together every single day, and she and Jefferson still talk to each other casually, though they're careful not to get too close. So far, her father hasn't made a fuss.

"Thank you," I say. "We'll put them in the wagon."

"No, we can load it." She leads her brothers off, casting another longing glance Jefferson's way. I don't blame her; he's become quite a sight. His thick black hair curls slightly at the nape, framing a strong jaw—inherited from his Irish da— that balances his sharp cheekbones perfectly. His sleeves are rolled up, exposing muscled forearms burnished dark with sunshine.

Therese's eyes catch mine.

"I'm ready," someone says.

I turn around. Widow Joyner stands in the back of her

wagon, ready to topple over the edge. The children's heads pop up behind her like prairie dogs.

I hurry over to help. So does Henry Meek. Together, we carry her to their wagon and raise her gently inside. Olive clambers over the backboard to be with her mother. Andy reaches up with his arms, so I lift him and give him a quick snug before putting him beside his sister.

"What do you want from the wagon?" I ask Mrs. Joyner.

"Food and water," she says. "And the small trunk—the one with my initials. Nothing else."

I gather all the supplies, but I grab her red-checked tablecloth too. I waste a precious moment gazing at the dining table, silently saying good-bye.

Cracks splinter the air as Jefferson attacks the Joyners' wagon with an ax. The Major feeds the pieces into his fire to bake his bread. I run over to take one last reading from Mr. Joyner's road-o-meter.

"Sixteen hundred eighty-seven," I say.

"What's that?" asks Jefferson.

"The number of miles this wagon has traveled since Independence."

"Is that all? I was worried it might be a lot."

"We aren't done yet," I point out.

Across the camp, Frank Dilley and his men are combining their own wagons. Like us, they're leaving half of them behind. Unlike us, they've packed the remaining wagons with pickaxes and shovels and mining supplies. I'll have to witch up some gold to pay for our own equipment.

"Are our fifteen minutes up yet?" I yell at him.

"You've got a few more if you want to come with us," he says.

I turn to Jasper. "What do you think? Do we hurry up so we can leave with them?"

"The oxen go faster, more consistently, when they see other wagons in front of them. And I know we've had our disagreements with those men, but all in all, I want to believe they're decent specimens of humanity. If something were to happen to one of our wagons, they'd no sooner leave us behind to die than we would them."

I hope he's right.

Tom approaches, his sweat-soaked shirt unbuttoned halfway down his chest. He takes off his hat and waves it beside his red cheeks. "You trust them more than I do," he says. "But the longer we wait, the weaker our animals will be."

That makes sense to me.

Major Craven hobbles over. "Do you want me to tether the weakest to the back again? Rotate them in yoke when we take breaks?"

"They won't get stronger by trailing behind," I say.

"So we yoke them all and let them pull until they drop," the Major says. We all nod in agreement. "Seems cruel, but the least cruel thing to do."

"Let's hook them up," Jefferson says.

We have the wagon loaded and ready to go by the time the last of the Missouri wagons is pulling out. Frank Dilley was yanking our chain with his "fifteen minutes" line, but I'm proud of how fast we worked and how well we all worked together. The smell of fresh quick bread fills the air as we square our shoulders and walk into the blinding, yellow-white desert.

"That's making me hungry," Jefferson says, walking beside me.

Therese sidles over, careful to keep me between herself and Jefferson. "If my mouth wasn't so dry, I'm sure it would water," she says.

We lead our horses. The dogs trot along beside us, tongues lolling in the heat. "How long do you think it will take us to cross?" Jefferson asks.

"According to the Major, about three and a half days," I say, looking at the sky. "It's Monday afternoon. Maybe we'll be across by Thursday at sunrise."

He whistles. "I was happier before I knew that."

"Think of it this way: Once we cross, we're in California. Give or take a mountain range or two."

Therese says, "Then we're practically almost there." Suddenly she tenses. Ahead, Mr. Hoffman has twisted on his wagon seat to stare at the three of us.

I almost glare back at him. Instead, I shift away from Jefferson, draping an arm across Therese's shoulders, like we're just two girlfriends out for a stroll.

"Thanks, Lee," she whispers.

"If your daddy asks, I specifically requested your companionship, you being the only female of appropriate age with whom to keep company. You couldn't say no."

She nods solemnly. "It would have been *rude*."

- - -

September days are still way too long. The heat is like a blanket on my skin, weighing me down and drying me out until finally the sun sets and the desert air starts to cool. The wagon train takes a short break to feed and water the animals, so we can push on through the night. We all have a few bites of the Major's quick bread and sip some bitter slough water. I'm feeding grass to Peony when I hear my name.

"Lee," Widow Joyner says calmly. Then frantically: "Lee!"

I run to the back of the wagon and peer inside. Her face is sheened in sweat that makes her look almost blue in the waning light. She pants like a dog in the desert, and a huge wet stain spreads out on the feather mattress beneath her.

"I can't hold off any longer," she says. "This baby wants to come right now."

A whip cracks in the distance, and someone yells, "Haw!" I peer through the gloom toward the front of the wagon train.

Frank Dilley and the Missouri men are leaving without us.

Chapter Thirty-Two

"*H*old on," I tell her.

Her hand darts out, and she plucks weakly at my sleeve. "Don't go."

The wagon already smells peculiar, and it feels too hot inside, too small. "I have to tell everyone," I insist.

"Lee, please."

My voice wavers as I say, "I'll be right back. I promise."

Our three wagons are pulled together in a little triangle. "It's her time," I say, confirming what everyone already guessed.

Ahead of us, the Missouri wagons slow. But they don't stop. Frank Dilley strides over to our group, thumbs stuck in his waistband. He squirts tobacco onto the ground at my feet.

"We can't wait," he says. "You're better off leaving her behind with one of your horses. Take her little ones and go on without her."

Major Craven shuffles forward and brandishes his crutch.

"You think we should put her down too? Like you wanted to do to me?"

"We aren't asking you to stay behind, Frank," I say quickly. It's not my place to speak for the group, but I can't stand one more moment with him. "You do what you need to do, and we'll do what we need to do."

"This is good-bye, then," he says. He takes one good last look at me, slowly from head to toe, which gives me an unpleasant shiver. "Though I suspect our paths will cross again. *If* you ever make it to California."

As he strides away, he circles his hand in the air and shouts, "Wagons, roll out!"

Reverend Lowrey has been short on words around me lately, but he's the first to speak now. "I came west to minister, so that the light of Christ might shine upon these miners, calling them unto salvation. God wills that I follow. But know that I will be praying for His blessing on the Widow Joyner as I go."

He doesn't give us any chance to argue. He hurries over to his own wagon, snaps his whipping stick over the oxen, and heads off after the Missouri men.

That leaves Mr. and Mrs. Hoffman and all their children. Mr. Hoffman's hat is crumpled in his hand. "I'm so very sorry," he says.

"Vati, *bitte,*" Therese pleads, and I don't know how anyone can say no to those big blue eyes. She puts her hands on Doreen's shoulders and presses a kiss to the top of her sister's head. "We should help those who have helped us," she murmurs.

"Es tut mir sehr leid," her father answers.

Everyone looks to me for a reply. Somehow, I've become the official spokesman for the Joyners.

The Hoffmans' oxen are weak. Any delay puts them in danger of not making it across. "You must go, for the sake of your little ones."

He nods, and I know that he was going to go anyway, regardless of anything we said. He herds all his children toward their wagon. At the last second, Therese runs back to us. She throws her arms around Jefferson, who hugs her fiercely. She grabs me next, squeezing like she can't bear to let go. I cling to her, unable to say "good-bye" or "good luck" or even "be safe" because of the tightness in my throat.

She steps back, blinking away tears. "I will be very angry if I don't see you in California."

Therese darts away before we can respond, and I barely glimpse Mrs. Hoffman and Therese looking back over their shoulders before darkness swallows the whole family.

A moan drifts out of the wagon.

"Coming, Mrs. Joyner!" I holler.

Quickly, the six of us gather around—Major Craven, the college men, Jefferson, and me. "As much as I hate to admit it," I say. "Frank had a good point."

"On the top of his head," Jefferson says.

"There too," I say. "But about the other thing. Leave the Major's tent behind, along with Peony and all the supplies she can carry. You fellows take Andy and Olive and the wagon and go on with the others. I'll stay with her until the baby comes, and then we'll catch up with you."

I startle at their response, which is a single, unified chorus of "No!"

"She may need my help," Jasper adds.

"I'm not leaving you," Jefferson says. "Never again."

"Leah!" she calls from the wagon.

I hesitate, unsure whether to argue sense into these fool men or run to Mrs. Joyner's aid.

"Go," Jefferson says. "We'll take care of things here."

I run to the wagon.

I climb inside to find the children clinging to their mother. Olive holds her mother's hand, as if in comfort, but her lower lip quivers when she sees me. Andy's face is swollen, and wetness streaks his cheeks. "Is Ma going to die too?" he asks, his right hand clutching my locket.

"Please," Mrs. Joyner says. "I don't want them to see me like this."

Olive is easily led to the back of the wagon, but Andy has to be peeled free. "Jefferson," I call.

All five men come running.

"Keep the children busy," I order. "Make sure they get something to eat and maybe put them to sleep in the tent."

The Major hobbles forward. "Come here, soldier," he says to Andy. He braces himself against the wagon and lifts the boy by the armpits. "Let's teach your big sister to make quick bread. Your ma is going to need it."

The other men linger, as if eager for something to do.

"Go away," I say, and they slink reluctantly into the darkness.

Mrs. Joyner sags into the soaked feather bed with relief.

"We'll get you cleaned up," I say, grabbing her hand. The wagon smells of blood and urine and sweat. "Then Jasper can come deliver the baby."

She shakes her head. "It has to be you."

"Me?"

"It was supposed to be Aunt Tildy. She was going to help me. . . . You're the only other woman here."

I open my mouth to argue, but a wave of pain takes her. Her eyes squeeze shut as her torso lifts from the bed. The last time I brought a baby into the world, she mooed, and I named her Gladiola, and she gave us milk a few years later. Surely this won't be too different?

Mrs. Joyner collapses when the pain leaves her. "Promise me, Lee," she whispers.

"Promise what?"

"Promise you'll look after my children. Make sure they know how much their ma loved them."

I lost my own mother less than eight months ago. Mrs. Joyner was already with child then. It seems so long ago. It seems like yesterday.

"Nothing is going to happen to you, Mrs. Joyner."

"Becky," she says. "Please call me Becky."

"All right," I say. "Becky."

"I can't stop thinking about the preacher's wife."

"Mrs. Lowrey?"

"Mary. Her name was Mary. A sweet girl. Not much older than you."

"I didn't know her very well," I admit.

"I only spoke to her a few times." She squeezes my hand. "You were wise to refuse the preacher's offer. Put off marriage as long as you can."

I almost ask why, but I'm not sure I want to hear more. Instead, I squeeze her hand in return.

"You don't know what it's like," she says. "Every time I . . ." She puts a knuckle to her mouth and bites down. It's not a contraction that's taken her, but something even deeper and more painful. She tries again: "My own ma died giving birth. So did my grandma. And last year, my older sister . . . Every time I lay with my husband, I thought, 'Becky, you will be dead in nine months.' I know it's God's will that women suffer, that we are saved through faith and childbearing, but sometimes . . ."

"Things will be fine." I squeeze her hand again, because one of us is shaking and I'm not sure which.

"You don't know that," she says. "That's the problem with pregnancy—you never know. My husband was a gambler. The fool man never considered that the thing he gambled with most was me."

All through the night, the contractions come slowly. Too slowly. I count the time between them, and they gradually grow closer together. She makes me check her frequently, which I do by candlelight. I can't see any way a baby will come out.

Between contractions, she dozes. Once, I try to doze too, but as soon as I nod off, a hand reaches under the canvas to tug at my sleeve, and I nearly jump through the roof.

"Is there a baby yet?" Jefferson whispers to me.

"No," I whisper back.

"Hampton is back!"

"Oh?" I brace myself for what he'll say next.

"Just walked right into our camp carrying a barrelful of water, like a peace offering. Found the empty barrel back at the sink and filled it up."

"Good," I say. Then: "No one is going to . . . I dunno, do something awful to him? Are they?"

"You mean the Major? Not a chance—not with the Missouri men gone. That extra barrelful might really help."

I loose a breath of relief. Hampton would have had a very different reception a few weeks ago, even from the families. But everything changes on the road to California.

Jefferson is silent, and I think he's gone away. I drift off again.

"You know, the Major isn't such a bad fellow," he says, startling me.

"Oh?" I blink to wake my eyes. "Even after the way he talked about Indians?"

"He told me he had to do *something,* or the Missouri men would have done worse. That stupid drill was just to keep them happy."

"Huh. You believe him?"

Another contraction snaps Becky Joyner awake, and

she gasps in pain. Jefferson yanks the canvas flap shut and disappears.

The sun rises and burns its way across the sky, and still there is no baby. I continue to sit with Becky, telling her stories about growing up in Dahlonega, giving her sips of warm, brackish water, squeezing her hand through contractions.

"It was this way with both the other children," she says after a bad one. Her skin is pallid and clammy. Salt streaks her face, and her hair is plastered to the side of her face. "With Olive, I was abed for thirty-six hours. Andrew was almost twenty-four."

"That sounds awful," I say.

She can't answer because another contraction takes her. I murmur meaningless but soothing words. This one lasts forever. I'm just starting to wonder if I ought to go get Jasper when her face relaxes.

"That was more than a minute," I tell her with forced cheer. "They're getting longer."

She nods and gives me a brave, brief smile. Then she screams.

The waves come, over and over, relentless and fierce. She was right all along; she's going to die. I check between her legs one last time. If there's no progress, I'm fetching Jasper, no matter what she says.

I see the tiny crown of a baby's head.

"Oh!" I say.

Her eyes fill with panic. Fingernails claw into the back of my hand.

"Your baby has curly black hair!" I tell her.

Joy like I've never seen lights her sweaty face, makes her almost beautiful.

"The next time you feel a contraction, you should push, right?"

There is no answer, only agony. A vein on her forehead pops out. Her low, guttural groan crescendos into an agonizing scream. I glimpse the baby's shoulders for a split second before its tiny body slips out, almost leaping into my outstretched hands.

"A girl," I whisper, staring. She's so little.

The slimy little bundle coughs, gasps, and then cries out, tiny but vigorous.

"Sweetheart," Mrs. Joyner sobs, reaching out her arms. I place the baby where she belongs, and all the worry and pain drop away from the woman's face like they never happened. The umbilical cord drapes across Becky's torso and ends on the mattress in a mess of afterbirth. News first, clean up later.

I open the canvas flap and see eight weary bodies clustered in the shade of the tent, which has been stretched out flat like an awning. Their faces stare up at me in anticipation.

"A girl," I say. "She's fine. Her ma's fine too." I blink against the brightness. When did everything get so blurry? Maybe it's because I haven't slept in more than a day.

Jefferson claps his hands. "Great. Can we start moving now?"

But I'm looking over his head at something I'm not sure is there. A silhouette in the distance. Skirts flapping in the wind. A woman staggering out of the shimmering mirage that is the horizon.

It's Therese. After five months on the road together, I would recognize her from any distance. She stumbles, gets up again.

I leap from the wagon and start running.

Everyone's else pounding feet are right behind me. I skid to my knees when I reach her. She vomits—a thin, yellow gruel followed immediately by dry heaving. One foot is bare and riddled with open sores. Her sun-scalded skin is hot and dry. I try to help her up, and I feel her heartbeat under my palms; it's as rapid and tiny as hummingbird wings.

"Therese?" Jefferson says. "Therese! What's wrong with her! Jasper—"

"Heat stroke," Jasper says. "Quick, get her into the shade and give her some water."

Jefferson lifts her by the armpits. I grab a leg; Hampton the other. She swings between us as we half walk, half run back to the shade of camp.

"*'Märchen von einem, der auszog das Fürchten zu lernen,'*" she babbles.

"I don't understand, Therese," Jefferson says. "Tell me what happened."

"It's a fairy tale, silly," she says. Her eyes meet mine, and her face gets a sudden clarity. She reaches out, as if to grab my arm but misses. "You have to help them."

"Of course we will," I say. We're almost to the tent.

"The axle broke," she says. "Everyone left us behind. Vati

tried to lead on foot, but Doreen was too heavy. He fell. Please . . . help . . ."

Her eyes roll back, and fear stabs through me. "Where are they?"

"I really wanted to see California."

"Therese, where are—"

She seizes. Her leg shakes out of my grasp and plops to the ground.

"Hurry!" Jasper yells. He directs us to lay her down and turn her onto her side, then he dribbles water over her skin.

"Therese," Jefferson whispers. His hand snakes out and grabs mine.

We watch, helpless, as she convulses for several minutes. It's like seeing a contraction all over again. Except when she finally stills, her eyes are wide and sightless, and no breath passes her lips.

"What happened?" Jefferson asks. "Therese!"

Jasper shakes his head.

Henry says, "She cooked to death in her own body."

It's not true. It didn't happen. Not to Therese. But she doesn't move. She doesn't even blink. I can't amputate the badness from her. I can't run to her rescue. I can't give her a golden locket to keep her safe.

Jefferson opens his mouth, but nothing comes out.

"What's going on?" Becky Joyner leans over the edge of the wagon, her new baby cradled to her chest. Olive and Andy peek out at her waist.

If I let out an answer, I won't be able to hold anything in.

"It's Therese," Hampton says gravely.

Jasper rises to his feet, his face stricken. "Her family is in trouble. She ran through the desert to get help. She sacrificed . . ." His jaw trembles.

I squeeze Jefferson's hand. Therese is a hero. Just like she wanted.

"Then we must go to them," Becky says fiercely. "Right away."

Chapter Thirty-Three

There's no time to bury Therese properly, not if we want to help her family, but we wrap her tightly in the Major's tent and weigh her down with rocks.

Her death can't be for nothing. It can't. So the only eulogy she gets is action. We have the oxen yoked and the wagon under way in record time. It heaves and jerks over the rocky trail, but Becky Joyner makes no complaint. She is so relieved to be alive that she cleans up and takes care of herself.

All through the night we press on, with only short breaks every hour to give the animals a few sips of water and some bites of bread. Peony's head droops. The oxen cry piteously. Near dawn, the first one falters. Jefferson and I run to unyoke him and leave him behind.

We find the broken wagon around nine in the morning. The axle is shattered, but there were no spare parts—everything was discarded to lighten the load.

Jasper is quick to take charge. "We'll organize our search

from here," he says. "We'll take the horses and ride out in circles until we see their tracks or find—"

"No," I say with certainty. The Hoffmans are not nearby. I don't sense their secret gold stash at all.

"We shouldn't separate," Hampton says. "No one can survive out here alone."

Everyone nods, except Jefferson, who stands with his head bowed, his shoulders slumped. I've never seen him look so defeated, not even when he was getting the worst of it from his da.

"Therese was clear," I say. "Her father was trying to get through the desert on foot before he collapsed. We'll keep to the trail until we catch up with them."

"Are you sure?" Jasper says.

"I would gamble my life on it."

Jefferson's head snaps up. "Don't say that."

Jasper says, "Let's grab the water barrel and any supplies from their wagon and go."

In minutes, we've stripped it of everything useful and are pushing onward. An hour or so later, another ox drops to its front knees, then keels over to the side. We're down to eight, with almost half of the desert yet to cross.

We pass one of the Hoffmans' oxen, collapsed and dead. Then another. Above, huge buzzards glide in lazy circles. They're the only creatures eating well in this godforsaken place.

The sun bakes us mercilessly as we plod forward—not just with heat but with light that sears my eye sockets. I'm so lost in the blaze of bright-hot determination, so focused on putting one foot in front of the other, that I almost miss it when my gold sense twinges. It's the barest tickle in my throat, the softest siren call.

The Hoffmans' hidden gold is at the absolute edge of my range. I close my eyes and concentrate. It's off to the left, over a rise and out of view.

"I see tracks!" I shout. "Leave the wagon here, feed and water the animals. Some of you come with me."

There are no tracks; anyone can see that, and I give a split-second thought to how careless I'm being, but it doesn't matter. We have to find the Hoffmans. I have to do one last thing for the girl who was becoming my friend.

I don't bother to see if anyone follows my instructions; I break into a jog and crest the rise. The rocky, ochre earth stretches for a mile. Beyond it is a shimmering expanse, like a lake of light. At the edge of the mirage are seven tiny, dark figures.

The silhouettes are as still as death. We're too late. Like Therese, they've—

One of the figures shifts, moves into the shadow of another. Jefferson, Hampton, and Jasper are suddenly beside me, and then Tom and Henry. Together, we pour down the slope toward them.

They're even farther away than they seem. We are heaving from effort by the time the figures become distinguishable—Mr. Hoffman laid out under a makeshift awning, Doreen curled up near his feet. Luther and Martin sit together with

Otto while Carl leans against his mother's side.

Martin waves as we approach, relief flooding his face, but Mrs. Hoffman is the only one who struggles to her feet. Her face is splotchy, like she's been crying, but her body has no wet tears to spare.

"Therese found you!" Her eyes search behind us for her daughter.

I try to respond, but the words clog my throat.

Mrs. Hoffman stares at me, and then she stares at Jasper, who shakes his head. She stands stock-still for the space of three heartbeats. Then she wraps her arms around her belly, eyes squeezed tight, and says, *"Gott hab sie selig."*

Mr. Hoffman remains unresponsive. Beside him is a giant, bulky knapsack. Its contents make my whole body thrum.

Jasper crouches beside him, pries open his mouth, and forces water from his own canteen between Mr. Hoffman's lips. He chokes, and his eyes flutter.

"We need to get back to the trail," I say.

"Ja." Mrs. Hoffman rouses her children. The oldest boys can walk on their own, but the three youngest children must be carried. Doreen staggers over and climbs into my arms.

"Oof," I say. She is too heavy, but all I have to do is put one foot in front of the other until we get back to the wagon. I can do it, for Therese's baby sister.

Tom carries Carl, and Henry picks up Otto. Jasper and Hampton drape Mr. Hoffman's arms across their shoulders. He tries to shrug them off, head lolling, but he doesn't have the strength to resist.

"They have supplies," Jefferson says.

"Grab any food and water and leave the rest behind," Jasper tells him.

Jefferson slips Mr. Hoffman's knapsack over his shoulder, staggering under its weight. "No wonder Mr. Hoffman collapsed," he says, reaching inside. He pulls two tarnished candlesticks from the bag. "Do we need these?"

"They're just heirlooms," Mrs. Hoffman says. "Rubbish. Leave them."

Jefferson drops them onto the hard-packed ground, where they roll a ways before lurching to a stop against a jutting boulder. He hefts the pack over his shoulder again. "Better. Let's go."

I hang back while the others head toward the barren slope and the wagon. Beneath that layer of dull brass, the candlesticks are solid gold. A small fortune, disguised for travel. And Mrs. Hoffman doesn't know.

I put down Doreen and pick up the candlesticks. They sing to me, vibrating through my fingertips.

"You heard her," Jefferson says, and I jump. "We can leave those behind."

"Mr. Hoffman has come so far," I say. "And he just . . ." I swallow hard. "He lost his daughter. I don't want him to lose these too."

His stares at me. Then at the candlesticks. His eyes narrow.

Ignoring him, I drop one into each pocket, and their weight makes my suspenders feel like knives at my shoulders. I gather up Doreen again. This time my "oof" is even more heartfelt.

Jefferson walks beside me. "I'm a better tracker than you are," he says. It's true. He always tracked; I always shot. We bagged dozens of critters that way. "I didn't see any tracks leading this way."

"I must have stomped over them," I say.

"That's your story?"

"We found the Hoffmans—that's proof right there."

He mutters something angry under his breath.

My heart races, with heat and exhaustion and guilt. Not telling Jefferson is one thing. But lying feels worse, somehow. Once an omission becomes a straight-out lie, you can never take it back.

We stumble onward. My lungs heave, and my legs are brittle and aching, like they're about to snap. Maybe this time, the Major will be the one holding *my* shoulders down as Jasper does his work.

Jefferson struggles beside me, carrying a supply bag even heavier than Doreen. His breaths are gasping and dry, and his steps skid and slide, like he doesn't have quite enough strength to lift his feet.

I think of Therese, and I keep going, one foot after the other.

When we arrive, the dogs lie panting in the shade of the wagon, not bothering to stir. Becky relinquishes her spot to the Hoffmans, and I'm more than a little relieved to hand Doreen over and drop the candlesticks inside the wagon bed. The oxen groan when we whip them forward.

Still so far to go. Everyone is weak, moving slowly, feet

dragging through the dust. Our lips are cracked, our eyes swollen, our skin bright with sunburn. Waiting for the Joyner baby cost us dearly, but maybe not so much as our dash to rescue the Hoffmans in the full heat of midday. I don't know how we'll make it.

After a mile of slow plodding, the Major pulls the wagon to a stop. "If we don't lighten the load, the oxen will die. How about we put the children on Peony and Sorry and let them ride?"

I stare at him, puzzled. "'Sorry'?"

"Ain't that the name of Jefferson's horse? Sorry mare."

"Sorrel mare," Jefferson says.

"Well, she's awful sorry looking, if you ask me."

I laugh, though it sounds more like a wheeze.

"We *have* been saving the horses in case we need them," Jefferson says.

No, I saved my horse because I couldn't bear to lose one more thing from my life before. "And now we need them," I say, staring at Peony's ribs and drooping neck. "Oh, Peony, my sweet girl."

Peony snorts and tosses her head when we put Carl and Doreen in her saddle, but with the children riding, the wagon moves a little faster.

Becky Joyner walks beside me for a spell, her tiny daughter swaddled in her arms. I can't believe how quickly she's on her feet after such a hard labor. Or maybe riding in the shade for so long put her in better shape than any of us.

"Have you given her a name?" I ask, even though it hurts to talk around my swollen tongue.

She shakes her head. "Not until she's lived long enough to earn one."

"All right." Some families are like that, especially during hard times. My baby brother never got a name.

"Listen, Lee, I said some things to you. In the wagon, when I was in my way. About being married and having babies and . . ." Her voice trails off.

"You did."

"They weren't proper," she says. "And I didn't mean them." Her finger traces a soft circle on the baby's forehead.

"She's so beautiful," I say, peering over at her bundle. She's been a good baby on this first day of her life, with wide-clear eyes and little fuss, which is a wonder given this godforsaken heat. Unlike her brother and sister, she's dark-haired.

"I shouldn't have complained. I ought to face my lot with faith and courage."

I'm plumb out of faith and courage. I don't think I have anything left but stubbornness. Maybe that's all I ever had. "Everyone's afraid of something," I tell her.

"Oh? What are you afraid of, Lee?"

I don't have to think even one second. "I'm afraid of my uncle Hiram, the man who killed my parents. And I'm afraid of being alone again."

Her smile is humorless. "And I'm afraid that my children will be alone."

"Well, I'm glad you're still with us."

"So am I." She sounds surprised by the fact. Then she looks up at the sky, where buzzards continue to circle. "For now."

We take a rest when the sun goes down. The moment we stop walking, everyone collapses to the earth. Jefferson plunks down beside me, back against the wagon. He folds his arms on his knees and lays down his head.

Major Craven half jumps, half falls from the wagon bench. He hobbles a few feet and lowers himself to the ground to massage the back of his short leg. "Only one barrelful of water left," he says.

One barrelful is not nearly enough for us and our animals.

"We should turn around and go back," Henry Meek says. He lies on his back, staring at the darkening sky. "Before it's too late."

"Are you daft?" Tom says. "We're more than halfway there. If we go back, we're dead."

"We're dead if we go forward," Mrs. Hoffman says bitterly. "If we go back, at least we *know* there's water at the end of our journey."

The Major shakes his head. "We'd never make it. We covered too much ground today, too fast, chasing after you and your family."

"If your husband hadn't run off after that Frank Dilley—" Henry starts, but Becky Joyner jumps in.

"They were just doing what they thought was best for their family!"

Her baby starts to wail. Jefferson raises his head for a

moment, but then drops it back to his forearms, shutting the rest of us out.

"Henry has a point," Tom says. "Therese would still be alive if—"

"Don't you dare talk about Therese!" Mrs. Hoffman yells. Her son Martin jumps to his feet and strides toward Tom, fists clenched and murder in his eyes.

"Martin! Stop!"

It's Mr. Hoffman, clambering, with Jasper's help, from the back of the wagon. He is wan and haggard, with red blisters swelling his chapped lips. Becky's baby wails and wails.

Mr. Hoffman sways on his feet. "What was that about Therese?" he asks. "Where is she?"

Mrs. Hoffman stares at her husband, unable to speak.

"She didn't make it," Jasper says gently.

"What? She . . . My girl . . ." Mr. Hoffman looks around desperately, as if Therese might suddenly appear. I see our group through his eyes: filthy lumps of weakness and despair, huddled low as if hoping the earth will swallow us and take us away.

Mr. Hoffman wilts, like a drying summer flower. He collapses to the ground and buries his face in his hands. His shoulders shake, and he rocks back and forth, keening in chorus with the Joyner baby.

"I'm telling you, we should go back," Henry says, shouting to make his voice heard. "We're falling apart here."

"No!" Becky yells.

Everyone starts arguing again, except Hampton and me,

who watch helplessly, and Jefferson, who ignores everyone.

"We're going to *die* here, don't you get it?" Henry says. "Fine. Go on if you have to, but I'm going back."

Fear tears through me. We can't separate. We *can't*. I open my mouth to protest, but I'm not sure what to say. I don't know that I have the right to tell someone how they ought to die, whether going forward or back.

Little Andrew Joyner, who has been huddled at his mother's side this whole time, rises shakily to his feet. His tiny nose is peeling from the sun, and his cheeks are flushed bright red. He ambles over to Mr. Hoffman, who continues to rock back and forth, back and forth.

"Herr Hoffman," Andy says, and for some reason, his quiet child's voice silences everyone. I didn't realize the boy had picked up any German.

Andy reaches beneath his shirt and pulls out my locket. He lifts the chain over his head.

Mr. Hoffman stills.

Andy holds it out to him. Solemnly, he says, "This locket has given me strength and courage. You should carry it for a while."

We all stare at him. Wind whips against the canvas of the wagon. A buzzard screeches somewhere high above.

As Mama's locket dangles between the little boy and the grieving man, her voice fills my head. *Trust someone. Not good to be as alone as we've been.*

Shakily, I unfold my legs and gain my feet. My limbs thrum—with the gold of my locket and with purpose. "Take it, Mr. Hoffman," I order.

He looks at me, back at Andy. Slowly, he extends his arm, and the boy pours it into his open palm.

"Now, get on your feet." I look around. "All of you. On your feet."

No one moves.

"Now!"

Becky Joyner rises first. Then Major Craven.

"I'm going back," Henry says. "I'll take one canteen and—"

"No, you're not, Henry Meek," I say. "You're coming with us, and that's that, because you're my friend, and I'm not leaving you behind. You wouldn't leave a man behind, would you?" I say, with a pointed look toward Hampton. "We go together. All of us. We'll help one another. We'll *trust* one another. Together, we can make it to California. We *can*. Even if we have to crawl on our hands and knees. Even if I have to drag you by that fancy beard."

Mrs. Hoffman is on her feet now too, along with her boys. To my surprise, Jefferson suddenly fills the space beside me. "Break's over," he calls. "Roll out!"

Becky hitches her baby onto her shoulder and starts walking west, Olive following at her heels. Martin Hoffman trails after them.

"Do you want to ride Peony for a while?" I ask the Major.

He leans on his crutch. "The rest of you are using two legs, but I'm only using one—I think that means I can walk twice as far." He heads off after Becky before I can tell him that's the worst logic I've ever heard.

One by one, everyone heads west, even Henry Meek. Even

Mr. Hoffman, aided by Mrs. Hoffman and Luther.

"My knapsack," he mutters to his wife. "We left it behind, didn't we?"

The candlesticks are so close that my insides hum. I walk over to the wagon and reach inside.

Mr. Hoffman's eyes go wide when I pull one out to show him. "How . . . ?"

"I know what these are," I say. "I . . . could tell by the weight. My father used the same trick once." Maybe it's the hunger and thirst, maybe it's the way everything else has been stripped away, but the gold purrs like a living thing in my hand.

Mrs. Hoffman looks to her husband, confused. "Those ugly things?"

I can't return Therese to them, but maybe I've helped a little. I put away the candlestick and fall back to allow them their privacy. The presence of gold fades with distance, but never leaves me. Maybe, in California, it will infuse me constantly, like the warmth of my own private sun.

I'm the last in line, giving me a clear view of everyone stretched out on the trail ahead of me, shoulders braced against the desert. The air cools rapidly with nightfall, and the stars brighten in the sky like beacons leading us onward. For the first time in days, I feel like we might make it.

Chapter Thirty-Four

We started across the Humboldt Sink on Monday evening. When dawn rises on Friday, we see the lush grassy meadows and bright waters of the Truckee River straight ahead. Real water, clear and running, not at all like the mirage that led the Hoffmans astray. It's September 14, 1849, and we are in California.

We unyoke the oxen and set the horses loose. Miraculously, every single animal finds enough strength to pick up their hooves and dash toward the river, where they all stand neck deep. The oxen cry rapturously. Peony and Sorry paw at the water and splash it over their backs with their tails. The dogs chase each other through the shallows, flinging spray that soaks a delighted Andy. We all drink deep of the clearest, cleanest water we've had in weeks. If all of California is this sweet, golden times are surely ahead.

We agree that we're in no danger of meeting winter in the mountains if we stay a few days and get back our strength.

So we let the animals graze their fill while Jefferson and the Major spend the days fishing.

It's tempting to let myself be idle, to rest up a bit, but I don't dare. Idle time brings idle thoughts, and mine turn inevitably to my uncle Hiram. He's probably in this territory already. He could be waiting around the next bend in the trail. It's a big place, I tell myself. You could fit three Georgias in California Territory. I might go the rest of my life without running into him.

I know it for a dangerous lie as soon as the notion takes me. So to keep my thoughts from my uncle, I busy myself with hunting. Game is scarce this late in the year, but I still bag a small deer, two snowshoe rabbits, and five golden squirrels. Becky makes stew from the squirrels. It's terrible—watery and oversalted, with spongy onions and a single shriveled turnip for flavor. We eat every single drop.

"You named that baby yet?" I ask her one night as we're scraping dishes.

"Not yet," she says.

As I set out to hunt the next day, I find myself remembering the people we've lost, like Therese and Mr. Joyner. Even Lucie, who left. So on the last day of our respite, I start collecting rocks. I pile them one atop the other until I've made a noticeable mound.

"What are you doing?" Jefferson asks, happening by.

I think of my parents' rickety wooden crosses. Soon enough they'll be gone, worn by sun and ice or toppled by wind. "We couldn't bury Therese," I say. "But we can still leave a marker for her."

"You didn't even know her!" he says.

I'm about to snap back, but the sadness in his face makes me say, "I'm sorry, Jeff. I didn't mean anything bad. It's just . . . She was going to teach me how to knit."

His frown deepens.

Quickly, I add, "What I mean is, I've never had a lot of friends. Just you. I feel like I lost a good friend before I even had her."

He stares at me, long and hard.

"I'm not going to mess up like that again," I continue, to fill his awful silence. "For every Hiram I've met, there's been a Therese or a Becky Joyner. People I end up taking a shine to, once we give each other a chance. And it's too lonely out here, if you don't give people a chance."

The pain in his eyes fades and is replaced by something softer and calmer. "Lee . . ." he says, searching my face.

An invisible force pulls me toward him, like molten gold lighting up my insides.

"I . . . I'll help," he says, and he's off before I can answer, bending to gather a few rocks of his own.

Hampton sees what we're doing and adds more rocks to our pile. Gradually, the rest of our company trickles over and starts helping. The mound grows, higher and higher until we've built a proper monument, something no one passing this way could possibly miss. Mr. Hoffman hacks down two large pine branches and nails together a rough cross, which we stake into the ground and bolster with more rocks.

Jefferson pulls out his knife. He starts to etch letters into Mr. Hoffman's wooden cross, but changes his mind. Using his sleeve, he wipes off the surface of one of the larger rocks and etches there instead: "Therese Hoffman." He stares at his handiwork a moment, then he adds: "Andrew Joyner. Mary Lowrey. Josiah Bledsoe. Athena the Cow."

We heave off the next morning, ready to tackle the Sierra Nevada.

For once, I expect the worst but get the best. The Sierras are even steeper than the Rockies, and we've no spare wagon parts left in case something goes awry. But the land is lush and beautiful, and we now have eighteen souls in our company, if you include the baby, and only one wagon to handle. We lose one more ox to sour feet, but the other animals thrive in the mountains, with its fresh supply of clean water and grazing.

Blue mountain jays flit between pine boughs. Trout dart through crystal streams, and late summer flowers bloom in wild meadows surrounded by granite edifices wondrous enough to make your heart stop. Lowering our single wagon down even the steepest slopes proves little burden when shared among us all.

In spite of all this, my soul is troubled. I keep to myself as much as possible, and I take every excuse to go off and hunt.

Becky walks beside me sometimes, content to endure my silence. She's different now. Lighter on her feet, with an easy smile. Sometimes she lets me hold the baby, who gazes up at me with bright-blue eyes as she blows little spit bubbles through her lips.

"What's wrong, Lee?" Becky asks one afternoon as we trek through a spongy alpine meadow. She has the baby against one shoulder and pats her bottom as she walks.

"Why do you say that?"

"You've been so quiet. You don't even talk to Jefferson much."

I bend down to pick up a pinecone that has rolled into the grass from the tree line. It's perfect and pristine, untouched by jay or squirrel.

"Still thinking about your uncle?"

"Yes." I reach between grooves with a forefinger and snag a pine nut. "Hiram will find me. Somehow, he will."

"Men can be relentless," she agrees, "when they think a woman belongs to them."

I don't have a chance to ask what she means, because Olive calls for her, and Becky excuses herself. I stare after her, wishing I could tell her more. Wishing I could tell someone. It turns out that a girl with all the friends in the world is still lonely when she's keeping secrets.

My gold sense is a tiny tickle on the eastern slopes, but once we cross the divide it swells, becoming ever-present, almost uncomfortable. I tell myself to pay it no mind, that there will be plenty of time for gold later. But once in a while, when no one is looking, I can't help crouching down and sifting through stream gravel until I find the thing that sings so clear to me. By the time the mountains give way to rolling golden hills dotted with oak trees, I have almost seventy dollars' worth in my pockets.

One afternoon while we're resting the oxen, I catch Jefferson scowling at me. He's right to be angry. I've been avoiding him. Having him near reminds me that I'm keeping secrets, that even though I wear Lucie's skirt most days, I'm still a liar.

The scowl on his face darkens when he notices me staring, becomes something deep and sorrowful. My chest squeezes with the realization: I'm _hurting_ him.

My feet stride toward him even before my mind registers my decision. I grab his arm and pull him aside under the cover of a giant sprawling oak. It's time. It's past time.

"Lee—?"

"There's something I have to tell you. A secret."

His face goes blank. "I'm listening."

Trust someone, Mama said.

My heart races. In my whole life, I haven't told a single soul. Jefferson is a good person to try it out on. The best person.

"Lee?"

I inhale deeply and say, "Remember how I saved those ugly candlesticks?"

"Sure."

I reach into the right pocket of my trousers. I pull out my hand and open my palm so Jefferson can see the fistful of tiny gold nuggets and flecks I've gathered. "Those candlesticks are made of gold. Just like this. And—"

"I know." His mouth quirks.

"You do? Did Mr. Hoffman tell—"

"I mean I know that you're . . . magical."

I stare at him, mouth agape.

He stares back, like he can see right through me. "I've known you my whole life, Lee. Still took me awhile to figure it out. But when you found that locket in the dirt, I got the most fanciful notion that you could sniff out gold the way Nugget sniffs out squirrels."

"I . . . see."

"Then I thought back to Dahlonega, how the Westfall homestead grew so fast, all those rumors about Lucky's stash. My mother's folk had dowsers, people who could find water or lost things. My da never believed my mama's stories, but I did. I figured that's how it was with you and gold."

He doesn't have to look so smug.

"You're not mad?"

Jefferson considers. "Well, now that you've told me, I'll get not-mad. Eventually." He reaches up to brush some of my lengthening hair from my eyes. "It's the strangest thing. People lie all the time, and it's nothing. But one little lie from you makes me feel so small."

"I . . . I'm sorry, Jeff."

"Thank you for telling me, finally."

I nod, swallowing hard.

His eyes narrow. "Your uncle knows, doesn't he?"

"Yes."

"Well, California is a big place." He sounds as uncon-vinced as I am.

"So I keep telling myself."

"We'll deal with Hiram Westfall when we have to," Jefferson says.

A smile slips onto my face. He said "we."

Less than a stone's throw away, a striped tawny squirrel skitters through the blanket of crunchy oak leaves, his cheeks puffed out with acorns, and I marvel at how golden everything is in this country—the squirrels, the fat marmots who spied on us as we crossed the Sierra Nevada, the wind-rippled velvet of these grassy hills.

Softly, Jefferson says, "You have the most beautiful eyes I've ever seen."

My heart stampedes in my chest.

"Did you know that sometimes they turn dark gold? Like the last edge of a sunset. I think it happens when you're sens-ing something."

"I . . . No, I didn't know that."

His eyes are so close, and the world disappears. There's just Jefferson and his familiar, perfect face and his knowing gaze and the way he's leaning forward as if to kiss me. My whole body thrums, as though I'm in a wash of glittering gold.

After a hesitation as quick as a blink, he brushes his lips across my cheek. It's brilliant and breathtaking and not nearly enough.

He steps back quickly. "Um, well, I guess you have to decide if you want to tell anyone else your secret. But we have some good people with us, and I think you might be surprised."

"Maybe so."

"And Lee?" His eyes dance. "You are going to be so rich."

On October 10, we reach Sutter's Fort. It's not as big as Fort Laramie, but it's a lot busier. Walls form a huge square. They're almost twenty feet high, but an even taller building peeks out from behind them, capped by a waving American flag. Three little girls play with corn-husk dolls just outside the entrance, and men and women kneel over cook fires. Laundry flaps in the breeze between wagons, and dogs run from camp to camp, begging for scraps.

Guns thunder constantly—men discharging their rifles to be let inside. As we approach, I see signs of wear on the fort itself: cracked adobe, a tilting well cover, gates that don't quite hang straight.

"Any sign of Frank Dilley?" Jefferson asks as we dismount.

"None," I reply, scanning the crowd. "It wouldn't make me sad to never see him again."

"Agreed," says Mr. Hoffman, walking beside the wagon. "Though I want *him* to see *me*. I want him to know we made it." Then, in a softer voice, "Most of us, anyway."

We park the wagon outside the walls and gather together. "I'll stay with the children," Mrs. Hoffman says. "You all go inside and figure out this claim business." Luther and Martin agree to help Mrs. Hoffman keep an eye on things, and the rest of us head up the slope toward the fort.

We haven't gone three steps before a voice rings out. "That's my horse!"

It's like being socked in the gut. My lungs refuse to draw breath, and my hands holding the rifle begin to tremble.

Slowly, inevitably, I turn.

Uncle Hiram stands straight and tall and impeccably groomed, wearing a shiny top hat and a black suit with silver buttons. Abel Topper stands at his right shoulder, a tall Negro at his left. Hiram took the sea route and arrived ahead of me, just like Jim said. Wouldn't surprise me one bit to learn he's been right here at Sutter's Fort for weeks, charming everyone in sight, knowing I'd show up eventually. By now, the entire territory of California probably thinks him a fine, upstanding gentleman.

I've been wondering what I'd do when I saw him again. Run like the wind? Shoot? Burst into tears?

Instead I say, cool as ice, "Hello, Uncle Hiram."

That name gets everyone's attention. Becky moves to stand beside me. Jefferson calmly begins loading his rifle. For a moment, the only sound is that of a ramrod sliding down a barrel.

My uncle puts up his hands. "Now, now, I don't want any trouble. But that's my girl you've got there, and I've come a long way to fetch her, so I'll be taking her back now."

"No, sir," says Henry Meek, stepping forward. His thumbs are cocked in his vest pockets like he's a man who knows his business.

"You've no legal claim here in California," Tom adds. "And

I'd be happy to see that adjudicated in the nearest court."

Uncle Hiram's answering grin holds no humor. "Maybe we'll solve this matter outside of court."

Mr. Hoffman steps up, crossing his arms. "Try it," he says. My uncle suddenly doesn't seem so large.

"It would be a strategic error," Major Craven adds.

Jefferson sets the rear trigger.

We stare one another down: Hiram and his two men, me and my traveling companions. A few passersby stop to see what the fuss is about.

Becky is the one to break the silence. "You see, Mr. Westfall, sir," she says, bobbing her unnamed daughter in her arms. "Leah is *ours* now."

Hiram deliberates, his eyes roving our small company, resting for the space of a moment on every single face. "I see," he drawls, slow and Southern and altogether false. "You realize, don't you, that you're harboring a runaway? She belongs with her family."

Becky laughs. "I knew she was a runaway the first time I laid eyes on her! But I'll thank you to leave us alone, regardless."

"She's with her family now," Jasper amends.

Hiram holds my gaze, and I hold his right back. It gives me an ache to see him; he's so like my daddy, except straight and strong and healthy. But he's half the man my daddy was. Less than half.

He seems to come to a decision, and his face darkens with determination. At last, he tips his hat to me. "I'll be seeing you again, my Leah. Very soon."

He means to scare me, but my breathing is just fine, thank you, and the hands on my rifle are steady enough to take him at two hundred paces. "For sure and certain," I reply.

Uncle Hiram turns his back and strides off, the other two men at his heels. He still wants what I can do, and he won't stop trying to get it. Mama and Daddy never saw him coming, but my new family knows what kind of man he is. We'll be ready.

I'm about to say thank you, and maybe hug someone, but everyone has already turned away like my uncle isn't worth another moment's attention.

"I still think you should call her Therese," Olive says to her mother as we resume our walk to the fort. It's a game everyone has been playing, trying to find a name for the Joyner baby.

"Or Lee," Andy says, with a shy glance at me.

"Or California!" Hampton says. "You can call her Cali for short."

"Elizabeth is a fine name," I put in. "It was my mother's name."

We continue to throw names out until we reach the gates, where we pause a moment.

Jefferson drapes an arm across my shoulders. "We made it," he says, gazing up at the walls. "We actually made it."

I'm smiling, fit to burst. Feeling richer than a king, I say, "Let's go find us some gold."

Author's Note

Eight years before the publication of this book, I moved from California to Ohio to marry the man of my dreams, a reverse migration, if you will. We loaded all my possessions into my car and drove across the United States, making the trip in six days—one day for every month it took a covered wagon to trek the same distance. The landscape we traveled was sometimes inspiring, sometimes tedious, always vast. I spent hours gazing out the window, already missing my home state desperately, even as I thrilled at the adventure of starting a new life in a new place.

It was then that the idea for *Walk on Earth a Stranger* germinated, but it would be years before I felt ready to write it. Sure enough, combining history and fiction is its own fraught adventure, and in order to best tell Lee's story, I took a few minor liberties. For instance, Dr. M. F. Stephenson's famous speech in Dahlonega's town square really took place in the summer of 1849, not in early winter as portrayed in the book.

And it's likely that the real-life citizens of Dahlonega would have received word of gold's discovery in California some months before Lee and Jefferson do. Occasionally, I allowed them to use words that probably hadn't found popular usage in the eastern United States, such as "nugget" and "mother lode" and "palomino."

Most significantly, I allowed Jefferson to propose to Lee when she was not yet sixteen, even though the average age of first marriage for women was twenty to twenty-two at that time. I allowed this because there is anecdotal evidence that women on the California trail married early, often out of necessity. Lee's circumstances seem to me to qualify.

I wanted the flexibility of choosing and directing my own characters, so very few historical personages appear in *Walk on Earth a Stranger*, and then only in cameo roles. The one character I couldn't resist, however, was James "Free Jim" Boisclair, an entrepreneur from Dahlonega, Georgia. Not much is known about him, though he probably set off for California in 1850, rather than 1849 as portrayed in the book. By all limited accounts, he was well respected, ambitious, and full of conviction. I hope I have done him justice.

Lee, Jefferson, and their contemporaries refer to Jim and other African-Americans as Negroes, as that was the polite term of the day. Likewise, they refer to Native Americans as Indians. I choose to use "African-American" and "Native American" in general conversation, but I will always honor someone's personal preference when informed of it.

There is some controversy over whether the term "confirmed bachelor" was used during Victorian times to refer to a gay man. While this euphemism may not be the phrase's only meaning, there are enough examples in the academic literature and within the LGBTQ community that I chose to use it with this implication. For more insight into specific terminology of the day, as well as some delightfully subjective commentary, I highly recommend the *Dictionary of Americanisms*, by John Russell Bartlett (New York: Bartlett and Welford, 1848).

No book is written in isolation. I am grateful to the following people for their many insights and expertise: Angela Thornton of the American Indian Library Association, who read an early draft; Marlena Montagna, an accomplished equestrian, who provided expert advice on horses and horseback riding; Jaime Lee Moyer, a critically acclaimed author of historical fiction, who helped me identify and sort through an avalanche of primary sources—diaries, lithographs, newspaper articles, daguerreotypes, etc.

For readers interested in learning more about the journey to California from the emigrants themselves, I recommend the following books, which I found invaluable:

Covered Wagon Women: Diaries & Letters from the Western Trails, 1840–1849, edited and compiled by Kenneth L. Holmes, with an introduction by Anne M. Butler (Lincoln, Nebraska: Bison Books, University of Nebraska Press, 1995)

Women's Diaries of the Westward Journey, edited by Lillian Schlissel, with a forward by Mary Clearman Blew (New York: Schocken Books, 2004 edition)

Most of all, I am grateful to my husband, C. C. Finlay, for reading this book multiple times, for applying his training as both editor and historian to key portions of text, and for listening patiently as his displaced Californian spouse waxed endlessly about her native state's many wonders and the Gold Rush that shaped it.

Walk on Earth a Stranger is so much better for these contributions; any errors that remain are mine alone.

Today, you can hardly visit any place in California without seeing evidence of the Gold Rush. I've rafted down the Tuolumne River through steep cliffs of layered sediment— the result of dredging. I've chanced upon ancient wagon wheels, half-buried in sod, while backpacking through Emigrant Wilderness. I've cheered the 49ers on to multiple Super Bowl wins, toured the mines and orchards of the Sierra Nevada foothills with my friends, spent days wandering the Golden Gate. Though this book deals primarily with the overland journey in 1849, there is much more of Lee's story— and California's—yet to be told.